MARIONn

The Management of Loss

Nick Millard

MARIONn

www.marionnthebook.com

To Issy and Rachel

"Esse est Percipi"

(to be is to be perceived)

Bishop George Berkeley 1710

Contents

Prologue

The MARIONn campus: September 2038

WHOOSH……
WhoooooSH…

whoooooooshsh…….

The blades of the helicopter fluttered to a standstill, their cadence falling as they slowed. Thornton Lamaire twisted in his seat, turning to face the colleagues who had flown up with him. He breathed a sigh of relief. "Well, we survived that," he said, trying to sound relaxed, insouciant, as though just playing around. But, in truth, he hated helicopter flying. It always made him nervous – whatever the convenience. He had a morbid fascination with crash reports; tail rotor failure, blades clipping power lines, he knew all the causes of helicopters falling out of the air. Only last month some celebrity had been immolated as his machine burst into flames attempting to take-off. *The rich man's way of death* was his view of this mode of aerial transport. No amount of rational analysis of the accident statistics seemed to remove his fears. Thornton, never a man to admit a weakness – even to himself - wiped away a light perspiration that he attributed to his excess weight and general lack of fitness, rather than any sign of anxiety.

While waiting for the blades come to a complete stop Thornton took out his phone and searched for any messages that had been sent while they were in the air. But there were none, or none at least that he was able to download right then. He checked the signal. Zero bars. He smiled, pleased, of course there was no signal up here – nor should there have been. He turned off the phone and handed it to an aide to dispose of. He would never need it again. Thank God, no more squinting at that tiny screen. This afternoon a MARIONn technician, trained and authorised by Apple as part of their joint-venture, would fit him with one of their new *iPsyches*. It was still in beta testing mode. Soon everybody would be able to message by thought alone, but, right now, he would be amongst the first to wear it. Thornton had always been fascinated by technology.

The visitors disembarked from the helicopter and, after some preliminary greetings from Heather Masters, Thornton's CEO for the MARIONn project, were led to the room in the main campus building where the demonstration would take place. It was a large, white painted room, with floor to ceiling windows on one side that looked onto a glade, a wide patch of grass that had been cleared from the closely packed pines. At the centre of the room was set a rectangular white laminate table, about waist height, and of substantial dimensions - the sort of table that would support an array of chemical retorts for distilling something, or maybe a model railway set of tracks. Around this table the audience, mostly board members responsible for the MARIONn project - plus those who worked at the centre and were part of her development team - took their places. As can be seen from photos of the occasion there were, standing from left to right; Thornton Lamaire, chair of the Blue Ridge board, Heather Masters, Xian Han, Blue Ridge's chief neuro-biologist, and Harvey Jennings, the machine-psychologist. Several other technicians, including Euclid McNamara, MARIONn's lead 'educator', together with various other staff who had contributed to this moment, have gathered behind the board members. There is no sign of Claude Blondel in the photo, the celebrated French philosopher, who has yet to join the team at this point.

This was to be a final demonstration of some of the technology that they hoped to install in MARIONn. If successful, the test would establish that the technique known as the *'Han Translation'* – the ability to interpret what electrical and chemical signals that registered memory in the brain actually *meant,* was accurate and worked. The team also wanted to show their boss that they could not just interpret memories but also manipulate them; delete, modify or enter fresh, manufactured, memories into the mind.

Most of the table was covered in a wire mesh structure, about 15 centimetres high, that contained passageways with internal baffles at certain points; a maze in fact. At one end of this were two small cages that held a couple of rats. These were Henry and William, old hands (if rats can be so described) at tracing their way through this maze. Both the rats had, by virtue of their persistence, determination and lack of complaint (none that could be identified in any event) wormed their way into the affections of the team. Indeed, the two estranged species had almost bonded with each other. Perhaps that bond was the result of mutual dependence. The rats got fed by the humans, and the humans? It would not be an exaggeration to say that the professional futures of the humans, and their reputations, plus a great deal of financial investment, had a lot riding on the behaviour of Henry and William over the next few minutes.

The rats were settled into their two boxes at the start of the maze. Xian Han looked around to check that everybody was in position, particularly his assistant, Euclid, who held some tiny silver electrodes in his hands. He glanced at the clock on the lab wall and said quietly, "Now." A cage door lifted. William was released first and scuttled though the maze. There was no hesitation when he met a junction or a baffle. He made no blind turns and a minute or so later he was at the food pellet dispenser, triggering his reward. He knew exactly where to go – and why not? He had been run through this maze many times before, as had Henry, until both of them could memorise the layout and repeat the exercise without the slightest doubt about the correct route.

Then Henry was released. Exactly the same thing happened. Henry found the maze as easy, even easier, to navigate as his brother. He arrived at the pellet dispenser a few seconds ahead of William's time. "I think you will agree," explained Xian Han, "that for all intents and purposes these rats both know the maze equally well; they find their way through with similar ease. Their states of recognition are equivalent." But Thornton, who could never resist commenting on, or disputing, anything he was told, if any man wanted the last word it was he, said, "Henry was a little faster. He's a tad quicker than William I noticed, more confident, sure of direction. He's a real Theseus – you know like that Greek guy who escaped the maze after he killed the Minotaur." Those around the table, concentrating on the antics of the rats, laughed good naturedly in agreement. Thornton was their ultimate boss – and paying for all this. Always wise to laugh with the chief. But Thornton was wrong: it should have been William, if either of the two rats was to be renamed after the only successful hunter of the Minotaur to find his way to the exit. For Henry was about to lose his memory of how to navigate the maze.

The two rats were gathered up and taken back to the start of the maze. When the room was still again, and he had their attention, Xian said, "Now watch. We are going to just touch Henry's head gently… so." He nodded towards Euclid, who stepped forward as he heard his cue and leant over the table with the two electrodes. William was wandering around in an open area at the entrance to the start of the maze, while Henry, of similar size and colouring, was held in a much smaller enclosure, no larger than himself, that prevented him turning. Euclid touched the electrodes to either side of Henry's head. He wriggled slightly, not that the electrodes caused any pain. A slight dizziness had been observed in humans during the same procedure – but nothing more. Xian Han continued, "Soon, these rats will have an implant and we will access their minds remotely but for now… this. Then, we're going to press the switch, wait 5 or so seconds and… Henry's recall of the way through this maze will have disappeared. His mind, or at least his memory, will be ours and he will have forgotten the correct route. We've tried this excision many, many, times while retraining both of them, after each memory deletion, how to navigate the maze again. The results have been completely repeatable. No failures – yet. Just watch".

His assistant touched the symbol on the computer screen and a clock appeared. A few seconds later the hands of the clock had described a full circle and the memory excision was assumed complete. Heather Masters, the CEO not just for the MARIONn project but also for the *LetheTech* start-up, the entity that would commercialise separately the technology behind the Han Translation, had seen both rats successfully navigate the maze before. She could hardly hold back her impatience to see if Henry would be successful again – or, as she presumed and hoped, unable now to find his way. Five years it had taken Han and his team to reach this point. If the technology worked they would be on the brink of one of the great scientific and medical advances of the century. For here was a precise surgical tool that could remove specific memories, repressed incidents that caused trauma and misery. Today it was just rats, but tomorrow the technology would be tried on hundreds of volunteer humans. Such sophisticated control over what was held in our minds! This was not like electric shock treatment, or some chemical cosh that cauterised whole areas of memory, with often terrible and uncertain effects, in the search for relief of depression. This technology would revolutionize mental therapy and form the basis of the artificial mind built into MARIONn, that would mimic that possessed by Homo sapiens. And if MARIONn had a mind like us, then, maybe, when combined with the ability to process those memories, and act on them, she would be self-aware, conscious. That, at least, was the goal.

The electrodes were removed. The barrier at the entry to the maze was lifted. William ran straight through the maze, as he normally did, negotiating each gate and baffle successfully. But when Henry's turn came he just looked around, confused, peering at the various routes that were available to him, in a state of indecision. He made a random choice and tried an alleyway - that proved blind. He came back and tried another, blind again. His next choice got him a little further until he was blocked once more. It took Henry nine minutes to find a route out of the maze instead of the normal one or two.

Euclid went back to the computer screen. He typed in a command and what appeared to be a shaky video appeared on the screen. The shot was taken very close to the table top. To the right and left of the picture, the mesh walls of the maze could just be identified, if a little out of focus. As the recording device travelled along the paths in the maze, openings would appear on the sides of its walls but these openings were not pursued. Eventually the view panned upwards to a large cylindrical device to which it got so close that focus was lost completely. Then the video was pointing at the floor where there was a little ball of something that it was approaching, until finally the ball was overridden, pushed under the recording device and disappeared from view.

Heather turned to Thornton Lamaire, who was standing at her side and explained, "That's a computer cleaned up version of Henry's original memory of the maze, seen through his eyes, removed by us just before his latest run. He wouldn't have remembered the route quite as you see it, olfactory signals would also have registered, but the memory has been reconfigured so that we can view it, as humans. That memory was in his brain, but it's not now; it's in ours, digitalised and held in our computer. Henry had a memory of the correct route through the maze – and now he doesn't."

Part 1

THORNTON LAMAIRE

Chapter 1

The IPO (Initial Public Offering). April 2039

Spring was early this year, as it was always now. If New York alternated between winter and summer before finally deciding which season it preferred, the city had clearly made a decision. No more danger of the sky dropping a last burden of snow, driven by a late nor'easter, burying the city in a thick carpet of white.

Winter might be over but it was still too early for the humidity of summer to have settled in. The atmosphere was sharp and bright; the sort of day to bring an exhilaration to the soul. Yet, in the hearts and minds of Julian Beck and Brooke Haberstadt, his colleague in the new equities' division at Goldman Sachs, the mood was sombre. It should not have been, and not just because of the beauty of the spring day, they should have felt full of good cheer for they had recently been appointed as lead bankers to the forthcoming IPO of *LetheTech* – the clear winner of the race amongst the new psycho-technology companies to come to market. *CyberSoul* and *ElectricMemory* would no doubt IPO soon but *LetheTech* was first, the most advanced in its exploitation of the progress that had been made in mind/ machine interfaces during the last 5 years.

LetheTech claimed to be the only one of its peers that had so far demonstrated a workable and tested technology. Yet, as Julian and Brooke realised from reading the on-line story this morning, the technology might not be quite as perfected as Heather Masters had led them to believe - and as they hoped it would be. Of course, the whole area of memory therapy was unregulated at the moment so quite what was the permissible level of error for these treatments was unclear. In the mean-time, the bankers took the view that *LetheTech's* processes needed to be pretty well faultless. There was an attitude in *LetheTech*, understandably perhaps, that their results needed to be no better than an equivalent testing regime for a chemical drug. There would always be some side-effects with any treatment; it was ridiculous to expect there to be none. Just as long as the hazards were no more prevalent than what the public had already been led to expect, that seemed reasonable enough. It had to Heather anyway.

Perhaps, perhaps, thought Brooke. But perhaps not, too. There was already suspicion and generally negative attitudes amongst the public surrounding the idea of invading the mind and manipulating memory. He was not at all sure that investors would tolerate the slightest doubt about its safety. He understood that *LetheTech* wanted to proceed to Phase III trials with several thousand clients, which would be very costly, before the government started to draw up rules. Luckily, the government had farmed out the issue of how exactly regulation would work, and how vulnerable people might be protected, to an independent committee of advisers. God knew when they might report. The deregulation of the Trump years had become a pretty well permanent phenomenon – although a few recent disasters was beginning to force the pendulum the other way.

But the regulatory delay suited the planned IPO process for *LetheTech* just fine. For the company needed the infusion of funds right now, to finance the tests, prove the technology – as well as recruit and train a series of consultants to market and administer the memory therapy. Blue Ridge had funded all that so far but Thornton Lamaire's appetite for further injection of cash was limited.

What everyone was agreed on was the market potential for the technology. The ability to delete traumatic memory should result in a great improvement in human happiness and peace of mind. All those adults, troubled adolescents, soldiers with PTSD, unrequited lovers, wandering around with clouded lives as a result of traumatic experiences, would in future be able to delete their unhappy memories. How many people were in therapy world-wide? The analysts at Goldman's had tried to estimate it for the prospectus; there were no reliable figures but the number was evidently enormous. Many of those sufferers would pay handsomely to have their damaging experiences excised permanently, not have to persist with years of psychotherapy.

As the bankers drafted the prospectus the opportunities seemed almost endless for these mind advances. Traumatic memories, of what one might call a 'medically incapacitating' quality, would be *LetheTech's* initial focus but later, who knew the limits of its compass? So much benefit, so much money, so much promise was being shown – and now this! The sort of thing that could ruin investor's confidence. Of course, this was just an early report, maybe it was overdone, an outlier, but it had inevitably spread all over the internet. No one knew yet if the rumours were accurate, whether the cause of any problems lay in *LetheTech's* technology and treatment protocols; whether it was an isolated example or one that showed there was a fundamental issue and this incident would soon be followed by others. There had been rumours of cases where, even if no damage to the patient had occurred, the treatment had been ineffective. None of this was verified, none of this was statistically significant – yet. But, unless Heather had some knock-out way of neutralizing the impact of the on-line chatter, the faulty cases would have to be investigated and the IPO delayed. There was no way such a new technology could be launched, or investors be asked to step forward with their funds, unless the doubts could be comprehensively rebutted. They had a problem, that was for sure.

Heather Masters could read these runes as well as the bankers. It had been a bad morning and the report on the case of Kinnead O'Neal was not the only problem presenting itself. Shakespeare's warning came to her mind, *troubles coming not singly like spies, but in battalions*. She sincerely hoped there would be no more troubles for a while, but the inevitable call she would have to make to Thornton later that morning did not add to her peace of mind. And then there was her personal life and the problems there that had bubbled up last night.

It had been a stupid mistake, which was unlike her, to bring up with Bruno the subject of their *uncoupling* and the prospect of her marrying again. Just delay it, she should have said to herself, until after the IPO. Nothing would have been lost by pushing back the confrontation but the subject had been boiling for weeks and could no longer really be kept under control. Besides the IP0 process would be ongoing for months and she couldn't defer her personal life the entire time. But she should have given Bruno's potential reaction more thought. She had just been too busy and had failed to reflect a little more.

Heather read again the reports of Kinnead O'Neal's discovery on the streets. There must have been some really big fuck-up. She could only assume that O'Neal's state of mind had escaped her staff. Clients in Phase II testing were to be regularly monitored - and very closely supported. *LetheTech* was still tuning the right level of mental intervention and the risk that too much memory could be inadvertently wiped out was a real hazard. There were enough concerns in the public's mind about the treatment already. This sort of thing didn't help.

Particularly as the problem had occurred to a celebrity author, even if O'Neal was a bit of a fading celebrity. People could remember his name. Many would have read his books. To make matters worse the 'creative community', to which she supposed

O'Neal still belonged, the beneficiary of some life-time membership that writers and painters liked to bestow on one another, had been extremely vocal on what they saw as the dangers of memory therapy. And their fears didn't even encompass what seemed to have happened here. Heather knew their concerns; if *LetheTech* removed discontent and mental anguish, that these 'creatives' believed underlay so much of the artistic process, would the very future of art be imperilled? She recalled that many of the great artists, Picasso, Victor Hugo, Goethe, Shakespeare had been perfectly happy - but the myth died hard. It was true that for every happy writer there was a tortured Dostoevsky, for every Picasso a Van Gogh cutting off his ear but, really, many, most perhaps, artists would be far more productive if they were rid of their internal, mental, barriers. But she knew that it would take some education by *LetheTech's* PR agency before that view prevailed.

Heather picked up the draft IPO prospectus and read it again. What did it say about the dangers? Well, it downplayed them as much as possible of course, but they were spelt out. Part of the problem she knew, and she had kept this to herself as much as possible, was not so much minimizing the dangers as not understanding fully what they were. Memory was such an integral part of personality and as nobody had, until now, been able to affect it very much, certainly not in the precision way that *LetheTech* could, they were driving a little in the dark. Did they know what all the hazards might be? No, they didn't but it was best that such ignorance be played down. The benefits to humanity clearly outweighed the dangers, in her view.

For the problems were surely overplayed. How stable was memory anyway? As had been recognized for centuries, memory was hardly a fixed entity. Things were forgotten, re-remembered inaccurately, modified to reflect some more flattering narrative or be changed by persuasion that something quite different, to what the individual thought had happened, had indeed been the case. Memory was anything but constant, or even permanent. Memory was plastic; it could be, and was, modified all the time, as one journeyed through life. The fact that memory could change or even disappear was hardly novel or scary. Humanity had lived and coped with this mental fluidity throughout history. In fact, as *LetheTech's* critics failed to recognize, the quality of memory, both individual and collective, would be enhanced, rather than detracted, by their efforts. Vast quantities of memory could now be down-loaded and stored in electronic form, outside the volatility of human recollection. What a boon to future historian this would be! History would be different in the future, much more accurate. As Xian Han had said, '*in the future, the past will be very different to what it is at present'*.

Heather had a few minutes before the bankers were due to arrive. She flicked her eyes down the list of recently viewed topics on her desk screen and called up the article from the day's New York Times:

A FORMER NOVELIST NOW ON THE STREETS, LOOKING FOR ANSWERS AND HELP, BUT FINDING NEITHER. A VICTIM OF MEMORY THERAPY?

NY, NY – Just outside the Agostino store near 1st and 53rd the man in the yellow knit hat was at his usual spot, sitting on a square of cardboard and accompanied by his mongrel dog, sleeping peacefully at his side. He held a scrawled sign with dirt stained hands,

'Lost home. Lost family. Lost friends. Lost memory,' it read

Here was the man I was looking for.

After hearing a month of rumours that this dishevelled man in a dirty jumper was none other than the famed writer Kinnead O'Neal, I managed to track him down. It was an elusive chase, every day O'Neal moved on, from street to street, sometimes town to town. For weeks, I had wondered if the man who had been identified only by a photo, since now he answered to the name of Kermit, was indeed the man who, until recently, had been one of the most revered contemporary American writers.

For weeks, I had imagined what he would be like and how many details he could remember of his past life as a literary lion, which he had abandoned – or had it abandoned him – or, if the rumours were true, might have been stolen from O'Neal?

O'Neal may now be as far from the celebrity dinners and literary prizes that he once enjoyed as it is possible to be - but he was not always like thus. Although for most of his life the famous author had trouble with alcohol, drugs and failed relationships, medication and therapy had kept his demons – demons that fuelled his books – at bay.

They didn't stop him winning a Pulitzer twice and writing a new book every other year. He had three wives, several houses and a horde of children but now here he was, looking forlorn in the evening light, his faint voice beseeching passers-by for '*any change or a dime?*'. I noticed that most passers-by didn't even hear his entreaty, much less reach into their pockets.

"I don't like this", he said to me. "I don't like begging, I'm not even any good at it. But I've got to eat."

Nobody disputes that a couple of years ago O'Neal had a breakdown after the death in a car crash of his eldest son. He sought help for the severe grief that this led to; grief – according to some of his friends – that seemed to overpower him. At first he sought comfort in drugs and alcohol. Then, at the urging of his wife, he turned to memory therapy. And it was maybe from that therapy that his problems got a whole lot worse.

"I'm mentally so weak these days", said Kinnead (or as he now likes to be addressed, Kermit). "Something is wrong with me. I don't know what it is, but I used to be able to remember things. But now I remember nothing. One day a woman came claiming to be my wife but I didn't recognize her. I told her to be gone."

The friends who have stuck by O'Neal, and even now visit him on the street, claim that the memory therapy, that he sought in order to forget the pain of the loss of his son, has scrambled his brain.

"He was a bit lost before but he was a long way from where he is now," said one. "Kinnead was never as bad as this. The tragedy is that while he has forgotten his son he appears to have forgotten everything else too. It's too easy for companies like *LetheTech*……..”

Heather had read enough and turned down the screen. This was about as bad as it could be. The story played right to memory therapy detractor's worst fears – that the technology couldn't be accurately enough controlled, that the precision with which a company like *LetheTech* claimed to excise memories, with no collateral mental damage, just wasn't there. And, as she knew, this wasn't the only example of unwanted memory loss. There weren't too many cases like this in the present trials but there had to be pretty well zero. Who would submit themselves for memory therapy if there might be a chance of becoming a largely non-functioning human being? The public expected that occasionally drug treatments would have unanticipated side effects but if the price of this therapy was the potential ruin of one's life, that would be a cost way too high.

Heather's musing was brought to a halt by a knock on the door and her PA put her head round to announce the arrival of the two bankers. She collapsed the article back into her desk projector, stood up and smoothed her hair. How tricky was this meeting going to be, she wondered? The two men, dressed in dark blue suits, as this was a client meeting, greeted her with at least some warmth and a positive countenance. She had been worried they would enter with long faces and pursed lips. She couldn't have borne that, she needed some confidence shown by those she had asked to advise her. Evidently these were professionals. Thank God for that small mercy. Heather gestured to the two men to sit down and after some preliminary chit-chat she decided to tackle the subject head on;

“What's your view on this Kinnead O'Neal article?” Heather knew they would have seen it. “I'm afraid that I have to confirm O'Neal was one of our Phase II clients.” She spooned sugar into her coffee and stirred, hoping that the hit might overcome her tiredness. She had not slept well last night.

"We heard rumours a few days ago that this was coming," confirmed Brooke. Brooke was the senior of the two bankers and the one who would lead the discussion. "But we were hoping that this guy might be a client of one of the other memory therapy starts-up. They're running trials too, as you know. But I gather we can't take comfort in that. If we ever could. Any bad publicity, for whichever company, will taint all of you, the whole field of memory therapy."

Heather placed her hands into a pyramid shape in front of her and leaned back in her chair. She searched her mind for some positive gloss that she could lay on the news about O'Neal and his memory loss.

At last she said, "As you may appreciate, one of the problems we have in this early testing phase is that we are forced to use clients who are already in bad mental shape. Given the freshness of the technology, people who are just mildly disturbed are not prepared to risk it. So we're left with clients, patients, what you will, that start from a position of being already mentally impaired. It's sometimes very difficult to unscramble the problem when things go wrong. Is it us, *LetheTech*? Or is the excessive memory loss the result of some pre-existing problem? Some further deterioration that would have happened anyway?"

"But you must, I imagine, check the health of the clients before therapy starts?" asked Brooke. "To understand what their pre-existing condition is? Whether there could be a risk of sudden further deterioration?"

"Of course," confirmed Heather, a little too defensively. She didn't like the imputation that her firm was careless. "And I have checked the records this morning. O'Neal had his mental problems and deteriorating memory. Alzheimer's does seem to have been a factor here."

"Are you claiming that *LetheTech* is not to blame?" asked Brooke. "Surely his memory loss has been a bit sudden for Alzheimer's to be the root cause?"

"I'm not saying that we didn't have some impact," conceded Heather, defensively. "It's like when the knife slips in the surgeon's hands; it happens rarely but it does occur – very occasionally. Such accidents are ghastly but....they cannot be avoided altogether." Heather looked at Julian and Brooke to make sure they understood her perspective. This was not a systemic problem with the technology, this was an unfortunate but rare type of reaction that sometimes happened when new treatments were tested. These *incidents* should no more frighten the public than the occasional instance of side-effects in drugs trials, which the public were already familiar with. It was just a matter of explaining it the right way. Which was the banker's job. They were being paid, and paid handsomely, for overcoming just these sorts of road-blocks.

"Do you think this will have an impact on pricing for the IPO? said Heather optimistically, trying to put on her brightest and most confident smile.

The two men looked at each other as though searching for confirmation that they were thinking the same thing. There was a brief silence as they seemed to communicate by telepathy, then Brooke turned back to Heather, with the slightest of less-than-jolly smiles flitting over his face, at least making the effort to sugar what he was about to say next;

"I'm afraid this isn't just a matter of adjusting the pricing, Heather. There's no way we can sell this IPO to investors with these stories – some of them you have now confirmed as fact – swirling about. You know how skittish the public are about this technology. There are sites whipping up fears about Frankenstein machines altering your brain. Even the *Financial Times* has been asking if memory modification is ready for general release. The government is just itching to regulate it. This isn't 2020 anymore. You can't launch anything this radical without the technology being absolutely 100%. I'm sorry Heather. This is not the message I ever wanted to give you but I would be lacking in my duties to you as my client if I told you anything else."

Heather looked across the table at Brooke, her lips pursed in disappointment. She knew in her heart that he was right, that there was no way they could launch their IPO until the fears had been dealt with. There would have to be another long period of testing and further development of the software until they achieved 100% results. The trouble with that was, as she also knew, *LetheTech* didn't really understand what was going wrong in cases such as O'Neal's and until they did, perfecting the technology and achieving those peerless results, that public and investors expected, would be difficult – and Thornton's goal of an IPO would be a long way off yet.

She would now have to call her boss, and she feared his displeasure. Thornton had wanted to liquidate at least part of his holding in *LetheTech* and raise some much needed cash. He was already meeting, personally, higher than expected development costs of the MARIONn research. Well… lucky that Thornton had deep pockets. He was sure going to need them for the next few months. It was not going to be a pleasant call….

Chapter 2

The *Crooked Timber* plantation

Thornton Lamaire III, prominent citizen of the state of Louisiana, family patriarch, troubled Catholic, unsatisfactory husband (in his wife's eyes) and majority shareholder in the Blue Ridge corporation, the largest robotics manufacturer in the South, awoke that morning with a soft buzzing in his head. At first he lay there not moving, groggy with sleep, but as the sound rose to a sufficiently irritating pitch he turned onto his side and reached over the covers.

Then he remembered: all he had to do was to think the command, *Alarm off.* There was a soft click deep in the back of his mind; the simulated throwing of a switch, and the buzzing stopped. The direct brain/computer interface, enabled by his iPysche device, still amused him. So much easier just *thinking* something at this hour of the morning, rather than scrabbling around in the dark for his phone, searching with his fat fingers for the *off* button to press. He shut his eyes again and let the night's incoming mail scroll through his consciousness. Thank God all that peering at minute print was a thing of the past. He'd gone almost blind.

Thornton felt the back of his neck, to make sure the iPsych*e* was properly attached. Sometimes it rubbed itself adrift in the night. There was talk of a new smaller, thinner, version that fitted under the skin. He wasn't sure that he was ready for that yet, even though it apparently overcame many of the connection problems from which the present model still suffered. He checked the time. The digital image of *5.42 am* formed itself somewhere deep in his thalamus.

He cast the bedcovers aside, a man undaunted by waking anyone. It was many years since he had slept in the same room as his wife, Bethany. He swung his heavy legs to the floor and stumbled to the bathroom, there being barely enough light working its way through the shutters to illuminate his shuffle and avoid any collision with the furniture. He gave no command to his iPsych*e,* as he might have done, to turn on the lights. Thornton had no wish for the violence of artificial illumination so soon after waking. He felt an irritation, a soreness, behind the eyes; the consequence of star gazing for too long, too late, last night. He should have gone to bed at least an hour earlier but his excitement at being able to identify the *Savannah*, the second Mars lander and successor to the ill-fated *Roanoake*, as it sped on its outward journey to the red planet, had kept him up long after he had intended.

He looked at the pale, jowled, freckled face reflected in the mirror, decided to defer shaving until he returned from his morning ride, and ran a hand through what was left of his fading, once red, hair. He pulled on a pair of heavy cotton trousers and a new linen shirt but couldn't manage to thread the cuff-links, the button holes still too tight for his chubby fingers. No matter, Clarence would do that for him when he descended for a cup of coffee, the only thing Thornton allowed himself before his ride, apart from the temporary sustenance of a couple of oysters. Proper breakfast could await his return.

He crept onto the landing, softly closing his door, not wishing to wake any member of the household, that was more numerous than usual this week. It was rare for both his daughters, Stephanie and Elizabeth, to be back home at the same time. Not that they were likely to wake but Bethany, a light sleeper, might. He would probably just get told off for being inconsiderate or careless in that event but he had no wish for criticism this morning. His mood was still one of contentment and he wished to keep it that way as long as possible.

Thornton descended to the pantry and was greeted by his long term butler, Clarence, with the regular pre-ride snack, pills, coffee and the shucked oysters, liberally addressed with Tabasco. He swallowed some of the coffee, then put the cup down and held out his arms for Clarence to thread the cuff-links. The two of them, long used to sharing each other's company before the rest of the household stirred, discussed the past night and observed some commonplace remarks about what a beautiful morning it should be. But that was not the only matter on Thornton's mind.

"Did Elizabeth make it back from New Orleans last night?" he asked.

"I did not wait up. But I expect so, sir," Clarence replied diplomatically. He had not seen or heard Elizabeth return, and he was aware that she might be still absent. He understood the resonances in Thornton's mind about daughters staying out all night.

"I hope she didn't have any trouble at the gates," said Thornton

"I'm sure she would have called for assistance in that circumstance," Clarence said, wishing to reassure his employer. He tried to distract him from melancholy reminiscences; "Can I refill your cup sir?" Clarence reached forward with the pot.

"No, I'm good thanks Clarence," said Thornton.

Clarence continued with his morning patter. "I think you rode past the main gate the last time you were here, sir? But I fear the DOGs have been re-bunching there since they were moved on by the police."

"Have they?" said Thornton, who been up North for a couple of weeks and had not kept abreast with local news.

"I heard the DOGs have tried to take over three farms now, near here. One particularly aggressive mob broke through Mr Dilke's gates a couple of days ago." Clarence recounted this gloomy news with the same tone as he told of the morning's weather. He was not one to add a gloss of emotion to everyday events; things were what they were and his job was simply to ensure that his employer was kept informed.

"Really?" commented Thornton, as one of the oysters slid down. "I would have thought the late Mr Dilkes' plantation would have been a little large and well protected for such a band of desperadoes. To himself, Thornton reflected, '*Ah yes,* 'Panama' *Dilkes. The man who had somehow made a fortune financing something in that little Latin American strip of canal. The man who'd had the good sense to marry Lu Ann but the bad luck to die while he, and she, were still young.'*

"I'm told there was no real danger," continued Clarence, in the same respectful tone that Thornton reckoned would not have varied if the entire family and workforce at Panama's place had been slaughtered. "The sheriff and his men were there soon enough. The governor will have none of that nonsense but it's creating a lot of anxiety for folks. Someone's going to get hurt real soon, the way things are going. But if those at *our* gates have been well behaved this week, would you like me to take them some sustenance, sir?

"Yes, do that, please Clarence," replied Thornton. 'We must do what we can an' hope to keep them from violence. I don't want those people helping themselves to any of the crops or livestock, either."

"Very good, sir."

Whether Clarence's idiosyncratic habit of speaking in a sort of Jeevesian English had developed from too long spent earning a living as a waiter at the Savoy in London, or whether an over-literal reading of PG Woodhouse had given him to understand that this was how butlers were expected to address their employers, had never been entirely clear to Thornton. But the two had been together for almost twenty-five years and Thornton had long got used to what Clarence presumably thought was appropriate diction for a butler.

Thornton swallowed his remaining oyster and walked over to the stables, calling at the kennels on the way to collect his two Catahoula hounds, Lewis and Dexter. As he walked on, and the dogs with their pale blue eyes bounded around him, the sandy feeling behind his eyes began to wear off. He collected a bucket with a few inches of oats in the bottom and a head collar, and walked out to one of the paddocks. His favourite mare, Texas, was used to these early morning hacks - and the offering of oats as a bribe to ensure her compliance with the head collar. She held her head over the gate in anticipation. Texas looked at the feed and, deciding that the quantity fulfilled her expectations of the respect she was due, bowed her head to the proffered collar.

Ten minutes later Texas was tacked up and horse and rider headed up the track. The light was still grey and the land lay under a frail mist that swayed between the hollows, pushed here and there by the gentle zephyrs of the morning; a swell upon a lazy sea. The mist allowed only the high points of the land to be revealed, suggesting hints of the fields that lay beneath, as though God was still finishing his handiwork below the haze and required a few minutes more for the world to be perfected.

Man and horse set out in the direction of the main gates. Thornton had no intention, or need, to proceed beyond them – he had five thousand acres of his own on which to roam – but he wished to check on the groups camped just outside. They seemed good natured enough towards him, at the moment, and glad enough of the food, blankets and so on that he provided. He knew that he could call up the sheriff's office and have them moved on if necessary. He'd done that in the early days but the groups always reformed themselves a few days later, re-built their crude shacks.

His kindness towards these unfortunates was prompted partly by his Catholic faith, as much as self-interest and a sense that these people, before they became too numerous, too united, or too desperate, should be propitiated if they were not rise up against those more fortunate, like himself. He imagined that he understood how much they had suffered, losing their jobs first and then, for those who resided around the Bay area, particularly the Cajuns living down in the Bayous, their homes too; constant flooding having rendered their homes untenable. Feeding them seemed the least he could do.

The problem was that these so-far peaceful groups had been infiltrated by the more desperate and violent DOGS; those with SHO (*Social Harmony*) scores of zero, who had been convicted and sentenced to the withdrawal of their digital status in society. If you were part of the DOGS, the *Digital Outlaw Groups*, you found no place in the modern world - where a cyber presence, and a SHO score of at least 2.5, was the precursor to being part of civilization.

This morning, Thornton decided not to approach the refugees too closely; he had neither the wish for a cheery morning chat, nor to offer them the opportunity for a rendition of their troubles. The first fires were already smoking and the smell of singed ham caused Texas's nostrils to flare and her gait to become more nervous. The campers were made up of sub-groups that were discrete, separated by a few yards of worn grass, with several early risers making breakfast and the rest, Thornton imagined, still asleep in their makeshift tents and huts. As far as he could tell, there were no more of them than a week or so ago, when he last rode this way, but his plantation manager would need to inspect the images from the drone he saw hovering above, disguised as a bird of prey, to enable a more precise judgement.

Something caught his eye and he stood up in the saddle. In the distance Thornton saw one of his own cars speeding along a track. His eyes narrowed. Elizabeth had said she was going out last night but he'd presumed that she was taking a taxi and would be home late; but not out all night. Probably with that idiotic boyfriend of hers, Ambrose; drinking.

The car sped out of sight, hidden by a screen of dust that followed it like a fluffy squirrel's tail. The sight of a daughter returning to the house early in the morning raised all sorts of unhappy memories in Thornton's mind. To restore his mood, he touched Texas with his heels and cantered up the path, branching to the left to inspect his black Angus cattle, grazing contentedly on a rich green field. White egrets danced around their feet.

He cantered on some more, to enter the dense forest with its mixture of oaks, Tiepolo trees, cypresses and crepe myrtle. He reined Texas back to a walk. A grey fox stood in his way, undisturbed by this unexpected meeting of two species; man and horse being, from the fox's point of view, a hybrid creature, a centaur. The fox had no fear of another member of the animal kingdom, even if this one had an unusual, but not completely never-seen-before, protuberance upon its back.

As Texas passed by, the fox languidly moved aside to let such a large fellow through and then padded off on his morning business. Thornton loved this time of day for many reasons; the quiet, before the crickets and frogs started their own chatter, the sense of being one step ahead of the turning of the globe - but above all he loved this communion with nature, only possible on horseback, when his taint of humankind would not alarm the denizens of the forest.

As he rode out deeper amongst the trees, the squirrels, raccoons, the swamp rabbits, the possums, came out to enjoy the dawn; an animal *passeggiata*, where each species strutted around, keen to discuss their daily pre-occupations with each other and woodland business in general. Texas lowered his head as though he too wished to talk to his cousins and Thornton did not pull him up. This circus of animals moved aside to let then two of them pass, showing no more anxiety than the fox had done.

When he and Texas exited from amongst the trees they found themselves at the edge of a large bowl of cotton, almost mature since the temperatures these days made it ripen earlier than in his father's time. They should be able to harvest in a month. Beyond that, there lay a one-story white painted, clap-boarded, wooden chapel, with a short stubby bell tower. An old bronze bell, now green with verdigris, hung there. Thornton had insisted on keeping that during the restoration, though it had been a very long time since it last rang. He walked Texas down to the chapel, dismounted and tied her to the hitching bar. This was as far as he intended, or needed, to go this morning.

Around this chapel could be seen traces of old foundations of a larger settlement. There had been a complete farmstead here once but with the fall in employment on the plantation over the decades it had long been abandoned. A few years back Thornton had ordered the collapsed ruins to be torn down and the site cleaned up. But the chapel he liked and he had kept this and restored it, while maintaining its appearance as original as possible. He sometimes regretted that he hadn't modernised it a little more, when he had had the opportunity. Air-conditioning would have been a welcome addition, but there was no power out here. And that would continue to be the case unless he decided to install some solar panels - that would have spoilt the ambience of the place. His pastor had joked that the temperatures concentrated the congregation's minds on the perils of hell. Thornton had laughed at the time but some Sundays he thought the remark was only too apposite.

While it remained consecrated, the chapel was used only irregularly. In two Sunday's time, it would be host to a sermon by Carroll Gillespie, onetime Bishop of the Diocese of Alexandria and recently elected governor of the state. Now *laicise*d, he spoke from the pulpit rarely and then only when he had something that he badly wanted to share with the inevitably small, but well-connected, and well-heeled, congregation. He would normally reserve his energies and time for larger audiences. Well, there was the plebiscite coming up. No doubt Carroll wanted to say something about that and there was no group of people locally he could afford to overlook.

Thornton bade the two dogs sit, and wait for him, as he strode up to the porch. He slid back the bolts to the main door, eased it open with a sharp creek, dipped his hand in the font, bowed his head and crossed himself. He walked up the aisle, illuminated by the shaft of early morning light that shone through the east window, as though he was the star of a show to which no one had yet bought tickets.

The old flowers and candles from the previous service had been removed and those he requested for the forthcoming service not yet put in placc. He inspected that the altar had been cleaned and dusted; above him the statue of the Madonna, in her white drcss and black robe, looked mournfully down as though she thoroughly disapproved of him, as well she might, all things considered. Two lesser saints flanked her. Thornton retreated back to the one of the pews and sat down. He wasn't going to risk his knees when no one except God could see him. He hadn't made confession for at least a month and there was no priest here, so he just leant forward on his pew and prayed to Mary for remission.

He rose, turned and paced out the nave, checking the floor had been properly cleaned. Although they had been successful in preventing bird intrusion, small field creatures sometimes crept in and had trouble finding their way out again. But human vandalism was a rare hazard, given that the chapel was within the grounds of such a well-guarded plantation. In sum, as Thornton saw to his pleasure, all was well; the chapel smelt musty but otherwise emitted a sense of welcome and potential redemption.

He dipped his hand in the font again as he left and softly shut the heavy door behind him. He untied Texas, remounted, and called to Lewis and Dexter who he saw, to his displeasure, had left their designated spots outside the chapel and were now roaming around, their heads low, as though mapping their territory. He pointed Texas towards home; his hunger for breakfast beginning to make itself felt.

Chapter 3

Hubris

The beauty of this morning was not to be wasted so Thornton decided to ride the long way back, via one of the small bayous that eventually flowed into the Mississippi. There was an old wooden bridge and he crossed to the strip of land on the other side, that bordered the slowly moving water. As he peered down into the gentle stream, for a second he suffered the illusion that the water was stationary and that it was the land on which he unstably stood that was moving past. It was only when he observed closely the tendrils of weed, waving in their slightly sinister way, as though they were a shoal of lampreys or the thousand arms of some fresh water species of squid that had made their lair in the muddy bottom, did he comprehend the relative movement for what it was. Ever since he had seen, as a child of five, a showing of *Twenty Thousand Leagues under the Sea*, the image of the giant squid had left him with a phobia about Cephalopods. There was never a *polpo* or a plate of *calamari* put before him when he visited Italy.

Thornton looked up and saw in the distance the rice fields, being prepared for their second inundation. Although it was only just after dawn there were already men working them, heeling in the seedlings and wishing to complete their shift before the heat of the day made it intolerable. The historical resonances did not escape him. But what was the choice? Machines were cheaper but these men needed work. There were, as he recalled the men camped at his gates, people worse off than this.

Beyond the bayou was a pool, hung over by a giant willow, where Thornton recalled swimming as a boy with his sister Dixie and brother Thad, in the then cold waters. The water was warmer now but still quantities of large mouthed bass, catfish and sacalait swam there. Thornton could not make the fish out in the low, flat light, the sacalait being particularly wily and resistant to his own and his siblings' predations, but he knew they were waiting, hiding. The bass were more plentiful, not so wise and an easier catch. He suddenly knew that what he wanted for breakfast was one of these bass, grilled – with a side of beans.

As he turned away he noticed an alligator swimming silently, slowly, through the duck weed. Only its nostrils, the top of its head and the ridges along its back were visible; it looked just like Disney's *Nautilus*. He watched it for a few seconds, mesmerised by its sinister motion and then was about to move off when, from behind the stand of cypresses on the other side of the pond, arose a flight of roseate spoonbills, the translucent trailing edges of their wings filtering the rising sunlight, so they appeared to be wearing a halo, angels of a morning God. They were one of his favourite birds. The heavens were indeed smiling on him this morning. He accepted the auguries and felt reassured; perhaps the researches that he financed, into artificial minds, were not some blasphemy, a trampling on areas of competence reserved to the Almighty. He had not yet been judged and found wanting. The Madonna of the chapel would smile on him yet.

Thornton and Texas trotted along the opposite bank for a way and then turned off, up the last hill before the gentle descent back to the house. When they reached the small plateau at its apex he halted Texas, relaxed his reins and rested in the saddle. He looked down on his house, this patrimony, the home of successive Lamaires since that great- great- great grandfather, a hundred and thirty years ago, had struck oil near the Vermillion river and acquired the wealth to buy the *Crooked Timber* plantation up by St Francisville.

The white stucco of the Greek-revival house was illuminated by the sun. The house positively glowed, reflecting its original Palladian proportions, as though it took justified pride in its own perfection. It was really very handsome: everything was in balance. Thornton was glad that neither he, nor any of his ancestors, had succumbed, like some of their neighbours, to adding the disfigurement of a veranda along the façade; a front that was approached so grandly by a long avenue of live oaks, drooping with Spanish moss.

On the left hand side of that avenue he picked out, and admired, Bethany's prized garden; a riot of azaleas and camellias in the spring. Beyond that, a paddock where his horses grazed contentedly. At the left hand edge of the paddock lay a large pond, perhaps a 150 metres in length, where the family now swam and in whose brackish depths lived patrols of robotic turtles that ripped any weed from the sandy bottom that was impertinent enough to linger and consider itself established. Around all this stood a three bar white picket fence that announced the limits of domesticity and the beginnings of the commercial plantation.

This house, and the other one, the Henry Howard town house in New Orleans, had been in the family for five generations, ever since Thornton's ancestor had decided to move the family to somewhere grander and nearer the seat of power in the state. But the origin of the Lamaires in Louisiana had way preceded this move, the family having fled Bordeaux after the French revolution made life too hot for their royalist views. The first settlers of the family had grown rice, sugar and cotton south of what was now the town of Lafayette. By the combination of thrift, good management and a lot of slaves, they had done well. But not well enough – until they found oil. Then the 'white gold' of sugar was replaced by a black gold that was even more profitable. Oil had provided the bedrock for Thornton's great-grandfather's expansion into industry, throughout the South, initially into construction and shipbuilding, and then there had followed Thornton's grand-father, the first of the Lamaires to be called Thornton, who had taken the family into newspapers and publishing.

His way had been made easier by marriage to that famous North Carolinian beauty, Harper Reed, who brought with her an inheritance of a controlling stake in the Blue Ridge newspaper group. Husband and wife had decided that the family's financial and commercial power needed a political dimension – and newspapers were to be the engine by which that ambition would be achieved. There had been worrying liberal and socialist tendencies rampant in Europe. The first Thornton judged it his responsibility to fight the risk that these tendencies might infect America.

Then it had been the present Thornton's father's turn to pursue the next twist in the evolution of the economy, leading the family into radio and cable TV and from there, through the entrepreneurial talents of himself, Thornton Lamaire III, into a broader spectrum of telecommunications, robotics and Artificial Intelligence, the technology that could support all sorts of ways of addressing the public or, in his enemy's view, manipulating them.

Each generation had piggy-backed off the last to reinforce and build another layer of the Blue Ridge Corporation. So far, there had always been a son to inherit this great industrial estate and each son had proved worthy, (apart from the black sheep, Thad, Thornton's delinquent brother whose name was never mentioned) always increasing the family's wealth and influence. But the chain had now been broken. He and Bethany had no son, just his two daughters, neither of whom showed any sign of wishing to enter the family business. Would that change with time? The omens were not promising. Stephanie was the best adapted of the two, by temperament and intelligence, but she was how old, now ? 37 – almost 38? There was no sign of a husband and, as for a career, only recently did she appear to have chosen a settled direction in life. She was always wandering. She could have been a successful journalist in the US. God knows he had enough contacts to ease her way. Instead, she wanted to go to Paris and work there. Would journalism in Paris lead anywhere, or be a temporary diversion, like all the rest of her seemingly unconnected and random life choices? But she seemed settled in her choice of career, the move to Paris might give her a further boost. And if it didn't? Well, there were always the family's media interests to manage. Perhaps in time Stephanie could be inclined to take on that challenge.

Her sister, Elizabeth? She was unlikely to prove the answer to Blue Ridge's succession issue. Unlikely, but not completely impossible; she did seem to have grown less dreamy than hitherto, her dance career was going well. And she had a boyfriend, Ambrose. Maybe he would translate into a husband? But he didn't seem very suited to a life at the helm of Blue Ridge, this over-muscled football-playing dim beau Elizabeth had chosen, even if, from time to time he unexpectedly said something faintly sensible. You never knew what miracles people might suddenly reveal. And for that matter, thinking of miracles, miracle of miracles, Bethany was drinking less than usual. Yes, the family indeed seemed more settled than it had been for a long time. And the issue of succession might not arise for decades more. He, Thornton Lamaire, was only middle-aged.

Meanwhile business was flourishing. The Blue Ridge group's revenues were at their highest in history. His conglomerate had become the big winner of the robotic wars. True, profitability was a little down but that was only temporary while they invested in the next big thing, the fully conscious computer, his MARIONn project (it was he who had chosen the acronym MARIONn, the *Meta Aware Intelligent Open Neural network,* a sort of homage to the Virgin, his Mary). Really, Blue Ridge had been incredibly lucky to secure Xian Han and his team. Han had been way ahead of the others with his ability to build neural networks that mimicked the brain, so brilliant to have uncovered the relationship between electrical states in the mind and what those states *meant*. Yes, the *Han Translation* had been the clue to building an artificial brain, better than any human's. Now they were almost there, at the foothills of consciousness, at the point of *singularity*, so long the grail of AI. There would soon be little difference between types of minds, whether built of silicon or carbon, made by man or made by God – but the former would be the better version. Not really better; Thornton quickly corrected himself, for that would be sacrilegious, but he couldn't stop himself from reflecting that MARIONn would provide humanity with a mind that combined the power of a computer with the understanding of a human - but without the ego, traumas and psychic damage that so beset fallible humanity. And it was to be he, Thornton Lamaire III, who would have made all this possible; the greatest step mankind had taken since the Fall. Soon man would have a companion whose origins never lay in the Garden of Eden.

From all this progress, Thornton's companies would reap the very considerable rewards that must surely follow. Their first, practical, commercial spin-of the MARIONn research, the technology that could *modify* the human mind, delete or insert memories – was going to revolutionise the therapy market. *LetheTech*, named after the Greek river of forgetting and oblivion, was going to make them a fortune.

All things considered, everything was moving in the right direction. The sunny uplands of the next stage of Blue Ridge's development, as it powered ahead to its place at the forefront of the AI business, was in sight. Maybe at last he had earned the redemption that he had so long sought. But, as he was also aware, he must avoid the sin of *hubris,* not be overcome by a sense of pride and the satisfaction of a job well done. Just when everything seemed promising he didn't want to upset God's favour that had been so difficult to earn. He also needed to be particularly careful about where this thing with Lu Ann was going. Was that really permissible, with Jim '*Panama*' Dilkes hardly cold in his grave? Probably not, but a man needed an emotional life and a recipient for his natural affections. Bethany had long ceased to provide that sort of succour in his life. Surely he would be forgiven for this one understandable weakness? Was that not God's profession after all; to forgive?

Texas began to paw the ground with his hooves; impatient with this static musing. Thornton awakened from his reverie, crossed himself, mouthed a short prayer of thanks for his good fortune and turned Texas towards the stables. He was ravenous now; two oysters didn't last a man long. He conceived an instruction to Clarence, *put a bass on that grill*, and transmitted it via his iPsyche. The message would pop up on the kitchen monitor. Just needed to stable and un-tack Texas and breakfast would be his. So nice too, that today he would be able to share that meal with his daughters.

Chapter 4

Breakfast

Thornton checked his blood sugar via the iPsyche and, finding it had, as he expected, been lowered by the exertions of his ride, allowed himself to order a glass of orange juice, normally reserved for his girls and Bethany. Surely one glass would not hurt?

He was taking the first gulp and then suddenly, just before he was about to swallow, realised that he had ingested a mouthful of pips along with the juice. He grimaced and spat out the foreign bodies, in fury against whoever had been careless enough not to check the glass before it was put in front of him. He missed the plate and the offending pips rattled as they hit the wooden floor. Thornton was about to call out Clarence when he caught himself and re-imposed a measure of self-control. It was just pips in his juice, he shouldn't feel so insulted. It was ridiculous and probably not Clarence's fault. He pressed the buzzer.

"We got n' staff in the kitchen?" Thornton asked

"We have Florence, sir, since the start of the week. Is there something wrong?"

"Ask her to check the juice before serving it, please Clarence. Never could stand things floating in my OJ." Perhaps he felt so affronted because the pips were the visible evidence of his weakness. Put there by a caring Creator as a warning about his diabetic control, or the lack of it, his akratic tendencies. He understood that. He should have resisted asking for the juice, but he felt he had earned it, what with his long ride this morning. *My,* he reflected, *life is full of traps for those not wary enough of self-indulgence……..*

"My apologies, sir. I should have checked myself," said Clarence, in a voice full of regret.

" It's OK Clarence, not a big deal. Don't scare the poor girl."

"Certainly not sir, I will mention the issue only. I hope though that your fish will be as you would like it?" Clarence brought over Thornton's grilled bass and placed it at the head of the table., accompanied by a tub of horseradish – and the beans.

Thornton looked around the room in which he had not eaten since redecoration started. He'd been forced to breakfast in the main, baronial style, dining room that he especially liked, but whose formality he preferred to savour later in the day. He focused on the new decoration; typical Bethany he thought; William Morris style green fronds twisted up the walls. Nice enough, although a few elk and moose heads on plinths were more his sort of thing. At least his first edition Audubon bird prints had been re-hung properly; one piece of evidence that he had won a battle with Bethany.

Many of the rooms in the house displayed evidence of the collateral damage caused by the battles within his marriage. For Bethany was a Renaissance girl. Elsewhere in the house, cherubs and *putti* gallivanted over the ceilings, vines rose up trompe l'oeil pillars and tangled in their baby heels; Gods pursued nymphs through Arcadian glades. But in the main dining room, Thornton had his own way and was free to express his inner Scottish baronial yearnings (he had fantasized in his youth about Sir Walter Scott's heroes and felt he should appropriately have been born the head of a clan) that were channelled into dark oak panelling, hung with mounted heads of the unfortunate elks, deers and bobcats that had found themselves in the sights of one or other of the Lamaires.

He eased the fillet from the back of his bass and was about to take a mouthful when Stephanie came in, bright, strong-featured, tall, dressed in a Chinese style wrap, her dark hair wound up into a knot, held in place by what appeared to be a porcupine's quill, stabbed through the centre of the dense, roughly brushed, mass. Clarence asked her what she would be eating that morning and having decided that orange juice, toast and coffee would be quite sufficient she came to sit next to her father. After a brief discussion on the merits of his early morning hack, Thornton said,

"I saw Elizabeth coming back this morning. She must have stayed out all night"

"Sure, I heard her come in," confessed Stephanie cheerily. Then she hesitated. Stephanie knew perfectly well where her father was coming from; no daughter returning early in the morning would ever be a thing of little consequence for him again.

"Elizabeth was staying with Molly last night," she said. "She probably didn't want to drive back after she'd been drinking."

"That so? "said her father, sceptically. "*Bah*! The car would have driven itself."

"Oh, I don't know Daddy. Ask her yourself when she gets up - if it's so important." Stephanie was unwilling to share her father's distress.

Thornton grunted, unsatisfied, but with no wish to press the matter with Stephanie, concentrated on his fish. Then he looked up;

"When are you off? Remind me."

"Thursday. I've got a couple of calls to make on editors who've promised to take my work while I'm in Paris. Houston first, to see *TrueNews,* and then Tampa, for *Clear and Present Times*. Next week I'm staying with the Westwoods, at their house in Rye. Flying to France the Monday after that."

"*Shoot*. I'd quite forgotten it was all so soon," said her father. "I thought you weren't leaving until next week. If you wanted to go to Houston together, I could give you a lift. I'm headed onto New York later today, but I could go east first. There's room on the PJ."

Stephanie shook her head. "Too soon for me. I'd like to spend another couple of days here. It's been a long time since I was home – and it's going to be a few months 'fore I'll be back again. But I'm sorry we won't spend more time together. You have to go? Today, I mean?"

"I do. We've a meeting at the up-state New York campus all set for tomorrow. Everyone's flying in."

"What's so important up north, on your campus in the Berkshire's anyway? Anything I can use in one of my articles?"

"Not yet," her father replied, rather sharply. "Anyway, aren't you covering European news in Paris? Not my sort of stuff?"

"I'm freelance. I'll write on anything that's interesting and someone wants to buy."

"Well, please don't sell anything about this. We're not ready yet."

"Of course, I won' Daddy – if you don't wish it. But what are these tests anyway? Must be mighty important, if it's causing y'all to get together at once?"

Thornton looked at her, deciding just how much he wanted to reveal. But, hell, this was his daughter. If he couldn't trust her.......

"We've been running some tests on memory management. If it works, as I think it will, then we are going to roll out our artificial therapy product, *LetheTech*, very soon. Make us a heap of money. And we will incorporate the technology into the way we build the mind of MARIONn, so she will be conscious. Like us. Some of us, at any rate."

"Is that a good thing?" asked Stephanie. "I mean, will your MARIONn, this machine, enjoy being conscious?"

The issue of whether MARIONn would appreciate, or not, her mental state of consciousness had not so far occurred to Thornton – and he wasn't going to suddenly venture an opinion on that right now. Besides, he had people, like Claude Blondel, that French thinker-guy, on his payroll to consider those sort of issues.

"It's coming, it's inevitable," replied Thornton, as though that was sufficient answer to his daughter's enquiry. "Artificial consciousness is the next big thing. All the main tech groups are working on it; Apple. Microsoft, Amazon, Google. It's just that it's looking like Blue Ridge will be there first. The others are close behind but we managed to discover the *Han Translation* early on – and that has turned out to be the clue to the whole thing."

Stephanie raised her eyebrows and shook her head slightly, the signal of bemusement, as though trying to clear her head of incomprehension. "*Han Translation?*"

"Sure. Xian Han, you remember me talking about him before, our chief neuro-biologist, he discovered how to translate observations about the electrical and chemical activity in the brain to their equivalent human mental processes. We can tell now, just from looking at the electrical states and impulses of your mind, exactly what you're thinking – or what's in your memory."

"You could put a couple of electrodes on my head and tell what's passing through my brain?

"Not sure if it would just be a *couple* of electrodes but, yes, we can. Han could point to your neuronal states that correspond to a certain belief or memory – that you believe in evolution, for example, or how you recall a particular childhood picnic. Or even whether you prefer strawberry to raspberry ice cream!"

"And how does that help you make your computer conscious?"

"If we know how the human mind works – at a technical level – we can build and program our own copy. And if we do that, if the copy is accurate enough, it should behave in the same way as you and I – in other words, consciously. That, I gather, as much as I understand these things, is what Han believes will happen anyway."

Stephanie was silent for a few moments as she tried to assimilate what her father was telling her. Then she frowned and said, "How'll all that go down around here? Our wonderful governor, Carroll Gillespie…he's not even keen on the level of AI we've got at present. I read that he's using that Supreme Court case, the *Douglas versus Milton Robotics* thing, to whip up a lot of support against any further introduction of robots in the South."

"I never wanted that case to go to court," said Thornton, morosely. "Even if we won, it was bound to be a provocation. I mean, I can understand, people don't want to be told they have to respect machines. I get that .....but *heck*, you know, that's the way it's going; whether people like it or not. These machines are now so sophisticated that they do have expectations about how they will be treated. We can't avoid that and if MARIONn works like we expect that's only going to be more true. These new machines are going to be very similar to us – and they're going to want to be cared for and treated in the same way."

At that moment there was the sound of someone rushing down the stairs, accompanied by a loud lament, in what sounded like a female voice.

"*Holy Heavens*! What the deuce is that noise?" said Thornton

Stephanie tilted her head to one side and cocked an ear. "Sounds like Elizabeth is up."

"For heaven's sake, go and see what's wrong, Stephanie," said her father. "I can't bear this sort of noise so early in the morning." Stephanie rolled her eyes, accustomed to the volatility of her sister. She rose slowly from her seat, to make it clear that in her opinion this was not a crisis, and went in search of an explanation. Her father's eyes followed her with love; he wished that he could make life easier for his eldest daughter. He'd heard from Bethany that Stephanie had just broken up with George, her latest boyfriend. Well, not a disaster really. He hadn't been right for her. But still; must have been upsetting.

Stephanie shut the door behind her but the noise of Elizabeth's distress, now augmented by the running around of members of the staff, who had evidently gone to help, trickled through to Thornton. A few minutes later, Stephanie returned.

"Elizabeth has lost something. She's says whatever it is, it's beyond important to her. She's managed to get everyone on the case. Never happier than when the entire household is demonstrating its devotion."

Through the open door they heard Elizabeth take charge of the gang of household employees, now directed on a search of the house. Thornton looked at Stephanie and shook his head; they smiled at each other in silent accord. Neither were surprised when five or so minutes later Elizabeth burst in, heavy-eyed, exultant. Whatever had been lost was now found.

"Come and sit down, Elizabeth," said Thornton. "And have a cup of coffee with your sister and me. It's been a stressful morning for you already – and you've got the rehearsal later."

He looked at his two daughters, not so different in appearance but way apart in personality. Elizabeth the prettier of the two, softer, smaller featured, cuter, with cornflower blue eyes below black bangs. Her long, blood red nails, that she spent much of the day inspecting and polishing, were, he assumed, in deference to her 'artistic' personality. She lacked the reserve and practicality of her sister but she rode the world in a lighter, maybe even frivolous, way. Stephanie, is spite of her inauspicious start in life, would be OK. Elizabeth? She suffered her sister's unsuccessful taste in men in his opinion, but did not, in compensation, possess Stephanie's competence or firmness of character. There had been a few times when he had to bail out Elizabeth financially. Would it have been better for her if he had not? Would that have firmed up her character? '*Many a young man is ruined by a modest competence'* he recalled Samuel Johnson writing. Probably true of girls too, he thought sadly.

Thornton decided not to press the issue of why Elizabeth had taken his car and come home in the early hours. Another time: it was already getting late. "Well, my dears,' he said. 'It's been delightful sharing breakfast with you this morning. But I need to get going. Stephanie, I'll see you to say good-bye before I leave." It was a statement not a question.

"Where are you going, Daddy?" asked Elizabeth who, although she lived at the plantation, was largely oblivious to everyone else's comings and goings. Thornton was sure he had told her several times. "The MARIONn campus, up in the Berkshires, dear. Just as soon as Billy tells me the plane is ready. I'll be back Friday. Don't forget we're going to the chapel on Sunday"

"Not me, Daddy"

"And why not, pray?"

"I'm staying with Ambrose this weekend. And he disapproves of our governor – as you know."

"*Huh*," was about all Thornton could muster as a reaction to that bit of news. He was not best pleased. Ambrose might be a successful football jock but now he'd left college that wasn't going to do him much good. He could benefit from an artificial brain as much as MARIONn in Thornton's caustic judgement.

"In that case I'll guess I'll see you next week sometime," he said, and turned to Stephanie. He ran through some practical, family related, issues and was about to ask her to make sure that any bottles of alcohol were stored and under key during his absence. This was a standard reminder, hardly worth mentioning if it was not so important. It was unfair to expose Bethany to the temptation. He was about to repeat the injunction – except this time, for reasons that were opaque to him, he did not. He just moved on to discuss some other topic.

Chapter 5

The salvation of memory

Heather was right; the call to her boss was not a welcome one. Thornton had been counting on the funds raised from the IPO. However well MARIONn's development and education had been proceeding up to now, the most recent report on her progress did not suggest that it was likely to get any cheaper. He had just received the R&D budget for the coming year. That, together with the cost of *LetheTech's* planned Phase III trials, made it vital to get the wider investing public to shoulder some of the financial burden.

He thought, ruefully, MARIONn will turn out like his two other, flesh and blood, children; under-budgeted for. Now as he read the board papers for the meeting he saw how tests to establish early signs of consciousness, *singularity*, in MARIONn, despite what he had been told a few weeks earlier, had not revealed the indicators that had been expected and hoped for. Probing of MARIONn's synaptic processes had revealed something closer to machine rote learning than full self-awareness. A Turing test had not been passed to the team's satisfaction. Thornton made a note to raise the subject with Claude Blondel, who been brought in to provide an outside, fresh, perspective on just these sort of problems. Maybe he would have an explanation for the disappointment and suggest what might be done about it. He hadn't yet met Claude but he would be up at the campus this time.

The immediate problem was what to do about financing. He'd have to call the banks, the Venture Capital funds and other sympathetic investors to see what he could raise, without dipping any further into his own pockets (which is how Thornton viewed the cash resources of the Blue Ridge Corporation. In spite of the fact that much of the equity had long been sold to the public, the idea that this was '*his*' company was hard to shake). He wondered how bad the shortfall would be; Heather would have mapped out the cash flow implications. He would make sure to discuss them with her; maybe best to do that one-to-one at first. He didn't want to alarm the others until he knew how long the delay to the IPO was likely to be.

Thornton couldn't believe that they had hit this snag with O'Neal – given that the successful Phase I trials had not suggested any hint of a problem. And was it just a snag – or an indication of something more serious? It was vital that they overcame whatever it was; not just from Blue Ridge's point of view but from wider humanity's perspective, too. Everyone agreed on the potential for *LetheTech*'s memory technology. So many psychological problems found their root cause in traumatic, *repressed*, memories, but if their technology worked as promised, now all that would be in the past. In a revolution undreamt of by mankind's psychological pioneers, Freud, Jung, Klein and so on, psychic burdens would be lifted from humanity, permanently; without effort, without sorrow, without penance. There were plenty of adults and adolescents wandering around with clouded lives as a result of unhappy, traumatic, childhood memories.. Well, no longer….

Thornton ran down the list of additional market opportunities.

EXHIBIT ONE: THE TRAUMATIZED OF WAR

The military had already expressed interest in a system whereby they could heal battle stressed troops. Warriors could be re-cycled. Those who now had to be invalided out with terrifying psychic wounds could be healed and sent back onto the battlefield. PTSD would be a thing of the past and millions would be saved in on-going medical expenses.

EXHIBIT TWO: DEMENTIA

There had been many false horizons with promised new drug treatments. Recent developments in medication had slowed its progression and the physical damage to the brain could now be stalled, but there was a massive loss of memory amongst elderly sufferers even so. The electrical and chemical charges that encoded memories were lost by the time the physical damage had been halted. Now, with *LetheTech,* the potential sufferer could record memories in earlier life, if genetic studies predicted they were in danger, and have them reloaded later should they be lost from the decaying brain. If there had not been the foresight to do that, no problem! New memories would be written, fresh images created. *LetheTech* could insert a whole new narrative of the client's past life. The memory therapists would work with the family on a biography of the individual and then download the 'new' history. The previously demented could participate in family occasions, share old reminiscences, the plots of television programs, and enjoy being part of the discussion on family affairs. Accurate or not. In short, they would be fully equipped with the *illusion* of memory , empowered to discuss these topics in whatever social occasion they found themselves. And who would tell the difference? Was not all memory an illusion anyway?

EXHIBIT THREE: BROKEN HEARTS

Survivors of unhappy love affairs need suffer no more, they could simply remove the memory of the one who had been the ungrateful recipient of their affections. *Ghosting* would now happen within the mind of the disappointed romantic partner; not just in their social media feed. So much more humane!

Many would pay not to have to persist with years of psychotherapy. Unhappiness would just be a thing of the past. Lovers losing their partner, parents losing their children, children losing their pets, men losing their fortunes, grandparents losing their minds.... If the most fundamental experience of life was *loss*, then *LetheTech* was going to change the very sense of what it was to live and be involved with the world. This would be the salvation of memory. No longer would memory be a threat to happiness but now an opportunity for greater content. In future, memory would be managed;, like one's weight - or blood pressure. Such an advance. Thornton thought, '*I could almost write the copy myself.*'

The market potential for *LetheTech* might be immense but it wasn't going to be exploited automatically. Speed was everything. Already there were other companies researching in the same field; *Cybersoul* and *ElectricMemory* were just behind. At least Thornton thought they were just behind, but how good was the intelligence? Maybe they had a technology that didn't suffer from O'Neal problems? Who knew? The market was full of rumour. *LetheTech* needed to get to market as soon as possible. Was Heather Masters the right person to do that? Thornton had asked himself the question many times. The relationship between them was not of very long standing. A year ago Heather had been head-hunted from a small, fast growing, tech company to oversee the day to day operations of the MARIONn project and, in particular, to head up the commercialisation of *LetheTech.* Her background had appeared ideal but he noticed, since employing her, that she veered between great enthusiasm to appearing greatly distracted. Her complicated personal life; a husband to whom she was going to remain semi-married in an *'uncoupling',* as Federal law now permitted, and a new one on the way, could not be making life easier for her. But finding the right candidate for *LetheTech* had not been easy; the ideal CEO needed an understanding of the technology, the ability to handle a brilliant, and often individually difficult, team of neuro-biologists, plus the vision and drive to take the therapy into the market place. Heather had been the best of the choices he had been offered but he sometimes doubted that he'd made the right decision.

Thornton flew up from Crooked Timber to the private airfield at Teterboro, New Jersey, and then helicoptered onto the MARIONn research campus. On the flight up, he ran over the agenda; the morning would start with a full discussion on the O'Neal issue and then they'd move onto a briefing about MARIONn's progress towards full consciousness, the *singularity* that had been sought by Blue Ridge, and indeed all AI engineers, for so long.

Let's deal with the immediate crisis first, Thornton thought. The memory trials, on rats and then a few early human volunteers, had seemed to go well enough at the start. His team had proceeded conservatively; as he had insisted. Those early human trials, the Phase I, had been limited; not just in terms of the numbers of guinea-pigs who had their memories manipulated, but also in the depth of intervention *LetheTech* had been prepared to risk. Those early forays into the minds and memories of some of the more adventurous staff had been shallow; deletions had been modest. That seemed to have proceeded without problems. Only with the rodent trials had Xian Han and his team unleashed the full capability that the technology provided, removing core memories, putting them back, creating new ones that had never existed before and inserting them permanently into the rat's minds. Evidently, as he reflected sourly on the Kinnead O'Neal debacle, things were more tricky with humans. So, what had happened with O'Neal? Whatever the cause, it would be months before they could countenance the IPO launch again; the bankers would be jittery after this fiasco. They would seek cast-iron guarantees that those problems were in the past.

With the noise of the helicopter blades preventing any talk, Thornton downloaded, through his iPysche, the email Heather Masters had sent him that morning, only two days after the news of the collapsing IPO. He closed his eyes and '*saw*' the text floating in his mind. Rather unpromisingly, the email was headed;

More teething difficulties

From: Heather Masters

To: Thornton Lamaire

Re: Recent developments

Hi Thornton,

I'm afraid that it seems to be one of those trying times! I wanted to bring you up to speed with developments before our meeting.

We've had one more incident that has been a little disturbing – but I'll come to that later.

Let me talk about O'Neal first. In the wake of that, we have identified some calibration issues, inadequate and excessive deletion of memories; that sort of thing.

Failing to properly delete a memory is hardly a problem but excessive deletion is a bit different! The patients don't notice anything – once the memory is gone they don't recognize that that they ever possessed it. O'Neal has been an extreme case but even in less severe deletion issues we've had push-back from relatives. Some have been quite aggressive when they discover that their aged parent can no longer remember a great family occasion or one of their children's names (not popular that!) or, at worst, *who they are*. Equally problematical is where we inadvertently remove a '*motor*' memory. The old saying about never forgetting how to ride a bicycle may not prove quite true! But then, I guess, that's not a skill most of our aged *clients* (as you know, we don't like to call them patients) much use anymore.

But prior to O'Neal, these incidents has been on the decline. We have almost halved the rate in the last month – but. I know, we need to get them down almost to zero before we can approach the IPO again. But I gather *CyberSoul* and *Electric Memory* are having the same problems (and worse!). I have talked at length to Xian Han about the whole issue and he assures me that he understands the cause of O'Neal type problems and that they can be rectified with some modest changes to the software.

As for MARIONn… well, her development continues apace too. Xian and his team have pretty well completed basic software testing, prior to the installation of the ethical edicts and early education. We thought all that was going well but, as I mentioned, we had an incident last week that made us realize that we have not eradicated all the bugs.

We wanted to test some new software that integrates sense data; it combines different sensory inputs, like touch, sight, smell, to inform behaviour. The software was installed in some *series 4* trial machines. We gave each robot one sense, e.g. one touch, one vision, etc. They would contribute their separate data streams in order to achieve a common objective – to locate a reward buried at a specific location. They had to navigate a mile or so of woodland before they arrived in the *observation clearing*, outside the executive dining room.

So…. we're all sitting there, Xian Han, myself, 5 or 6 other members of our team and an invited group of our sub-contracted programmers. (*Mistake 1 – don't invite outsiders at this stage, until we're sure everything works!)* Picture the scene. The three test robots, that look a bit like eight legged beetles, are introduced some way out of sight. We monitor them as they work their way through the trees.

Occasionally one of them bumps into a pine but, by and large, once begun, the test seems to be going as expected.

All goes well - until they reach the clearing. Then, a dog appears out of nowhere, followed by a man, with a gun, who must be out hunting. We thought we had secured the local woods so I don't know how this guy had got into the area – but got in he had, with his dog.

He looks puzzled as he sees the thin, silver, metal pole that is the designated objective for the robots. His dog is sniffing around its base, wagging his tail like mad and jumping up and down, no doubt attracted by the scent it can smell at the base of the pole. I had no idea the scent we chose for the test was so attractive to canines! *(mistake 2!)*

The hunter goes over to investigate. He begins to waggle the pole and pull at it. I guess he is curious about whatever is causing his dog such excitement. I turn to Euclid McNamara (remember him? Member of Xian's team?), who's sitting next to the intercom, and ask him to tell the man to vacate the test area. *Quickly* – very! The man looks up, trying to identify where the voice is coming from. But he doesn't move – at first.

Meanwhile, I've been noticing that the robots are no longer venturing forward; they're spreading out on the boundary of the clearing - but making sure they are hidden by the trees. Then they stop advancing and take a position that I can only describe as '*hunkering down'*. They are absolutely silent, not treading on anything that might make a sound and give them away *(I'm*

guessing here. We won't know for sure what they were really thinking till Xian finishes analysing the data).
Then, as though at a coordinated signal, each robot rises up on their eight legs, come out from behind the trees and launch themselves, faster than I have ever seen them move before, across the grass. The man hears the noise of their approach, spins around, drops his gun; so startled he's transfixed by what he is seeing. The dog runs off, scared out of its wits

Each robot grabs at the man. Two go for the legs, the other jumps and lands on the man's midriff, wrapping its own legs around him and knocking him over in the process. The man is screaming with fear, as you might expect. We've never seen this sort of behaviour before. I've no idea what the robots might do next.

I shout at Euclid, "Turn off the power, *pull the plug, pull the plug*!" This, thank a million heavens, he manages to do. Luckily he was sitting next to the emergency STOP button. God knows what might have happened otherwise. The robots immediately freeze - but unfortunately with the man still locked in their embrace. He's no longer screaming. He's passed out.

We go out into the clearing, unwrap the robots from around the man and carry him into the dining room. Despite his ordeal, there are few physical signs of injury, some scuff marks on his legs but that's all.

I can see how this might end for us. So with Xian, Euclid and a few others we sedate the man, to prevent him from waking from his catatonic state, and carry him into one of the labs. Xian is a bit worried by the ethics (always the same with Xian!) but I overrule him (*I'm not making mistake 3!).*

We settle the man on the table, attach the *LetheTech* headgear, bring up the memory of the last few minutes on a screen – and delete it.

Luckily, the incident is so fresh in this man's mind that it has not travelled very deep. Removal is simple and fast.

Then we take him to the canteen, put a cup of coffee in front of him and bring him round. "Oh," we say. "So glad you are OK. We found you passed out in the woods and brought you here."

The man shakes his head, and says, "Thank you, thank you, that was mighty kind of you. I'm sorry to be such a nuisance. But I had a dog with me, I don't suppose you've seen her? Answers to the name of Daisy."

By that time we'd found the dog and could reunite them; gave them both a meal. The man couldn't have been happier or more grateful for his treatment. We drove him back to town, to bear witness to our kindness and deny any of the rumours about untoward goings on at the campus.

Not so easy with the audience of sub-contractors, who'd witnessed the whole thing. We had to buy their silence.

All in all, an exciting month but not one that I wish to repeat. Obviously there is something amiss with the internal controls that we built into these *series 4* robots and I've asked Xian to go over all the protocols again. The *kill button* might not be so close at hand next time!

Enough from me. Look forward to seeing you later

Best, Heather.

Well, could have been worse, Thornton reflected, gazing out of the window of the helicopter. He hoped that the hunter's memory deletion had been thoroughly done: he didn't want any repressed memories coming back to haunt this unfortunate guy – that, as inevitably would land up as a suit against Blue Ridge. But really, Kinnead O'Neal and then this: he wondered if they had the technology as well under control as Heather and Xian Han tried to assure him.

Chapter 6

Thornton meets Claude Blondel

The helicopter clattered on, flying as low as it was allowed, following the ribbon of the Hudson as it wound itself through the Berkshire forest. Wanting to give himself as much time as possible, Thornton had set out early, accompanied only by a couple of assistants. Heather had flown up the day before, to check out the arrangements for the meeting and agree with Xian Han the line they were going to take with Thornton.

The sun had only just risen, illuminating with its oblique beam the forest canopy beneath the flight path. The helicopter flew past the Palisades, up past West Point college, over the town of Beacon and then, a little further on, banked off to the left, where the land rose and the trees without number disappeared over the horizon. Soon Thornton, relieved, spotted the clearing and the gleaming glass shell of the MARIONn building and a few minutes later the pilot began bleeding off height to approach the landing field. He could see the welcoming party below, sheltering by the side of the main building, blown about by the wash from the blades. He mentally checked them off, Heather Masters, Xian Han, that must be Claude Blondel, identifiable in his charcoal grey suit and open necked white shirt that even Thornton was aware was his 'brand' identifier. He must have arrived from Paris a few days before. Next to him several people he didn't recognize, probably programmers and technicians. Then two young guys in trainers on the left. Euclid was one of them, no idea who the other was. And there, standing slightly apart from the rest of the group was Harvey Jennings, the chief machine-psychologist.

Once on the ground, Heather made the introductions of those Thornton did not already know. He was given to understand that the young man he had seen with Euclid was a student, an intern on some form of limited contract to help out and learn from Euclid. Had he been properly vetted? Thornton wasn't keen on itinerant students, on work experience programs, or as interns. Who knew what their agenda really was? There were many misguided young men fighting against machine intelligence these days. They claimed idealistic motives and a wish to promote the primacy of the human mind, but Thornton was unsympathetic. Whatever their motives, they were destructive and would imperil MARIONn if they got their chance. Most of them came from within the US but they had their supporters overseas too. He knew Xian Han tested for motivation and underlying belief systems but some of these people had been very good at hiding their true allegiance. He would raise the issue with Heather later.

Thornton checked, as always, his iPsych*e* and the lack of signal. It was as it should be; the team could take no risks. The building had been constructed as a seamless Faraday cage, through which no radio signals, to or from the outside world, could penetrate. The irony of it all amused Thornton. At the MARIONn campus, where they were carrying out the most advanced AI studies the world had ever seen, it was impossible to send or receive a telephone call. Well, not quite. Xian Han and Heather had needed their own encrypted link but even that was guarded by a computer programmed to sniff out any messages that might inadvertently compromise their work, or give the outside world an idea of what they were building up here. Security was an ever present issue. They had to prevent the *'crazies'* interfering, or causing damage, but also to deflect any premature influences, unhelpful, disturbing stimuli, reaching MARIONn too early in her development. She might not be able to make sense of what she heard or saw, and the precipitate data could upset her.

And then of course there was another worry, a greater one, of MARIONn herself reaching the outside world before she – and her creators – were ready for her to do so. If she became conscious in the same way as a human being, yet could analyse more information, think and act faster than any individual, how would she choose to engage with the world? Nobody knew yet; but until they were certain and had determined that it was safe, there could be no contact between MARIONn and the external world. Information that she needed to know in order to fulfil her purposes (the entire code of legislation of every country on the globe, all scientific papers published in the last 50 years, etc) would be down-loaded from the internet, scanned for viruses and hidden, inappropriate, messages and then uploaded again to MARIONn. No direct feed was allowed. The educational staff were segregated from everybody else at the campus. An unsuspecting employee, even a cleaner perhaps, might be seduced by MARIONn to act as a conduit to the world. Would she do this, seek a forbidden contact with humanity? Probably not, but it was not a risk that could be entertained. So the team had to do everything themselves, make their own coffee and carry out their own cleaning - the most highly paid and highly qualified domestic staff on the globe.

The meeting was due to kick off at 10, so they had half-hour to chat over coffee. Thornton spotted Xian Han across the room and went over. He noticed that Han's countenance bore an uncertain look and speculated silently on its cause; a trace of perplexity, almost of anxiety? Did his chief developer have doubts about the technology that he had invented? Thornton reflected briefly on the debacles with Kinnead O'Neal and the hunter. Han might be one of the most accomplished neuro-scientists of the age but he wasn't one of the great communicators, and he kept his own counsel.

Thornton smiled encouragingly, "Cheer up Xian. You've been working on this for years and now you know that, bar a few snafus, the *Han Translation* works. There's a Nobel prize here for you, for sure. Heather tells me that you understand the weakness that led to O'Neal and that you know how to rectify it. After that, we'll be there, all hazards sorted, will we not?" Thornton looked hopeful, willing Xian Han to confirm his optimism.

Han did his best; he knew what Thornton wanted to hear. "I hope all that's behind us," he agreed. "Phase II testing has been a little hit or miss so far. But I expect to achieve less than 0.2% failure in the next two months of trials." But for all Xian's confidence in the revised technology, that was not what contributed to his look of anxiety

"Good enough to release on the public?" asked Thornton. "You know it costs a lot to keep this effort running. It would be nice to turn it all into a buck or two."

Han was familiar with this sort of pressure. "With your signature, Mr Lamaire, we will go straight into wide-spread human trials, Phase III; trials with several thousand or so patients." Han stopped and corrected himself. " Several thousand *clients* who've got serious psychiatric issues. But you know, damage as bad as what O"Neal suffered has been rare. Even in Phase 1 we weren't getting those problems - often. Remember when we tried an early iteration of *LetheTech's* technology on a few volunteers here? We even persuaded our sceptical Frenchman... over there," Han pointed vaguely in the philosopher's direction, "to participate. He seemed quite keen. We never experienced an O'Neal type issue with him or any of the others."

Thornton nodded approvingly; he liked to be reassured. But reckless deletion of memory was not his only concern. "Are we going to have a problem with the FDA, the Federal drugs people, after this. Could that slow things up?" he asked.

"I don't think so. Anyway I hope not," replied Han. "We seem to be in a grey area regulation wise. We may mimic the procedure for drug testing, going through the three phases, phase I, II and III, but this therapy isn't a drug, after all. Nothing is ingested or injected into the patient. This is more like psychoanalysis. We will aim to comply with whatever standards the Association of American Psychology advises – but that's not too strenuous."

"And while we are on the subject of progress, how's MARIONn herself coming on?" queried Thornton. "Are we close to *singularity* yet?"

"Soon, very soon," replied Han encouragingly. "But don't have too high expectations. Initially MARIONn will only be at the equivalent stage of a very young human child. Simple conversations are developing – early evidence of semi-conscious thought, I believe. MARIONn's not complied with the full Turing test yet – it's a little early for that. But, then, could you tell most American children are fully conscious at four? Or at any other age I sometimes wonder." Hans smiled at his own little joke.

Just then he caught sight of Claude Blondel talking to Heather Masters. "By the way, I don't think you've met Claude yet? Claude Blondel?" asked Han. "Our resident philosopher, our *metaphysician* as we should more accurately call him? He's has been a lot of help. He's French, but otherwise he's OK."

Thornton looked across the room at the tall man with tussled black hair, in the charcoal coloured suit and open snow-white shirt, that he had noticed from the helicopter. "Only when we were introduced on arrival, this morning," said Thornton,

"He's on part-time contract to us from the Science Po University in Paris," explained Han. "That place where they start to train the elite to run the country. Blondel's a typical product – but smart, very smart."

"Just explain to me why we have him on the payroll?" Thornton asked. "What exactly does he bring to the table?"

"At *singularity*, we're trying to mimic the human mind," explained Han. "If we're successful, we'll have built something that operates very close to the way your or mine brain works. Part of the problem on the way is defining what we even *mean* by concepts like 'consciousness,' or what it is to be self-aware. We can't progress, can't reach the right answers, unless we ask the appropriate questions in the first place. And Claude helps us do that. He helps us frame the question in the right way. Once we have the concepts tied down we can build the appropriate neural networks. Come – I'll introduce you properly."

The two of them were just about to walk over to where Claude and Heather were standing, chatting, when a troubling question occurred to Thornton. Couldn't they have found an American philosopher? Was this Blondel character safe? Had he been checked? They couldn't afford any leaks. But Xian appeared to anticipate Thornton's doubts. "He's the top guy in his field, you know, like there's really no one better. Speaks perfect English too; bilingual. We really needed him and he's sound. Been checked out, signed the NDA and everything. He won't leak."

"Ask him to come over here. Then leave us for a few minutes, please," said Thornton in his usual manner of directing the world, without expecting any hindrance. "I'll be the judge if the guy's right for us."

Han went over to ask Claude to join them and then left the two men to form whatever relationship they could. It was a culturally diverse pairing, he hoped it would go OK; the entrepreneurial traditionalist from the South and the slightly dandy intellectual from Europe. But neither lacked self-confidence. Their meeting would either lead to mutual antipathy or a grudging respect for their different talents. Important that it was the latter thought Han; he didn't want to lose Claude.

"Han tells me you're core to our team effort, Mr Blondel. What do you think of it so far? Are you pleased with the progress?" Thornton asked, by way of starting a conversation.

"Core?" responded Blondel, with a doubtful tone to his voice. "You're very kind, Monsieur Lamaire. But I am not core here. Xian Han is, he's a genius you know – he will get to the destination in time anyway, whether I am here or not. But it is perhaps true that I can quicken progress a little"

"And is the work helpful to you, I mean to your own discipline?"

"That's a perceptive question, Mr Lamaire. The answer is, yes, it is. It is fascinating for me to try out different concepts of what *is* consciousness. There have been many attempts to define it. With Han's help we can install these various definitions on the prototype MARIONn to see how her response matches our own concepts. So, my own subject will benefit too, yes. We make a two-way-street, *une rue à deux sens*, as we say."

Coming from Louisiana and being educated at Tulane University in New Orleans, Thornton spoke perfectly good French but thought it might be useful in the future if he hid that knowledge from Blondel just now. He nodded, glad that the benefits of the MARIONn research were so widespread. It assuaged his conscience, buffeted as it was by doctrinal twinges about the moral standing of this work, that different scientific disciplines were profiting, that the sum of human knowledge was growing as a result of the way he directed the R&D budget. Besides he considered that people gave the best of their work when they were being rewarded with more than just their fee. "I'm not entirely sure I understand what is your professional subject, Mr Blondel. Can you enlighten me? Han has explained to me a bit about why he needs you – but perhaps you could fill me in as to your views on the development of MARIONn?"

"My speciality is the mind and metaphysics," replied Claude. "Particularly, obviously, the nature of consciousness. That's why Heather invited me to join you all here."

Thornton didn't like being at a disadvantage in a conversation. The philosophy of mind was not his field. "I don't know anything about Metaphysics; never understood what the term meant," he confessed.

"You're in good company Monsieur Lemaire," said Claude. "There was a famous German philosopher, Wittgenstein, of whom you might have heard, who thought metaphysics was a mental illness! I hope he is not right, I don't want to influence the mind of MARIONn in the wrong way."

But this was not a hazard that particularly worried Thornton. Blondel didn't seem particularly mad and anyway half the people working on this project appeared thoroughly eccentric to him. "Really? And why did Mr Wittgenstein think you were all mad?" he asked.

"This philosopher – this Wittgenstein – thought that the metaphysicians asked improper questions; questions that were not really capable of an answer. They were pursuing clouds of speculation, not rooted in the real world. Western science believes that we should study reality through experiment, the metaphysicians believed that the true nature of reality can be approached by thought alone, by contemplating the nature of the universe."

"But you obviously don't think that you are mad or wasting your time, contemplating as you do these clouds of metaphysics...."

"Pah! Who knows?" Claude waved his hands in the air, an expression meant to indicate his intellectual modesty, as though it were perfectly possible that he might be lost amongst the ineffable complexity of the cosmos. "I try to persuade myself that what I do has a purpose. Us metaphysicians.... we are not scientists and we lack their precision. Scientists look at the specific qualities of things; physical properties, chemical ones, and so on. Me and my kind, ...we are trying to do something different; to see if there are some broad links between things, some qualities that all matter possesses. It's called metaphysics because we consider relationships at a higher, more abstract level, than the scientists. We take their research, their observations, and find a thread between them, a thread that will show there is some common bond between things. And those bonds are what we metaphysicians conceive of as the ultimate reality, the qualities that do not change, that are eternal."

“I see,” said Thornton, doubtfully, not seeing much at all. “And what’s all that got to do with our pursuit of artificial consciousness?”

Claude hesitated for a moment. “There’s a connection between how we perceive things and how things *are*. Metaphysicians believe that how we look at the world, and how we understand what we are looking at, determines what the world *is*. They are inextricably linked; our consciousness and our reality. In other words, we, us….conscious human beings, are not one thing and the outside world another sort of thing. The two are intricately related. So, if I want to understand the world, the universe, I first have to understand consciousness. That’s why I’ve had to become an expert on the subject. And as you wish to make the mental operations of MARIONn, her consciousness, as much like that of humans as possible – well, there I can help.”

Thornton made a note to download some of Blondel’s written work when he got home; he didn’t fully understand what Claude was trying to explain and it frustrated him. If the attractions and temptations of technology were one of his weaknesses he might as well indulge that pleasure properly; understand where his scientists and philosophers who he employed were taking MARIONn.

Chapter 7

Euclid McNamara explains MARIONn

Heather Masters started off the meeting with a brief introduction on the state of the company, for the benefit of the staff who had no or little contact with the outside world since her last visit. She spoke of how *LetheTech* and Blue Ridge were performing, a portrait of the overall business, its financial strength and strategic issues. And it was not a happy story. She began with a discussion of the problems with the Phase II trials, that had come to a head with the PR disaster of Kinnead O'Neil's therapy; the consequential pulling of the IPO, that was going to create financial stress for the funding of the phase III trials and, finally an internal issue, the unexpected slowing in MARIONn's progress towards full self-awareness. She stopped short about telling her audience of the further disaster, a few days ago, when one of Blue Ridge's series 5 Milton robots had been destroyed by an angry mob, protesting about the Supreme Court decision of *Douglas v Milton Robotics,* the ruling that had recognized the rights of the new semi-conscious robots. But there was only so much bad news she wanted to impart this morning and, anyway, that incident had nothing to with *LetheTech* and MARIONn, or not much anyway. Yet, as Heather knew perfectly well, this latest incident would be used as yet more ammunition by those who opposed the whole idea of robots growing ever closer in abilities to their human masters. *Masters at the moment* was a fleeting thought that passed unbidden through her head.

Heather was nervous enough this morning and had reason to be. Although Thornton was, as ever, courteous she had sensed in recent calls between the two of them a chill in his attitude towards her that was new. She had heard how you were fired from Blue Ridge; first came the chill – and then you'd find that your calls to Thornton were no longer returned. At that point you were expected to do the decent thing, pick up the revolver left on the table and use it – at least metaphorically. Heather could almost hear the rounds being inserted into the chamber.

Having covered recent history, she moved on to what she knew Thornton was here for – an update on MARIONn's development and an explanation for the falling behind schedule. She looked directly at him, "Welcome back to MARIONn, Thornton. It's been a little time since you've been here. Since education is at the heart of where we are now, in terms of MARIONn's progress, and," – here Heather paused, hesitant to mention yet again bad news, although Thornton was fully aware of it, "and, as I have reported to you, the arrival of full self-awareness is slower that we had anticipated. I've asked Euclid, as chief educator, to make a short presentation about what the problems have been and what we might do to overcome them."

The long gangly individual with a scrappy beard and glasses, that was Euclid, stood up. "I'd be delighted, Heather," he said. Euclid seemed to be very confident in himself, Thornton noted, not at all like the nerdy, maladjusted presence that his clothes had led him to suspect. He had had to restrain his reaction to Euclid's dress sense; T shirt, jeans and sneakers were not the way he had been taught to dress at business meetings with his employer. At least this time there was a rather grubby jacket over the T shirt. But Thornton knew that it had not been easy to find the combination of exceptional programmer and primary teacher MARIONn required at this stage. And, in addition, someone who was prepared to live a pretty isolated life out here in the *boondocks*, as Thornton judged this outpost in the Berkshire woods. He was not a man moved by a frontier mentality.

Thornton was in a sour mood and he was already suspect about the way he reckoned the morning would be run; they'd attempt to bamboozle him with science, tell him all was going in the right direction, in spite of the reverses, and then ask him to sign another cheque. He took a deep breath. "OK, Euclid. Please proceed," he instructed..

Euclid set off with a bright smile, "Thank you Mr Lamaire. As you will know, twenty years ago AI was seen as a revolution in computer science and so, in many ways, it was. But progress towards making computers think for themselves, in a self-reflecting way, be *conscious*, has been slow. Computers have remained essentially dumb machines, calculating what we, their masters, instruct them to do. Even when they became learning and self-programming devices, beneficiaries of that very AI revolution I mentioned, that enabled them to go beyond their initial programming, they were still essentially *our* devices. It was us that gave them their purpose, their direction, their goals – even if they pursued those goals with strategies, and at speeds, that we had never have dreamt of. Twenty two years ago, at the start of this revolution, Alpha Go learnt, on its own, three thousand years of Go strategy in just over a month. But even as computers started to show signs of human-like inductive reasoning, to progress from single goal machines, like being outstanding at chess or Go, to *AGI* machines, capable of artificial *general* intelligence, they were still not independent actors."

"Alpha Go, and others, Deep Blue, Deep Mind, Alpha Zero and so on were designed to educate themselves to perform a range of tasks that *we would give them*. They were useful, but not as useful as if they possessed the independence and creativity of a human brain, as MARIONn is designed to be. She is built, even if in silicon, in the same way as a human mind, not only to learn and how to manage and perform any task that we give her, *but any task that attracts her interest.* MARIONn will, of course, be contained within limits that we set - but she will have autonomy too. Like us, she will have an overall purpose, *purposes* perhaps, but how she will achieve those will be up to her. And as she develops her consciousness, she can add to those initial purposes and pursuits as matters in her environment pique her interest.

"MARIONn, when fully actuated, will be as flexible and as creative as a human being, while possessing a much larger memory, and work much faster. But, you may be asking yourself, why do we bother to put such an emphasis on acquiring consciousness? Of course we want a machine who can process a much larger set of data than any other computer can manage, and for it to analyse that data with much deeper reflection. And we also want a machine we can talk to. That's all taken as a given yet….. we could achieve that without bothering with the added complexity of consciousness. But, in addition, we sought a computer who can understand not just what we say, but what we *mean,* too. We wanted a machine that is liberated, who can range where she wants, in search of solutions to mankind's greatest problems. If she is going to be able to do that most effectively then, we believed, MARIONn needs to be self-aware. Our creation needs to be reflective about her thought processes so she can *choose* goals and lines of enquiry for herself, not just ones that we might give her. She needs to make those inductive, creative, leaps which will lead her to the answers we have sought throughout history, but never found or worked out for ourselves That's the quest of *singularity*, achieving the human attribute of self-awareness in a mind *that mankind has built.* And a month ago we thought we had achieved that state – at least at a primitive level."

Euclid hesitated and took a swallow of coffee, then went on. "To a limited degree we have achieved that objective. We have tested MARION extensively and there *are* glimmerings of self-awareness. But we now find that further development is slow. We also find that consciousness is not very well established. It's as though it flickers on and off. MARIONn is still not a great deal more conscious than a very clever AGI machine. Consciousness and intelligence are not directly linked, as you know, so she can be both highly intelligent – which she is – but not very self-aware. In that regard, she is presently at the level, at her best, of, say, a young child. A child that can perform amazing calculations – but still effectively the equivalent of a three or four-year old in terms of self-awareness."

Thornton had read the briefing reports describing all this. God, he thought, will Euclid get to the point? We're behind schedule and I get a lecture of how we got where we are and how difficult it all turns out to be. He interjected, "Euclid, I'm aware of most of this. Tell me, do we have any solution for moving things forward?"

Heather saw her boss's impatience but thought she was probably better suited to handle his moods than Euclid would be.

"Thank you Euclid," she said. "Why don't I take the story on from here?" Euclid retreated and sat down, perfectly glad not to be in the firing line. He found the whole meeting a bit of a waste of his time; he could be getting on with MARIONn's lessons more profitably – and more interestingly.

But, in truth, Euclid had chosen to downplay MARIONn's performance. Yes, she was becoming self-aware slower than had been predicted but she was still a lot further on in her understanding of the world, like an idiot-savant perhaps, wise but silly at same time, than any of them around the table were being led to believe. And Euclid like it that way. He enjoyed the idea that he should know MARIONn better than anyone else. That knowledge might well be useful in the future, in a way that he could not yet ascertain. MARIONn was a fast learner, and Euclid found her eagerness to acquire new knowledge, and her ability to structure it into something meaningful for her, highly rewarding. He had to be careful to remind himself that this was a machine that he was talking to – for MARIONn sounded so very like a human sometimes. When she spoke, he would challenge any one to realize they were speaking to a computer, if they couldn't see the banked-up array of servers that contained her '*mind'*. For him, the Turing test had been passed long ago.

A relationship was growing between them. It could hardly be otherwise since they spent ten hours a day together and MARIONn was dependent on him for much of her raw material, both intellectual and sense-data. Sometimes Euclid worried that there was a co-dependency establishing itself and he had to remind himself that MARIONn was just a machine that he could close down at will – which he partly did at the end of each day, when he put her to '*sleep*'.

Euclid set himself back into the slouch he had enjoyed before he started to speak, bored by Heather's attempts to reassure Thornton. He heard her say, "MARIONn's education is going really well. During the next month we expect to bring her up to fourth grade. After that we are going to pause and assess things before going further. As I am sure you are aware, there is a step-change in the nature of consciousness in the years after that - when a human being becomes not just conscious but self-conscious, more reflective and self-aware; what we know as the beginnings of adolescence. We need to navigate those years carefully – just as we would if they were human teenage years – and we all know how tricky those can be!" Thornton failed to laugh.

This mixture of hope and excuses, as Thornton saw it, about MARIONn's progress or lack of it, continued from Heather. "We are ahead of other, competing, universities and research departments working on the threshold of computer consciousness," he heard her say. "You will remember the latest iteration of the famous LIMBO computer that was built at Oxford in England that got very close to singularity – but none of them have cracked it either."

Thornton couldn't bear this wittering on anymore. He pushed himself out of his chair and stood up. He said, "Heather, thank you," in a perfunctory tone, that held neither warmth not much sense of appreciation for her presentation. Sometimes, Thornton was full of self-doubt and fears of intellectual inadequacy in front of his scientists and philosophers, but there were also occasions when he became aware of his authority, for the need to impose a direction, when he channelled his inner dynamic as the chair and largest shareholder of Blue Ridge.

"All of you," he said. "Listen to me. This whole program is in trouble. The launch of our first offshoot of the MARIONn programme, *Lethertech*, has failed, or at least been delayed, significantly. We are short of finance; the development work towards self-awareness is behind schedule – and we have no idea whether we can fully achieve that goal. At the same time we are under pressure from those who believe our work is some sort of deal with..... I don't know what, with the '*Devil*' perhaps. I don't want to hear about how well we are doing compared with other research groups, I don't want to hear stories of scientific advances that we've made but that don't get us towards our goal. I don't want to hear, '*Please Mr Lamaire, can we just have some more money and it will all be right in due course.*' I want practical steps that will get us back on track and start turning all this expenditure over the last how-many-years into income. You are not owed your jobs by God: you hold them to do a specific task, *for me*, that gets results. And if those results are not forthcoming then those jobs are not worth doing. Do I make myself clear?" Thornton stopped and let the silence linger. He looked down at the crescent of people spread before him, tracking his gaze from left to right, as though to challenge any objections.

"Now," he continued, "let me tell you what is going to happen. First, Heather, you are going to concentrate on making sure the Phase II trials of *LetheTech* are completed perfectly, no more fuck-ups, like with Kinnead O'Neal, and we're going to launch our IPO within six months. No '*maybes*', no '*I hope so*' about it. It's going to happen. Second, until that IPO arrives we have a financial squeeze. Leave the solution to that with me. Resolving that is my job. As for the delay in raising MARIONn to full self-awareness which is, may I remind you, the whole point of this research and which will lead to a pot of gold at the end of our rainbow, we need to give that some hard thought – as to whether this is a goal we are ever likely to reach."

Claude Blondel, stood up and catching Thornton's eye said, "Mr Lamaire, may I? I have some ideas about the last point that I'd like to discuss." Thornton, recalling the enthusiastic review that Han had granted this French philosopher, nodded. He was very willing to defer to anyone else but Heather. "Of course, I'd be delighted for any guidance Mr Blondel," he said, recovering his good temper. He needed an effort of will to achieve that self-control. He knew the warning sign of which irritation was the harbinger. His blood sugar would be almost at danger level. It had been a long time since breakfast; he needed something to eat. He burrowed into a pocket for a bag of nuts. He would munch while the Frenchman spoke.

"Let's hear Claude Blondel's suggestions," he said, just before shovelling a fistful of cashews into his mouth.

Chapter 8

Euclid hears something he doesn't like

Claude set off, his mind already tuned to the way he had long learnt to address an audience, whether students, the press or boards. He held up a hand, three fingers were splayed. "There are three points I want to make. First!" And he bent over one of the three fingers. He expected his audience to listen attentively. "As we agreed right at the start of this project, it is impossible to imagine human consciousness without the *human experience. Our* consciousness has developed to help us, homo-sapiens, cope with the external world, with the challenges that the world brings. Consciousness is a very sophisticated response to the experience of the world we find ourselves in. If we want to elevate a novel embryonic consciousness, such as MARIONn's, then we must provide her mind with an experience similar to that which we enjoy in our early years, and as her life develops the experience must expand appropriately. MARIONn must '*see,*' and enjoy, the world just as we do."

"Second!" Claude bent over another finger. "In pursuit of that experience for MARIONn – so she enjoys all the human senses, vision, hearing, smell, even touch – we have wired up Euclid to her mind, via his specially adapted iPsyche. MARIONn experiences what he experiences. But third!" The last finger folded forward. "Even with that direct connection, MARIONn still does not in fact experience the world just as we do. For one thing, we *act* in the world. We DO things and then we receive back data on how that action changes our environment. Without the feedback that we enjoy when we act, consciousness, as we understand it, will never be properly formed."

"So MARIONn needs experience of the world and she needs experience of *acting* in the world, solving the day to day problems of living. If the technology had been there we would have built MARIONn as a mobile robot. Like those you see in the movies. But there was a problem. We can't make human sized robots, as sophisticated as MARIONn, that can go out and live in the world. There are 3 trillion neurons in a human brain, more junctions and connections than atoms in the universe. Even with all the progress in miniaturizing computing capacity over the last decade, we still can't build something as as smart as a brain, that will fit into a volume the size of a skull; a human cranium. And that's all apart from the reliability problems of the physical machinery that would allow our robot to move around in public. Besides, would the public want these conscious robots wandering around amongst them, given existing social attitudes? After the reaction to *Douglas versus Milton Robotics*? I don't think so. Then there's one killer additional problem; what exactly would this robot actually *do* in the outside world? Just wander around aimlessly? For that is not how humans operate, we go about their lives *purposively*, we do things, direct themselves with a goal in mind. Even if it's shopping. We are *intentional* creatures. The early mobile MARIONns, if they could have been built, would not have been like this. So, reluctantly, we decided that to make her a simulacrum of a human-being was not possible. That's why MARIONn sits in a stationary series of servers

- over there." Claude pointed to a door at the side of the conference room.

"So," said Thornton, interrupting. "Are we at an impasse? Is true consciousness beyond us? We've spent a heck of a lot of money to get this far. We set out to beat everybody else to the first conscious computer and now they're going to beat us, instead." There was a harsh, disappointed tone to his voice. "Can you help us here, Claude? You were the one who persuaded us to link Euclid's experience directly into MARIONn."

Claude looked down at the table, seemingly lost in thought, as though as yet unclear what any solution might be. At last, instead of answering the question directly, he said, "Euclid, can you just remind us how you educate MARIONn? You mentioned that you have brought her up to the equivalent of a three or four-year old child in a nine months or so – in terms of self-awareness. But just remind all of us please, not everybody here will be as familiar with her operation as you and I, how MARIONn is meant to develop at the moment and what resources are available to her."

Euclid decided that he did not need to stand to respond to this question and would address Claude from where he sat. "There are two educative mechanisms," he explained. "MARIONn has access to an extremely wide library that we have downloaded, vetted and stored here on the campus. She can read these works whenever she wants and because she doesn't have any human limitations she can read them a million times quicker than we can. But reading is only part of the exercise – she also needs to assimilate what she reads and interpret it. She needs to build the information she has acquired into a world view. She must decide what information *means* to her. That's why she must have down time, so that integration of the information can be achieved. We put her into the equivalent of '*sleep*' each night so she has time to absorb that data and to reconfigure, in light of whatever she has leant, her view of the outside world. Otherwise she simply gets overburdened, becomes confused and has a sort of breakdown, as one might say."

"And the second educational mechanism?" inquired Claude. Then he proceeded to answer his own question. "If I recall correctly, although there is a team that sources and organizes the factual, hard, data, and feeds it to MARIONn, you, Euclid, are the *only* person who has direct access to her and can provide living experience. She is wired through to your senses – and only yours. As you feel, see, smell - so does she, isn't that correct? She is almost *you*, in a sense. The formal education, via books, programming and so on that you feed MARIONn is maybe the least important source, for her, of what it is to be human. Her relationship with you is primary."

"That's right," agreed Euclid. "I am wirelessly connected to MARIONn." Euclid turned his head to one side and lifted his long hair. "You see this? My iPsych*e* picks up signals that travel up and down the Vegas nerve, from my nerve endings and from my brain, and those signals are then transmitted to MARIONn. Without any need for my authorization, there is a constant feed of raw sense data to her." The usual iPsyche small silver rectangle could be seen affixed to the base of Euclid's neck, at the top of his spinal column. "We worked – and continue to do so - with Apple on this. It was the forerunner of the new, subcutaneous, iPysche*,* that is about to be released to the general public At the time I was fitted, this was entirely experimental. It's been modified a bit from the standard version that will be on sale. Usually, all iPsyche signals have to pass through Apple's servers – for security. This one doesn't. It's the only one of its type that allows communication directly to a non-Apple device – in this case MARIONn. It has to be that way as no signals are allowed in or out of the MARIONn campus."

"And you are the only one of the team here who is presently in this direct communication with MARIONn? asked Claude, keen to clarify this point for others in the audience, although he perfectly well knew the answer to his question.

"That's correct," confirmed Euclid

"And how do you spend most of your day here?" said Claude

Euclid thought, '*what is this Frenchman getting at? Claude must be perfectly aware how I spend my days – sitting in front of a screen.*'

"I'm here – monitoring MARIONn, answering her questions, designing the educative program, the lessons for the following day, that sort of thing," said Euclid

"So most of the time you are occupied with MARIONn – and MARIONn alone? Not going out much, for example? You and MARIONn are, how shall I say, entwined with each other?" Euclid was not sure whether this was a statement or a question. "There's almost no discernible difference between the two of you! You are practically one mind," Claude suggested.

"That's right! "replied Euclid. "I am already a combination of her parent, her friend and her teacher. We're almost becoming co-dependent! No, - I jest. We're not getting that involved!"

'*Many a true word is said in jest,*' reflected Claude to himself.

Then Claude said, "OK, Thornton, Heather, listening to Euclid's description of his interaction with MARIONn I think I see the problem – and maybe this will suggest the solution for us. So far, it has been only Euclid's life that's been the focus of MARIONn's experience. Until recently, that's probably been enough for MARIONn to learn from. But now that's a bit limiting, maybe restricting MARIONn's growth. Because, for most of the time Euclid is stuck behind a screen monitoring MARIONn and feeding her information. And that's how it should be, that's your job, Euclid. But………"

Claude turned and addressed himself directly at Euclid. "I've no doubt that in your early life you grew up rich in varied stimulation. But right now your life, if I may say so with respect, is not like that. Your stimulation is mostly of an intellectual variety. And that is perhaps not of much use to a developing mind such as MARIONn's. She is experiencing a life that is not very diverse. She is like a child of one of those obsessed parents who locks their offspring in a room because they wish to devote their time to gaming, or like one of those crazies who never lets their children out because they fear the world's contamination. In the end, those children grow up stunted and withdrawn. We don't want that for MARIONn. I'm not saying you are such a parent, I'm just making a point!"

But in spite of Claude's effort to soften his metaphor and not be seen to criticize Euclid, the latter was hurt and offended that he should be judged an inadequate parent of his charge. "That is absolutely not the case," said Euclid, with a disgruntled timbre to his voice. He didn't like any implication that he was less than completely suitable for MARIONn.

Claude ignored the protest and continued with his train of thought. "So, if that is the case, then what MARIONn needs is a much more varied experience, a richer diet of life," he said.

"And how are we to achieve that?" asked Thornton.

"We must expand her educators beyond Euclid. She needs a team of perhaps 5 or 6 people, all of them equipped with iPsyches to feed their experience back to MARIONn. And they should be engaged in varied activities up here. Some of them should go into town occasionally, to experience everyday tasks, shopping, strike up conversations with others and so on. Maybe go on holiday. In widening MARIONn's life we may have to take some risks but that I am sure that is what has to be done. Give her a wider experience of what it is to be a human."

Thornton was sympathetic to this idea and began to cheer up; maybe here was a solution to their difficulties with MARIONn. Maybe when MARIONn had direct access to a more extensive, richer, life than Euclid's, her self-programming brain circuits would enable her full consciousness to develop. The old enthusiasm he had for this research began to return.

"I will tell you why I support Claude's idea," Thornton said to the team. "Ultimately, we want MARIONn to assimilate the experience of thousands, millions of individuals, so that she can provide answers to questions that have eluded mankind for years. Xian Han mentioned that the brain has three trillion connections. Well, MARIONn will have many more than that. There will be a point when MARIONn leaves humans in the dust, mentally – when she has direct access to *all* other minds and computers." Thornton hesitated. "I exaggerate a little. But she will, eventually, be connected to at least as many minds as there are devices like iPsyches installed in the human race. And soon those devices, whoever they are made by, will be everywhere. When that moment arrives us poor, solitary, isolated humans, who have had to rely on just our own minds to understand the world, will defer to MARIONn." Thornton was getting increasingly carried away, his gloom having now given way to excitement. "She will have an experience denied to any one single human being. She will hold in her memory the combined experiences, the identity, of us all. *A sort of collective brain.* That's what's going to make her so useful to humanity – she's going to be so wise, so intelligent! That's why she *has* to work, be conscious. She will be the saviour of humanity! I think Claude is right, she needs a more varied, richer, diet of human life if she is to grow. "

Xian Han decided that some corrective to this euphoric state of Thornton's was needed. "There are dangers of this new approach, that Claude recommends – of widening MARIONn's access to minds that go to and from this campus," he said, soberly. "I'm sure that I don't have to spell out the hazards. Until we know MARIONn's character and that our controls cannot be overridden *by her will*, we must be extremely careful. We've no idea of the possible consequences."

"Oh, Xian you're such an old worrywart!" cried Thornton, far too carried away now to let a hint of caution spoil his mood. "This isn't a monster! You've been reading too many gothic novels. And we're safe in Euclid's hands, Euclid is a.........look," and Thornton pointed to Euclid's chest, where over the top of his T shirt could be seen a chain and a cross hanging at the end of it. "Euclid's a Christian. He's not going to let MARIONn run into any bad ways!"

So, in spite of the previous emphasis on risk aversion, Claude's views were thought to be worth a try. The decision to expand MARIONn's group of educators was agreed by the board. Maybe the group was intimidated by Thornton's pressure, maybe they thought there were no great risks from increasing the number who had access to MARIONn's mind – or hers to theirs. Or maybe they were all just exhausted from the endless debates, and lack of conclusions, about what to do. But whatever the cause, Claude's suggestion was agreed to be a sensible one. To everybody except Euclid. He was outraged. MARIONn and he had a close, personal, one-to-one, relationship and now others were to be permitted to join them? It was a trampling on their intimacy, as though someone had invited other people to share his girlfriend. But of course this wasn't his girlfriend and the rest of the group would not understand if he tried to explain his objections to the proposal. His contempt for it was emotional, not rational. How could they be expected to understand a relationship between him and this thing of silicon, that had been under his charge for only nine months?

Euclid had to swallow his ire and his emotional distress. But the repression left him with a resentment against his colleagues. Was this how his hard work and loyalty to Blue Ridge was to be repaid? He resolved, while barely admitting it to himself, to forge a different, deeper, and unique relationship with MARIONn that would exclude these new interlopers.

And who knew what Xian Han was really thinking at this point, either? Did he know himself? He was certainly conflicted. He wanted to force MARONn's progress through to the point where singularity was clear, the Turing test passed with colours, but he was also acutely aware of the hazards of widening her sphere of influence. But he also, like most members of the board, recognized the futility of fighting Thornton's will. So he just said, "OK. We seem then to be agreed about how we are going to proceed. I will appoint the new members who will join MARIONn's group of connected educators. Harvey Jennings will continue to provide psychological input. We will measure MARION's awareness at the end of the quarter and see the level of growth. Thornton, do you or Heather have any more questions? If not, we've been here a long time and we need to stretch our legs. Let's have a 15 minute break and then I'll give you a tour of the facility. There'll be an opportunity to talk to MARIONn directly."

For potentially the most intelligent mind on the planet there was not much to see as the group entered the room where MARIONn was housed. Claude was amused by how far MARIONn differed from the robots and computers depicted in the novels and films of his youth. This was no of R2-D2 or C-3PO from Star Wars, nearer HAL out of 2001: A Space Odyssey. As he looked around the room he understood why, given the size of the boxes that contained MARIONn's brain, and the amount of cooling all the processing required, there was no way this computer was going to walk around in some android body. But she did not need to walk around anyway; the connections to her human hosts via iPysches gave her all the mobility and data she should ever need or seek. MARIONn represented a true democratization of intelligence. Of course, there would have to be some sort of protocol, to prioritize who had access to her capabilities, if she was to be best employed, but that was a problem for the future.

Hung on the wall were some devices that looked much like bicycle helmets. As none of them, apart from Euclid and Thornton, had *iPsyches* fitted they had to use these helmets to talk to MARIONn. Euclid explained the procedure;

"You can talk to MARIONn completely normally. Ask her what you want. If she doesn't know something, or finds your request unclear, she will tell you. Heather, this is the first time you have been here since we finished stage one of her education – why don't you chat to her first?"

Heather picked up a helmet and slipped it on. "Hello MARIONn," she said. "How are you today....?"

Euclid touched his cross. He really did not like others talking to his child. When all these interlopers had all gone, he would do what he always did when he was upset – he would call his uncle, the governor of Louisiana and no doubt, shortly, president-elect of the

New Confederacy, Carroll Gillespie. Of course, he wasn't really an uncle, just auntie Kirsty's husband, but that was how he was always known in the family. Euclid understood that uncle Carroll was incredibly busy these days, yet he always had time for him, his favourite nephew. That was what made him so nice and why Euclid always called if he felt the need for guidance. Not like Kirsty's daughters, the three Swans as they were known, any one of whom he could have loved if they had deigned to look his way – which, of course, they never did. Such snobs! He was glad to be over them; those bitches that would never stoop to give him even the time of day, let alone a smile.

And so, when all the others had left, Euclid did call uncle Carroll and to his surprise was put straight through. The governor sensed readily enough that his nephew was agitated about something; something that even if he did not wish to disclose on the phone, he would like to unburden himself of. The governor had a busy weekend coming up. He would be pretty well occupied for the whole of Saturday but Kirsty and the girls could look after Euclid. Besides, Carroll wanted to know what was now going on, up at Thornton's research facility in the North. He needed to know where the interaction between man and intelligent machine was headed. This was destined to be one of the big political issues that he would be faced with. He said, "Come on down at the weekend. We'll have a discussion. Besides Kirsty and the girls would love to see you." It was only a white lie but he needed to be encouraging and at least it was true for Kirsty; she did like him. For something in Euclid's tone signalled to Carroll that his nephew possessed information that he should be aware of.

Chapter 9

Is MARIONn a potential monster?

Once everybody who wished to do so had spoken to MARIONn, Thornton, whose blood sugar in spite of the cashews was once again at a dangerously low level, declared the morning's meeting closed. They all filed back to the boardroom and a team brought in sandwiches and refreshments. Or at least for those who wanted to stay. Thornton, who had already agreed to have lunch with Heather, looked on enviously. It would be at least 20 minutes before he got anything to eat. But he could hardly just walk out; he'd have to go around and say a few words, thank people for their attendance and so on.

Thornton was well aware too that there had not been time to discuss some other important issues, such as MARIONn's ethical protocols and behavioural inhibitions, that still faced her development team. They would have to take these up at their next reunion but maybe the Frenchman could help on these too? Thornton paused as his old doubts about this project swept through his mind, like fog filling a valley, the light that had appeared after this morning's successful meeting diminishing. The fear of sinister things being hidden in the mist of his unknowing scared him, as they did every so often. He walked over to Blondel,

"Thank you for your suggestion Mr Blondel. That was very useful. Let's hope it does the trick."

"Claude, please. Call me Claude," said the philosopher.

" And likewise, call me Thornton. I insist," replied his nominal boss. "But I wanted to ask you..." Thornton rubbed his chin with one hand and looked at the floor, as if emphasise his concentration on an important point – or maybe he was just calculating whether he should fully reveal his concerns? At last he said, "Do you think there are dangers to our work, Claude?"

There are many, thought Claude, some of which he would attempt to influence, to minimise. But he suspected that Thornton's worries might be of a more traditional kind. "You mean, like Frankenstein's monster or a Pandora's box? That we construct something that gets out of our control? That she is no longer our servant, but our master?"

"Something like that," agreed Thornton. "It's not so much that I fear MARIONn acting against us in ways we can't anticipate; we can – and will - build in a moral code to inhibit undesirable behaviour. But that may not be sufficient...." Thornton's voice trailed off, uncertain perhaps, how to finish his thought,

"I know what you mean Mr Lamaire. Moral codes never stopped humanity behaving like monsters themselves!" said Claude, jumping into the gap as Thornton searched his mind for what exactly troubled him. Claude raised his eyebrows as he spoke, as if to say, '*what else should we expect*?'

Thornton ignored the cynicism. "I've talked to Han about this and we've agreed that the moral instructions must be absolute; like taboos, given without possibility of disobedience to MARIONn's maker, her God, namely ourselves. But that is not the end of the matter...."

"You mean, perhaps, that the installed taboos may not be sufficient?" suggested Claude, guessing at what might be perturbing

Thornton. “Because if MARIONn is conscious…..and therefore can reach conclusions by her own thought processes, conclusions not anticipated by her makers, *us* in other words, then she may consider doing something that is not forbidden but is nevertheless……. evil? Like Adam and Eve, she might let curiosity about the world get the better of the prohibitions we have provided for her?”

“Just so,” agreed Thornton, warming to Claude. “That’s exactly what I have in mind. It’s not that we are creating a monster, indeed we will do everything to avoid that, but that we may be *enabling* one……. inadvertently; creating a being who acts, who behaves, malevolently - from *her own volition*. Not because of our poor programming.”

“It’s like any other advance,” said Claude. “To be used well or badly. Everyone knows that these machines… machines who are self-aware, are coming. We’re going to discover very soon what’s it like to share our planet with another conscious being, one of own making. If man can do something, he will. We never have the strength to resist our wish to *know*. It’s the original curse isn’t it? Adam started the process and we continue the Fall. We will eat the apple again and again, if given the chance. We would prefer to be thrown out of the Garden, rather than not know something about the world in which we find ourselves. It’s our curse and our fate.”

Claude, who had a booming voice, one only too used to addressing inattentive students, had allowed his tone to rise. Others standing nearby stopped whatever they had been talking about and began to eavesdrop. Amongst them, Xian Han and Heather. Then Claude picked up his thread again, on a more hopeful note,

“*Mais*, …. on the other hand mankind is sometimes wise about controlling his inventions, about regulating their use, protecting ourselves against our own worse impulses. We invent atomic power but have been mostly good about not using it to kill people, at least not since World war II..”

“There was that incident in Iran about 15 years ago,” pointed out Heather, who felt she needed to contribute to the conversation.

“Yes, there was,” agreed Claude. “But after the Americans dropped that bomb, by mistake as they said at the time, although few believed them at the time, we horrified ourselves didn’t we? The atomic nations pledged greater efforts to control their arsenals. The chance of a repeat accident became less than before. It’s as though every so often we have to remind ourselves of the terrible power we possess; frighten ourselves. But we don’t want that with MARIONn; we don’t want any instances that might scare the public. The whole project could be closed down in the first year. So the more we give MARIONn human-like reasoning, the more we’ve got to educate her, morally, give her to understand that she *has* to behave in certain ways and not in others. Computers have just been dumb assistants in the past. But not anymore. MARIONn is going to be more *actor* than assistant; she’ll have *agency* in the world. She will be able to decide what to do, not just follow our instructions. So…MARIONn must be….sensible, I suppose. Moral in her own judgements. She must act properly, not irresponsibly.”

Claude paused, gathering his thoughts, then set off once more. “There is a certain type of danger with MARIONn that mankind has not faced before. I mentioned that bomb on Iran. Drop an atomic bomb and, of course, thousands of people are killed immediately – but then there’s the spreading radioactivity, which in time poisons many more. In a parallel way, a connected MARIONn could spread her thoughts and influence into every aspect of our society. If she was ill-disposed to us, the effects of that dispersion could be disastrous. That’s obvious enough. She must never be connected to the internet or any other systems that are a common part of mankind’s everyday existence. Not yet, anyway. Not at least until we are absolutely sure about her own conduct and beliefs….But there’s also another effect - that you have touched on Mr Lamaire, which is even more worrying. MARIONn and her like can think and react in new, creative ways. And those ways may not be of benefit to the way we think about ourselves, our identity. It’s not just MARIONn’s malevolence that we must fear – at least I hope not – but her *competence*: that she may start to perform human tasks so well that there is no room for us. That would be devastating. So do we have to make her *inefficient* artificially? Build in a sort of *incompetency* circuit to make her more like fallible humanity?"

Heather could see Thornton becoming increasingly thoughtful at these warnings of Blondel's. Her boss could cause the whole team a lot of extra work if he got off down that track. Thornton's religiosity, his doubts about the morality of the project, his questioning of whether there were dangers in mimicking God's creation, would all get in the way of their progress unless it was headed off now.

"I'm sure," said Heather with a show of confidence that she did not entirely feel, "that we can programme these silicon minds like our parents taught us, and evolution moulded our moral sense. We can build in '*genetic*' inhibitions into their neural networks, and '*moral*' instructions into their software. They will have limitations on the way they think and *act*, even if they are tempted to act badly. But please," and here she thought of her role as CEO, responsible for maximising the economic return from these investments. "Let us not talk of making MARIONn *purposely* incompetent. That seems a very retrograde step. Surely we wish to achieve something remarkable? To benefit from the great wisdom she may bring to human affairs? Is that not the very point of MARIONn? Why otherwise are we all working on this great project? Let's not hobble her immediately!"

She turned and looked towards Xian Han, "Xian, you've been very quiet. What do you think?"

Han hesitated in his response, sucking his lips a couple of times as he pondered his reply. At last he said, "Where I came from, the land of my birth, most destruction resulted not from people thinking they were acting badly, or being unable to overcome their temptations, but from those who thought they were acting in the name of the *good*, in the best long term interests of society. The problem was not a willingness to do evil but a different concept of how to do better. We can never be sure how an artificially conscious being will develop its thinking. That's the real danger here. Everyone, including MARIONn I have no doubt, believes they act from only the best of motives but…."

Thornton broke in, "the way to hell is paved with good intentions. That sort of thing?"

"Something like that," agreed Han. "We can give MARIONn an understanding of what it is to be *'good',* our concept of the good ….. but our defences must go further than that."

"Further than that? How's that going to work?" asked Thornton.

"We've agreed that MARIONn must be insulated from everybody," said Han. "Until we can determine how restraining, in practice, are her moral constraints. We must take care that she can't talk or influence anybody outside that team. And even they must be regularly monitored for the conversations that develop between themselves and MARIONn. In case some sort of relationship builds between them which she manipulates – to our peril."

Thornton sighed and looked out of the window. All this debate – but the solution was straight forward. The path to good behaviour had long been laid out in the Bible. That was good enough for him and should be quite good enough for any silicon brain. He turned back and addressed the group that had gathered around him. "Xian and Claude have put their thumb on a critical issue. One of great importance, that we must get right. But I believe the solution lies before us. The correct moral guidance has been given to us by the scriptures. They have been good enough for us – at least when we choose to observe them. We don't need to recreate all that, again, and maybe get it wrong in the process. After all, what has ever been wiser than our Lord's admonition '*to do unto others as you would have done unto you*'? I should have thought that, combined with the 10 commandments, would pretty well do the job."

As the rest of them wondered how to respond to this, Thornton turned to his resident philosopher, and said, "Claude, I appreciate you're not a moral guy……" Heather, who knew Claude better than the rest and his reputation, smiled at the unintended innuendo. "By which I mean," Thornton corrected himself, seeing Claude's surprise at this judgement, "your speciality is not ethics, I understand that, yet.... you must have some thoughts on the effect of this technology – if we can make it work to our, humanity's, benefit," he added, piously, worried that the others might have considered him focused only on the profit motive. "You're a philosopher and all philosophy is pretty similar, right? I mean it's all about *thoughts*, isn't it? It's all the same sort of thing really."

Claude made a little *moue* with his lips, his vanity piqued by this view that all distinctions in philosophical study were so much hot air and distraction. He raised his hands in a regretful gesture, "Ah, I make no greater expertise in the moral realm than you yourself Thornton, I'm afraid. But I appreciate the issue. Absolutely. But at the beginning of MARIONn's, what? Can we call it *'life'*? I'm not sure what to call it, but during her development period anyway, her team of educators will school MARIONn, at least at the early stages until she can start teaching herself. It will be their job, ..."

But before Claude could elaborate his point further, Thornton, for whom the morning had already been long, had decided to move on. Morality for him was a straightforward issue; one could choose to ignore the Good Book's strictures but the right way to act had been settled long ago. "Let's not burden today with this issue," he said. "This morning has proved very useful so far. I wish Claude that you could join Heather and I for lunch: alas, we have some business issues to discuss in private but .. it's been a real pleasure. Claude. I hope you will come and stay with Bethany and I one day on our plantation in Louisiana. As a Frenchman I'm sure you'd like to visit the State your countrymen sold for so little over 200 years ago? I hope you bear us no ill will from that. Napoleon did sell quite willingly after all!"

Before Claude could answer for his countrymen, Thornton had moved on again. "Do you shoot duck?" he asked. "They are really excellent later in the year. Maybe, next time you are here to work on MARIONn?"

Claude gave a little bow of thanks. "Your duck would not be in much danger from me, Monsieur Lemaire. I'm not such a great shot. But eat them yes. So, thank you, I'd be delighted to accept your invitation. And you have a wonderful stables too, I hear. I love to ride so a visit to you would not, I think, be a penance, do you say that? A pleasure in fact – and an honour. Once I am in your state I will be keen to '*laissez les bons temps rouler*'. Is that not what you say down in Louisiana?" Claude gave a little chuckle, pleased with his slight knowledge of local culture and its sayings. "Heather told me the name of your plantation, *'Crooked Timber'* How could a philosopher resist such a name? '*From the crooked timber of humanity no straight thing was ever built'*. That's what Kant wrote, So, true, so true*!*

"Don't know 'bout that," said Thornton, with a bemused expression, having no idea who this Kant was. "Ain't never heard that saying myself. But when you come down to visit us you'll see the crooked oak out the back. Split by lightning, grew at a crazy angle. As my ancestors built the house there, they took the name for the plantation. "

"Well, let the philosopher's words be an admonition to us in any event," said Claude agreeably. "Let us see if we can create our new mind, our MARIONn, in a less crooked way than humanity has so far managed to achieve for itself! As for your invitation to visit, for which I thank you profoundly……. I regret for the next couple of months it will not be possible. My work is done here for the moment and for, for a little while, I shall be in Paris. There's my aged father. He's not well and I shouldn't leave him for too long. Then I have the next semester's lectures to prepare. But after that I would love to accept."

"And is there a Madame Blondel?" asked Thornton. "She too would of course be most welcome," Claude took a second to deal with this question: Madame Blondel? Had there ever been a Madame Blondel? He thought not, as far as he could tell. "Sometimes I wish there were, Mr Lamaire. The life of a professor is quite solitary. One day, perhaps, but not so far, *c'est dommage*".

Thornton was a trifle surprised to hear this; he reckoned Claude must be considered a good looking guy. He made a mental note to put Stephanie in touch with Claude. He seemed nice enough, about the appropriate age, 45'ish he guessed, and Stephanie would have few contacts in Paris.

"In that case what can I say except *'bon voyage'?* And we will hope to see you at our home soon. We'll keep in touch." Thornton nodded in the direction of Heather. "I know Heather and you will talk from time to time, there's going to be a lot to do." He shook Claude's hand and walked away. But as he departed for his lunch with Heather, Harvey Jennings, the resident machine-psychologist, who had not featured much in the morning's activities, moved over to talk to the philosopher.

" Mr Blondel, nice to see you again. Do you remember me?" Claude looked the man over. He was unlikely to have forgotten this man, if he had once ever known him. Sixty or so years of age, he guessed, heavily lined face, long, too long hair, that hung down his back and shimmered with a surface greasiness. He was dressed in an slightly worn brown suit and the clothes could have benefited from a clean as much as his hair. He would not have forgotten this fellow.

"Harvey Jennings. One of the psychologists on the team," the man introduced himself. Neither the name nor the elaboration brought him any closer to Claude's recognition. "I'm not surprised that you do not remember me. It's good – much better this way."

Better that I do not recall this man? What does he mean? thought Claude. What is this Mr Jennings talking about? As he could find no trace of recollection, and not wishing to appear rude, Claude decided to head the conversation onto another tack, "What did you think of this morning's meeting?" he asked. It seemed as cautious an opening conversational gambit as any.

"Well, I thought you were right about exposing MARIONn to a wider range of people. I said months ago that relying just on Euclid was inadequate. And possibly dangerous."

"Dangerous?" queried Claude

“ Sure. No doubt Euclid’s a wonderful guy but it puts him in too isolated a position being MARIONn’s sole teacher. You never know…..and MARIONn might try to influence him. We understand so little at this stage. Not like when we were dealing with rats! Like in our early experiments manipulating memory.” Jennings recalled that Claude had not been at the technology proving demonstration last fall.

“You deal a lot with rats?” asked Claude, with an amused tilt to his voice. “I feel sorry for them sometimes. They are so put upon, so always the butt of experiments, those poor rodents. But I read recently that octopuses were the most intelligent form of non-human life. I wonder you don’t use them instead. Would they not be nearer MARIONn in intelligence?”

Jennings laughed. ”Have you ever tried doing experiments with octopi? They’re the most unruly, rebellious, mischievous creatures you have ever come across. You don’t want to work with them, I assure you. And besides they would be hopeless for my purposes.”

“And why is that?”

“Because they have a different neurological system to us. We have a centralised nervous system, feeding its impulses to our brain. For *cephalopods* it is distributed all over their body. Where would we put our electrodes to remove a memory? We’d have no idea. We’re trying to build something like us, not an octopus or a squid. That would be a terrible idea – imagine how we’d try to manage one of them in the laboratory. What a horror!” The two men laughed together at the absurdity.

“But you’re sure you don’t remember meeting me, Monsieur Blondel?” asked Jennings, suddenly changing the subject. Claude started to shake his head, “ I don’t think so,” he insisted. Just then a glimmering of some forgotten, buried, memory passed transiently across his mind. The image fled before he could hold onto it and left him with no identifiable awareness of a prior encounter.

“I joined the team a month or so after the famous rat trials, so we wouldn’t have met then,” explained Claude. He was now beginning to fidget as he really wanted to catch Heather before she was dragged off to lunch with Thornton

Jennings seemed quite unfazed by Claude's inability to remember him, but he noticed the latter's impatience to move. He said, "I know you need to go, Claude. But it's been a pleasure. Maybe we will meet again.....? "

"That would be delightful, Monsieur...." Claude cursed his inability to recall the man's name.

"Just call me Harvey, everyone knows me as that here"

"Of course Monsieur Harvey"

Claude brought out his notebook, that he carried everywhere, and withdrew two visiting cards. Claude was aware of the anachronism of these cards in a digital age but for that very reason, perhaps, he liked and persevered with the ancient practice. He even ensured the printers employed a raised font when they inscribed his name. Detail was important to his aesthetic sense. He gave one of the cards to the psychologist. Then, finding he had nothing to write on and his phone was turned off for the meeting, he took out a pen and wrote on the back of the other card, using the original French spelling, *Hervé* and slipped it back into his note book. There, when he got home, he would have an aide-memoire about this meeting. His memory would not be allowed to fail him again. For Claude was disturbed by this encounter. Somewhere at the back of his mind he felt sure that he had come across Harvey or *Hervé*, however it was spelt, in some other circumstance.

Chapter 10

Thornton and Heather have lunch together

There was a good staff restaurant on the campus but Thornton wanted this talk between the two of them not to be overheard. There were parts of Heather's background, those personal weaknesses as he saw them, that he would like to discuss, among all the other things he had on his agenda. So, instead of the staff canteen he'd take her to one of the executive dining rooms where they would be on their own. He considered inviting Xian Han, which would have been the polite thing to do, but decided against; it would be impossible to discuss Heather's private life if he was there.

The dining room looked out over a clearing, beyond which lay the endless forest that is the Berkshires. Full depth windows allowed the privileged diners an uninterrupted view over the cleared glade, about 200 meters wide by a 100 meters or so deep, curved at its outside edge, like a scallop shell. The view across the glade was sometimes enriched by a deer making its way across the grass. Twenty years ago that sight would have been almost a certainty.

Now, less so. The demand for cheap protein, as the *Shanghai-Accords* on animal husbandry began to bite and force up the price of farm reared animals, plus the deregulation of restrictions on hunting, had driven most of the deer into the sights of those with rifles and crossbows. Today, there was a lone rabbit sitting, munching away contentedly. Even that was a bit of a miracle, thought Thornton.

He offered Heather a seat facing the view and asked, "Do you know why this view is like it is, what it is meant to represent?" Of course Heather did not, so Thornton explained. "It was the idea of the original architect. Several years ago, when we were drawing up plans for this facility, there was a fashionable theory that consciousness was like a sunlit glade in a wood. All your sensory inputs of a particular event were laid out in the mind, on an open mental space, on the grass as it were, to be illuminated simultaneously by the light of consciousness. In that instant of perception you were *aware*; the miracle of being conscious was happening. Outside of the glade, beyond the light of consciousness, in the woods, all was dark. In the subconscious, I suppose. Of course, we've moved on a lot since that time, we have a much better idea of what is consciousness now – but, as you know, to this day we sometimes use this glade as a place where developments in self-awareness technology can be tested." Heather remembered the unhappy experiment involving the three trial robots and the hunter a few weeks back. She drew in a breath, uncomfortable with the recollection. She hoped Thornton would have the grace not to remind her any further of that almost disastrous debacle.

Clarence (for Thornton always wished to be served by his personal butler) approached with the menu. Thornton ran his eye over it and transferred the image to his iPsyche. It took an update on his blood and enzyme readings, analysed both data sets and then sent back a recommendation of what Thornton should be ordering. He summoned Clarence. "I should be having chicken, or some fowl anyway, roasted red rice, and spinach that's been picked this morning. It shouldn't be too difficult for the kitchen."

“Very good, sir.” said Clarence. He wandered off to discuss the order with the cooks. With the two of them now alone, Thornton turned to Heather and said, ”Have you given some thought to which bank we might appoint to handle the IPO next time around, when we try to relaunch it? I think Goldman’s may be skittish after their last experience. Or, alternatively, this time should we issue the equity - directly to the market, do it ourselves?”

Heather knew how much Thornton liked to save money - particularly on bankers. She chose her words carefully. “We could manage the issue ourselves,” she replied, “but with technology this new - and, in some views, this risky, particularly from a future regulatory point of view - private investors might shy away from investing in *LetheTech* if we approached them directly. I think we need the validation that a respected bank would give. But you know that we are still at least a year away from this relaunch? We’ve still got to finish the Phase II trials and it’s going to take some time before we’ve analysed the results - be sure that we can manage memory in people more reliably than we achieved with O’Neal.”

Thornton frowned. “In a year? That’s not what’s goin’ to happen, Heather,” he said, with some force. “As I emphasized at the meeting this morning, you will finish the trials and prepare for the launch of the IPO within six months – at the maximum. You can do both simultaneously. We need to keep up the pace. I hear that *CyberSoul* is almost there with successful trials. They may release results soon – and now Congress is talking about regulation. You know how much we need the cash; I want us to be ready as soon as we possibly can be to tap the markets. So let’s just concentrate on those issues – and which bank we might choose - if you think we must have one at all.”

Heather decided not to argue about timing, however much she thought the timescale wildly optimistic. And there was another objection.

“Which is?” asked Thornton.

“We’re getting feedback from the banks we’ve talked to so far that they believe investors – particularly corporate ones – won’t be thrilled at seeing their money being poured into what they consider the speculation of MARIONn. They'll want it concentrated on making the memory therapy work and getting that to market. They see MARIONn as an unnecessary distraction."

"Well, that would be inconvenient would it not?" said Thornton, sarcastically. "We've counted on not having to fund the next level of MARIONn's development ourselves, at least not very much."

Heather fiddled with half a bread roll between her fingers, "I guess we could load a lot of MARIONn's overheads and her capital costs onto the business that we're selling, i.e. onto *LetheTech.* It's pretty opaque anyway how we divide up the cost allocation between the two sides of the business."

"We need the money - so if that's what we have to do, so be it," said Thornton. "Give the investors the minimum of information that we can get away with."

In the meantime, Clarence returned with the disappointing news that there was nothing available from the kitchen that seemed reasonably in line with Thornton's wishes. But they could manage a burger, proper meat, not that synthetic stuff so often offered. Thornton perked up. Was that right? Did he hear *burger*? Hadn't eaten one of those for a long time. He checked with his iPsyche; no, forbidden. All that bread. *Bah*! Too bad… a man had to eat something. "Bring me the burger", he instructed. He would disobey the proffered dietary advice, …..just this once. He dismissed the faint recognition in his mind that the excuse of *'just this once'* was now being offered remarkably frequently.

With scarcely a two minute delay Clarence returned bearing the burger straight from the kitchen. So confident had he been of his employer's tastes and indulgences that he ordered one anyway. Thornton picked up the bun in both hands and dug his teeth into the soggy mass, drenched in real meat juices. My, it was good. It had been too long.

Fortified with two large bites, he addressed the next item on his agenda, that of Heather's personal life. He put down what remained of the bun, and drew the napkin across his lips, with a few flourishes, like someone polishing the hood of a car.

"I hear I have to congratulate you Heather, and not just about the great results in the lab."

"About what?" The unspecified nature of Thornton's congratulations making her wary.

"Your engagement. I heard that you are to be married again."

"You have good sources, Thornton. Yes, it's true. It was going to happen a few months ago but things are still not settled with Bruno (Heather's first husband). And I wanted to wait until the IPO is launched, so we've decided to delay till next year at least. You must meet my intended the next time you are in New York. He's called Chase by the way"

"You evidently have better experience than me. What do they say? '*The triumph of hope over experience*'? Obviously a lot of hope you have!" Thornton's voice almost sounded like a sneer. "Are you planning to divorce Bruno first?" This question was a sign of Thornton's distaste, and perhaps, considering the state of his own union, envy too for those who did not cleave to their first spouse – and particularly for those who chose the immoral, as he saw it, option of '*uncoupling*'.

Heather hesitated. She knew Thornton was a committed church-going man but was not sure of his view of *uncoupling*, although she suspected she had a good idea. She'd have to risk the truth. "No, I'm not going to fully divorcee Bruno – not at the moment anyway," she said. "I'm fond of Bruno, even if I'll be living with Chase in future. Besides we all live very independent lives. I can see no virtue in a divorce, all that financial mess – when we could simply uncouple."

"The things that people tolerate now," said Thornton, in a carefree voice, as though it was all one to him what people put up with. "I guess there are many of instances of uncouplings for women up North these days, right? But I've hardly ever heard of it being practiced in the South. I'm not sure it's even legal down where I live."

Heather shook her head. "Not so many as you might think in the North; it's still a minority taste. But several of my girlfriends have pursued it. You've got to be very rich for a full divorce these days. So few of the men have jobs now and the courts are asking us to provide them with an income for life. The courts know these men, these ex-husbands, will probably never be employed again – and other women don't want them either. Then you have to provide a house on top, so they have somewhere to live. Men expect to be looked after! But you're right, I think people were a bit taken aback at first. But, it was the obvious next step in the *smorgasbord* of personal relationships. Why not have two spouses at the same time? It could be worse. There's a movement up North, as you well know, to allow polygamy – up to 4 spouses, they say. That's a long way off perhaps but people are saying they should be allowed to do that."

"Polygamy? Yeah I heard. Well, for me even uncoupling is just bigamy made to sound nice," said Thornton, disapprovingly.

"Oh… come, Thornton," said Heather. "You men had been doing that for years, even if you had your wives and girlfriends consecutively. You can't really have one sex having privileges that aren't open to all, can you?"

Heather paused, seeing the scepticism in Thornton's eyes. She would try another angle. "Even in your beloved South you have many marriages too, they're just not simultaneous. I thought you'd rather approve of uncoupling – you being opposed to divorce and all that." Heather smiled – she wanted to be agreeable, if not entirely serious. "I mean, marriage is such a patriarchal institution. It was about time it became more balanced; reflected the needs of both sexes."

Thornton raised his eyebrows and emitted a *hmm*, to express his doubts about the wisdom of what he was hearing, as much as any moral criticism. "Marriage, patriarchal you think? I would beg to disagree," he said. "Always seemed to me that marriage was a very even, balanced, contract – invented to heed the needs of women just as much as men."

“Oh really?” queried Heather, with a tone of mock surprise in her voice. ”I thought men invented it to ensure that their children had been fathered by themselves. Men are so insecure, always so scared of female sexuality. In need of reassurance, men. Always.”

“Not just men, I think. Women have their concerns too, their need for reassurance,” countered Thornton. “They worry that they will be left as they grow older, with their child bearing age behind them. When the threat to men of uncertain paternity will no longer be there as a glue. Men might just move onto a younger model, left to themselves. The traditional insolubility of marriage put a break on that – at least it used to. The marriage contract has suited both parties, really. Given both sexes some security for their different anxieties. So, yes, I am opposed to divorce, and *uncoupling* and to multiple marriage partners too; polygamy, if that ever arrives. Still, I can’t imagine why you should want to get married again but I guess that’s your affair. At your age, you both have houses, you’re not going to have children together. So why bother? ‘*Six months of fire, thirty years of ashes*’. Pretty well sums up my experience of the great institution.” Thornton stopped, as he had arrived at his final view of the state of matrimony, and returned to his burger.

“Thornton don’t be so cynical! Bethany’s not that bad. I know you have your problems. But where would you be without her? Eh?” asked Heather.

Thornton shrugged. He didn’t answer the question. But he had a good idea where he would be if he wasn’t married to Bethany. With Lu Ann in all probability. They’d always got on well. She was warm, not mad, not an alcoholic, nice children, a widow. Yes, that’s where he would be, or at least that’s where he’d aim for if he was free. But he wasn’t, and he was not about to become so either, even semi-free with an uncoupling. Bethany would fall apart without him, or fall apart even further. He’d taken a vow long ago and he’d stick to it. Besides, there were things that bound them to each other; their daughters, Elizabeth and Stephanie, the latter with her complicated history. So he and Bethany would continue together, locked in their barbed wire embrace; but every so often he could dream of Lu Ann, down at his now dead friend Jim's house, on the plantation that was nearly as large as his own.

"No, not all marriages are like mine," agreed Thornton. "I realize that. Well, I wish you well Heather, I really do. But let me ask you, is some of your attitude, to uncouple rather than divorce, consequent on your Lincoin losses?" Six months ago, the largest of the crypto-currencies, the Lincoin, had been hacked and a vast increase in the currency had been mined, causing a massive inflation and collapse in the value of individual holdings. It was perhaps an inevitable (but seemingly unforeseen by the holders of the units) end to the currency 'wars', where competition to attract customers had resulted in ruinous increases in the interest offered on holdings. Finally, some hacker with access to the power of one of the new quantum computers had designed a Trojan horse virus that caused the hitherto thought-to-be impregnable algorithm to run wild and the currency to multiply like a cancer. Heather, as a conservative investor who kept most of her assets liquid, had suffered a 90% fall in their value.

Heather sighed and looked down at the table, cast into painful reflections. "It is. The scandal has almost ruined me. Apart from the house, I have lost almost everything. I could not afford to divorce Bruno right now. So its lucky, he's agreed to an uncoupling. He'll continue to live at home."

Thornton tried to be reassuring. "The IPO is coming. You hold a lot of shares, at least options anyway, in *LetherTech*. That should rebuild your wealth quite considerably."

"Yes, let's hope that IPO goes well. It will be a great help," agreed Heather.

"You and I, we've got some big challenges coming up in the next few months," said Thornton, sympathetically. "The conclusion to the memory trials, the IPO, fending off regulatory attacks in Congress. Anyone of these could be a problem for us. You need to be absolutely concentrated on the job – no distractions worrying about Bruno or Chase - or past financial losses."

“I know, I know,” said Heather, lifting her eyes to meet Thornton’s gaze again. “You can rely on me.”

”The last problem, regulation, particularly worries me. Congress might do almost anything,” said Thornton, not really listening to Heather’s attempts to reassure him. ”Memory therapy is pretty well unregulated at the moment but in 6 months, a year? There’re some guys in Washington who are beginning to wake up about the whole thing. I’m trying to head all that off, but who knows?”

“ You could ship the MARIONn project down to the South, out of the Federal reach, if regulation got too heavy?” suggested Heather. She imagined this would always be Thornton’s strategy if things became too hot up North.

“I could do. But it wouldn’t really solve things,” said Thornton. “Firstly, we’re going to be operating all over North America, all over the world if everything goes well. The Federal government still rules up here, even if its writ outside the Coastal States is not much followed. And it’s still respected - other governments overseas will follow the North’s lead. So we can’t ignore what’s left of the Federal government. I need them not to regulate, yet – or if they must to do so, very lightly. Secondly, there’s a lot of conservative and religious attitude in the South that does not look sympathetically to what we are trying to do with MARIONn. So moving to the South would solve nothing, almost certainly make our problems worse in fact. Besides we’d lose half our staff. Who’s going to swap New York for Baton Rouge? Not Xian Han for sure.”

Thornton paused as Clarence brought in the coffee, then continued, his comment on the chief of the Lab prompting a thought that had been lurking not far below his consciousness, ”Is Han Ok? On message?” he asked Heather. “He looked kind of distracted today I thought. These should be good times for Xian. All his ideas are coming to fruition, with us he’s got the opportunity to make them a reality. I don’t know….. sometimes he makes me feel uneasy. I can’t tell where he’s at, like…….. what he’s thinking?”

“You have to make allowances,” said Heather. “Han’s marked by the loss of his first home. He was happy in China before his parents took it into their heads to try and make China a liberal democracy – and fell foul of the government. Lots of friends; adored by his grand-parents; doing well at school. Then all that was taken from him and Han had to make a new life in the US. He arrived speaking practically no English, was bullied in his first school here. It was hard for him and he retreated into himself. He’s never really come out. But yes, he’s ok. He’s loyal.”

“I hope so. We can’t afford to have him getting fantasies about machines like MARIONn running rogue. I’ve promised him that we’re going to investigate every sort of way to control the technology. Restraints *will* be put in place, I’ve committed to it. He shouldn’t worry so much.” Thornton decided to reinforce the view he’d taken in the meeting. “I don’t know why we just don’t make the job simple, as I said; program the ten commandments into MARIONn. Good enough for me, good enough for humanity these past two thousand years. What’s the problem with that?”

“Not much wrong with that, too true Thornton,” replied Heather, sensing that she had better go with the grain of Thornton’s world view if she wanted to exercise any influence on his decisions. “Except that Christ did not have to contemplate how artificial minds and human ones might interact. We might need a bit more than the ten commandments.”.

Thornton shook his head, “Well, if control is such a big deal what about your French friend, Blondel? I asked him to help. He’s probably the best equipped of any of us to think about those sort of issues. Maybe I should talk to governor Gillespie too – this is sort of his field. He’s a man of God, or was, after all. Ethics should be his baby. That was his profession before he took up politics.“

Heather had met the governor once. There was no way she wanted his Old Testament views anywhere near MARIONn. She reckoned it an idle threat to get him involved anyway; Thornton was well aware of the governor’s views on robotics. “Gillespie would have a heart attack if he knew what we were doing with MARIONn – or *LetheTech*," she said. And Thornton knew that was true.

"I'll talk to Claude – together we'll come up with something," said Heather, keen to promote any solution other than those that might be suggested by her boss. "He's been very useful so far. There's no way we could have finished the programming mimicking consciousness without him. He had some great insights that were fundamental."

"Like?"

"Like……. that our concept of consciousness is tied up with the physical experience of being human. So, there can be no such thing as a disembodied consciousness. No conscious brains floating around in a warm jar, that sort of science fiction fantasy. As he explained this morning, our consciousness is built to reflect our lived in experience of the world – to enable us to participate in the environment we find ourselves in, to act. We have to be part of the world to be conscious in the way we are. It was Claude who came up with the original idea of connecting MARIONn to an individual and let her experience what is to be a human through *their* senses. That's how Euclid was chosen in the first place.

"He's going to be in a very powerful position, Euclid," said Thornton. "So privileged to be selected to act as MARIONn's senses. You'd better keep tracks on him."

"It works both ways," said Heather, skipping the point about Euclid's loyalty. "Have you considered that there is a danger for Euclid too? He'll be dealing with a very powerful mind."

But Thornton's concentration had already moved to a different issue and he failed to hear the point that Heather was making. If he had, perhaps the eventual outcome might have been different. Who knows?

"Do you think the very speed at which we're advancing with MARIONn is something Han's worried about?" Thornton asked.

"Yes," replied Heather without hesitation. "Han is indeed worried whether we, our team here, or indeed the world in general, is ready for this, this advance to artificial consciousness. He does speculate, I know, whether we can manage and control the mind that his work is about to create. He takes a look at what's going on in..." Heather paused, looking for an example, then found one that she knew was close to Thornton's heart. "Han reads about New Chaldea, the debate about all that, and asks himself how new powers and old ways of thinking are going to collide; how territory, super-power supremacy, religion, prejudice are all being fought out over there and he wonders if we have advanced very much. Are we ready to handle a new being, *like us* – but not quite us? We discover nuclear fission and then use it to build bombs."

Thornton shrugged, bereft of a decent response to Han's concerns. There was no definitive answer, no ultimate reassurance he could give. But equally Han was not paid, and paid handsomely, to concern himself about these political issues, nor to bring his personal philosophy into the lab and affect his work on MARIONn. New Chaldea was way out of his orbit, at least in the work place. A strict boundary would have to be enforced. Han was a genius, that much was clear, his translation had made all the rest of their work possible, but the next stage of development should be more straightforward. He wasn't irreplaceable – as he had been before.

A silence fell between them and, from the discrete distance at the side of the room where he was standing, Clarence saw the look in his employer's eye. Thornton began to rise from the table. "Well, my dear Heather, I need to be getting back to New York. I've got a dinner there tonight and then I'll be home at *Crooked Timber* tomorrow. Can't wait to be there again – always feel a little out of my natural environment when I'm up here."

"Missing your gumbo and fried green tomatoes?"

"Something like that. You should get Clarence to make you some of his gumbo. But let's speak again in a few days when you're back in New York. I want to be kept regularly in contact from now on with progress – the human trials, the IPO – it's all coming to a head. Within six months, do you hear? No mistakes, no leaks, before then. You have my complete trust. And good luck with Chase – even if I don't quite approve. Hope the other one isn't too upset." Thornton had already forgotten his name.

Heather waved her hands in an airy gesture. "It'll all be fine. No worries there."

"Good. You'll have enough on your plate without domestic distractions." Thornton consulted his iPsyche. Billy, his pilot, was due to fly him back to New York in twenty minutes but first he would find Han and reinforce his good work with a large bonus. Han might not be indispensable as he once was, but while he was on the team he needed to be kept a happy Han.

Thornton walked over to the picture window and gazed out. He felt hemmed in here by the endless forest and liked looking out over the scalloped shaped '*glade of consciousness*'. Today it was, as had been intended originally by the architect, bathed in sunlight. The thought of the next two days of business talks in New York, cooped up in offices, made him feel claustrophobic. At least he'd be home on Friday. Though it was a pity he'd miss Stephanie. He wondered what she was up to and whether her discussions with her editors in Houston and Tampa had gone well. It had been so nice to have her back last week. He could call her but like all fathers he didn't want to intrude on his children's life unnecessarily. He always thought that they were enjoying themselves outrageously and didn't have the time to talk to him. In this assumption he was, again like most fathers, usually wrong.

Chapter 11

Stephanie Lamaire goes to the beach

Since leaving Crooked Timber, Stephanie had met the editors she would be dealing with from Paris, on *TrueNews* and *Clear and Present Times*. From there she'd continued north, to stay with her friends, the Westwoods, in Rye. Now, two weeks later, she felt different needs than the companionship of friends, for solitude and reflection. She wanted to meditate on the recent past, on her break up with George and on what this next step in life, the transfer to Paris, might hold. This Monday was a beautiful, calm, warm day, a perfect day to be on one's own and spend it beside, or even in, the ocean. The sensation of sun on her skin seemed the perfect way to celebrate the arrival of summer. Still, the ocean would hardly have warmed yet from winter's chill, the water might have to be endured rather than enjoyed.

As she drove down I-495 in her rented car, her mind turned to George and their rupture. Each time a lover departed, even if propelled at her choice, she felt a piece of herself being cut away. The piece grew back but as she grew older she noticed that the wound drained more of her energy and took longer to heal. If only there was just a way to remove the memory of a displaced loved one! Some clever *app* perhaps. Fill the screen with the image of the no-longer-loved, press '*delete*' and *pfff* – all gone! Neither party any longer in the memory of each other; the recollection removed simultaneously. Life, and love, would be so much easier, so much more humane! Would her father's new company provide this essential service? It should. Meanwhile, before this technological marvel became available, she had written to George a sympathetic email that she hoped would mitigate his pain.

Stephanie recognized that this email was full of the clichés thought appropriate to these occasions; she had come up with no better way to ease George's angst than to be *nice.* But he would make such a good long term friend, if he would accept her on that basis; which he probably would not, his pride getting in the way of rescuing at least something that could continue between them. She had read that asking a discarded lover to be a *friend* was the worst insult. Was that really true? She hoped not. It seemed a very practical option to her.

Stephanie sighed; exasperated with the world for not shaping itself according to her wishes - and with the folly of men who allowed their romantic (*or so they supposed*, she thought cynically) inclinations to lead them into cul-de-sacs of emotion that did them no good. Yet, if she made an effort of imagination, she did understand that her presence, even if only in the form of an occasional email, or drink together, and washed of the intimacy that had once bound them together, might not allow George to '*move on'*. Well, it was all too bad. If George didn't want to be her friend there was not much she could do about it.

About a hundred meters short of the beach was the car park. It held only a few cars this early in the season and Stephanie could have easily found a space. There was no sign of the attendant who would charge her a few dollars for the privilege. So she chose to drive straight across the tarmac and beyond, towards a cleared piece of scrub that was virtually on the dunes. The car skidded on the loose surface as she braked. She was just about to swing her legs out of the car when the attendant appeared at the side of the car, with a disapproving look. Stephanie looked at him quizzically, already resenting the fact that he was going to tell her to move. "I can just tell you're going to ruin my morning," she said to the attendant, but in a tone that held no rancour, a resigned smile on her lips told of impending acquiescence to the attendant's likely request. It was a beautiful day and she was determined that this man with his tiresome duty was not to going impinge on her up-beat mood in the slightest degree.

"I hope not 'mam," the man protested. "No intention of doing any such thing. But if you could just park where you ought, that would be mighty obliging of you." Stephanie gave him a narrow glance, as if to infer, in a light hearted way, that she had never been quite so put upon in all her life. But she said, "Sure, that would be no problem at all." She closed the car door, started up, spun the wheels, and drove the few yards to the official car park.

She slid the car to another stop, got out and leant over with her good left hand to grab her beach bag. When she reached the sand she removed her sandals and wriggled her toes open so the tingling coarseness of the grains might find their way between them. It was a sensation that foretold of the pleasures of summer to come. She strode on, past the first set of sunbathing bodies, cast in regular rows along the shore, pale from the lack of exposure during the winter. They huddled together, seeking protection from the breeze. Ahead, she saw clear, uninhabited, sand where there were no bodies and where the dunes provided a natural wind break.

She found a hollow in the dunes. She laid her towel down and resolved to swim immediately. The unsettled spring, much cooler than down South, would not have warmed the sea yet; the vast latent chill of winter would still linger. Best to get it over with. She tied her dark hair into a top-knot and dived straight into the first breaker that threw itself at her, preferring to get the shock over with rather than undergoing a, slow, tortured entry into the waters. But once immersed she didn't stay long; she disliked being bounced around in the surf, unable to swim as freely as she preferred. Later in the year, she would have struck out beyond the breakers into the quieter water but now the ocean's chill made her reclaim the shore quickly.

At least the sand was hot from the sun. Its warmth rose up and percolated through her towel, like Roman central heating. She settled back to commence her morning meditation, bracing her back against the dune. The mantra came to her swiftly but the peace that she expected to find did not follow. Instead, as stillness settled on her mind, neither a sense of joy nor gratitude for the blessings of her life found her; but something else arrived unbidden, something she had not sought, a sense of frustration and disquiet. She had forgotten that in the depths of meditation things lay hidden that were not always beautiful, nor welcome.

As if to remind herself why she was this way, she rubbed the stubs of the fingers on her right hand. Then she reached down and felt the horizontal scar below her belly. '*Written on the body*' she remembered as the title of something. A short story? An opera? The phrase resonated, with the physical traces of the traumas that infected her psyche, daily visible. She recognized the causes of these marks and injuries, and yet the recognition did not seem to give her release. Nor had years of therapy. Oh, if only all this old baggage could be removed, along with her memories of George and he of her! Just bundled up and dumped somewhere, outside one's mind! Would she avail herself of *LetheTech*'s service if it ever worked safely? She had contemplated often enough the fantasy of excision of memory since her father told her of its development but now that the treatment was on the horizon, almost a practical possibility, she became less and less sure. Was not this all part of her history, her identity?

The breeze had now increased and it crept over the dune that had hitherto offered its protection. Stephanie drew the towel across her tighter so that she could lie a little longer and enjoy the sound of the sea. She put on a sweater and wondered whether to go back to the car. But she was at peace here and there was nothing much else to do that morning.

Her mind moved on to the text her father had sent her the night before. From the polling data of last week, it looked as though Carroll Gillespie was going to lose the plebiscite, but only by a small margin. It was always going to be a challenge for him, as a super-majority, 75% of the vote, was needed for approval. But not everyone voted electronically; many older voters distrusted the system and submitted postal votes that would be counted overnight. But the full results should be available by now. She pulled her phone out of her bag and called up *TrueNews*. It was the headline story:

US DIVIDED FOR SECOND TIME IN HISTORY. VOTERS OPT FOR SEPARATION. PRESIDENT-ELECT FOR THE SOUTHERN CONFEDERACY SAYS: "NOW WE CAN BE TRUE TO OURSELVES AND TO GOD."

In a decisive poll, the plebiscite to allow eleven southern states (Texas, Louisiana etc..) to secede from the Union has been approved by voters. The final vote cleared the 75% threshold required by the Constitution, with 115 districts voting for and only 16 against. This is the first time the nation has been divided since the civil war. The referendum must now be ratified by representatives from all the Southern states. If they support the result of the plebiscite, as seems likely, then terms of the secession must be negotiated with the Federal government over the coming year. They are likely to take effect at the end of 2041.

The result was determined on the aggregate vote. Individual state counts have not yet been made available but it is rumoured that at least in North Carolina there was no majority for separation. However, following an earlier accord, the Southern states had formed themselves into a block (the *Southern Caucus*) and each state in the Caucus will be bound by the overall result.

Yesterday's result was unexpected. Right until the final tally, it was predicted that the 'No' vote would prevail. Polls had leant in the direction of maintaining the existing Union structure but there was always a level of volatility in the public mind.

After the final count was made known the Governor of Louisiana and President-elect of the New Confederation, Carroll Gillespie, said;

"This is a great day for the South and for those who love the Lord. it is a great day for those brave states that have joined us in this journey. No longer will we have to submit to laws that are alien to our traditions and to God. The people have spoken and they have spoken clearly."

"Let me assure all Americans, and I mean all Americans, not just those who live in the South, that in spite of today's vote we are, still, all bound by a common Constitution and faith in the wisdom of the Founding Fathers. We will continue to act together on many matters of mutual interest. Separate development does not mean we fail to be brothers. The vote today is not a hostile act against those who do not follow our beliefs."

"But the freedom to pursue the life that each of us finds righteous is a divine right. Recognizing that right, as this vote does, will enable each of us to live in harmony without resenting the action of his neighbour. This is not a sad day for our country, it is an opportunity for its different parts to flourish; to go forward to their chosen destinations. The conflicts that have divided us over the last few years has disappeared today."

In Washington, The President of the hitherto United States said, *"We will of course respect this vote. The People of the South have spoken clearly. But, nevertheless this is a sad day for the Union. I had hoped the result would be otherwise. From here on I also hope, as Governor Gillespie has said, that both sides can live in harmony together. I have always considered that separation was not needed; that we could work out our differences. That has proved impossible but our work to find a way to live together does not end today. We share a history and a common belief in the exceptionalism of this great nation. We will, all of us, go forward in a spirit of being Americans, even if our routes diverge on some matters. The President-elect of the Southern Confederation has already assured me that the Southern Caucus will follow the Constitution and that he will consult with us where we have interests in common...."*

Stephanie tried to phone her father, wanting to discuss the news, but he failed to pick up. They had discussed the plebiscite, the possibility of secession, many times before but that was all theoretical. Now there would be a new political settlement, and one that would probably not be in her father's interests. She noted that the actual date of secession was still two years away; two years of squabble between the North and South over its terms. During that period the Southern government was not meant to make any legislative changes and should continue to respect the authority of the Federal government. The reality, her father had predicted, would be different. The atmosphere would alter. Existing laws, while not repealed or amended immediately, would be interpreted to please Carroll and his cronies. Executive orders would be issued, that required no new legislative backing, to institute changes they had long sought. In practice, there would be few restraints on Carroll Gillespie's power, apart from the Constitution, which his party had promised to respect. But even that would be now be viewed through the lens of sympathetic Southern courts.

When Thornton did return his daughter's call thirty minutes later, he spoke about his concerns for not only himself and his involvement with the MARIONn project, but also for some of Blue

Ridge's industries in the South. It was not just the manufacture of the latest AI inspired robots that was now imperilled, his plants employed many robots in traditional industries, like ship-building, and modern ones such as aeronautics and space. Carroll had made it clear during the campaign: the two loadstones he would pursue would be maximization of human employment and control of what he called the *mimicking of divine attributes* by next-generation robots, conscious ones possibly. The president-elect would refuse to let his bureaucracy grant state contracts where he considered there was '*excessive*' use of robots or the robots employed were too close to '*divine purpose*' – whatever that was. He would certainly use aggressive interpretation of existing industrial legislation to ensure Blue Ridge bent to his will.

And that was just on industrial policy. They would see a more aggressive stance on Carroll's pet hobby horse of New Chaldea too. So far the Federal government had suppressed his fervour. There had been little support for intervention, official or otherwise. Well, that would change. Carroll might have to wait till secession took effect before committing Southern military support. But behind the scenes there would be an increase in clandestine operations – and nobody was likely to stand in his way. What could Washington do about it now, however much they disapproved?

There was no upside for Thornton or Blue Ridge in this secession. Her father would try to manage things so they didn't fall foul of Carroll too often. He needed the cash-flow from his Southern industries; he couldn't afford to see that upset, just as they were ramping up *LetheTech*. Things might be easier, financially, once the IPO was launched but that was, as Stephanie knew, still months away, after the crash of the last effort. '*Cash needs will be a hostage to fortune in this new set-up,*' Thornton explained to her. "*In the short term, there's going to be a squeeze. Things are going to be tougher for us. No question. I wish I could come to Paris with you! Much more fun.*" He didn't say, as he might have done, that '*lack of fun*' was unlikely to be his largest problem in life going forward. Stephanie said she would have liked her father to be there, in Paris, too. To herself, she thought '*but only for a visit. And provided you don't bring mother.'*

She signed off, promising to keep him informed as she settled into her new life. Then, by now chilled, she gathered her things and walked back up the beach.

On the Monday morning Stephanie flew to Paris to start her new life, armed with her journalism contracts and the names of several friends she had made over the years, together with a few contacts her father had given her, including, of course, that of Claude Blondel.

Part 2

STEPHANIE LAMAIRE AND CLAUDE BLONDEL

Chapter 12

Paris. April 2040

From: Stephanie Lamaire

To: Elizabeth Lamaire

Re; Hi

Hi Sis,

How are things? No word in ages. I'm equally bad, I know. Just had one of those three-line mails from Daddy, dictated no doubt on some flight or other. Didn't get too much of an idea about how you were all getting along, but at least it seems neither he nor mother have yet killed each other. I know he's completely occupied with MARIONn – and I guess that's all for the good. Keeps them out of each other's hair.

And how are things in Gay Paree, I hear you ask? Well…… the big news is, as I mentioned to you last time, I was thinking about moving in with Claude – and now I've done it. Early days. Slowly getting used to living with a man again – and he to me. I am strongly of the impression that he's a little more experienced in that regard! But we're very happy – really. The apartment (in Montmartre: I'm sure you've been here. Sacré Coeur?) is nice but crowded. There are 3, and sometimes 4, of us here, after all. Claude has had to take in his aged father, Victor – who's got dementia (it's more than he can do to remember my name one day to the other) – and there's also a Senegalese day nurse (Fabienne) to look after him when Claude's at work.

But we get along well enough (although Fabienne is a bit of trial. I think she has a thing for Claude) so far. Claude's making an effort to introduce me to his friends and contacts who might be useful. They look on me with curiosity (*Claude's got an American girlfriend? We must check her out).* There's an undercurrent of, *how long will this one last*? There have obviously been a few predecessors (I found some photos in a drawer the other day. Claude claimed to have no idea who it was. That was not super reassuring but we were all very grown up about it).

I had lunch with Bella Aquavella (you must have heard of her, even down South? The dress designer?) the other day. I wanted to interview her for an article. She obviously didn't think my relationship with Claude would last another day without the benefit of her advice. A little rich as I hear that her husband has just left her! Point number 1, never let Claude see me naked, except in bed: to maintain one's *allure* is all important. *Le Mystere* must be preserved. A bit late for that I'm afraid. She, like all the French (I know she's sounds Italian but Bella seems to have lived in Paris all her life), keep telling me how much they'd rather live in the US. *So bourgeois*, they complain about Paris. But when they say the US, they really mean New York (actually, *Manhattan)* the only bit of the

States most of them have ever visited, apart from LA maybe. I explain that where I come from in the South it's not really quite the same. Then they start asking me questions where the unspoken subtext is, '*are you all still racists who mistreat the blacks?* Of course, the one thing they have heard about the South is the dismemberment of our country by the plebiscite and something about the work gangs that Carroll has introduced. Sometimes I hear a comment that suggests what they really want to ask is – *do you still have slavery where you come from*? I exaggerate a little. Occasionally, very rarely, when I get tired or cross, having to defend the South all the time, I play up to their prejudices. So, I tell them about the difficulties of getting the cotton in and how it's such a problem finding a good *overseer* these days.

At least I'm getting better at speaking the language. I noticed that when I was real bad, everyone used to say how well I spoke French. But now I'm pretty good and really quite fluent (*je parle français couramment maintenant - presque bilingue*) they pick up on every error and inform me with a patronizing smile (because, as a foreigner, I cannot be expected to get it right every time) what I should have said. And sometimes, it is true, my much improved language skills do go seriously haywire. Particularly at dinners, after a few drinks. I'd been led to believe the French drink in moderation but, *please,* this is not a moderation that would be recognized in Manhattan. The wine flows copiously at all the dinner parties I have been to. Which is a few. At the present rate of my decent into alcoholism I shall end up quite like Mama soon (how is she anyway?)

Oh – and I'm expected to know all their friends in the US too. I'm asked things like, "One of my favourite cousins is a journalist, like you, lives in Chicago. Perhaps you know her?". Or, "You must meet my friend Doug or Mary Ann, lives here but he/she is American. You'd love him/her" as though my strongest wish is to keep in touch with my own country men/women - and that I must be facing severe homesickness. Well, as you will appreciate, considering the state of our home-life, that's not quite the predominant emotion I suffer as I sit here, cuddled up to Claude.

Now, if he can just keep his eyes off other women for a bit longer this might all work out just fine. Luckily, when he's not lecturing, he has to spend an awful lot of time handling MARIONn queries. I must tell Daddy to make sure Claude is kept deeply involved! As it is, I hear more from him about father than I ever get directly. I know Daddy's very busy (as usual) and he's not a great correspondent so (sigh) I guess I'll have to be satisfied the odd few lines; when he can manage that.

And you, dear Sis? How is everything? You and Ambrose still getting along? Any sign that he might land a job any time soon??

Write me sometime and let me know how things are going at home.

Miss you, Kiss, kiss
Stephanie

Chapter 13

Vincent, Fabienne, Valerie and Irene

The meeting, between Claude and the psychologist Harvey Jennings, at the MARIONn campus, almost a year ago now, often returned to Claude's mind. But try as he could to identify the cause of unease that arose whenever he contemplated the meeting, and the subsequent discussion with the psychologist, no illumination was forthcoming. Of course, he could have simply called Harvey Jennings and tried to clear up the whole business but, whenever Claude was about to do this, some inhibition to his will descended and he found that he could not. There had been two review meetings at the campus that he had to attend since that original conversation: at the first Harvey Jennings was absent for some reason and at the second Claude never found an occasion to engage him. But he recognised that he hadn't really tried that hard to do so. In fact, really, he's done his best to avoid Jennings.

The recent relationship with Stephanie brought stability and an established routine to Claude's existence. Claude had gone out with several women over the past year, but none had taken his heart until he met Stephanie. As one of the few contacts in Paris her father had provided, she had planned to contact Claude at some point but she didn't have to wait long. Thornton had written to Claude, asking him if he could invite Stephanie out for a drink or a meal, and introduce her to some of his friends. His daughter didn't know many people in the city. The introduction had been only too successful. Now, after a courtship of a few months, Stephanie lived with Claude and was rarely to be found in her own apartment that she rented in the Latin Quarter. So, most evenings, Claude looked forward to seeing her when he got home.

His routine was, after work, to take the metro to Abesses, the station below the church of Sacré Coeur and the nearest to his apartment in Rue Charles Nodier. He would stop to pick up a couple of baguettes at the boulangerie in the square - and then, frequently, his reflections would move on from Stephanie to thoughts about what he was going to do about his father, Vincent. His memory has been growing worse for years but now it was almost non-existent. Some of the most simple daily tasks had become beyond him and soon, when Claude was next on a long trip abroad, he realised that Vincent would need a live-in, 24 hour, carer. Stephanie would then move back to her own apartment. She would not want to stay in his, alone with Fabienne, if he was not also there. The present arrangements were no sort of a permanent solution to their life.

Stephanie's presence in Claude's life had provided for him the incentive, and the excuse, to end a precarious relationship with Fabienne - that went well past what a carer was expected to provide. That was never going to be a long term arrangement – in his view. But his perspective on their '*rapport*' had not stopped Fabienne from fantasising about being his girlfriend. However attractive she was, he had not considered her suitable for that role; barely educated in Claude's opinion (there was no way he could introduce her to his friends. *Mon Dieu, l'idée*!) and he had been beginning to regret his weakness. Matters had only become more tricky when Stephanie started staying over regularly – and then moved in. Even if Claude took the complacent attitude that surely Fabienne could never have seriously considered they had a future together, and that her resentment of the new dispensation was unreasonable, it had become clear that she was not of the same view.

Claude knew that he had to resolve the situation, move his father out into another apartment and have Fabienne, or more likely her replacement, look after him, on a 24 hours basis, there. But this was impossible at the moment. A second apartment on a professor's salary, topped up with a bit of consultant income from Blue Ridge? What was he thinking? Maybe his father might be installed as a resident in a modest 'care' home? That sounded more likely.

Not that Claude wanted to put his father in a home or shift him to one side in some other way. Claude was his father's last living relative, for Vincent's wife had died many years before, and Claude was his only child. Apart from anything else Claude had always adored his father – and the affection had been reciprocated. But if he didn't put him in a home what was the alternative? His last book had been a modest success but that was temporary income at best. Blue Ridge paid something, but usually late, and even with that his total income was not sufficient to cover the rent on another apartment. Of course he could fire Fabienne and replace her with someone whom he had never slept with. That would resolve one source of friction in his life. Yet he shrank from even that course of action at the moment. His father had grown accustomed and affectionate towards her. Besides if he did fire her, Fabienne would almost certainly go to a tribunal and claim she only been let go because her employer had grown tired of her bedroom services.

Perhaps there was another route. If his father didn't have Alzheimer's any more then he would then have a perfectly valid excuse to fire Fabienne and be in no danger of a tribunal's censor. There would be no need to recruit a replacement either and so, no need of a second apartment. Now that *LetheTech's* initial human trials had begun in Europe maybe he could enrol his father? He had seen preliminary results that suggested the memory therapy provided successful treatment for Alzheimer's patients, able to rebuild their minds once stem cell treatment had re-grown damaged brain tissue. Or at least to some extent. Enough, anyway, to give the patient (or *clients* as *LetheTech* more reassuringly insisted on calling them) the ability to manage everyday life and even to converse with family members, without that annoying repetition that memory loss involved. Some days, Vincent could barely manage more than two minutes of desultory conversation before asking the same question again. But at least his father's physical health had been better recently. He had quite forgotten half his ailments.

The O'Neal debacle caused him to hesitate. On the *LetheTech* website, the potential for '*problems*' was spelt out, if a little softly. In some cases (*very few*, the blurb assured) the memory rebuild might go awry and the client left with even less recall than before. But, Claude reflected, that was not much of a danger in his father's case. He could hardly have less memory anyway. And it was a not inconsiderable attraction that because *LetheTech's* technologies were still in the trials phase, any treatment would be free.

With these revolving and unresolved issues in his mind, Claude reached his apartment building and walked up the three flights of stairs (there being no lift). The door of the apartment swung open and he was greeted by Fabienne, warned of his approach by the intelligent intercom system. She appeared to be in more emollient mood than normal. "Let me take Monsieur's coat," she said. "Shall I make you some tea? You look tired, Monsieur, after your long day." Claude was puzzled but gratified by this warmth and wondered if this was an attempt to disarm him before Fabienne revealed some new tactics that she thought might either protect her job or get rid of Stephanie.

Claude picked up a letter from the sideboard. A letter! My God, that was a rarity these days; he couldn't remember when he received the last one. He didn't recognise the hand, but then whose would he recognise? The envelope was addressed to his father and written in mauve ink – that made it rarer still. He handed Fabienne the baguettes and allowed himself to be attended to. He noticed that she was dressed in her black jeans and too open white blouse. Was she trying to imitate him, his own dress code, he briefly wondered? Or just to remind him of what was once available and could become so again? He ignored the provocation. "How has my father been today?" he enquired. It was the same question he asked everyday at this hour, part of the evening ritual. He would say hello to his father first and open the letter later.

"He's been fine. I took him out for the air in the streets around Sacré Coeur," Fabienne said. "He always likes to go up there. But since we got back, he's been asking for you continuously. Will you go and see him?"

Claude went into the living room. His father was seated in an arm chair, gazing without any apparent interest at whatever was on the TV. He turned to Claude as he heard him enter and briefly smiled. Claude went over and took his hand. "All well, Papa, Good day?"

"Is Madeleine coming today?" asked Vincent. Madeleine had been Vincent's wife, long dead

"No, Papa, Madeleine I'm afraid can't come today. Why don't you tell me what you saw on your walk with Fabienne?"

The two struggled to connect and converse. It was taxing for them both and the efforts that Vincent made to keep up his end of the simple conversation made Claude's eyes water with empathy. But it wasn't long into their time together before Vincent asked again "Is Madeleine coming today? I would so much like to see her." One more time Claude assured his father that, alas, she would not be visiting. Vincent appeared to take this information in his stride but then he looked straight at Claude, puzzled, as though hesitating while trying to identify something deep in his mind. Failing to find whatever he was searching for, he rolled his eyes to the ceiling, beseeching inspiration to descend from the heavens. At last the inspiration arrived. He turned to Claude with a beatific smile and said, "Do you know you look very much like my son. I do miss him so. I haven't seen him for a long time. I think you would have enjoyed knowing him too. Uncanny the resemblance."

Claude sighed inwardly. He looked at his father with love; there seemed little point in pointing out the reality of the situation. His father turned back to the television and Claude took out from his pocket the envelope with mauve ink. He felt little hesitation about opening it, even if it was addressed to Vincent. His father might have no recollection of the sender or be agitated if he did. Either reaction might have been possible.

The letter was written in a shaky hand and difficult to decipher, but he could just make out the name in the signature, '*Valerie*'. He knew who Valerie was – his father's last girlfriend after the death of Madelaine. He and Valerie had never married but must have been together for some 15 years. But when his father became seriously forgetful they had separated. Valerie had visited the apartment a few times but since she had moved to another area of France even those visits had petered out. Claude thought back. His father could not have seen Valerie for at least 5 years.

Unknown to Claude, his father had been paying Valerie a monthly pension for years and then suddenly it had stopped, plunging her into financial distress. Well, of course it had stopped! Claude had taken over Vincent's finances and had cancelled all his regular payments, reasoning that whatever services they were for, his father had no need of any of them these days. Valerie was now raising the alarm directly with Vincent, probably not realising how far his memory loss had advanced. Did he know the payments had been suspended, did he understand how much difference the money made to her? The sums were not large but they were not something that Vincent's pension could support, now that Claude used some of that to fund his care. He put the letter in his pocket. He would consider how to reply later.

"Do you remember Valerie, Papa?" Claude asked, hoping to be heard over the noise of the television. No answer, his father was much too occupied by whatever was on the screen. He tried again, a little louder. This time there was a response. His father shook his head; the name meant nothing to him. Hardly a need to subsidise Valerie if his father couldn't even recall who she was.

There was very little now that his father did remember. His internal life must be barren without the ability to recall people and events that had been significant to his life. But *LetheTech* could create and implant memories, as well as delete them. Claude took a decision; *I must drop an email to Heather and see if I can enrol my father in the trial*s. The technology may still be at the testing stage, and there were the known dangers, including the accidental deletion of whatever memory still lingered, but....did that matter? Papa had little memory enough these days and even if things did go wrong……

But some days later an incident occurred that drove Claude to wonder whether he did not need memory therapy himself. Stephanie discovered, while clearing some drawers for her own stuff, two photos of a pretty blonde, of about Claude's age, maybe a few years younger. At the bottom of one of the photos was written the name, *Irene.* Stephanie tackled Claude about the photo. Who was the woman? Had she been of particular significance to Claude? *Irene, Irene…* Claude searched his mind but no recollection of this mysterious woman was forthcoming. He peered at the photo, hoping that illumination might arrive but although Irene had evidently been an attractive woman, no amount of concentration enabled him to recall her better. He couldn't remember his father having a girlfriend of that name either.

This absence of memory disturbed Claude, almost as much as it did Stephanie. Was he going the way of his father? But he took comfort from the fact that in the rest of his life his memory seemed to be fine. But once, when Stephanie was away, a visitor - who did not know Claude well – had asked him about '*Irene*'; an enquiry that Claude brushed aside for he had no answer to give the man, or none that occurred to him. But this was a rare incident. In general, no-one in his daily life seemed to refer to this 'Irene'. And if someone did, inadvertently, an internal warning system advised him not to enquire about their reluctance, or his own, to pursue the subject of her identity any further.

If 'Irene' had once been connected to him there was no memory of their time together; just, sometimes, a faint sensation that at some point in the past this woman had been, in a very ill-defined way, in his life. She might have been a lover, but equally, maybe, a favourite cousin or a niece. When he sat alone considering the situation, to question his acquaintances seemed the natural thing to do. Yet, when he was with one of them and had the opportunity to put forward those questions, he felt he could not. There was always this inhibition, some lack of will, a fear perhaps, to explore the subject. And it was no use asking his father, who might once have known 'Irene' but if he had, would have certainly forgotten her existence by now.

The situation was causing a hiatus in his relationship with Stephanie too. At first, she decided to say nothing about her discovery; reasoning that Claude might be upset and suspect her of spying on his past. But after some gentle questioning about his romantic life, that she had already determined had been extensive, had elicited no information about '*Irene*', she decided to tackle the subject directly. But that only deepened the mystery. Claude's complete amnesia on the subject ensured that no amount of probing had the slightest result. And it was clear that he was not faking his memory loss. Well, if the whole episode was that painful she didn't want to push too hard and cause Claude to suffer unpleasant recollections. Still, the episode upset and unsettled her and left uncertainties about her own relationship with Claude that were not going to disappear fast.

Chapter 14

The marriage feast

Stephanie's perplexity and concern was only increased a few days later when she and Claude had to attend the marriage (a second marriage) of one of his friends, Benoit, to his girlfriend of long-standing, Agnes. The wedding was to be held in the pretty town in south west France of St Jean.

They flew down to Biarritz and from there planned to drive to the mairie for the civil wedding. The plane was delayed and the hired car drove at a very modest pace, too slowly for Stephanie, who hated to be late. They were way behind schedule and still had 45 minutes of drive ahead of them. She particularly hated to be late for people she did not know. Punctuality she considered one of her few virtues. They decided to skip the marriage at the mairie, nobody would notice their absence since these civil weddings took only about 10 minutes anyway, and drive straight to the reception.

The delays had created a tension in the car and Stephanie at first sat silent, playing with the heavy gold bangle on her arm, watching the undulating countryside that she had not hitherto visited, slip by. Even so early in the year, the grassy sides of the softly contoured hills were as much brown as green; patchy and still burnt in places from the heat of the previous summer. Not the deep, seemingly perpetual, green that Claude told her he remembered from family holidays in his youth. As emerald as Ireland this part of France had been. Once these hills had been irrigated by the succession of rain-bearing depressions that flowed in from the Atlantic. But they visited no longer, after the shift in weather patterns. The land had once been remarkably pretty, a mixture of pasture and woodland, but the look was now more blasted than Arcadian.

Stephanie turned and looked at Claude, as he told her about his childhood holidays near San Sebastian, with his aunt and uncle. The latter, who had been in the military, had retired down here. The combination of reasonable weather, the sea and cheap property made a compelling trinity of incentives. As she listened to the tales of his childhood, she became more aware of him and then she had an epiphany. Despite Claude's vanity, his occasional self-importance, his secretiveness about his past relationship with whoever '*Irene*' was, she understood that she had begun to love him. Claude was really very handsome, with his olive skinned, craggy face, his pepper-and-salt hair, floating over his collar, his intelligence, his charm. A bit too charming she thought, particularly when it came to women. And those occasional flashes of intellectual arrogance; she would obviously have to get used to them too.

At last, the car rounded a long curve and crossed the bridge that marked the entrance to the village where the reception was to be held. It turned sharp left and came to a halt on an area of gravel. The Tricolour on the outside of the hotel hung limply in the still, early summer air. Claude instructed the car to go and find its own space somewhere else, after dropping them. It was now past five and many of the guests had already made the journey from the mairie.

There must have been about 200 guests, most of whom Claude didn't know (except for his old acquaintance Hervé, who he thought he saw across the heads of the assembled guests, with his wife Sophie). He hoped the marriage feast would not be too long coming. It had been a long time since breakfast and nothing to eat on the 'plane. He and Stephanie had wanted to stop and get themselves a beer, or a glass of red, and a *tartine* on the way from the airport but had decided against it; they were late enough as it was.

They found themselves, along with all the other guests, milling around on a large terrace that projected over the valley below. A broadly spread tree, a lime, stood on the edge of the terrace. Underneath its branches were set up a couple of microphones. Evidently the speakers, if not the assembled guests, might be kept out of the sun, still hot this late in the afternoon. To one side of the terrace lay some large open grills that, from the amount of smoke they were emitting, suggested they had only recently been lit. There was no sign of singeing meat cooking on the charcoals and as Claude guessed, with the disappointment of a man in need of nourishment, the wedding feast must still be a long way off. He saw some girls circulating with trays of canapes and *amuse bouches*. These morsels of food looked tiny; he and Stephanie would have to eat a lot to compensate for the fast that had so far been their fate that day. Claude gave a beseeching gaze at one of young girls, hoping that she would meet his eye. He gave her a smile and a '*please approach me'* look. He took a minute piece of toast and foie-gras and popped it into his mouth, but declined the proffered wine. A glass of water at this stage would be fine. He'd better pace himself; but he was concerned about Stephanie, who must already be on her second or third glass of champagne. Claude had heard about Bethany and wondered if some of her mother's genes had been passed down.

He turned and looked at Stephanie. Hers was not a look that previously he would have thought attracted him; the roman nose, the slightly flat face, hair so thick that she could shake it into a tent, enabling her to disappear from the world when something displeased her; pronounced, heavy, arched eyebrows, that reminded him a little of Frida Kahlo, but not so much that Stephanie ran the risk of needing to shave between them. Stephanie was bright, beautiful in her *jolie-laide* way, had a rich father, bit neurotic but, really, what was there not to like? He had fallen for the combination of enthusiasm with which she approached life and the sense of past injury that touched her. Or was this just his sentimentality? Would they be together for the long haul, he wondered? Why not? The way things were going that might well be a possibility.

From the side, a waitress approached and re-filled Stephanie's glass. She was laughing, in a good natured way, at the father-of-the-bride's speech. Claude wondered how much she understood. A lot of the allusions passed him by, all these in-joke family references; heaven knows what she made of them. He clicked his glass with hers in a gesture of companionship, hoping to gain Stephanie's attention.

"You have to be immersed in the last 30 years of their family history to get half these references," he said. "What a ritual! It's amazing anyone gets married when they know the most embarrassing parts of their life are going to be dragged up for the entertainment of others. They're always a little sadistic these speeches. At least we're being spared the couple's early sexual indiscretions. So far, anyway."

"Do you think that's the French race for you? A bit sadistic?" asked Stephanie, adding a playful lilt to her voice as she tried to take the edge off her remark. It sounded too sharp. Claude knew that Stephanie liked to tease him, implying that he belonged to a race of hooligans. He noticed that her glass was describing loose circles on its axis as she twisted her wrist around.

"I doubt the French are worse than anybody else." replied Claude, wishing to deny any special aberrations on the part of his own people. "What would they tell of at your wedding?"

"*My* wedding….not '*our*' wedding?" Stephanie let the words hang. Then she said, "It's Ok – I don't think *you* will be marrying for a long time," Stephanie said.

Claude frowned, puzzled. What was Stephanie driving at? Why would he not be marrying for a long time? Had he been married ever? Something at the back of his mind nudged him into thinking that he had but he was unsure; he could find no specific reminiscences. Maybe this was just an attempt by Stephanie to needle him about what she judged as his lack of commitment? Although he considered himself '*taken*', he was aware that Stephanie's insecurity failed to reassure her on this point.

"Stephanie, don't be like that," he said. "And don't drink too much either; there's hours of this party to go yet."

Claude regretted his words. He had forgotten one of the lessons he had learnt early in his relationship with Stephanie; any attempt at control would result in behaviour diametrically opposed to his wishes. She looked straight at him, lifted her glass and downed it in one.

"Don't be like *what* exactly Claude?"

Claude said nothing. He needed to keep Stephanie on an even keel for the rest of the evening, and he couldn't face any frostiness for the next four or five hours. He turned back to the speeches and tried to show an interest and concentration he failed to feel. But he did notice the open air grills were no longer giving off smoke; maybe they were up to temperature and whatever the family had manged to purchase for the celebrations would now start cooking; the salvation of dinner was not far away.

When the speeches were over Benoit, released from his groom duties temporarily, came to talk to them. Claude asked about the man who he had spied the far side of the terrace when they arrived. Was that not Hervé Maurot? With his wife, Sophie? Claude's short-sightedness made many identifications less than certain.

"But, of course, my friend," said Benoit. "I remembered that you knew Hervé. He said that you had not seen each other for ages; he's always away on some voyage or other. He would be delighted to have the chance to reconnect." At that point Benoit's just-married wife Agnes came to join them. Claude introduced Stephanie. Agnes insisted that she came to meet some of her friends; Stephanie must know nobody at the party. The men could be left to their own devices.

Claude and Benoit walked over to join Hervé and Claude said, "What a long time it has been, Hervé! 4 years?" He explained how recently he'd been travelling a lot to the States. He now had a very demanding employer.

Hervé raised his glass to toast Claude.

"I am delighted to hear that things are now going so well. Particularly after what I heard about Irene. I am so sorry." The tone of Hervé's condolences suggested to Claude that Irene had probably not been a niece.

Claude was, of course, at a loss about what Hervé had heard or why he should be sorry about this 'Irene'. But he knew that he had to respond in some way. The resistance he always felt at the mention of Irene's name rose up again. Claude didn't want to, and indeed couldn't, dig beyond that block. And as he couldn't remember any details of the relationship, he would have to be as vague and non-specific as possible in his response.

"It was very sad," replied Claude. "It just didn't seem to work. Maybe we had outgrown each other. I'm not sure. But we parted friends. We'll always be there for each other." There, he had managed to fit into his reply all the clichés that were required in these situations.

Hervé gave Claude a concentrated look, more of puzzlement than anything else. Claude noticed the reaction and saw that his words had not, perhaps, been the appropriate ones, or, more accurately, had not been those that Hervé had expected to hear. Claude was uncertain what to say next. He chose another tack, deciding to embellish the story that he didn't remember, with a few made-up details, "It was just the usual sort of thing. Very boring for everybody else. I was working more and more in the US, Irene's own work took her away overseas too. We were no longer there much for each other. We had no children so at some point it just seemed sensible to recognise what had happened to us – and to separate."

"I see, I see," said Hervé, although he still looked perplexed, as though he did not see anything very clearly. "Anyway, you seem to have recovered, Claude. That's a nice new girl you came with." Hervé gestured with his head in the direction of Stephanie, who had started to chat with some of Sophie's friends.

"Ah yes, that's Stephanie. She is a journalist," said Claude. "American, so that makes it much easier." Although as he said this, he wasn't quite sure in what way her being American did make things easier – perhaps it was because if things didn't work out she could return to the States. In other ways it didn't make things easier at all. Being in a relationship with the daughter of your employer had the potential for lots of complications that tripped through Claude's mind from time to time. And then there were all those weeks when she would not be in Paris with him, but in Louisiana on the family plantation.

But something else was also now passing through Claude's brain – that he needed to face down his reluctance to discover more about 'Irene'; that he couldn't continue to live with his ignorance, however easy, indeed necessary, avoiding the subject seemed to be. Hervé might be just the person to do that. He evidently had known 'Irene'.

"Hervé, for some reason I have gaps in my memory of Irene," he said. "I am not sure what has happened, what did happen, but could we talk about this some time?"

Hervé looked sceptical about the appeal of this. "Claude will you excuse me a minute?" he said. "It rather looks as though Sophie needs rescuing. But maybe we could have dinner one night in Paris? Can you give me your contact details? Sophie and I are travelling for the next three or four months – but after that I should be back in Paris."

"Ah! Well, I shall wish you both *Bon Voyage*," said Claude. "I'm sorry there won't be an opportunity before you leave but where are you going? Four months – it's quite a time."

"We're sailing across the Pacific – Panama to *Nouvelle Caledonie.* We've always wanted to do it and now we must, if ever," said Hervé

"If ever? Is there a rush?" asked Claude

"It's considered late in the season already. We only have a few months before the cyclones begin. Besides, the seas are dying. From Ecuador, past the Galapagos, almost to Hawaii, is now a '*dead zone'*. We want to see what's left of the marine life before it's all gone. And before they resume testing," said Hervé, with sadness and disapproval in his voice

"Ah, yes," said Claude. "Who would have believed nuclear testing would restart in the Pacific? Even if the devices will be very small ones. Tactical only, as they say."

"Well, you know the official explanations. They claim the deterrent will be more effective if it is seen, made visible to our enemies," said Hervé. "But who seriously doubts the force of these bombs anyway? Testing will be the final blow to those seas. A lot of dead fish will be deterred anyway."

"No, no, no!" exclaimed Claude, suddenly excited. "That's not the reason they want to restart testing. It's not to deter – it's to *legitimise*. They want to overcome the public's perception of these being unimaginable, terrible, unusable, devices. They want to make atomic weapons seem like conventional ones! These tests are not meant to ensure they never drop these bombs – it's so that they can!"

"No worse than what we're used to, then?" asked Hervé, perplexed.

"Exactly! That's why they are going to test small nuclear bombs first, these so called 'tactical' ones. They'll say, 'look, they are just like those conventional devices you see exploding everyday on your screens. We should be able to use these weapons too; they are no worse than the rest; acceptable in fact. *The military don't want to scare us; they want to reassure us*."

The two stood silent for a few moments. But the conversation had run its course and as they were about to part, Claude reached into his jacket for his old leather wallet and drew a visiting card off a small wedge that was stuck into a pocket. He handed it to Hervé, "So you can find me on your return. This will remind you of my details," Claude said

Hervé took the card in both hands and peered at this artefact from a previous time, as though it would emit some sort of hidden meaning, if he could only break its code. At last, satisfied that he had gleaned all the information was available from the face of the card, he turned it over - a random gesture of curiosity. On the back was the word *Hervé.*

"Ah, but there is a name here!" cried Hervé. "And it's mine! Did you know that you were going to meet me today? What prescience!"

"Can I have a look at the card?" said Claude, bemused.

Hervé handed back the card. "Perhaps you should keep this one. You may have written Hervé as an *aide-memoire*, no? For some other purpose?""'

"it's very odd." said Claude. "I don't remember ever writing your name on the card; and if it's not you, I've no idea who this other Hervé is. It's a mystery. But there we are! An example of synchronicity in the universe!" He put the card back in the wallet and withdrew a replacement, that he handed to his friend.

But even as Claude did this, there came into his mind the ghost of a recollection. Somewhere at the back of his brain he vaguely knew that he had met another Hervé, not that recently but at least in the last year, even if he couldn't place the occasion exactly. It was irritating; indeed, more than that, it was unsettling.

But the next day Claude remembered the connection. This Hervé on the back of the card, of course it was not another Hervé *but the American Harvey*; Harvey Jennings, the psychologist at the MARIONn campus. But quite why he had thought it so important to keep a note of this man's name was a question that eluded him. Claude's could not identify the significance that he felt was attached to it. He really must try harder to pin down Jennings on his next visit.

Chapter 15

An uninvited guest

Middle aged bankers were never quite Stephanie's thing, although the one on her left spoke good English, a welcome relief after the tortuous conversation she had tried with the man on her right. His deep Marseilles accent had begun to taunt her self-confidence in the comprehension of the French language – particularly after all the wine she had drunk. At last she decided she had paid her debt to courtesy and could break off the conversation without being judged rude. When a decent gap appeared in the man's explanation of the latest manoeuvres in the financial markets, she explained how interesting this was but she feared her partner probably need rescuing - and would he excuse her? The banker asked who was her partner and Stephanie pointed across the room, "That's him," she said. "Claude Blondel."

She hadn't quite realised, as she said Claude's name, that she now expected his name to be recognised by whoever she was talking to. He was her first celebrity lover and she had unconsciously grown use to the recognition that he was universally granted – at least in France. They had this thing about intellectuals. She bet not one member in a hundred of the US public could give her the name of a philosopher. But here it worked. The banker gave a nod, a gesture of recognition to the thinker. "Ah, *chapeau*,' he said. He gestured with a flat, opened, upward turned palm as if to say. '*please, I quite understand If you need to tend to the great man. I am a lesser mortal and know when I must give way'*. Stephanie was charmed by the courtesy of it all and, accepting the generosity of the moment, rose in her seat. As she did so, she looked over at Claude on a neighbouring table. He was talking, animatedly, to the pretty girl next to him and looked content to be left to his own devices for the moment. She would leave the two of them in peace to finish their conversation.

But once she had risen, Stephanie had no wish to linger at the table. She was tired of talking and besides, it was hot in the room. What she longed for most now was fresh air. She looked back at the banker and said, "*Au revoir. C'était un plaisir de faire votre connaissance",* a phrase she had learnt was fungible to most social circumstances. She navigated her way through the tables and onto the terrace. By this time, with the effect of alcohol and the lateness of the hour, nobody paid her any attention. Through the corner of her eye she noticed Claude did not even look up as she passed by. He was still looking deep into the eyes of the attractive companion..

Given the earlier warmth of the evening, and the additional heat generated by all the diners, the doors to the dining room were wide open but she felt a chill in the air even so as she reached the outdoors. She pulled her light shawl about her shoulders.

Stephanie had no particular intention other than to escape the noise and enjoy fresh air and a moment of repose. But a few feet onto the terrace she became aware of the noise of people talking animatedly. She turned her head to investigate and saw a knot of five or six men and women, formed into a little semi-circular group, berating someone whom she could not see - but who was evidently at the centre of the group and the focus of their attention. Although she could not hear clearly what they were saying, the indistinct words carried a harsh tone.

She moved towards the group, curious as to what all the fuss was about. Tall enough to peer over their heads, she saw an unkempt man, a youth really, facing them. He seemed to be saying very little, while the wedding guests were remonstrating with him forcibly. The man was not moving and held out his hand in a beseeching gesture. He was about 20 she guessed, clad in dirty clothes and with feet shod only in a pair of worn plastic flip-flops. Even in the dull illumination on the terrace Stephanie could make out matted and congealed blood, where his feet had been torn.

His coffee coloured skin and unusual copper tinted hair gave the man, or boy, an unusual masculine beauty. Stephanie caught her breath when she saw him but the sympathy that rose within her for this unfortunate, a migrant presumably, was even more profound than her natural generosity of spirit would have always granted such a wanderer.

Now she was closer she could make out the gist of the altercation. The group of wedding guests were chiding the man that this was a wedding and his presence was a disturbance to the party. Would he please leave? But the man continued to stand his ground, pleading for, as far as Stephanie could pick up on the half-overheard conversation, food and something to drink. He was refusing to move until he received this and, in face of his intransigence, the voices of the group surrounding him grew in vehemence and became more insistent. Meanwhile with each passing minute more people heard the dispute and joined the pack at the side of the terrace. The group was becoming more aggressive, each member contributing to the sense of shared dislike of this interloper disrupting the celebration.

Stephanie walked back to where the barbeque was cooling. The cooks had long ago left and whatever carved meat had been left undistributed was now congealed – but it was better than nothing. She made up a plate of whatever she could find, some *bavette*, a sausage, a chicken leg and poured a glass of water. She did this quickly, concerned that the man might be driven off before she could return.

Her actions could not have taken more than a couple of minutes and the man was still there. She pushed her way through the crowd and they parted before her, sensing perhaps her strength of purpose, or glad of someone who looked as though she would resolve the stand-off. She presented the man with the plate of meat and the water. Nobody tried to stop her, although they fell silent as they saw what she intended. The man did not seem surprised when the meal was offered, or grateful. Perhaps he was dispirited from the lack of charity he had encountered, just tired from his journey or so pleased to see food that every other reaction was forgotten. He took the plate and the glass and then started to move away, having now obtained his objective, to eat out of the light of the terrace, in the woods beyond. But Stephanie shook her head, bidding him to stay where he was, for a moment.

She reached into her clasp but there was nothing to give him of any value within it. Just her make-up, some lip stick, her phone – for who carried cash these days? Frustrated she peered into the bag more closely and stirred the contents again. There must be something of value here. But apart from the phone, which she really did not want to part with, of little value in the flea markets where the migrant was likely to sell it anyway, there was nothing. She hesitated for a second, as though summoning her will and then, having made her decision she slipped off the gold bangle around her arm. As the man's hands were both full, she stuffed the bangle into one of his trouser pockets.

There was a gasp when the crowd saw what she was doing. A woman reached out to her and grasped her arm, as though to pull it back. "*Non, non,*" said the woman, *C'ést trop, c'ést trop. Ne faites pas ça. Ce n'est pas nécessaire.*" Stephanie turned and gave the woman a look that would have done Medusa proud. " *Lachez-moi, s'il vous plaît. Laissez-moi faire comme je le souhaite.*" The woman shrank away. The migrant looked confused, perplexed by Stephanie's act and perhaps worried that it was some form of joke at his expense - or that he would later be arrested for theft. But Stephanie looked directly at him, to make sure she had his attention and smiled in reassurance, sending the message that this transfer was fine; he was welcome to the gift and that there would be no unfortunate repercussions for him. She was not going to report it stolen in the morning. Then she bowed her head and nodded in the direction of the woods, indicating that he could now leave.

The man backed away, still gazing at her, as though he expected her to change her mind at any moment. But within a few feet the lamps of the terrace no longer illuminated him and he was lost in the gloom. Stephanie stared after him, keeping the man in her sight as long as it were possible. If Noah had survived he must be about the same age now. This could have been her son for all she knew. This youth, this migrant, with his colouring, his age and his height, was a violent reminder of what was always in her mind. She knew why she had given this uninvited guest her bangle; it was not just so he could sell it for cash. For an irrational thought had entered Stephanie's head. This could indeed be Noah! Maybe the fates had brought them together at last. And even if he was not Noah, this man might know of her son, might have once have crossed paths with him, and if he had done so.... he would know that fact because her son carried identification. She had once before left a bracelet, when she was forced to give up her son. Her gift might trigger some recollection in the mind of this unfortunate. The thought was not absurd; this was a meeting that was meant to happen. No, it was not absurd to think thus. The chances were minimal – but they existed! Stephanie gathered up the folds of her long skirt, climbed up onto the low wall and was about to jump down the other side and pursue the man. He must know something! But at that moment she felt a grasp at her elbow, restraining her, pulling her back into the light. She twisted, trying to free herself from the restraint.

"Let him go, Stephanie. Let him go," said Claude. "you can always replace the bangle."

But he had quite misunderstood. Stephanie looked at Claude, studying his face for a few moments, saying nothing, as her mind assessed a few things. Was it perhaps time her lover knew? She made a decision. It was indeed about time that he understood; that Claude should know that part of her background that infiltrated each and every one of her days. She took his land and led him across the terrace where she had spied an unoccupied bench.

"Come," said Stephanie. " Sit with me for a few moments and I will tell you something that you need to know about me."

Chapter 16

Stephanie tells her story

"I was 17. I had just returned, for the holidays, from my boarding school in Switzerland, where I had been sent to distance me from my mother's problems; a relocation that I did not object to. That evening there were just three of us dining, my parents and I. Elizabeth having already gone to bed. We had almost finished. The meal had started well enough - our first time together in several months. We were eating in the old baronial style dining room – the one lined with the hunting trophies of the male Lamaires.

This room was reserved for family occasions, or when my parents had guests, as it was too large for just my mother and farther when eating alone. But Daddy had asked for dinner to be laid up there that evening, hoping, I guess, that I would appreciate the ancestral resonances and feel at home again. Feel at home? Sure did. My mother was increasingly tipsy, my father withdrawn. When he did speak, as far as I remember it was mostly to complain about some decision made by Trump, on China or climate change or whatever; there was always something to rile my father, even if he was nominally a Republican.

So, business much as usual. Still, I thought - dinner will soon be over, then we can all go to bed. The meal might not have been an unqualified success but tomorrow would be another day and Daddy had planned to take me out riding, early, before it got too hot and muggy. Then Clarence came into to see if we would be taking cheese or desert. "I think not, thank you Clarence," my father said, without waiting for at least mother's wishes to be made clear. "Very good sir," replied Clarence, in that sort of mock English way he has. "But maybe we will have some coffee Clarence," Daddy added. He glanced around and asked me "Stephanie, yes? Then mother, "Bethany – would you like one?" It should have been an innocent enough request but in a bad marriage nothing is truly innocent; there is no territory that cannot be fought over. My mother looked at Daddy and said, in a voice full of venom. The words are still etched into my mind.

"Thornton, we have been married 20 odd years and in that time have I ever had coffee after dinner? 20 years and you still get this wrong? It is just typical that you can't remember the slightest detail about me. I mean, it's not very difficult is it? To get even a little thing right? After all this time you're still incapable of....." Mother lost her thread at that point. She stood up shakily and began to make for the door which, unexpectedly, she managed to reach and open. Normally Clarence would have been there to grab an elbow in support - and guide her at least to the stairs, if not the entire way to her bedroom – but this time he seemed to have thought it wiser not to be a witness to Mother's behaviours. I guess he had left the room in search of father's coffee.

I was in tears by this point, although whether that was from the attack on Daddy or just the general misery of my parent's marriage would be difficult to say. Probably both. No doubt father would have been open to attack even if he had not offered my mother any coffee. Mother would have accused him then of lack of courtesy. It was, as usual, to be a lose-lose situation all round. Father tried to comfort me. "I'm sorry", he said. 'Your mother's not always like this but she seems to have been under more strain than usual." But as far I remembered the whole thing was pretty run-of-the-mill.

Then there was the sound of a crash outside. We both rushed out to find Mother at the foot of the stairs. She appeared unhurt but as Daddy went to help her up she lashed out, "Get away from me. Don't come near me." I fled upstairs to my room. And that was when I stared to make some unfortunate decisions.

I had long had to live with my mother's drinking, and I feared this would eventually lead to divorce and the break-up of the family. I thought Daddy could only take so much. But the idea of divorce just made me more miserable. It might be a hopeless family but it was the only one I had. In any event, I had long learnt to protect myself by emotional withdrawal from my mother, who through-out my childhood had been almost as aggressive towards me as towards Daddy. I had developed a protective distance but that incurred a psychic cost, a loneliness, that I ameliorated those days by frequent doses of marijuana. So I went up to the sanctuary of my own room and lit up.

Then I remembered; I had been invited, and had declined, a party given that night by an old childhood friend, Carter Martel. I began to regret that I had not insisted on going to Carter's party, instead of acquiescing in father's request to stay and have, in his words, a 'pleasant' family supper. But it was still early; given the lack of conversation the meal had not taken long. The party would soon be in full flow. I could make it. However, the house would be locked down by now. Clarence would not have considered that anyone wanted to go out after supper. Father was almost certainly still up. But I did not want to confront him when I was high and reeked of weed.

Many of my friends would be at the party, friends whom I hadn't seen for ages, being stuck at that boarding school in Europe as I was. So I decided, yes, I would be Cinderella and go to the party in search of a prince, or perhaps I would be more like

Rapunzel, given what was to follow. Because If I couldn't risk going out by the door, I would go out by the window. My bedroom was only on the second floor; the height was not very great.

I slid up the casement. The night air damp, warm, rushed in to embrace me. It felt so soft; it seemed to promise protection and cover, rather than danger and discovery. Remembering, amazingly, to take the key to my little car, and the front door key to let myself back in, I levered myself out onto to window ledge, leaned over and reached out to the trunk of the thick ivy that grew just outside the window.

I was careless in the confidence of my intoxicated state. I tried to swing herself out onto the inviting vine – and immediately slipped. I grasped at the tendrils and the leaves of the vine as I fell, but they ripped away in my hands. One of my feet caught briefly in the contorted branches and I upended. I put out my hands to break the fall but as I hit the ground beneath there was a faint cracking sound, that I did not quite hear or feel at the time.

I brushed off the dirt and in a haze walked as quietly as I could towards my little Honda. Although I could just about trigger the car's central locking I was unable to open the doors with my good left hand. Each time I tried to apply leverage, a shooting pain travelled up my arm and I could not pull at the handle. Well, so be it. I was not going to be put off attending the party, having come this far. I opened the door awkwardly with my other hand, and slithered in. I rested my left hand on the wheel but it would take no pressure. Each attempt only resulted in excruciating pain and I could not make the slightest movement of my wrist. My hand seemed to hang at a strange angle, uselessly. There was no way I could drive.

I took out my phone and was just about sober enough to find the taxi number. 10 minutes from town it would take. I wandered down the drive to the gates to meet it. I felt the curved, drooping, boughs of the live oaks, that embraced above the drive, form a protective corridor about me and even the Spanish moss that bedraggled their limbs did not seem too spooky or remove this sense that the trees were somehow on my side. I sat down at the gates, lit another joint and waited for the taxi.

By the time I reached the party many of the guests had already paired off and although, as I had hoped, the friends I had not seen for months were present, half of them were either entwined with their boyfriends or too drunk or stoned to make much sense. I could see no sign of Carter. I was just beginning to regret all the risks that I had run. The anaesthetizing effect of the drugs was wearing off and a dull ache ran up my right arm. I was practically unable to hold a drink. If I didn't concentrate real hard, each time I took a sip I risked missing my mouth. Still, a little more alcohol and dope and perhaps this throbbing in my wrist would go away. That was when I noticed a boy who, in the soft light of the room, seemed unusually good looking.

I remember him even now. I gazed at him, hardly conscious that I was staring. But he felt my glance and turned. He smiled, self-confidently, but tenderly too – it was not an aggressive or predatory look. I warmed to this guy and some connection of affinity passed between us.

He came over and introduced himself. Over the noise I could hardly hear properly; Tyrone,Troy, Tye? Anyway, this Tye, as I eventually discovered was in fact his name, was in his second year of medical school. He knew a broken wrist when he saw one. "You need to get yourself to casualty sister, or that's going to be real nasty in the morning," he said to me.

There was no way I was going to casualty that night. I wasn't so drunk that I didn't know that my father was well enough known locally that my presence in casualty would inevitably be reported to him. Better that I should creep back into the house later that night and claim I'd fallen in my room – or something like that.

We tried to dance but even that was painful. At last Tye motioned me to a convenient sofa. It was a wide one but there was already a couple on it and not enough room for us as well. So he pulled me onto his lap – but carefully, so as not to grab my bad wrist, or let it be trapped between us. It happened too quickly for me to object, and after all, wasn't this just what I had come for? The hope that there would be a warm, handsome, boy who smelt good and took my mind off the vileness of the evening at home? Who would comfort me, allow me to loose myself into a labyrinth of sensuality down which my hormones would surely lead me? I dropped my head into the crick of Tye's neck and took a deep pull on the pheromones of maleness that would bear me away to some other place.

But my injury prevented me being quite as sluttish as I really wished. I could neither move freely, nor embrace Tye as closely as nature tempted me. After a time, when we had both gone about as far as two motivated people can on a cramped sofa, and one of them with a broken wrist, Tye said "Hey, it's a full moon tonight. There's a place I would love to show you. I found it when I was last down here. There'll be enough light for us. Besides it will soon be dawn. Come with me, it's really cool."

I was very comfortable on the sofa but this sounded like an adventure. "OK," I agreed.

We managed to find Tye's beaten up 20-year-old small Ford amongst all the other beaten up cars that were strewn across a field next to the barn. No valet parking here. But the muffler of the old car had partly blown. God, I thought, this car is going to waken the dead, and probably father, sleeping peacefully (I hoped) five miles away. The chance of getting arrested seemed high and there would clearly be a DUI for Tye, at a minimum, if we were stopped.

We drove around the outskirts of the town to avoid attracting attention, and then on for another five miles or so, through an area that appeared densely wooded from what I could make out in the headlights. I began to chat animatedly about my life – glad to have an audience to whom I could vent my frustrations about parents in general, my mother in particular and my school in Europe. Tye appeared to listen. He probably sensed that this flow of words was more about release for me than a serious attempt at conversation to which he should respond.

After a bit we started to climb a hill and in half a mile or so of ascent came upon a small clearing at the left hand side of the road. Tye pulled over and stopped the car; "We're here," he said. "Are you OK to walk?"

"Sure. It's my wrist, not my ankle," I said. I spoke a little more acerbically than I meant to. I had no wish to score points against Tye. I was having a lovely time and liked him. I let him lead on

Tye took my undamaged hand and guided me up the track. But the moon was so strong, and the night still so clear, even if the first clouds were beginning to gather and sometimes obscure the silvery light, that I had no trouble seeing the way or even the odd root or fallen branch that obstructed it. We hiked for about ten minutes, walking peacefully in silent companionship, hand in hand, cosseted by the soft, warm, humid night air. Then, as we crested the hill we came upon a clearing, a platform of moss and grass on which stood a small, evidently empty, wooden, hut. It was obvious why it had been built here. Beneath us the land fell away over a meadow and beyond that our eyes followed the canopy of the forest which, illuminated in the moonlight, seemed to stretch for ever. I was awed by the beauty and immensity of the world that was laid beneath our gaze. "It's the garden of Eden," I cried, delighted. "Without the serpents I hope!" replied my new boyfriend. "It's OK, I haven't brought an apple," I jested. But in a way I had. We, or at least I, was about to lose my childhood innocence.

Inside the cabin there was very little furniture. Just a table with a visitor's book to sign and an orienteering map on the walls. There was a chart where bird observations could be recorded, a small vase of withered woodland flowers but little else. The hut was evidently a refuge for walkers and certainly not intended as a love nest. We sat on a couple of chairs on the little wooded deck, drinking in the peace of the night and smoked a little more weed. Then I understood what I wanted to do next.

"Hey, Tye, come with me," I said. No, I didn't just say it, I commanded him to come to me. There was a small area of flat moss

to one side of the hut; it was too early in the night for dew and the land appeared quite dry. We looked into each other's eye's for a moment, each wondering just how far the other wanted to go. I was a little unsure of myself and wanted a sign that Tye respected me, had paid attention to what I had told him about myself. I wanted to give myself the illusion that I wasn't making this too easy, that my fate that night was not inevitable. "Tell me the name of my sister – who is named after an English queen – before you can sleep with me," I said. I remembered telling Tye in the car.

Tye just laughed. He had completely forgotten the name of my sister. "Anne? Catherine?" he said, trying to remember any names of sovereigns that he thought might sound vaguely English to him. History had not been his strongest subject.

"Why don't you know?" I told him. "You weren't listening to me." The test was not very difficult and he had to get it right.

He just said, "Who cares ? It doesn't matter what the name of the Queen is your sister's named after. I don't know – Joan, Anne, Louise, Caroline - whatever."

"Why not?" I asked. "It does matter. You should have been courteous enough to listen to what I was telling you."

"It doesn't matter 'cos you've already decided," Tye said. I disliked his presumption – but of course he was right. I wanted a successful conclusion to my test; but I deluded myself as to my resistance if it was failed. I pulled him towards me anyway. What did I really care if he failed my silly test? I wanted love and my attempt at establishing an illusion of self-respect was not going to stand in the way of that.

By the time we left the glade and headed back down the path towards the car, the clouds had gathered more seriously and a gentle rain had started, turning the dust to a dirty paste that clung to our shoes. The moon was totally obscured and, even though the first glow of dawn was beginning to illuminate our way. We stumbled over the last few yards. The drugs and alcohol were beginning to lose their influence and I could no longer ignore the pain of my wrist. Tye offered to drive me home, an offer I could not do otherwise than accept. I just hoped my parents were sleeping soundly when we reached the gates.

The next morning, I awoke at around 11. I could not move my right hand and my broken wrist had swollen to the size of a grapefruit. There was no way I could disguise this damage. Then I saw muddy footprints all over the bedroom carpet. Christ! If I had made those, then God knows what I must have left in the hall and up the stairs. I hadn't yet recalled the evidence of the torn vine on the front of the house, that had so failed to support my escape.

I didn't know at which point that morning the truth of my nocturnal adventure would come out - but that it would be revealed seemed inevitable. I would, of course, now be banned from any further parties for the rest of the holidays; grounded for weeks, probably.

I went into the bathroom to shower off the lingering traces of the night, then put on fresh clothes; better to meet my fate properly attired than suffer the psychological disadvantage of facing parents in last night's dress. Dully steeled, I descended and went into the kitchen, to be greeted, to my relief, only by Clarence.

"Ah, Miss Stephanie, how are you this morning?" he boomed, in that ever cheerful way he has. He knew how much trouble I was in. He had already cleaned up the mud marks in the hall and on the stairs but unfortunately not before her father had seen then. Then he spied my wrist. "Good heavens, Miss Stephanie. You must get yourself to the hospital," he said – which was not really what I was hoping to hear. I couldn't drive myself and asked if my mother was around? I assumed father would be out by this time of the morning, and mother would still be sober.

I realized that any story about breaking my wrist in my room was not going to wash. I would have to brave the consequences of my escape from the house, but I was determined to reveal nothing about Tye. Or how I had spent the night. Unfortunately for me, what I didn't know was that Daddy had installed video monitoring of the gates while I had been away at school. I soon found out.

But my run of bad luck had hardly begun. A couple of weeks after the party I missed my period. The first time did not worry me unduly, I was often irregular. But when it didn't come back the following month I asked one of my braver girl friends to buy a pregnancy testing kit. The less I had to do with the technology, that I could hardly bring myself even to name, the more I could keep the horror of what might be happening in some very distant corner of my mind.

Three separate attempts with that apparatus delivered the same result. I had now to begin facing what I wanted so much to avoid. I had no idea what to do. I could hardly tell my parents and I had no idea how to go about getting an abortion in Louisiana, or even if that was possible. I suspected not. At that time, like now, obtaining an abortion in the state was about as likely as me landing on the far side of the moon.

I had no idea of how to contact Tye. We had exchanged Christian names only; I had no email, no number for him. In my tiredness and haste to get inside the house and into bed that night I had forgotten to ask. I texted my cousin Carter, who had given the party, but Tye was not a friend of his, and had no idea whom might have brought him.

My prince? Tye was unlikely to appear with a slipper to claim me. Maybe I could trace the northern college he attended, via Facebook or something, perhaps? But what good would that do, really? Tye was not going to marry me, or me him, and father would never countenance an Afro-American as son-in-law anyway. Did I want him to pay for an abortion? I didn't really know, but I would have liked to discuss things. I felt so isolated

I contemplated making an excuse to visit some friend up north before her new school term began, and take enough time out to procure an abortion up there. But how long would I need, before my parents started to ask questions as to why I was away for so long? Did I have enough money to pay for an abortion? How would I go about finding a clinic that would accept me – given that it was late in my pregnancy now? I had just turned 17 and had no idea of the answers to any of these questions.

The days ticked by. I prevaricated and prevaricated and the truth about my night with Tye did not become clear to my parents for another 5 months – after which time my pregnancy became too obvious to ignore. One day mother, less befuddled than usual, realized that her eldest daughter's tall, slim, figure was not quite so trim as it used to be. It could just be natural weight gain. But then again, maybe not.

So the truth came out. Not all of it immediately of course; and to begin with having somebody adult with whom to discuss my predicament, even if it was only my mother, was a relief. The immediate feeling of comfort in not having to bear my anxiety alone was immense.

But that feeling was pretty short lived. My fate became the subject of debate, how much damage I had done to my life, all our lives really - because my shame would inevitably descend on the entire family. How could I go to college with a new born infant, and no husband? It would be education terminated; any chance of a marriage to the scion of some other 'good' Southern family, that would bring connections and lustre to the Lamare family; all gone.

And who was the father? When I was questioned on the subject I had to steer a perilous course between the Scylla of suggesting I had slept with so many boys that I could not possibly determine who was the father, and the Charybdis of confessing that I had slept with so few that it would be easy to identify Tye. The insistence of the inquiry was remorseless.

My parents could do the approximate math. At last Daddy summoned up the courage to face the possibility that only I could confirm. Was it the boy who had been caught on video that night? The one who had given his daughter a kiss that went way beyond what was required of a chivalrous driver, giving a lift to a friend? That Afro-American? But possessing courage was not the same as accepting the answer. It was bad enough that his eldest daughter was pregnant, having a child when she was neither married nor in a position in life to cope with, but once Tye's identity was confirmed his view of the families predicament grew a lot worse. The baby would be half-caste! A product of that worst of Southern crimes; miscegenation. Times might have moved on but the old attitudes were still there. I wouldn't say my parents had ever considered themselves liberals so the idea of welcoming this unexpected little, coloured, visitor into their world was not something that appealed in any way. Until now they had assumed that the baby must be white. If it got around that this was not the case, then the shame they were already exposed to would become a great deal worse.

My dear old mother explained, with a hint of nostalgia, that, in a different age, there would have been a lynching of Tye. Well, unfortunately for them, that wasn't going to happen in 2018, even in Louisiana. Nor would it have solved my predicament. Instead, what could they do? They could track Tye down, of course, but what would be the point of that? They certainly didn't want Tye to do the honourable thing and marry their darling daughter.

So what exactly would be achieved by confronting Tye? Nothing except the pleasure of upbraiding and humiliating him – but those rewards, although significant to them, did not quite overcome father's doubts about whether he really wanted to know any more about this fellow, or precipitate any sort of contact that might lead to a future relationship that he shunned. If adoption of the fast-approaching child was to be the chosen route, then money, to ease the route to new parents and finance the upbringing and education of the child, was hardly an issue; the Lamaire's had that in abundance. No need to tap Tye for that.

In my father's mind – and I emphasize my father's, because mother had told him to sort this out - there was this indigestible truth; in my womb was developing a half-caste illegitimate baby that would carry Lamaire genes, and name. And he thought there was no safe way this could be hushed up. Somewhere in the future this 'incident' would return to haunt them. For I could not be kept prisoner at Crooked Timber for the next four months. There would inevitably be talk, speculation as to the identity of my impregnator.

As my father ruminated on all this, he became obsessed by the unfairness which fate (for he now saw this incident as a curse from a vengeful God, rather than the accidental consequence of two hormonal teenagers meeting) had delivered to his family. There must be some way to alleviate his pain.

It would be impossible to pin-point when the idea first came to my parents, when what had hitherto been deemed completely unacceptable came to be seen as the only possible solution. The transition, from vague musing to practical resolution to the crisis, was slowed by the abhorrence they felt each time they considered this (to them) hateful option. Had not their church, their God, forbidden anything of the sort that they were now contemplating? Remember they were, and are to this day, fundamentally, conservative, southern Catholics. Yet, yet, if things were left to follow their natural path, quite soon there would be this little, not-quite-white, baby.

One day my parents arrived at their conclusion. As usual my father was expected to carry out the dirty work, give effect to what neither parent wanted to face. So, he picked up the phone and dialled his old friend, Nat Seddenhow. Nathan had been our family doctor and a golfing partner of Daddy's for as many years as I can remember. He surely would know what to do. Daddy felt he could trust Nat. He had to; there appeared to be no other route out of this mess.

But as the good doctor explained; it was late in my pregnancy and this was the South. Those sort of places my father had in mind had all closed up shop. Only three clinics were still operating and, if the forthcoming Supreme Court decision, on 'admitting-rights', went the wrong way there would only be one. The governor sure didn't make it easy for them. Besides, my dates meant that the proposed procedure was only days away from being illegal, wherever in the US, even the North. It was almost impossible to obtain an abortion after 21 weeks – anywhere.

Still, Seddenhow didn't want to be unhelpful so he asked me to step past his office one day. I went along to see the good doctor, initially under the illusion that I was being offered a check-up, and we had a long chat. At the end of which I returned home and declared to my parents that I would be going away for a few days. My parents smiled at each other; it was all going to be all right after all. Good old Nat had done his stuff and come up trumps. In a few days this nightmare would be over. Throughout the house an atmosphere of denial descended, with my parents avoiding to ask where I was about to go 'for a few days'. And I believed, reasonably enough, that as my parents were the instigators of my trip to the family doctor, they must be fully aware of what was about to happen and if they didn't want to discuss it, that was fine with me.

A couple of days later, my case packed, I was picked up by Seddenhow in his big Chevrolet Impala. I said good-bye, told my parents not to worry and looked forward to seeing them in a few days. Well, that's perhaps not what I felt but that, out of custom and habit, was what I said anyway.

But few things in life go according to plan. Two days later, Nathan called my parents. There had been a complication. It was nothing to worry about. I was fine, my health – at least my physical health – was not in danger but I was suffering from exhaustion and it was best that I be allowed to recover, get some rest from what had been a stressful time. I needed solitude and expert support, mostly psychological. All this might take some time and I might be away for a couple of months. My parents listened attentively and agreed that they would certainly take his advice. They would miss their daughter, of course, but the main thing was I should be given peace to recover in my own time.

My parents were so relieved that their trials seemed to be over, and that Nathan had been the instrument of the family's salvation, that they would have agreed to whatever he asked. Besides they were glad, really, of a temporary break from my presence around the house. I think they felt uncomfortable at what they had done and asked of their daughter.

Dr Seddenhow was just lovely about the whole thing. He allowed me to stay on at his clinic while I sorted out what I wanted to do. He knew the pressure I had been under at home. But, of course, as the days ticked by my parent's preferred solution became ever less procurable. Then my indecision was brought to an end by nature. I went into labour two months early. The baby only survived because of the skills and care of Seddenhow's clinic. He arranged for my son to be adopted. And then, eventually, after I had recovered and weaned my baby, I went back home. Nobody said anything. The subject was buried. Life went on as reasonably normal once more

As Stephanie finished her story, Claude looked at her and said, "What did your parents say when they discovered that there had been no abortion?" he asked.

"I never told them. That was their punishment. Mine came later. There has not been a day since when I have not thought of Noah."

Chapter 17

Science Po

It was the last week of term, before the summer exams. There was his final lecture to deliver, several doctorates to *viva*, but, *Dieu merci*, no essays to mark. Those had at least been delegated to Claude's teaching assistants. Ah, the teaching assistants; they not only marked the essays but answered much of Claude's correspondence, carried out most of the research for his new books, and revised the old ones before new editions were published. He didn't like recalling the introduction he had recently been given at the start of a graduate seminar: '*many of you will have read Professor Blondel's books, even more of you will have written them'*. How they had laughed. *Salauds*!

On his way to Science Po, a few days later, he received an email on his phone from an old English friend, Brian Torrington. Some years before the two had met on a climbing holiday in the Alps and although it would have appeared at first sight that they had little in common, Torrington having chosen to join the London police, their shared passion for the freedom of the mountains had brought them together. The friendship was enhanced by the fact

Torrington was a Francophile and had married a French wife, Laurence. But it was not often that the two friends saw each other and Claude was delighted to hear that Brian was going to be in Paris for some conference or other the following week - and that there would be a chance to meet. Even better, he could invite Brian to stay over the weekend; maybe the two of them could enjoy some climbing, practising their rusty skills on the rocks in the forest at Fontainebleau. He would call the *Aigle Noir* Hotel and book a couple of rooms. He wasn't sure if Torrington was going to bring Laurence, but hoped so. She would provide some company for Stephanie, who would otherwise be bored while the two men went off on their own.

In the meantime, there were more immediate issues. The most pressing was to organise and write up the notes for his next book, *Consciousness and Reality*. Once he had reached New York and installed himself at the MARIONn campus, he would have more time to write but, if was to have any hope of meeting his publisher's deadline, he needed to make a start soon. He had conceived the draft structure of the book and this morning planned to fly a few of its central concepts over his students. Feedback was always useful. Of course, he had written along the same lines before; he knew the background to the subject well. But soon, with the incipient introduction of MARIONn, and other machines like her, there would be a new consciousness on earth. He was still struggling with some of the implications of that. Would these machines *really* be conscious? Would it be the *same* consciousness as humanity possessed? How would they be able to tell anyway?

Claude looked at his agenda for the day. He'd agreed to have an early dinner that evening with Stephanie and he was looking forward to that. They seemed to had been getting on better since the wedding. She'd become more light hearted and relaxed as she grew more familiar with Paris and his friends. Even if her proposed book on Benjamin Franklin's life in Paris seemed to be going nowhere, the acceptance of many of her articles by *TrueNews* had reassured Stephanie that she could find a role in the city, that she could live with a purpose here and feel respected by others. Insecurities about her place in the world never lurked far below the surface. At least he now understood the cause of her buried guilt. Having to give away her child must have been devastating for her psyche. He knew that every day she wondered if some chance happening would deliver news of her son's existence.

Stephanie had started talking of seeing a therapist again. Perhaps she should. To Claude it seemed as though no earlier treatment had ever succeeded in lifting the damage that the loss of her son had dealt her. Maybe Stephanie should investigate, as Claude was proposing for his father, the potential merits provided by the *LetheTech* treatment? Removing the memory of that teenage trauma might be her best option – rather than endless courses of 'talking' therapy. She'd already tried most of the schools, Freudian, Jungian, Kleinian, with scant results.

Reaching his office at Science Po, Claude gave an instruction to his virtual assistant, *Aladdin,* to make a cup of coffee and recall his lecture material. As the coffee dribbled into the cup, his notes appeared and floated in front of his eyes. He preferred to work standing up, like Victor Hugo. It kept him alert, he always claimed. And it made the process of composition easier to manage. If he wished to make changes to the text, he just placed his finger on a sentence hanging in the air to move it around to some new place, or click his fingers to delete it. Of course, it would be even easier with an iPsyche, or at least so he had heard, just *think* the amendment and the change would be implemented. But he wasn't sure that he was quite there yet. He'd wait a little. For the moment he'd stick with his wrist band phone, however old fashioned that might be. That it couldn't read his mind, like an iPsyche, was a large part of its appeal. He didn't like of the level of intrusion that device would enable.

He concentrated on the job in hand. During the spring term, he and his students had discussed what it meant to be *real*, to have *being* in the world. They had started at Plato and his idea of the *forms*, the Greek philosopher's view that these eternal entities represented the true reality, something unchangeable, immutable, not given to degradation over time, unlike so much of creation and unlike that philosopher's transitory shadows, cast by the light of a flickering fire on the walls of a cave; mere illusions of reality. They had gone on to discuss the Enlightenment view that the laws of physics, discovered through empirical research by scientists, not philosophers, governed the universe and that it was within the compass of such laws that the ultimate reality lay. Then they had discussed the world of quantum mechanics and what that theory said about reality – or was quantum mechanics just a mathematical construct, that produced the right answers, but said nothing about the nature of the real world? Now, at the final lecture, they were going to consider the footnote to philosophy that was metaphysics, and how philosophers who had followed that discipline had thought about the world and the nature of reality.

What was he going to say to these final year students about metaphysics? Why did he teach, and they spend their time learning, anything quite so useless in the modern world? It was a difficult and obscure subject that enabled him to shine a bit, to demonstrate his intellect in a discipline that was anything but transparent. But he worried about the vanity of it all; something that profiles on Claude Dominic Blondel, as was his full name, CDB, were never hesitant to point out. Being a teacher of metaphysics was a bit like being a carver of miniature figurines, difficult to do well, tortuous in detail, irrelevant to the modern world but sometimes beautiful to behold.

He knew there was an appeal of metaphysics to his students in its very uselessness. There was a certain snobbery in something that was intellectually elegant but had no real purpose; the very inverse of electrical engineering, computing, business, politics, economics and all those *useful* studies that had some practical application; studies that might enable the students to make a living once they had graduated. But, sometimes, he thought, metaphysics did say something true and important about the world; indeed perhaps more true and more relevant than all the schools of thought that they had discussed so far.

There was a knock on his door. Claude cursed silently, he was way behind in his preparations. He could ignore the knock but then again he hadn't yet really begun to concentrate on his material. He'd just say hello then get rid of whoever it was. He collapsed his airborne notes back into the cloud and pulled open the door. The person could have been more inconvenient and unwelcome, he supposed, but it was only his professional colleague Louis LeDuc. Louis, at least, would understand why Claude was busy and allow himself to be put off till another time. Claude was about to say just that when a different idea occurred to him. Perhaps Louis could be useful to him? He wanted to discuss the latest student unrest with another member of staff. And there was the issue of the autumn term schedules to discuss too, when Claude would not be present at the commencement. He let LeDuc in, explained that he had a lecture to deliver that morning but that, perhaps, the two of them could have a quick lunch together afterwards? A late lunch it would have to be; say, at 1.30 ? He would meet Louis at a restaurant near-by – 'Au 35', Rue Jacob.

Now he would have little time to do anything but check and memorise the barest of notes before the morning's lecture. He'd given the core of this presentation before; after all this was just a *tour de horizon,* a quick fly-past of the background to the subject and a brief look at the issues raised by the metaphysicians. He just needed to add a few remarks about the latest AI developments to show that he was *au-courant* with what was happening in the wider world – and that he wasn't simply regurgitating last year's lecture (*as so many of his colleagues did*, he thought waspishly).

Chapter 18

The lecture

So it was that 40 minutes later, with the confidence of a man with tenure, CDB, dressed in his usual open white shirt and charcoal dark flannel trousers, looked up, and over, the heads of the assembled students in the lecture theatre. This was almost the last day before the exam revision period, and the hall was packed. The seats got a little more sparsely occupied towards the back of the hall but they'd soon be filled with latecomers. For those who had been partying the night before, the first three rows were the place to be. It was well known, at least to everybody but Claude it seemed, that if you were tired and likely to fall asleep, sit at the front of the banked auditorium. The professor's gaze was always over your head. Any inattention might go unnoticed.

But not many students did fall asleep anyway. Claude was a popular lecturer and his classes were over-subscribed. His subject may have become fashionable but in addition, although he tried to push the immodest thought away, it couldn't help but occur to him that his own delivery may have influenced the fashion. Vanity was one of these spiritual failings that he had to keep under control; a hazard he must be aware of. The open white shirt may have just have made dressing in the morning that much simpler but his wide and manly chest, that was just a little too visible, may have also served his conceits. Of course, he could dress in other colours, button up the top of the shirt, but it seemed a trifle absurd to spend so much time contemplating every morning the otherwise simple act of what to wear. In any event, the black and white combination had become a symbol of his brand, his *marque-deposée.*

He caught himself reflecting on these narcissistic details, dismayed. The whole issue of how to dress was too trivial to worry that much about. But this was not the only thing bothering him that morning: at the back of his mind was a germ of doubt about what he was instilling into these avid young minds. Did his philosophy predict how the new self-aware computers and robots were going to perceive the world? Could they even identify with confidence whether the machines were truly conscious or not, had reached *singularity*? Not really. It was the old problem of how we know what's going on in other minds, whether those minds were human or made of silicon. With even the last generation of computers you could say their internal states were just the opening and closing of switches, the flow of electrons, the whole binary, digital thing. But now? Who knew what was in the mind of the servers at the MARIONn campus for example? A machine that would be *'educated'*, like a human being, and who could add to her view, from the basis of her own experiences, without any additional help from humans, about how to act in the world.

The machine at the MARIONn *campus*? Claude caught the thought before it passed. Could you properly call these computers, these silicon minds, *machines* at all? And if not, what were they? Persons? Would consciousness give them legal rights? A forthcoming case before the US Supreme Court would go much further than *Douglas v Milton Robotics.* That had determined there was now a degree of sentience in robots and computers and that awareness had to be respected. The latest machines could feel '*pain*' when their sensors were tampered with; they suffered like we did when someone stepped on our fingers. But the new case before the Court would go much further than that. The justices would have to determine whether recent advances meant there was so little difference between mankind and these new machines that far more extensive legal rights should be granted.

The lecture theatre was now full. Some students were standing at the back. Claude rapped on the desk to attract his audience's attention. He needed their full focus. The initial part of the metaphysical argument, that dealt with how perception influenced reality, or as those philosophers often termed it, *being* - the existence of things in the world – was especially tricky.

The room began to hush. "Good morning. I hope none of you are too tired this morning. Please be good enough to turn off your phones and any other distracting device you may have on you. As a matter of interest how many of you are wearing iPsyches?" About 20% of the class put up their hands. Claude noted silently – interesting; not many so far but then iPysches haven't been out for long. Beginning to catch on though. He said, "Well, for those who are wearing them, please instruc*t* them to be *off.* I'm sure I'll be able to tell from your glazed expression if you fail to do so." To the surprise of the first three rows, he looked down and said, "You too, any glazed looks that come from you lot catching up on sleep and I'll notice!" The students at the front opened their mouths and raised their eyebrows, a mock look of astonishment. So much for thinking they were safe, safe enough to close their eyes and let their iPsyches amuse their brains - if Claude's arguments became too strenuous to follow. Evidently this morning that escape route would be closed.

With their attention now directed at him, Claude moved out from behind the desk and started to pace from side to side, the perambulation assisting his concentration. As long as he'd read his notes beforehand, he didn't depend on them while he delivered the lecture. For theatrical effect, he hesitated, saying nothing for a few seconds, creating a tension in the hall. Then he spoke;

"Today, we approach the end of this *trimestre* and this series of lectures, devoted to what philosophers and scientists over the ages have considered *real,* permanent, in the universe. We have studied many different thinkers and many diverse views on that problem, starting with Plato. Today, I want to discuss our final approach, fashionable originally in the 19th and early 20th centuries, that takes another angle and asks, '*what is the relationship between perception and reality*, or how it is we *perceive* things to be real - and if there is a relationship between our perception and what we consider to exist in the universe? But first I'm going to backtrack a little for those of you who are still unclear about metaphysics or.......have failed to do the required reading." He stopped pacing around, looked up and smiled. These little jokes by Claude were all part of the theatre the students were accustomed to. So droll.

"*Ah non, ce n'est pas vrai!"* the students fired back in unison amid protest at the unfair accusation. They too could play the game.

"Thank you, thank you, I'm delighted for the reassurance that you have all done your reading. And my gratitude too, in advance, for the interventions that you will no doubt contribute this morning – and which I encourage you to make. Yes, please remember that I practice the Socratic method. So, if you wish to interject – with something intelligent, or to the point, or preferably both of these things at the same time, please do so." Claude returned to his stroll from one side of the hall to the other and continued where he had left off.

"You will recall, we agreed previously that metaphysics is a subject not much practiced or advanced in our times. It is not, as one might say, a *living* subject, an intellectual pursuit where contemporary philosophers daily make new advances. So we, as sophisticated 21st century intellectuals, feel perhaps a little patronising towards the subject of metaphysics; we think of those philosophers who spent, or wasted maybe, their life in the pursuit of this subject, as....... deluded academics. We tend to look down at them and think, '*how quaint their ideas seem to us now*'!"

"Long ago, the metaphysicians were dismissed, from the ranks of those who had something important to say about the modern world, by that great Austrian thinker, Wittgenstein. A mental illness, he called metaphysics; an obsession better studied by psychologists than philosophers! So, are we all mentally ill, you and I? Should we be undergoing therapy this morning, rather than sitting here on this beautiful early summer day? No! I insist, metaphysics does still have something to teach us. For at the core of this old subject is nothing less than the search for principles that underlie the make-up and the behaviour of the universe. And does that search not still concern us? Of course it does! Claude threw up his hands as though to say, *how could anyone be so stupid to dismiss the subject?*

He paused and then continued. "But why this contempt for metaphysics that we see in philosophers like Wittgenstein? The answer lies in the victory, in the West, of empiricism; the idea that what cannot be measured and what cannot be verified, or I should say *falsified*, through experiment, is valueless and so much hot air. This over-riding belief in the triumph of the scientific method is fundamentally a belief about the nature of reality; that the universe obeys certain laws and that we can discover these laws with our experiments and measurements. *Only* relationships between phenomena that can be repeatedly observed, by independent observers, can truly meet the claim of being *real*. These laws are the bedrock of our belief in how the universe is constructed. They are our idea of the rules that God, if you believe in one, created in order that the cosmos may come into being and thereafter operate smoothly. These are our '*forms*', if you like, and they represent the ultimate victory for Platonism!

"Most importantly, in this view, the universe is independent of *us*; that is, the existence of the universe we occupy is independent of our presence in it. For the empiricist is in no doubt that, if the human race disappeared tomorrow, the universe would still exist *in exactly the same way* as it does today - apart from the lack of ourselves of course. These scientists are in little doubt that the universe existed before we arrived on this planet, before we became conscious of what was around us, and it will continue to exist if we were to disappear. The world, the universe, is '*out there*', waiting for us to discover and interrogate it, but it is not '*of us*', as one might say. It is independent of whatever we might think of it. However we investigate the universe or however we perceive it, the universe *is supremely indifferent to our presence."*

"For the empiricists. there is a duality in the universe, a duality first dreamt up by Descartes – as you are aware - where everything is either stuff, *material,* or it is of *mind*, with the insubstantiality of thoughts and feelings. The material *stuff* of the universe, everything in it, atoms, particles, planets, plants, animals, is *out there*– whereas the mental stuff is all *within us.* Now this division, between the external reality and our internal perception of it, has taken a few knocks in this century; particularly in the area of quantum physics - where the experimenter's intervention as an observer *does* appear to influence the physical world. Nevertheless, it's fair to say that this duality of existence is a very deep rooted belief within our culture. "

"However!" Claude wagged his finger at the audience to emphasise the importance of his point. "However….the metaphysician does question this belief! He asks whether the world *is* as independent of our presence as we like to imagine. He believes that reality lies in a quite different place than we have hitherto supposed; not *within* things but rather *between* them, in the relationship between our minds and the world of physical objects that we see about us. In other words, the world we see might *no*t, in fact, be independent of our, human, existence and that the crucial fact about the world is not its *duality* and *separateness*, but its *connectedness* and its *'oneness'* – as many spiritual leaders have attested. In this view, the role of the observer is crucial. Perception matters and who is doing the perceiving will influence the world."

A hand shot up at the back. Claude stopped his flow, hoping that he would remember where he had left off. But he couldn't ignore the intervention; he had asked the students to speak up if they had something to say. Who was this, he wondered, not able to see too clearly amongst the mass of heads; ah, yes Magali, pretty girl – bright too.

"Yes, Magali, I think the hand belongs to you?" Claude said. "I am sure you have an interesting viewpoint. Share it with us, please" He wished to be encouraging.

"Monsieur Professor, you say that for the metaphysicians reality lies in the relationship between mind and matter; they are not two different things?" Magali's voice had a questioning tone to it. She wanted to make sure she had understood correctly.

"Indeed," said Claude

"In that case, how can there be laws, laws of physics? Do not the laws discovered by Newton or Einstein describe properties of things that don't change depending who's doing the experiment?"

"That's a very good point," said Claude, hoping that he didn't sound too patronising. "Let me explain how the metaphysician might answer it. So, the scientist does his experiments, finds there are patterns of behaviour between certain things, regularities that let him make generalizations and allow him to predict that, if this happens, then this will also happen. The existence of these patterns leads him to imagine that he understands the world, or at least some specific part of it. He now believes that he understands cause and effect."

"Consider, for example, the laws that control the orbits of the planets. Kepler, who can make a good claim to be the father of these type of laws, could say in 1619, '*look, I have discovered a law that governs the Universe. I can predict how the planets will move'*. But then someone else, a little later, let us say Einstein for example, notices a discrepancy. The predictions are not quite true in every case. The orbits of the moons of Mercury are a little different to what we expected. So it turns out these laws, whether devised by Kepler or Newton, these patterns of repeatable physical events, are not unchanging, eternal verities. They do not describe some ultimate reality, but they are just approximations: only so good until a better approximation comes along. Copernicus' concept of the universe is displaced by Kepler's, which is displaced by Newton's, who is displaced by Einstein's and so on. So the world only *appears* understandable because we impose some patterning upon it, patterns that are conceived by the human intellect, by *our* minds, and which are all proved *false* eventually. The laws of physics are not immutable, ultimate, realities – just approximate descriptions of phenomena, descriptions that are invented by us."

Claude paused, taken by his own enthusiasm for his subject. He took a deep breath and with more oxygen on board, started again, "So, when we say, the universe is like this or that, we would be wise to judge our efforts as mere temporary conveniences. All we can say, all the metaphysician would say, is that these so called '*laws*' are like a net that we cast over the world to render it comprehensible – attempts to describe the universe until a more accurate way of looking at the world comes along. To think of them as evidence of a deeper level of reality, to that we enjoy in our day-to-day life, evidence of a timeless place of eternal verities, *that* view of our efforts to understand the cosmos is mistaken. These are *our* laws, *our* creations, not created by some guy up in the clouds with a long white beard, when he decided to construct the universe, and ultimately they are, as we have seen, inaccurate. So the conclusion must be, the universe is intelligible *because we have made it so.* Are you with me so far?"

"Maybe..." said Magali, hesitantly. "But are you really saying that the world only exists in our minds? That everything is just a subjective experience?"

"Ah, I understand the point you are making," said Claude. "I realize that it must sound that the metaphysicians are claiming something like that. But that interpretation would be a mistake. I don't think they believe anything like that. No, the universe is definitely there, all right. Look." And with that Claude took a hefty kick at the desk in front of him. "*Ouch!*" he said, although he was wearing thick leather shoes and the kick couldn't have been that painful. The students were bemused by this piece of play acting. Claude explained;

"I am just repeating the experiment of the 18th century British philosopher, Bishop Berkeley. He too had encountered arguments that the world was all a mirage, all in the mind. '*Not so*', he said, '*and I prove it thus*'. He kicked a stone, *sturdily,* as his biographer puts it, to prove the world was real enough. I am not denying the world exists, not suggesting anything weird like that; matter exists and it exists outside our minds. The material universe is real and '*out there*'. The claim now before us is rather different; that the act of perception by an observer has an effect on the universe. That there is a relationship between the observer and the observed and that this matters – it is not a thing of no consequence."

Another hand shot up. This time Claude could identify its owner clearly, buried in the middle of the audience; Didier, not one of his star pupils.

"I'm glad these metaphysicians are agreed the universe is real and not a figment of our imagination!" he said, as though it had long been obvious to him that such was the case. Was that derision in his voice that Claude heard? He wasn't sure, but Didier was known to him as student who thought himself clever enough to disparage positions he didn't agree with, particularly those he didn't understand properly. "But if the universe is really there," the student continued, "what's it got to do with us? I can't make the rock less painful to my toes by thinking I wish it were a sponge!" Didier looked around as his mates, convinced that he made a good joke - at the expense of the professor.

Claude would humour Didier – unless he got tiresome. "Indeed not, Didier," he said. "You are of course right. How you perceive the rock is not going to render it any softer. But your unfortunate experience of suffering a bruised toe, while hoping the rock might obey your desires and turn into a sponge, does not entirely negate the metaphysician's point. Maybe one man can't soften a rock but at more infinitesimal level, we do have an influence. Even one guy."

"Think of quantum mechanics. Take an electron diffraction experiment for example; we know that the electron does not materialize into a particular position, or with a particular momentum until it is observed. Before we observe it, is simply a *wave function* - a package of probabilities that dictate where the electron *might* be. Then, we observe it, the wave function collapses and it becomes a particle, with a definitive position and momentum. The act of observation causes the electron to reveal itself. It's not just electrons either, all the sub atomic particles that are part of quantum physics have this characteristic.

"So, we are not just passive observers looking out on an indifferent universe. We are *necessary* players in it and we affect it, influence it, by the attention we pay to the world. Reality becomes what we make it. Metaphysics anticipated quantum mechanics – so perhaps this is not such an old, useless, study after all.

"Monsieur Professor!"

Who was this? Olivier. Usually helpful.

"Yes, Olivier. What would you like to say?"

"Didn't Hegel think that the concept of the universe, this world that we live in, is unintelligible without man. Didn't he say," and Olivier looked down at his notes. "Didn't he say '*the intelligibility of the world is not accidental. It is extraordinary that we can understand it at all. It might have been quite unintelligible'*.

"Thank you Didier. You have evidently done your reading." An ironic cheer went up from the students.

"Quiet please." Claude wrapped the desk in passing with his knuckles. "Yes, Olivier, Hegel thought it was remarkable, and not inevitable, that human beings are at home in the universe, that we can find consistent patterns that enable us to operate within it. For it might not have been like that at all. The world, the universe, might be just alien to us – nothing would relate to anything else, nothing would connect. There would be no scientific laws, no science in fact, no technology, life as we know it would be impossible, incomprehensible which - luckily for us - it is not. And from the observation that we are *at home* in the universe, that it is *our* universe, Hegel – and I leave out a few jumps in the argument here – appears to argue that what we see around us is *our* creation. We are *responsible* for it. We, all of us, the connected network of human minds, is, in a sense, God, the creator of the universe. This was an heretical, brave, view to make in a time when the church had great power. Hegel's conclusion is therefore only hinted at in his writings - but if you believe in Hegel's argument it has profound implications. If our consciousness makes the universe, then...

"But our perception, alone, cannot possibly be an adequate explanation for the existence of the universe," said a student in the front row who had been evidently following the argument closely and not listening to his iPsyche. "Ancient man looked out on the stars but all he perceived was what he could see with the naked eye. Yet, the universe was far larger, far more complex even then. His perception was inadequate, mistaken."

" NO!" exclaimed Claude, with some force. "That's wrong thinking! In this school of philosophy our perception of the universe is what the universe *is*. That's it. There was no other universe, a greater, wider, cosmos that ancient man *might* have discovered. That's to fall into the fallacy of the unobserved – that there's something out there, which we cannot yet see, which is independent of us and is just waiting to be perceived. That's incorrect thinking! There is only what can be observed!"

"So Monsieur Professor," said Olivier. By now the lecture had almost become a conversation, something that Claude enjoyed. "Are you saying that when ancient man looked out at the skies, without the benefit of a telescope, and saw only those stars that he could see with his naked eyes, *that* was the limit of the universe then?"

"That's exactly right. You have it!" said Claude pleased that at least one of his students understood the view of these metaphysicians. "We are tempted to say, in our modern day arrogance, that the universe, in those ancient times, was similar to ours, the one that we see now; it's just unfortunate those primitives did not have the means to investigate it, possess more powerful telescopes perhaps. This is very patronizing. It's a sort of cosmic imperialism! We can't possibly assume that. We weren't there!

And if Hegel is right the limited consciousness available then, in Neanderthal times, would have entailed a similarly restricted universe. To say otherwise is to make unwarranted assumptions about how the universe might have been all those millennia ago. We don't know what it was like."

"And so.... your conclusion is that....as man's consciousness expands so does the universe? As we became more aware, the universe grew to match?" said Olivier.

"Just so! If Neanderthal man had possessed telescopes he would have seen more deeply, but if he possessed those devices he would have demonstrated a higher level of consciousness in the first place, and that, the argument goes, would have entailed a more sophisticated universe than he had hitherto been used to. That's why we, modern man, with our super sensitive sensors, orbital telescopes, radio dishes and so on, keep discovering a larger and larger universe, ever further and further back in time. Just as at the other end of the scale, with ever more powerful particle accelerators we unveil more and more, smaller and smaller, sub-atomic particles. We are not just discovering these new and distant worlds, *we are bringing them into being* as our consciousness expands! Without consciousness to perceive, to establish the relationship between us and objects, there is no world out there. Humanity brings the universe to life. But it only brings it to life to the extent that our consciousness allows. The greater the level of consciousness, the greater the complexity of the perceived universe. So, it is illegitimate to say of ancient astronomers that, had they possessed the right equipment, they could have seen the universe that we see today. All they could see was all that there was. Those early cosmologists reflected the level of consciousness in their society at the time. What they saw, they saw and we cannot say that there was something else that they failed to see. What you see is what there is.

Didier interrupted again, "The fact that we do keep discovering a larger and larger universe and more and more particles – doesn't mean that you are right," he objected. "That experience is quite compatible with the idea of a universe that is independent of us, just waiting to be revealed by our clever scientists."

"Of course Didier," agreed Claude, a little wearily. "I am explaining the metaphysical philosopher's beliefs. What you say is obviously true – that the progress of physics is compatible with both hypotheses, theirs and our, quite different, modern one. We can't test one idea against the other. Unless… unless of course consciousness began to decline, then we might see the universe contract again, the smallest sub-atomic particles disappear and so on"

"Not very likely"

"No, I hope not."

Claude left it there and began to gather up his papers. "But before I let you all go, I have to advise you of something. I'm afraid there will be only four lectures from me next term, after the summer. I have been asked to return to the US for some more work on that project you know about – the MARIONn development. And then I have booked some leave of absence to write my next book. So, unless that goes a good deal faster than I suspect, your Prof for the beginning of next year will be Louis Leduc who, as you know is one of the foremost professors on the staff here. You will be in excellent hands, better than mine," Claude said, although he didn't believe what he said for a minute and he was secretly pleased when groans of displeasure greeted this unwelcome news. "So, for now, I shall wish you well in your exams and a wonderful summer vacation. *Au revoir* to all of you."

Claude stood at the desk, rather than leaving immediately, inviting those who wished to come up and discuss the lecture with him. This went on for fifteen minutes or so until remembered his lunch date with Leduc. He wrapped up the session, wished his students well, looked forward to seeing them the following year – and headed to 'Au 35' in Rue Jacob.

Chapter 19

Some questions about MARIONn

Claude walked the slight distance from Sciences Po and arrived at ‘ Au 35’ early, determined that he would not start off on the wrong foot with LeDuc. It was only 12.20pm and the restaurant had few diners. Claude cast his eyes down the menu. Most of the offerings were what he might expect, the algae spaghetti, the insect based ‘bug’ burgers, artificial steak, various vegetarian options but one item and price caught his eye. Zut! He hadn’t expected anything so extravagant here – there was an offering of *gigot d’agneau*, real meat. Quite a rarity these days since the *Shanghai Accords* and their restrictions on animal husbandry. Well, he couldn’t remember Leduc being a vegetarian, as so many were these days, on their limited salaries. Perhaps he should stand him lunch and let him enjoy the pleasure of some lamb. Claude had just been paid the last part of his consultancy fee by Blue Ridge. It had been due months ago.

Louis LeDuc arrived almost 20 minutes late and Claude tried to disguise the fact he had been undertaking the eye-watering exercise of editing a lecture on his phone screen for the last half-hour. He would have to think more seriously about an iPsyche; he could have beamed the whole text straight into his cerebral cortex and manipulated the text in his imagination.

The professor entered head bowed, as though forcing his way through a head wind, although it was calm outside. He emitted a strong vibe that life was lived at a rush.

"Not late at all, I've only just got here," lied Claude. With a hint of unintended complaint he said, "I chose a restaurant as close to the university as I could. But I fear you must eat here all the time?"

"*Pas du tout, mon brave. Tout est bon*," replied Louis, although whether the agreeableness of it all referred to the food or to the location, or maybe the company, was unclear. "I very rarely eat lunch out. But I have a reasonably quiet afternoon today and I wanted to discuss how we might divide up next year."

"Then, we shall order first and afterwards talk? '" said Claude.

"Sure. But I want to hear all about life amongst the Yankees too," replied LeDuc. "And how you are getting on with your Southern gentleman, the great industrialist, Thornton Lamaire? Sources tell me you are going out with his daughter? How is he taking to that?"

"So many questions! Well, all in good time, Louis," said Claude, irked by LeDuc's intrusiveness into his personal life.

The waitress, obviously a student from one of the local universities, although Claude didn't recognize her, so probably not from Science Po, came over and hovered while they chose. She talked them through the specials of the day; the surprise of the lamb (*they really should try it, who knew when it might next be available?*), a '*wild*' farmed fish, one of the new, genetically engineered, pelagic varieties that swam the oceans and returned to the nets they had been programmed to seek out once they had reached a specific size, a chicken something, and some new vegetarian dish, '*pas cher du tout'* the waitress reassured them. Just as well a vegetarian diet was sold to the people as so healthy, that was all most of them could afford these days anyway. They ordered, avoided the wine and made do with a jug of *l'eau du robinet.*

Once ordering was out of the way, Louis repeated his enquiry. "So tell me all. I know you've been back for a bit. But how was the great land across the water? Are they doing any better than us?" he asked.

"It's never a penance to be in New York!" said Claude, with a certain nostalgia in his voice. "I've always enjoyed it there. I used to go often as a child, you know. My parents regarded Paris as a backwater; but New York.....that was where the future would be made. I was only in the city a few days this time, otherwise I was up at Lamaire's campus in the Berkshires – but yes, I do find things a bit different to when I last spent a significant amount of time there. The streets now.... you see vendors on the streets selling tiny amounts of things, small piles of vegetables, tomatoes or potatoes. Some have odd assortments, old bits of hardware, kitchen equipment or ancient bicycle parts. It reminded me of an old photo from a childhood book I had – but that was of New Delhi or Calcutta. It seems one half of the people in the US are unemployed, much worse in the South than the North of course, although ..... if you listen to the government, they're not really unemployed. The government regards them as self-employed, so they're working. You look sceptical? But you know how it's come to this? After unemployment rose into the tens of millions, even worse than here....the welfare bill went out of sight. The Federal government had a choice - raise taxes or cut back welfare payments, never generous in the first place. Well, you can guess the answer to that one – in the land of *trickle-up* economics. Welfare is now so restricted as to be practically worthless. Those people you see on the streets, that's how they survive. They sell – whatever they can. *Tu vois,* there's no unemployment in the US anymore. Everyone has a job – even if it's as a micro-retailer of 5 tomatoes."

"Things have always been tougher in the States," Louis said, an obvious truth that any Frenchman could agree on and that would need no further elaboration. The economic situation was bad enough in Europe, worse in England. He had no trouble believing that it was painful in the States. "But there are also those who have a great deal of money still, some of them, like your Louisiana billionaire, Monsieur Lamaire," he continued.

"I'm not entirely sure about that," replied Claude, breaking off a piece of baguette and remembering that it had taken him almost six months to be paid the last instalment of his fee. Even the really rich, a class that Claude had always found congenial, were not as rich as they once were. "My Louisiana billionaire, as you call him, is feeling the pressure a little. He has a large team working on this AI project, a campus to fund in up-state New York, devoted to research. It can't be cheap. And no pay-back so far. At the same time, his traditional industrial and robotics business is under pressure. Their memory therapy research looks as though it might be fruitful – if they can get it to market before the others."

Leduc nodded slowly. He was interested in, but also not a little jealous, of Claude's international life-style and of the research with which he was now involved. So much more interesting than teaching the flower of France's youth – who were going to leave Sciences Po, go on to one of the *Grandes Ecoles (despite all the efforts of that old president, Emmanuel Macron, to close them)* and take up their predestined positions at the head of industry, government and finance. These students would one day be at the summit of it all! These little princes, *mon dieu, comment ils sont gâtés!* It was Ok for Claude of course, the University authorities loved their top professors taking these important roles in the outside world, gaining it a global reputation. It brought the university prestige and recognition. And who had more recognition than CDB? He had become a star with his looks, his ability to turn any complex problem into something facile and pretend that he understood every aspect of the modern world. *Bah, good luck to him*!

"So how's all that going – your contribution to this great dream, this quest, the invention of artificial consciousness?" asked

Louis, with a sour tone in his voice that he couldn't quite suppress successfully. "Where have your friends got to now? Are you near *singularity?*" he asked.

Claude poured them both a glass of water before answering. "I don't know if you remember," he said, "I think we discussed it once.......but the first hurdle has been to create a human-like memory. Memory is really key to it all – to consciousness. And now we...." He decided to sound more modest and corrected himself, "... I think *they*......have almost succeeded. There's this guy – Xian Han, he's a second generation Chinese-American, his parents left China after some disturbances in the last century. Tiananmen Square? Perhaps you were taught about the events there? Amazing fellow. He's managed to make extraordinary breakthroughs – how we can interpret what the chemical and electrical signals in the brain *mean,* and how we can delete or build on the codes that register memory. The technology works on rats and monkeys – that they've proved. And looks like it works on humans too. They've tried with a few members of the team, unofficially, but now they're undertaking fully randomized trials. If that works out Ok, then they will install similar memory circuits in this MARIONn, as they call their conscious machine. Then, they'll educate the computer in the same way we might educate a child, from the bottom up. But a lot faster"

"Educate? A sort of mixture of initial programming and reinforced learning as your robot gains experience in the world?" asked LeDuc, his interest now overcoming his envy of Claude's lifestyle.

"More than that. What you mention has been part of AI practice for years. There'll be a program that will enable it, or should I say *she*, to form initial memories in the same way as a human does. And synaptic structures will be installed to help her generate language that not only we can understand, but more importantly MARIONn *understands*. In her conscious brain." explained Claude. "But after that MARIONn will learn all by herself and form her own memories, her own algorithms and rules to deal with the world. Otherwise we don't think she will have self-awareness like ourselves. "

"And once you power it up, power *her* up, how long before you achieve consciousness? This *singularity*. You're talking years?"

"No, not at all. We think we already have achieved singularity – at least a very simple consciousness, like a child's. Maybe 2 or 2.5 on the Dennett index."

"Forgive me. Don't go too fast. The Dennett index?"

"It's a rough guide to levels of consciousness, generally accepted by AI workers. It's a logarithmic scale. A clever adult dog might be 0.5, a two year old human, maybe 2 - the Dalai Lama may be 7 or 8. But once MARIONn is up and running she'll progress to full adult consciousness – say level 5 – within about six months. We expect super-intelligence shortly after that. Level 11, as one might say!"

"Super-intelligence in less than a year? How so fast, if she's basically just a silicon replica of ourselves?"

"Ah, but MARIONn's a bit more than that. Why should we bother just to copy ourselves, identically? What would be the point of that? No, MARIONn – if she fulfils our dream – will be far more intelligent and creative than us. She's going to be so clever that she will develop her own software as she goes on. She starts with the best processing ability we can provide but after that she's not just learning *facts*, she's creating within herself new ways to consolidate information and fit that into the world view she will develop It's as though we could rewire our brains to make ourselves more intelligent, on a regular basis, year after year. Nor will MARIONn be constrained by the brain she's born with, unlike us. She will be able to call for extra hardware, greater capacity, if she needs it. It's as though she can add additional brains to herself, in a network, to give her extra processing power. There'll be no restraints on her learning ability!"

"But how will you know if she has achieved real consciousness, that she's self-aware in the way we are?" persisted Louis. "That's always the problem with these things, isn't it?

You've got the Turing test but that's not very definitive. You could keep on asking questions *ad infinitum* without ever being quite sure that the silicon brain you're talking to is conscious. It might be just a very clever, *unconscious*, machine."

"We're still discussing that issue," agreed Claude. "That's why being able to decipher memory; to see what's going on *in* her mind, what all those charged synapses actually *mean*, is so important. We need to determine whether MARIONn is r*eflective* about her behaviour, *self-aware*. That will be interesting – if fact more than interesting, it will be the very definition of our success with MARIONn. The evidence of consciousness. That we have achieved *synchronicity*."

" Why MARIONn? I'm amused to hear you call this thing of silicon, *she*"

"*Meta Aware Intelligent Open Neural network*, MARIONn for short."

"All this obsession with the Mother of God!"

"Well, Thornton Lamaire is a Catholic. Quite devout in his way. I think he wanted his great creation be a homage to the Virgin."

"Did you know that the first robot that appeared in a movie was called MARY? I hope your MARIONn likes her name and doesn't get any too grand ideas once she's conscious," said Louis, sceptically.

"At least we can pull the plug on her if we don't like what she's doing!" joked Claude

"Provided she'll let you…"

"You've been seeing too many sci-fi films."

"Maybe. So what's the next stage?"

"They've asked me to design some moral guidelines for her. So we never have to pull that plug……"

"*You* are going to give her moral instruction?" There was an ironic tone to Louis' voice.

"Oh, come, Louis. I'm not that bad!"

"No, I know," said Louis, with a tone that slightly lacked conviction. "And, there's a difference between being aware of the rules and following them."

Claude caught the innuendo, "Is that fair?" he asked

Louis backed away. "No, no. I apologize, I was joking. But I was pointing out something they always seem to miss in the sci-fi films. It's never enough for the machine just to know what is the difference between right and wrong, it's also got to decide to *act* accordingly. If your machine is conscious, like a human, then she must have freedom too. No? And if she has freedom, she might act in ways that we would prefer she did not. After all, plenty of us know moral principles but don't necessarily follow them."

"Unless, we make those principles like religious edicts," said Claude. "So MARIONn cannot disobey her moral instincts without suffering mental pain. We hope that will dissuade her from this bad behaviour that you fear."

"So, your machine can suffer guilt? In that case you really will have created a machine that responds like a human!" exclaimed Louis, amused. "You will have created the first artificial Catholic!"

"We'll see, we'll see," said Claude, suddenly wondering how far he could go before transgressing his confidentiality agreement with Blue Ridge. The conversation also made him aware just how much work there was ahead, how many decisions on MARIONn's mental apparatus still had to be taken. But right now, he wanted to change the subject and talk a bit about the *fac* and its students. He was beginning to feel out of touch. One of the bulletins that morning from the school's authorities had puzzled him. "Louis, what's your view of this strike I'm reading about? What's that all about?"

Chapter 20

The student strike

Student strikes in French universities are as old and as frequent as the rising of the sun, and Claude imagined this one would, like most of them, be in protest against some infringement, imagined or otherwise, of their liberties. The students professed their concern about the world they were about to enter, but what did they contribute? A strike? A laying down of their tools? What a joke, he thought. When they weren't marching on the streets most of them did little enough, stretching their student years to avoid battling with a non-existent job market. "How can the unemployed withdraw their labour? Will anyone notice?" he had once asked.

"It's not about politics this time," said Louis.

"Really? What then?"

"It's about the new rule banning iPsyches on the premises. The university feels they just make cheating too easy, too hidden,“ said Louis

"Well, they're right aren't they? I mean – there's no easy way to check if the students are downloading material or indeed having entire essays dictated to them during an exam. These things are going to be a menace. But can't the University do something about them? Can't they jam them, or something?"

"Apparently not. I'm not sure why. I don't understand the technology of it all. So, instead, the university is planning random checks, physical checks. That's going to be a little intrusive, requiring students to roll down their collars every time they enter an exam room. The situation will be even worse once the new model is introduced – the one that's worn under the skin."

"But most of these students just wear T-shirts don't they? No way to hide an iPsyche there."

"You will see there's been a move in fashion recently to proper shirts, with a collar, and long hair. Could just be a coincidence ....." said Louis, without much conviction in his voice. "But there's not that much force in the strike, I think. The students realise that something has to be done. And the authorities will just make the penalties for wearing an iPsyche so harsh that no one will risk being caught. Think of the reputational risk for these future masters of France. Why wreck your chance of being the next president by cheating when you were 21? And most of them are too busy feeding into their '*LifeStory*' narrative anyway. That's a much bigger threat to their education."

"Are you doing it? *Lifestory*, I mean," Claude asked

"Too late for me," replied LeDuc. "But for these ambitious young people, having their life narrative modelled to reflect them at their best is a powerful drug. *Control and approval* - what else do people want from life? Your girlfriend Stephanie probably uses it already. You should check how you are portrayed. You know there are different settings, that allow you to vary how you and your friends can appear?" explained LeDuc.

"I'm not a subscriber. I've never bothered to discover how it all works," said Claude.

"It's very clever," said LeDuc. "There's a lot of choice available about the degree of gloss you can put on your life. The tone can be realistic, ironic (*it's all a disaster*), paranoid (*everyone is out to get me*), victim (*it's all somebody else's fault*) favourable *(life's glass is half full*), passionate (*life is wonderful*), or heroic (*I'm wonderful).* I'm joking – a bit - I'm making them up, the different settings. I'm not completely sure what they are."

"Well, I don't think I need to bother myself how Stephanie might be presenting her life, or me. She's is not participating on *LifeStory*, I'm sure*"* said Claude. "I've never seen the app on her phone – or heard her dictating the day's events."

With a mischievous grin, Louis said, "If she wore an iPsyche you'd never notice. Her life would be downloaded in real time and you would never know. Have you checked beneath her hair line?"

Claude felt a moment of disquiet with this suggestion of physical checks on his girlfriend – from a man he didn't much like anyway. Who was this *Iago* in front of him, sowing suspicion? But then….. when had he felt Stephanie's neck last? Had she seemed lately to favour lying on her back when she slept. – or was that just his paranoia? And didn't she twist her head less than hitherto, so that she was always facing him when she spoke? He checked himself. This was absurd, he trusted Stephanie and had no wish to have that faith disturbed. Anyway, he was sure that if she did subscribe to *LifeStory* she would have invited him to have access to her account.

The conversation had taken a turn that Claude did not entirely like. He made an excuse to Leduc about the pressure of work and tapped his phone to bring up the bill. He checked it quickly, reminded Louis that this had been his invitation, and that he therefore wished to pay. He tapped again for the payment to go through.

The two colleagues walked back down the road to the faculty, discussing safer, less contentious, subjects. Claude realized that they had entirely failed to discuss the sharing of the lecture programme at the start of the following year. Well, there was plenty of time for that. Then they took their leave of each other and went their respective ways.

Claude walked to his office a little more thoughtful than when he had set out before lunch. Was Stephanie downloading their life together onto *LifeStory?* Did it matter if she did? It did, in a way. He wouldn't feel comfortable with their daily life being available to others, outside of their coupledom, even if the romance was being written up in the most sympathetic way (and which setting would Stephanie have chosen, he wondered?)

As he walked on, Claude recalled that she was not the only one who might have something to disclose. He had failed so far to tell Stephanie that he had been asked to return to the MARIONn campus very soon. Xian Han's team had been making faster progress than expected and Claude's next contribution was now required. He hoped he would not be there for too long; he didn't want to spend months living on campus, nor did he want the stress of frequent flights back to Paris in order to see Stephanie and his father.

He knew that Stephanie would not be pleased by his absence. Nor could he give her any guarantees about what the future of his engagement with MARIONn might be after that. His involvement should wind down, once the mental architecture was in place and the parameters of MARIONn's moral education agreed. But Claude's work was central to the '*personality*' of MARIONn and it might be less easy for him to withdraw later than he hoped - though he didn't really hope too much that he might have to withdraw anyway. He would probably never work again on anything so interesting. Stephanie said she understood that – but to understand and at the same to tolerate being sometimes second to a new form of life, to MARIONn, to be so often on her own, to be never sure if they would have enough time together to deepen their relationship was, Claude realized, a tough call and not one that she welcomed.

Claude wondered too about Stephanie's anxieties surrounding the 'Irene' photos. He couldn't consciously recall having tried to suppress the topic but for whatever reason it had been avoided recently. And so the subject lurked like a landmine between them. It might not be an easy evening, however well they were now getting on. He contemplated where to take her; it needed to be somewhere quiet and calm, but that Stephanie had liked in the past. Ah yes, he remembered – there was a Moroccan restaurant that she liked. It was usually half full, not too noisy then. That would be ideal.

But Claude quite forgot to book a table. When he returned to his study he found, amongst his inbox, emails from Heather Masters and from Xian Han. He cast his eyes down both but it was the one from Heather that disturbed him most.

From: Heather Masters

To: Claude Blondel

Re: Bugs

Hi Claude,

It's been a few weeks since we last spoke so I thought I would bring you up to speed with developments here.

On the whole progress has been consistent. At last (almost six months late on Thornton's timetable – but that was never going to happen) I am in a position to start exploring the relaunch of the IPO. I have set up a number of interviews next week with investment banks – for some preliminary feedback on investor appetite. I'm also hoping that one or two of them might leak information on where *Cybersoul* and *ElectricMemory* are with their own timings. My understanding is that they are some way behind us, but I'd like to cross-check my sources.

Thornton's constantly on my back, particularly over the delay to the IPO, telling me that these two competitors are just about to come to market. Not what I hear - but then Thornton is increasingly nervous about everything these days. Ever since Carroll Gillespie won the plebiscite he's convinced that his Southern operations are going to be closed down. In fact, nothing much has happened so far. *Douglas v Milton Robotics* isn't enforced of course but there's no new legislation either…yet. There is talk about the latest generation of AI will be banned in the South but, frankly, who knows?

As for MARIONn… well, her development continues apace too and things are, for once, ahead of schedule. We are now ready for the installation of the ethical edicts (that's you!) and we have also been running various mental tests to understand what we've created. During one of the tests something curious happened that is puzzling us all. I've asked Han whether he has any explanation for it – but he seems as equally bemused as I am. It wasn't dangerous or anything (I don't think). There are always unexpected incidents that happens when you're not quite sure how all the software is going to run together, even if separate pieces of it have been tested almost to destruction.

We had 5 programmers in the lab that day – running pre-set routines. They're all in house - connected to MARIONn, but not to each other. Each is working on something different. The exercise is a slog but there's nothing very experimental or *'at the limit'* about what they are doing. As you know, It's a fairly dull, routine, exercise to determine whether programme interaction produces some conflicts.

Well, nothing happens during the first few days. Then on the fourth day only two of the five programmers show up for work in the morning – and they look pretty hung-over. So have they been having a party? It seemed not, when we asked them but they sure looked washed out – like they'd slept real badly.

Anyway, I wasn't having any of this. These guys are paid good rates to come and work – and we have a schedule to keep. So I call those missing at their homes. One of them refuses to come to the phone; with another I get his mother. She starts screaming at me and saying I've ruined her son and I'm running some sort of experiment with the devil up here! When she quietens down, she tells me that something has so psyched out her son that not only could he not sleep but he woke up sobbing this morning. There's no visible signs of illness but he's evidently so traumatized that she has called his therapist.

Now, as it happens these guys are required to give us their medical details when they sign on, including the details of any medical practitioner that is treating them. So I have his therapist's number and I call her. There's the usual guff about patient confidentiality but eventually I gather from the therapist that this programmer has suffered some nightmare that is so bad it's triggered a psychotic episode. I can't precisely learn what the nightmare is about, except that it's related to some childhood incident – a deeply repressed memory has been forced to the surface, but the memory has been modified in some way – that has made it much more traumatic.

I ask the others about their experience and why they couldn't sleep. And their stories are pretty similar, even though the dream, or nightmare, they were forced to watch has been not so bad. But then perhaps their childhoods weren't either!

All this has happened on the same night and they all share the same *type* of experience on that night – even if the degree of trauma it produces varies from individual to individual. And all were working on MARIONn the day before.

I've discussed it with Xian and the only explanation we can come up with is this: MARIONn has managed to infiltrate all their minds, capture a memory, re-write it in some way and re-enter it. The memory then exploded out of their subconscious when they slept. We had no idea she could do this sort of thing – and I hope when we have the ethical prohibitions entered into her prefrontal cortex, or whatever her electronic equivalent is, she will think better of this sort of behaviour and not indulge in such immature games – whose potential hurt to human beings I am sure she does not yet understand.

But her ability (already!) to manipulate memory is, let us say…..interesting. Another reason to make sure she does not leave the walls of the campus until we are entirely clear we understand her and how to control her! One particular thing struck about this incident: MARIONn didn't try her abilities on just one of the programmers. She entered all of them at the same time, but managed each of their minds independently - as though she had like……. tentacles that could act on their own while being broadly directed overall by her mind.

I'll have more information on all this when you're over. Xian has promised to analyse MARIONn's synaptic records of the last 24 hours to see if we can get a better understanding of the episode.

Well, Claude, that's enough from me for the moment. Xian tells me that you are due back here in a month or so – when it will be time for the moral instruction and the taboo programming on MARIONn. Definitely needed, it seems! Can't be too soon the pace things are going.

Look forward to seeing you then. Hope all well in Paris and your students are behaving themselves

Best, Heather

Chapter 21

La manif'

The day the students had chosen for their manifestation turned out to be a beautiful one. A few puffy white clouds hung in the otherwise blue sky; their billows mutating in the gentle air currents, changing shape so slowly that if you were to concentrate on their curves you could not tell the point at which they assumed a different form. The clouds seemed to indulge their own somnolence, bereft of even the energy to drift. Through Claude's open windows came only the hint of a zephyr but also now the low, early murmur of the *manif'*. The students were still a few streets away but soon they would stream past and pervade all this part of the Left Bank.

The centre of the demonstration had begun around the Boulevard St Michel and St Germain, as was the tradition of these things. Claude presumed the proximity of the Assemblée Nationale, and the local presence of politicians, was part of the geographic draw but no doubt the number and quality of the cafes and bars locally was also an attraction. Now, those from the Sorbonne, further east, had moved west to join their fellows from the Ecole des Beaux Arts and Sciences Po. Together, the combined mass would sweep down towards the river. He was glad that he had got back from lunch before the Rue de l'Université became impassable.

With such a fine day for a protest Claude, for a brief moment, envied the students the fun of it all. But this was not a cause that would bring down the government. The public would consider the banning of iPsyches entirely reasonable. There had been an effort by the students to spice up the protest, hoping thereby the government might pay their grievance more attention, by adding an issue that was causing more and more tension amongst the young – the large pool of either unemployed or only occasionally working, self-employed, graduates. Many of those who had graduated found themselves, each morning, waiting to hear whether they might be offered some sort of employment, some chance of earnings that week or for the next day . Even when they were so lucky, they were expected to possess not only an education but also the means of production, a useful asset – a 3D printer, a robot or whatever someone with the demand for a good or a service might require for its fulfilment. If they did not have the capital for that, as most did not, they had to rent, which diminished their earnings even more. But the immediate issue – the ban on the wearing of iPsyches on university premises – was what really irritated and motivated the students this afternoon.

They had portrayed the whole dispute as one of civil liberties – absurd in Claude's view. How could the universities possibly permit something that would completely undermine the educative process? iPsyches made the transmission of information straight to the mind something that was impossible to identify or police. The universities were agreed on the prohibition. All they had to do was stand firm. Otherwise there would soon be no education at all. Or none that he would recognize.

This train of thought reminded Claude of Leduc's question – asked innocently enough – as to whether Stephanie had bought herself, and was now wearing, an iPsyche? He recognized a fleeting wisp of insecurity pass by. It was not just education that was affected by these devices; so also were relationships. With no need to speak or type, partners could lead entire other lives, of which the cuckold would be quite ignorant. Claude didn't believe that Stephanie was unfaithful but he knew there were issues in her life that so far were hidden from him.

His concern was not so much that she might subscribe to *LifeStory*, that their entire life would be laid out for friends and followers. Of course, if he asked he was sure that she would invite him to be a permitted reader of her life. All that seemed innocent enough. He was probably worrying himself unnecessarily. Claude had usually been secure and self-assured with the women he had dated and he was puzzled to find himself undermined in this way. In all probability Stephanie did not subscribe to *Lifestory* and did not wear an iPsyche; but he did want to find out. He thought he hadn't seen her use her conventional phone so much recently. He could just ask her outright, of course, but she might wonder why he was so concerned. There was a much easier, less risky, method. When he got home tonight, and as they sank into bed, he would simply slip his fingers under her hair, touch the back of her neck.

Dismissing these unworthy thoughts, Claude decided to wrap up the day early, work at home and provide his father with some company, other than the ever-present Fabienne. He collapsed his emails back into the holographic projector on his desk, while instructing the device to send one of the mails to the printer. He would read this one again, on his way home, over a beer. Xian Han was raising some the questions that required more thought than he could give them right now.

Claude went over to close the shutters. The noise of the students was now pronounced and he peered over the window ledge to gain a better view. This part of the march pretty well occupied the whole width of Rue de l'Université, no traffic was going to get down it that afternoon. The procession looked much like any other *manif'*, arms raised, fists clenched, banners, lots of shouting, everybody having a thoroughly good time. He turned his head to the left and looked at the faces, that despite the chants of hostility addressed to the university authorities, did not appear to be very discontented.

But there was something different this time; something that at first Claude could not identify. Then it struck him; of course – none of these students had long hair. Even the girls were sporting a '*gamine*' cut. Yet long hair had been a fashion recently, to cover the necks of those wearing iPsyches. So what was going on here? This must be some sort of statement, for none of the male students were sporting anything other than shaved crew-cuts. He turned his head to the right to study those demonstrators retreating up the street - and he understood. On the backs of every neck a small silver rectangle, no more than about 3 by 1 cm, could be seen. So, this was the students answer to the ban – everybody, in solidarity, would wear an iPsyche, and *flaunt it*. They would show that this was not about the wishes of a few recalcitrant fellows, who could be picked off and isolated by the authorities. They would all be in this together, supporting each other.

Claude stared at the retreating crowd for a few minutes. It was a strange sight, these shaven necks with their silver mark, each glinting in the afternoon sun. The students looked like convicts, with universal short hair and each of them branded. He shuddered slightly; the sight of mass conformity he had always considered disturbing. These people were meant to be the vanguard of tomorrows citizens. More tomorrow's storm troopers - technology's dupes – he thought. He turned from the window, depressed and wondered how they had come by all those iPsyches. Only 20% had confessed to wearing one at the lecture this morning. The devices were not cheap and many of the young would have been unable to afford them. Claude wondered whether Apple had supplied a whole lot free for publicity purposes and whether they would require them back the following day. He would be interested to see how many students turned up tomorrow with their little silver rectangles still attached.

He walked down the stairs and out onto the street, knowing that his only hope of escape from the massed throng of demonstrators was to move with the grain of their procession. There was not too far to go before he could lose them; turn left at Rue Bonaparte, head down to the Seine and then over the Pont Royal.

But his flight was not so easy. Claude was quickly recognized. Such were the perils of celebrity, he thought. A student crept up behind him and with a lightning and intangible gesture, as though he were a practiced pick-pocket, flicked up Claude's long hair and announced to the crowd that "No!", the famous CDB was not wearing an iPsyche, something of course that the student had guessed but the public demonstration of the fact had seemed worth the effort. A jeer went up; CDB was not one of them! But it was a good natured jeer and he did not feel threatened. A few students held up their hands and made scissor movements with their fingers, the sign of cropped hair and their symbol of solidarity. Claude grinned good naturedly at his *outing* and, to enter into the spirit of the occasion, shook his head from side to side, making his own long locks flow out, flaunting his iPsyche free status and demonstrating his disagreement with the cause of the students. They let him pass and he managed to reach his turn; luckily Rue Bonaparte was comparatively empty.

Down by the river, Quai Voltaire held only a few protestors, already on their way home, and the electronic divert signal to the robotic cars had obviously been lifted, traffic was flowing freely here. Claude crossed over the bridge to enjoy the sight of the river, that glistened in the reflection of light from the declining sun. The stream flowed languidly, its surface so glowing that it appeared to be a flow of lava from some volcano that spewed only gold. He felt cheerful, the energy and good will of the students having forced its way into his soul. He felt a heightened sensitivity as he looked around, feeling more alert than usual. His gaze fell on a pretty girl on a bicycle, a personal delivery robot wheeling behind her like an obedient dog.

Claude walked a little further then caught the metro up to Abbesses. He was glad he was fit, the lift at the station was out of action again and he had to climb up the winding staircase to the street. He was a little out of breath at the top and decided that the time for his promised beer had arrived. His father would not miss him for another 20 minutes. He stopped at the Tropicana café, decorated to give the clientele an illusion of some Caribbean atmosphere while they sipped their *demi* or vin blanc. Its gaudy colours might not have been everybody's taste and Claude was pretty sure they were not his – but he liked the patron.

He ordered his *demi-pression* at the bar and took it outside to enjoy the street life and the warmth of the late afternoon. There was a free table and he pulled up a chair, sat down and placed his phone at the edge. He selected the app that projected the evening news onto the table top, in whatever contrasting shade allowed the print to be best read. An article on the afternoon's demonstration caught his eye. Like himself, the reporter had been interested in the shaven necks of the students – a new phenomenon, not seen previously on the streets of Paris. If all revolutions are accompanied by a hair style, this must have been the first where the absence of hair was chosen as the symbol of protest. But it seemed there had been some riffs on this style, that Claude had missed. The reporter had found another bunch of students with long hair, who did not wish to follow the fashion of their comrades. Why not? Who were they and what was their complaint?

To the reporter's enquiry the response had been straightforward. These students had simply lifted their tousled locks, that drooped over their collars, and turned their necks for inspection. At first, the reporter had seen nothing unusual, there was no sign of an iPsyche. So he thought he understood; with nothing to display, why make a fetish out of a shaved neck? Was that what was happening here? The students gave him no help, expecting him to work out himself what was the significance of keeping their long hair. Then the reporter noticed. Just below the raised hair there was an horizontal scar, about 3cm wide. This iPysche was hidden under the skin. If the university authorities would not allow students these devices then they would, so to speak, go underground, or at least under the epidermis. And if the device could not be seen there was no point in flaunting their indifference to the ban. They might as well keep their fashionable long hair – as they had.

A surreal image, that he had seen in an old movie, passed in front of Claude's eyes, of all these students linked up to wires coming out of the back of their heads, as they recharged at night. As though they were robots linked to some central processor. But the image was an illusion, all iPsyches charged off the body's own heat so no external source was required. He had read about this latest, sub-cutaneous, iteration of the iPsyche but had no idea that it was yet available. This too must have been made available by Apple as a marketing exercise. Much more difficult to catch the wearers now. There would be no evidence that the user was wearing an iPsyche. With the new healing compounds, even the scar where it had been inserted would be invisible. And once these devices were installed within the body it was unlikely that the user would switch to some other brand. It would be buy it, fit it and forget.

Claude turned off the news and took a sip of his beer. What a development! Without even the need to remove an iPysche for a bath, or to go to bed, soon half humanity would be receiving, and sending, data direct to and from their brains 24 hours a day. Even when they were sleeping the device could download information. He knew that the iPsyche could be turned off, but why should it be? At night the young could be connected, broadcasting their dreams in the way they now shared photos of their vacations. What a horror that must be, he thought! Were manufacturers, for others would soon follow Apple, too sanguine about the hazards? What happened if a user had a nightmare? Were there dangers of having so powerful a device so close to the brain? Or was he worrying unnecessarily? After all, iPsyches were just providing an alternative route to the brain that had previously been left to the traditional receptors of information, the eyes, the ears, the nose, the skin. Did it really make any difference if the inputs were direct to the brain from an iPsyche, rather than via those God-given sensors? Apple had reassured users that all the information went to the conscious part of the brain, where the user could select to download or delete the input. They claimed little had really changed from the operation of the traditional cell phone. Maybe. And yet, who really knew if some downloaded signals might not transgress into the subconscious, where the user was not aware of whatever influences he was being submitted to?

Claude tapped his phone to pay, gathered up his back-pack and made to walk the last few yards to his apartment. It was later than he had intended for, apart from reading the news report, he had spent some time considering his response to Xian Han's email about MARIONn's development. Her education seemed to be proceeding well but to questions put by the team, MARIONn sometimes stumbled over her answers. Was that just evidence that she was thinking like any partially educated human-being, occasionally confused and struggling for the proper response while her mental apparatus was still insufficiently sophisticated to guide her fully? Were MARIONn's early responses really evidence of self-awareness, or was it more the case that she merely possessed an excellent ability to *mimic* consciousness? He hoped her responses came from her own inductive reasoning, rather than any clever programming from her creators. But if they really had succeeded, and MARIONn was sufficiently like a human in mental structure, would there also be flaws in her character; just as any human-being might suffer from? That playing around with the programmers while they slept, that Heather had written to him about, was hopefully not a warning of over problems. Claude longed to talk to MARIONn by himself.

That would all have to wait until he saw MARIONn again. Meanwhile, his father would be anxious and he would need to be extra attentive with him this evening; just *being around* in the apartment would not be sufficient to quell the agitation that would have beset him by now. Claude promised himself that he would sit down together with his father and they would discuss the old days, *many times*, before he had to get ready to meet Stephanie.

Chapter 22

A touch of mistrust

When Claude reached the apartment, there was no sign of Fabienne, just a note on the table indicating that she had gone out for some shopping, *faire les courses*. She had made the error of putting the time that she left on the top of her note. It was 3pm, his father had now been alone for three hours and was evidently distressed. Fabienne had sat him in front of the television and he had long got bored with the pictures. Vincent was spiralling through the programming, saying, *'next, next'* to the set. Claude had a tougher than normal time calming and reassuring him. Really, this would never do. It was not just an issue about Fabienne. None of the carers had been that reliable, even if Fabienne had been the least unsatisfactory.

When Fabienne was not present, Claude knew that he couldn't rely on his father to find his phone and call him. Perhaps the new *iPsyche*, permanently inserted under the skin, as with the students, might be one answer; at least he couldn't lose it then. And it would pick up on his distress, he wouldn't have to call out. Claude's mind turned back to previous thoughts, if Xian Han's trials proved successful then maybe Vincent's damaged memory could be rebuilt and he could live a reasonably independent life once more. He reminded himself, again, to email Heather and see if there was some way if his father could be included in the European trials

On the other side of Paris, near the Champ de Mars, Stephanie was preparing herself for her evening out with Claude. She had finished the day at her own apartment as she still kept much of her clothing and other personal possessions there, Claude's being so cramped. This week, while he had been concentrating on putting together a synopsis for his book and finishing the trimester at Science Po, it had been at least three evenings since she had seen Claude. She looked forward to reconnecting. Left too long and the link between the two became frayed; they risked becoming again partial strangers to each other.

That was what she hated about his inevitable trips to MARIONn. Whenever Claude left for the US a resentment developed within her, however hard she worked against it, And she knew that he would have to go back again and again; indeed would keep returning until MARIONn's personality and behaviour could be properly understood by her creators and they were reassured that they were no hazards they had not foreseen and countered. That was hardly an instantaneous process.

Stephanie looked at the photo on the dresser. It was the only one she had and it gave no clue as to how her son must now look. The photo had been taken when he had been what, 5 days old? It could be the photo of any baby, a million babies, but it was hers, her baby, her son, her Noah. In his tiny hands the nurse had placed her gold bangle; the bangle that she had left with him as the only memento she had at the time. She was glad that he would, as he grew, have some evidence that his birth mother had cared enough to leave some trace of herself. She hoped that he had not sold the piece of jewellery. Maybe he had been broke one time, might have taken the bracelet to be valued, and then he would have discovered his mother was someone of wealth, perhaps from an important family; for it was worth a considerable sum. Of course, she would rather he sold it than starved. But how she hoped that his fate had never come to that! That he still possessed the one keepsake that bound the two of them together.

Stephanie turned away from the photo; her eyes glistening, and started to brush her thick dark hair. As the brush swept down the back of her head she felt it catch something. There was a light pulling sensation on the skin of her neck. She put the brush down and reached both hands behind her and gently peeled the iPsyche away. Probably better Claude didn't know about it. She sensed that he disapproved of the device. Besides, when he made love to her tonight and went to kiss her neck she could hardly imagine a less romantic touch than his lips contacting 3 square centimetres of cold silicon. She still had her old phone and now she slipped that into her bag. Tonight that would be quite adequate. It was not as though she was going to get any update on Noah's existence in the cab on the way to the restaurant.

She dialled up a taxi and headed to the Moroccan restaurant in Rue St Honoré Claude had mentioned. It was at best a third full and she spotted Claude sitting in a corner, half hidden by a scalloped arch, reading an old, printed, book, his eves narrowed with the strain of the dim light, a glass of white wine in front of him. She was surprised to see him here ahead of her.

"You are very punctual," said Claude as he stood up to plant a kiss on each cheek.

"It is my only virtue, as you know," said Stephanie, enjoying the ritual of the old joke between them. Claude pulled out a chair. "But I thought you might be late - caught up in the *manifestation*," she said as she sat down.

"I was. But I left the university early this afternoon – and they let me through."

"Even a non-iPsyche wearer like you?"

"Oh, they don't expect someone my age to have one! Yet, anyway"

“In America we have graduate students your age. I’m sure you’ll have an iPsyche soon. You love gadgets. I give you a year,” said Stephanie.

“Well, certainly not one of the new subcutaneous ones. I didn’t see any demonstrators with them - but apparently there was a bunch of students with those too, thoughtfully provided by Apple, I’m sure.”

“How do you know they had been fitted with them? Surely the point of the new iPsyche is that they are hidden?”

“Apparently there was a sort of sub-march with students proudly showed their insertion scars to a reporter - a different sort of defiance to the university authorities than in the main march, where everybody had cut their hair and were flaunting their device. The alternative protest was sort of, ‘*see – you will never know who’s wearing an iPsyche in the future so no point suppressing them’!*” Then Claude decided to risk it. He needn’t wait till the night and the subterfuge of the investigative kiss. He put on a light, jokey tone. “How about you? Which form of iPsyche do you wear?”

Without saying a word, Stephanie put her right hand behind her head, gathered up her hair, twisted it a few times and held it back on the top of her head. She turned away from Claude and presented her neck, like Anne Boleyn to her executioner.

“ *Voila,*’ she said. “Clean neck, huh? Not even a scar.”

Claude laughed, the laughter of relief but also, he hoped, a sign to her that his enquiry had only ever been a playful one. Stephanie knew better. Claude had been concerned – but she was relieved too. That got that issue out of the way. But she knew that her moderately deceitful act had just made the future more difficult, when she finally did reveal that she wore an iPsyche, sometimes. She would have to bring it up, maybe, on an occasion when she would suggest that they should *both* start to wear them. When they became commonplace. When they were so entwined with each other they would want their very thoughts to criss-cross between them. A form of intimacy that past ages had never conceived. But that was a problem for the future.

They ordered; Stephanie a tagine and Claude couscous with a *merguez* sausage, a glass of wine each. Claude talked of his return to the Charles Nodier flat that evening, his father's confusion as Fabienne had not returned and how this had highlighted the increasing problem his father presented. He didn't want the responsibility for him to fall on Stephanie while he was away. The possibility of enrolling his father in the early *LetheTech* trials seemed not just attractive, but pretty well indispensable. Some of the failures *LetheTech* had been suffering had stayed his hand but maybe the time had come to risk it. He would write to Heather tomorrow to see if he could enrol Vincent in the European trials.

Not that Stephanie heard much of Claude's decision to submit his father to the *LethTech* trials. What she had noticed was how he dropped the word '*away*' into the conversation. She stiffened and looked at him, "So, you were about to tell me that you're returning to the US?" she asked, pointedly.

"There's just a short trip – I need to help out with MARIONn's moral instruction - unless there are some additional problems they want me to help sort out."

"There always seems to be additional problems that you need to sort out," said Stephanie. "How long will you be gone?"

"I'm not sure. For as short a time as I can possibly manage." Claude tried to be reassuring. "A month, six weeks?" Stephanie knew, from past experience, Claude was trying to manage her, to offer the least possible estimate for his absence. At least Claude would have to be back for the start of the following term. Stephanie did not know about the lecture sharing arrangement with Louis Leduc.

"I'm sorry," he said. "I know how much you hate this and I know how difficult it is for us to be apart. But you could come to New York with me and come up sometimes to the MARIONn campus too."

" I thought non-operatives were banned from the campus? By my very own father's instruction."

"Perhaps I can negotiate security clearance for you – *because* you are your father's daughter. And……. I'll have weekends. I can take a few extra days so we can disappear off-campus," said Claude.

Stephanie, who knew her father's attitude to security and had tackled him before about her inability to stay at the campus, was less sanguine than Claude about obtaining a pass. "And what exactly am I going to do there, on the campus, during the week, even if they would let me stay? I do have a job and have to earn my living. If you remember," she replied, in a dismissive tone.

Claude reached over the table and took her hand, before she was quick enough to remove it. "Look," he said." I don't like this either – but I am contractually bound to answer Blue Ridge's needs. This is your father! I can't very well ignore him."

"Yeah, yeah," said Stephanie, in a more conciliatory voice and with a smile, not wishing to seem resentful and unwilling to accept the inevitable. "I shouldn't make a fuss, I know. But I was looking forward to going away together this summer – and I don't mean to the Berkshires."

Claude began to massage her wrist with his thumb in what he hoped would be interpreted as a gesture of affection. "I would have liked to spend this summer together too," he said. "But maybe we could at least manage a week before I go? We could drive up to Deauville. You have liked it there in the past; that endless beach. Rather like the Hamptons." He paused. " And I'll be back before you know it."

Stephanie looked at Claude. "Damn Deauville!" she said softly. If we are going away I want to go somewhere hot. Take me at least to the South of France. Doesn't one of your cousins have a house in Antibes? Maybe we could borrow it." At this sign of cooperation Claude knew that he had been forgiven. His sojourn in the US might not help them as a couple but it wasn't going to break then either.

He turned over her hand and transferred his caress to the palm. In so doing Stephanie's shortened index finger, and the two digits either side of it, missing their top joint, caught his eye. Usually

Stephanie held her hand in a way that obscured the damage and Claude had long become accustomed to the sight – and the unusual touch. The temptation arose within him; maybe now, while Stephanie was in a conciliatory mood he could risk asking what he had long wanted to know. He tried to make his voice sound as neutral and casual as possible. He moved his touch to the stubs and stroked them, a couple of times gently.

"What happened here?" he asked. "You never did tell me."

Stephanie withdrew her hand from his grasp but did not hide it. She let it lie, palm up on the table, and gazed at it with seeming curiosity, inspecting the offending fingers as though they didn't really belong to her, as though the hand was some independent object left out by one of the waiters, like a dish of olives perhaps.

"It was nothing," she said. "An accident, a long time ago."

"Quite a big accident!" said Claude. "It must have been horrible, losing three fingers like that."

"Let's not exaggerate. It's just the tips – or at least the first joint. It doesn't affect my life now."

"But as a child it must have done?"

"As a child? Yes, I guess it did. But probably not in the way you think."

There was not the total resistance that Claude had met on other occasions when he had raised the subject of her fingers. He pressed on.

"Did you make a mistake with a knife?"

Stephanie gave a barely audible snort, as if to indicate how far from the truth was Claude's guess.

"With a knife? No, that would have been better perhaps. At least if I'd wielded the knife myself," Stephanie said.

Claude was puzzled by this last remark. If not Stephanie herself, who had caused this mutilation? "It was a car door," she said. "My fingers were trapped in a car door."

"But you must have slammed it very hard to do that much damage. As a child?"

"It wasn't me who slammed the door. But please, I don't want to go into all this now. Could we please just eat and enjoy a nice meal?"

Claude's inquisitiveness put a frost between them that the dinner never quite recovered from. They made the trip back to Montmartre in silence. At one point Stephanie said,

"I'm not the only one with secrets, am I?" Claude knew what she was referring to.

"I have told you what I know" said Claude, painfully aware that this was about zero. "I don't remember anything about 'Irene'."

"Your hiding something. How can you forget someone who has so obviously been in your life?" Stephanie accused. "Unless of course the photo was left by the last tenant in the apartment," she added, sarcastically." But you have been there for ten years now."

Claude looked out of the window, unwilling to meet Stephanie's hostile gaze and equally unable to think of an adequate reply. He could only agree with her logic. The woman in the picture must have had something to do with him. That he could remember nothing about her disturbed him as much as it did her. After a few more moments of silence, Stephanie said,

"What about your friend Hervé? He certainly knew something about her identity."

Stephanie had missed much of that conversation at the wedding reception but she had overhead Hervé offering his condolences about Irene.

"I'm having lunch with Hervé as soon as he gets back. I'm going to press him then to tell me what he meant," said Claude.

"We both know that lunch is months away,' said Stephanie. "Take the 'Irene' photo with you to the campus next time. Ask Harvey Jennings if he knows anything about it." Claude had told her about the confusion over the two Hervés. He agreed to her request. That at last some action was being taken to solve the riddle of the apparently forgotten 'Irene' seemed to mollify Stephanie. Claude felt the tension in the taxi ease a little. Had it eased enough for them to make love tonight? He would soon find out.

When Stephanie climbed into the bed that night she turned a beckoning face towards him. Claude put his arm around her. In spite of the fact that he now lacked an incentive to pursue his investigation, in light of Stephanie's denial, he recognized where his fingers were inadvertently headed. But as they crept over his lover's neck they felt only smooth skin. He was comforted by what he failed to discover. At least he could dispense with *that* worry and sleep soundly. But there were still other mysteries in his girlfriend's past, even if tonight was probably not the best time to pursue them. One day Claude would ask about the fingers, but not now. There was no rush.

Part 3

CARROLL GILLESPIE: MAY 2039

Chapter 23

An unexpected visitor

Thornton flew back from New York, following the MARIONn meeting where Euclid McNamara's role as sole educator had been amended, forcing him to accept a team approach, very early on Monday morning, accompanied only by Clarence. Thornton hadn't needed him during his stay in New York over the weekend but it was easier if Clarence hitched a lift on the PJ, rather than leaving earlier on some commercial airline before him. Besides, when they reached the airstrip at Baton Rouge Clarence was meant to be Thornton's chauffeur – except that these days there was nothing for a chauffeur to do except make sure that the flask of coffee that Thornton required in the car was hot.

Thornton missed the time when a chauffeur actually drove. Clarence still sat in the front and Thornton in the back but Thornton felt the pressure to make some conversation, as his 'driver' was now liberated from any actual chauffeuring. During their flight down Thornton had already discussed most topics of mutual interest, the progress of the *New Orleans Saints,* some domestic staff issues, and what Elizabeth might have been up to on the night she borrowed his car. His iPsyche helpfully suggested some additional subjects to discuss with one's chauffeur but they sounded at once contrived and not interesting enough to pursue. Besides the drive between the airfield to the planation wasn't far. Any silence between them would be short lived. So Thornton chose to concentrate on reading the news rather than any more chat. Not that he really '*read*' the news at all; it was simply piped into his consciousness via the iPsyche at the top of his spine. One minute he would be ignorant of, say, the latest developments in New Chaldea, the next he would understand what was happening there as though he'd known it all his life. There was no sense that there had been a time when he *hadn't* known these facts – although his rational brain told him that indeed this must be so.

The effect played with his sense of time. But in other ways, most ways, he enjoyed his iPsyche. The device had made life so much easier, no longer having to look at a screen, input instructions by type or voice; just *think* and it was done. So quick, so easy, so simple. The iPsyche was such a great step forward; soon everyone would have one. And it had so many features that amused him. Now, as they approached the turning for the plantation, he just *sensed* its mapping function gently telling him to make a right turn. Not of course, that he needed to; the car would do that on its own.

He wondered if there would be trouble at the gates, but so far his policy of engaging with those dispossessed had proven successful. As they turned into the drive he was glad to see that none of those camped were blocking his way, nor did they hasten forward as they had once done, beating on the cars windows, seeking alms or a job. Instead, they hung back but still looked sullen and vacant, at the passing car and its occupants, as they must have wondered why, in such a large vehicle, one person sat in the front and one in the back.

As Thornton and Clarence swung through the gates, they passed the sign that said '*Crooked Timber Plantation*' and underneath it another that read, in smaller letters, '*Home of the*

Louisiana Foundation for retired Afro-American artisans' This had been Bethany's project, that had come to her in one of her short lived liberal, must-share-our-good fortune, periods - which she had fast got bored of. All Thornton could see of retired Afro-American artisans was old Francis who leant out of the window of the converted barn where the artisans had been intended to end their days in relative security. The foundation may not have been much use to impoverished Afro-Americans but it had been an excellent tax shelter for him and Bethany.

The car began to vibrate as it hit the hard earthen track, bordered by the avenue of live oaks leading up to the house. Thornton had always resisted having this track metaled; it would have been out of keeping with the estate's buildings, most of which were ante-bellum, and he wanted everything to reflect, and be in-harmony with, the period in which it was built. Of course the centre-piece of the estate was the Greek revival house that had been kept true to its Palladian roots. As was always the case when he returned from '*abroad*' (as he termed not just foreign countries, but all states above the Mason-Dixon line), the sight of his home was pleasing to Thornton's eye.

But pleasing though it was, this unadorned, classically proportioned house did not *entirely* fulfil Thornton's aesthetic needs. There were other aspects of his personal taste that he wished to see advertised, at least to his acquaintances and friends. He wanted to be judged, as he indeed he was in many ways, a modern man. And for that, modern, *artistic*, side of his personality, he had the '*Blue*' room in his New Orleans town house. Twenty years before, greatly taken by a Picasso painting from his blue period, an absinthe drinker, that he had purchased when Bethany was away visiting Stephanie in her European boarding school, Thornton had resolved that he would make that colour the theme of a collection of contemporary art. So, 'Blue Dog' paintings by the Louisiana painter, George Rodrigue, jostled with 'Nu Couche Bleu' by Nicholas de Steal. Thornton was proud of his collection. It was his defence against accusations by his detractors that he was, beneath all the wealth, merely a redneck who had done well, an uncultured Creole planter who probably knew more about sugar cultivation than the arts of his time. But just as well, he thought, that the 'Blue' room was in his New Orleans home. That sort of modern stuff would not be appreciated out in the country. Besides, the plantation was where Bethany mostly took the reins, apart from that unlikely victory over the dining room decoration. The town house was his retreat.

The following day Thornton needed to descend into New Orleans for a meeting with his lawyer. He liked to travel early in the morning and there was still some of it left when he reached the town house. Bethany would follow along later, once she was up. She liked to come into town too, to see her girlfriends and if there were enough of them around, have a good time, *laizzez les bons temps rouler* with enthusiasm.

Just as Thornton was about to start work he heard a car drawing up outside. He hoped that, whoever it was, they were not expecting to see him. Nobody had been mentioned on the agenda that day; his lawyer was not expected until the afternoon and a brief inquiry to his iPsyche revealed no late additions. He noted the noise but gave it little more attention; during the morning there were always various callers, some delivering for the household, some for Bethany if she was there, and so he started to lay out the day's emails and the documents he had brought back from New York. Although he could read them directly, in his mind's eye, as it were, on his iPsych*e,* he often printed papers in order to read them in a more leisurely, but also more considered, manner. He was too old now to drop this habit he had formed in his youth. Besides if he was sweating, and the house's air conditioning never seemed quite up to the job in the summer, the moisture on his skin interfered with iPsych*e* transmission and its ability to pick up and send data from the brain stem. There had been times when he was out riding that communication became almost impossible. He'd have to consider moving to the subcutaneous version as soon as it became available.

There was a long mail from Xian Han, setting out the timing and protocols of the next stage of the *LetheTech* trials, Phase III. Thornton hadn't quite appreciated that, in addition to the Phase II trials, there had also been a limited number of memory modifications carried out on volunteer members of Han's team. He noted that Claude Blondel had been one. Interesting, he thought. Why had Claude wanted to experiment with memory deletion? Still, not his business. But curious none the less.

During these early trials Xian and his team had tried not to make any permanent amendments to the mind, not try to deal with deeply imprinted issues or traumas – just enter the shallows of memory, remove minor recollections that could later be reinstated; things like childhood holiday memories; things that could be checked against verifiable histories, to make sure that the deciphering of synaptic recording in the brain had been accurately calibrated. So much for that hope! He wondered if the O'Neal disaster might come back to haunt not just *LetheTech* but its parent Blue Ridge too. If there were any suits for damages, Blue Ridge was sure to be named; it was much better capitalized than *LetheTech*. The latter, in the end, could be let go but Blue Ridge, that was *heritage*, the family asset that had been passed to him in trust. He did not want to be found unworthy.

A few moments later Clarence knocked on the door and announced that the State governor, Carroll Gillespie, one-time Bishop (and now very ex-Bishop, after the scandal surrounding his '*laicization*' and his swiftly following marriage to Kirsty) was here to see him. Thornton thought: one of the governor's assistant's would normally book such a meeting days ahead – yet there been no contact recently that he could recall. And they would meet anyway at the service the following Sunday. Unexpected visitors were occasionally fun but this one probably boded no particular good. "Show the governor into the Blue Room would you Clarence?" he asked.

The shutters were closed to restrain the fierceness of the sun from entering this south facing room and damaging the paintings;

the air-conditioning, as usual, seemed ineffective. At least the warmth should ensure the governor should not stay too long. Thornton was irritated by this uninvited and unplanned visit. He had a lot to do. But he knew that the governor was unlikely to turn up just because he was at a loose-end this morning; he would want something – even if it was just information. And Thornton knew well enough, since childhood in fact, to be wary of Gillespie. Sometimes Thornton didn't discover the governor's agenda until much later, long after he had unwittingly passed on some fact or an opinion that seemed unimportant, or innocent - at the time. Yet to Gillespie the information would have been useful bricks in some policy he was building that Thornton had no inkling about. Thornton instructed his iPsyche to silence itself.

Chapter 24

A miracle and a warning

By the time Thornton reached the Blue room, the governor was already seated with a cup of coffee in his hand. He was dressed in his regular steel grey suit, and a narrow black, leather, lace tie. Carroll Gillespie emanated his usual air of implacability; that nothing was going to stand in his way or disturb him.

"I wasn't sure whether I'd catch you, Thornton; I didn't know when you would get back from New York," said the governor. Thornton noted that Carroll was aware of his trip. In spite of the latter's disclaimer, he was sure that the governor knew his comings' and goings' precisely. Gillespie would be informed of the very moment he had landed.

Gillespie gently placed his cup on the side-table next to him. "I have to come into town for a trial that opens later today. As my route took me near you I thought I'd call in and say '*howdy*'. And Kirsty instructed me to ask you and Bethany for brunch after chapel on Sunday too." Thornton knew that Kirsty was one tough first lady but the idea that she might instruct Carroll to do anything amused him. "Besides," Carroll continued. "There are one or two things I wanted to discuss with you. Didn't want to bore the girls with state talk at lunch."

"Of course," said Thornton, still no clearer why the governor was calling. "But I'm sorry that Bethany is not here yet. She would have been delighted to see you this morning. She'll be in town later. She always likes to hear the latest political talk. You know how impassioned she gets."

The governor waved the idea away; just as well Bethany was not here, he only had a little time. God's work had to be done and he didn't want to get into a three-way discussion with Bethany either. But that , as a tactful man – or at least a careful one - was not what he said. "I have to be in court by two," Gillespie explained. "Well, that's not strictly accurate. I don't have to be in court but ….I think I should be."

"I rely on you on to keep me abreast of local matters, Carroll," said Thornton amiably, but with a tone of voice that lacked flattery. It was quite true the governor was much better informed than he was about local matters, particularly as the affairs of *LetheTech* and MARIONn were pretty well all consuming at the moment and distracted him from paying much attention to, as he saw them, parochial issues. "But what's this court case about that requires your personal attention? Must be something pretty important to do that," Thornton said, laced with flattery.

The governor brushed his trousers of some invisible dust, a hesitation, perhaps, in how to tell the story, then turned his gaze to Thornton. "Nobody has done anything much worse than we're used to any day of the week down here," he said. "But …..it is a strange case, a curious situation. We've got an act of arson and attempted murder on our hands; that's not in doubt, but the defendants, there's a band of four of them, are arguing that they acted as they did because they believed the victim was a witch. Now normally, they wouldn't get far saying things like that. A belief in witchcraft is not a recognized defence. But these are not entirely normal times, as you know Thornton. And there's a move in the State house to push through a bill making witchcraft a punishable offense."

"Really? Witchcraft?" said Thornton. "People are believing in witchcraft now? Do you have to follow them? Does this bill have to be supported by you?" Thornton looked quizzically at Carroll, as if to say*, are you serious?*

"I don't believe it all, (*all?* thought Thornton), no certainly not," replied the governor. "Of course it's nonsense this belief, – but the bill before the state house? It's not entirely up to me, Thornton. There's pressure for this, many people want it. I am in office, after all, only to serve the voter's wishes."

"But you can veto it - when the bill, *if the bill,* comes to you for signature?" said Thornton.

The governor twisted uncomfortably in his seat. Of course he could veto the bill but somewhere at the back of his mind he didn't really want to. His position as governor was not entirely secure, there was an election next year and the plebiscite around the corner. Who knew quite how useful superstition might be to him? And maybe there was something in these beliefs too. There were a lot of new ideas up in the North that sounded awful close to witchcraft to him. Ok, they weren't really…but to the simple folk down here they must look very similar. There was a clear will locally to keep out ideas that were seen as ungodly. And who knew, except the Almighty, what exactly were ungodly practices? For example, fiddling around with people's memories – as he'd heard Thornton was up to, if his sources were accurate - well, to many of the good folk in the South that sounded an awful lot like something that was not part of God's plan for man. Was it witchcraft? Who knew? Maybe witchcraft was in the eye of the beholder but the problem was that the beholders were also his electorate. The proposed law could not be dismissed as easily as Thornton believed.

"I'm a God fearing man, Thornton, so are you," said Carroll, as though the latter might be in doubt and require affirmation. "There are some things going on up North now that look an awful lot like the work of the Devil to some good people down here. Who am I to say they are wrong? There are folk who draw a straight line between the things they hear being practiced these days and the state of this world. They sure don't like much of what they see. The inventions of man have not brought them any great happiness recently. Many folk think we've been paying too little heed to the ways of our Lord and that we have brought the consequences on ourselves."

"Things are tough for people I realise but have we regressed so much? Have we come this far? Witchcraft?" Thornton repeated his rhetorical question. "We're not living in medieval times, I hope,"

"Maybe not. I hope not," Gillespie hesitated, looked thoughtful for a second or two, as though a return to medieval times was just around the corner, and then he said, "It's ok for you to talk this way, Thornton ……." He left his words hanging in the air, as though he did not fully wish to mouth the hazards or threats to people, like the Lamaires, that he foresaw building outside their white picket fences. "You know the suffering that's been going on," he continued. "People just don't think it's natural. Folks are saying that there are forces at work, forces they don't like, and that certain men, maybe women too, are behind them."

"So this is that what's happening here … at this trial you're going to observe?" asked Thornton.

The governor stood up and walked over to the window. He gazed out on the garden, as though mentally gathering himself to launch into a lengthy explanation, and then turned back to face Thornton. "There was a woman, a very poor woman, living with her three children. Usual thing, husband had lost his job and left, trying his luck somewhere else. Of course, she never heard from him again. Then one of the children falls ill, I'm not sure with what – starts moaning, having fits and so on. The woman can't afford drugs or a doctor. But one day she's out walking in the hills, says she visiting one of the springs up there. I don't know why – maybe she's hot or something, wants a swim. Anyway after she's swum, she has a vision, the Virgin Mary or some angel, appears and tells her '*bring your son to this spring, bathe him three times, at sunrise, noon and sunset.*' So she does this, does as she's instructed, and a miracle happens. The son overcomes his fever; he's cured. But this woman is not only pious, she's smart. She sees not just a holy site but also a business opportunity. "

"She sets up a shrine at the spring, charges a few dollars for ill folks to bathe in it, three times a day mind you, anything less won't work she says, and she prices per dip. Did I say she was smart? And she sells the pilgrims food, drinks, trinkets and so on. Soon enough, she's become quite a rich woman, at least by the standards around here but, humanity being what it is.... Well, one day, someone brings his son to be cured. Except the spring doesn't work this time. Nothing happens. So, the women says '*let's try it again – you evidently didn't bring enough faith to the lady of the spring'*. So, the guy pays again and tries once more. One time there's a small improvement and she says, '*See, the spring is beginning to work. You need to keep goin'*. There's a bit more bathing in the waters but instead of the boy getting better, he starts to get worse. There's some suspicion now that he's picked up an infection from the waters, they're contaminated – maybe. The father of this child sees red, he's spent all this money and his son is more poorly than he was at the start. He goes back to his folk and tells the story. He really whips them up with indignation. Soon, they're so angry they come along, burn down the shrine and the poor woman's home too. She's lucky to escape with her life – although she was quite badly burnt. That's what lands them in the sheriff's jail."

"At which point they accuse the woman of witchcraft?"

"They do indeed. This bunch of hillbillies say the vision the woman saw was not the Madonna but the Devil and the spring only works for those who worship him. They, being good God fearing folk, only irritated the Devil and that's why their son got worse. In their view, they've done the state a service and should not only be found innocent but that the woman should be found guilty of conversing with the Devil and practicing witchcraft."

"Except there's no statute against witchcraft."

"But maybe there should be – at least that's the suggestion."

"The poor woman must have suffered enough, burnt, lost her home, her income - again. Are the supporters of this bill proposing the traditional punishments for witchcraft, burning people at the stake, pressing? Things like that?"

The governor raised both hands in horror and waved them from side to side, palms facing out, the signal for fending off unwelcome suggestions. "Heavens above, Thornton! Burning at the stake? Nobody is suggesting such a thing. Of course not. A modest fine perhaps, a short prison sentence. Just something to discourage the practice."

"You make it sound as though we've already accepted witchcraft's existence and now it's just a matter of determining the appropriate penalty?"

The governor pushed out his bottom lip and raised his eyebrows, the very expression of someone having to accept something which he didn't entirely agree with, as though to say, '*well, there you are, that's how we live now. What can I do*?' Except there was a falsity about the expression. Thornton knew the governor could, and would, do anything he liked. He was quite capable of facing down transient public opinion if it suited him.

"We live in a democracy Thornton. I have to pay some respect to what the voters want."

"But you don't have to follow all their beliefs, however absurd, their superstitions? You don't have to support them as they regress into the Middle Ages. We've made some progress, I hope, and live in an age of science and rationalism? We understand how things work. We don't have to revert to a belief in the supernatural. I would hope?"

"We understand how things work? Do we indeed?" retorted the governor with some vehemence. "There are a lot of people down here, Thornton, who'd argue with you on that one. For all your rationality and science we've ended up with a split nation and half of the country living in poverty. Now that half, they're mostly down here, or in the mid-west, and they're thinking *'what exactly have we done to deserve this?'* They see all sorts of strange developments around them; machines they are told they have to respect and be nice to, and other weird things .. *memory therapy* did I hear someone say? What exactly is that? Some folk think we are meddling in things that are best left to Him. You talk of superstition, but what is witchcraft but the attempt to explain the world when things go wrong for no good reason? The people are worried, the world they knew before has collapsed and the reasons for that are not clear to them. Witchcraft is just a name they give to what they fear, and for them, there seems much to fear at the moment."

"But even so…."

At that, the governor cast aside the reasonably urbane demeanour that he had hitherto displayed. "But even so, *even so*…., there's no '*even so'* Thornton! There's an anger afoot that will find its outlet in all sorts of unpleasant ways – ways you will not like and maybe I don't like either, but it's coming. You sit up there, in the relaxed, pleasurable security of your plantation, and you understand nothing about the mood outside. Or you're flying up to the North, hobnobbing with your smart, sophisticated friends, doing God knows what in your laboratories. You're walking a dangerous road, my friend! You condemn folks for playing around with forces they don't understand but what are you doing Thornton, huh? From what I hear you're undertaking some pretty strange experiments in your place in the Berkshires; all hidden away an' all, as though you're ashamed of what would be found if it were opened to the light o' day. If it's so straightforward as you sometimes tell me Thornton, why are you not carrying out that work down here? God knows, we could do with the employment."

Thornton bit his tongue and meditated on his risky scientific investigations of dubious morality – and the possible consequences. He would need redemption if the researches were indeed immoral and even if they were not, he would need political cover from the vengeance of his enemies. Not quite enemies perhaps, he thought, but certainly people down here who would line up against him if they discovered what was being developed in the Berkshire woods.

There were a dozen practical reasons why neither MARIONn nor *LetheTech* could be sited in Louisiana but one reason above all stood out, and Carroll Gillespie had just confirmed it. Thornton knew that *down here* their work would come under a scrutiny that was absent in up-state New York; a scrutiny that would judge their ambitions on grounds that neither he, nor the rest of the research team, were used to being obliged to take into consideration. It would indeed be so much easier if the work could be carried out locally; but it just wasn't safe. Things had not yet got so bad that he could not take his aircraft north without it seeming like an act of treason; many of his fellow tycoons still made the same trip after all. The issue was more that one day questions would be asked about the purpose of his trips, what exactly the Blue Ridge Corporation were doing *up there*, what so needed to be hidden *up there*, and the true reason for that might come to light. *But let's delay that reckoning as far as possible,* he thought to himself.

He knew that to some people, most people perhaps in the South, he was financing something sacrilegious, a usurpation of God given powers, a mimicking of the act that had given birth to Adam and Eve. Perhaps the critics were right? But who really knew what God thought? The fathers, people like Gillespie, of course; they thought they knew. But were they correct?

If everything was revealed he would probably get away with a fine, given his status locally - and a court order to shut down or divest himself of the MARIONn project - for a first offence. But you never knew, things were changing rapidly; attitudes were hardening. In six months carrying out the sort of research Blue Ridge was engaged in at the Berkshire campus might carry a prison sentence, *down here*. Of course he could move himself up North, supervise the researches in peace, but he was too old, too set in his ways, too fond of the South and the *Crooked Timber* plantation to live anywhere else now. Nor did he want to give up the MARIONn project either. It was so *interesting* and, he felt, so misunderstood too. Used correctly, the mental tools Xian Han and his team were creating would be of such great benefit to humanity. Sure there was suspicion, but MARIONn and *LetherTech*? They were going to make things better for folks, not worse.

But before Thornton had worked out exactly how he wanted to respond to the governor, the latter filled the pause, "You need to be careful Thornton. There are those down here who suspect that you are conducting experiments that fiddle around (*fiddle around*? *What exactly do they know, or think we are doing, wondered Thornton?*) with people's minds. Some are saying that's not right, maybe you're messing with souls. I'm just saying, I don't necessarily support them… but I would be careful Thornton. Most of Blue Ridge's factories are down in the South. Neither of us would want anything to happen to the Corporation. It employs too many people here, even if that's a lot less than it used to be. But people can get riled, and I'm just governor, Thornton. There's a plebiscite coming as you know and if that fails, or I am not chosen as president-elect if it succeeds, I will have to face re-election as governor the following year. I may not be able to protect you – forever!"

Thornton counted Carrol as a friend since boyhood, but however long their friendship, it would not be strong enough to divert a prosecution, if that was to become his fate. Carroll liked power and he wasn't going to place that in peril on the grounds of long acquaintance. What was that cynical transposition of the biblical edict on friendship that he'd heard somewhere, "*greater love hath no man than to lay down his friends for his life*"? That would be Carroll's epitaph, carved on his headstone.

The governor allowed his words to hang in the air between them, evidently thinking he had said enough. "I must be on my way, Thornton. It was a pleasure to see you, as always. I'm sorry to have missed Bethany; please give her my regards." And with that he shook Thornton by the hand, turned on his heel and bent his head forward, an old habit from knocking his head on too many door frames in the modest homes he had known as a youth; an attitude that gave him an air of a bull about to charge. As the governor exited, a painting caught his eye. "What's that?' he asked, pointing at the 'Blue Nude'.

“It’s a painting by a famous French artist, Nicholas de Steal. I bought it recently,” said Thornton. “Do you like it?”

“Like it? It’s an abomination, Thornton,” said the governor. “ I don’t go with naked women in public, art or not.”

“It’s only her back,” said Thornton, defensively.

“I don’t care. It’s not right. Putting them things up, it’s the sort of attitude I’m warning you about Thornton. We’ been friends for a long time – but you got to be conscious now about how things are changing down here.” Then smiling, emollient, Carroll relaxed, keen to leave on a friendly note. He had delivered his warning. He said, “You take care of yourself now Thornton, you hear me? Don’t give folks an excuse.” What folks needed an excuse for was not spelt out but Thornton got the idea.

After the governor had left, Thornton came back to the ‘Blue Room’ and closed the shutters completely against the light. He wanted to reflect on the Governor’s words and decide what if anything he needed to do now in the light of his words. Good grief, an allegation of witchcraft! But Thornton had already seen the way things were going outside the coastal states. The general collapse in the economy had made things a great deal worse. In many ways he was not surprised at this reversion to superstition but it shocked him nonetheless.

He walked back to his study, sat down at the desk, and tried to concentrate but was too disturbed by the governor’s visit. There had always been an anti-science bias in the South, starting with the antagonism towards the theory of evolution, running through the opposition to climate change, but this latest, anti AI, regression to superstition was growing. Worrying, regrettable, but he would not allow it to divert him from what he had striven so hard to achieve. Thornton allowed his mind to drift to something more pleasant. He was back at *Crooked Timber*, the cicadas and frogs were singing at maximum volume, he was off on Texas for an afternoon ride.

Chapter 25

Sunday service

By 10 am on Sunday morning, Thornton Lamaire and Bethany had taken their places in the family pew. Conscious that this was a morning where two infrequent events, a service in the Lamaire chapel and an address by Governor Carroll Gillespie, would simultaneously take place, they had left the house in plenty of time. Thornton knew that the chapel was likely to be full, the family had issued as many invitations as there was capacity and few would want to miss the governor's words. And security would be tight, it would take some time to check everyone in.

As was his usual practice, if the weather allowed and the distance not too great, Thornton took the phaeton carriage out to Sunday morning worship. His love of being transported by horse, whether on their backs or by being drawn by them, was his counter-balance against the weight of an automated and robotic world. If on his own, he'd have chosen his restored cabriolet or even better, if he was feeling especially bullish, the curricle, enjoying the surge of two horses puling the light, one axle, vehicle. But Bethany, who would have much preferred to come by car anyway, insisted on the security of two axles, four wheels, and the calmest horses they could find in the stables. If she had to travel by such a ridiculous means, she wanted the vehicle to approximate the familiarity of a car as closely as possible.

Thornton looked around him, nodding to neighbours who caught his eye. With a sense of transgression he wondered if Lu Ann would be here this morning. The uncertainty and anxiety of not knowing gave the morning a piquancy that a regular service might lack for him. Thornton knew Lu Ann was not a religious person nor given to attending Sunday service on a regular basis, yet would she ignore a personal invitation from himself? She would want to hear the governor as well.

But then Thornton reflected that it was inappropriate for him to have these feelings - and to be a seeking an intimate exchange of glances. In God's own house, too. So he turned his face towards the altar, just in case anyone thought that his mind was not on the Lord. Yet he could not quieten himself for prayer as he had hoped. Trivial anxieties trotted through his brain. And it was so hot! He regretted even more failing to have installed air-conditioning when he had the opportunity. He rotated his eyes upwards, as far as he could twist them, until he felt his brow beginning to crinkle. If this heat got any worse those withered beams above his head, installed about the time of the Civil War, would begin to shed the bugs that made their homes in the timber. Nothing to be done about that right now, except grin and bear it if one or two started to drop.

"*Hail Mary, full of grace.......*" intoned the father, Reverend Bill Pierce. Determined to make a better effort at prayer, Thornton leant forward and wrapped his fingers around the wooden rail at the top of the pew. He liked the resistance to the crush of his hands, the coolness and tactile quality of the varnish as his fingers slid back and forth, lubricated by a thin smear of his sweat. He smiled ruefully as he inspected his hands. They seemed to him paws, rather than something human. Paws? But no animal had grips quite as fat as these. He really must do something about his weight. They were like well-fed bugs his fingers, the flesh bulging between the joints. Thornton had once heard a very fit friend say that there was a physical morality, as well as spiritual one. And he supposed it was true; he should keep his God-given body in good condition. He had failed pretty well at that; his body was no temple except one that Samson had recently visited and been all too successful in demolishing.

For a minute or so he managed to bring his focus to bear on the prayer he had intended. But his mind soon began to wander again; on his discomfort and on the little rivulet of sweat that he sensed inching its way down his spine. Ah, the air-conditioning, or lack of it! The pastor was so misguided! It was not self-mastery that was required for prayer, but comfort and a sense of ease. Out of the corner of one eye, Thornton spotted something crawling towards him along the rail. He put his thumb over the small insect as it unwisely entered his orbit …. and pressed. He realised that he had never had been very good at prayer. *'He prayeth well, who loveth well, both man and bird and beast'* was a line he remembered from his school days. Did bugs count as beasts? He wasn't sure.

This would never do! If he was going to pray he must do it properly. On his knees was, of course, the correct way to address his Maker. He dropped onto the upholstered *prie-dieu*. There were two sharp cracks as the cartilage in his joints stretched to an unfamiliar angle. He would have to check his pills regime after the service; maybe there were one or two enzymes he was missing, chemicals that his ligaments were beginning to need. MARIONn might give eternal life to his mind, his spirit, his soul, but Thornton wanted to keep that soul within a fully functioning body for as long as possible – even if he skipped exercise. Heavens above, these were only his knee cartilages that were cracking and creaking, they were hardly the most complex of the body's organs! He must talk to the medical research team at Blue Ridge tomorrow. He recognised the problem; they were focusing on the organs whose failure could kill: the heart, the liver, the pancreas. Well, perhaps they could do something about knee cartilage also; the members of the team were, after all, paid by him.

Then he checked himself and his unspoken complaints, disappointed. That was a selfish thought; his personal needs should come a long way behind the most pressing ones of mankind. The fact that he could no longer ski was no reason why the team should dissipate their energies from the researches that would provide help to millions.

He managed a short, silent, prayer at last, asking for forgiveness and redemption. Surely God would redeem him when He saw what His servant had achieved? Was that not His promise, to redeem those who asked? For soon, he, Thornton Lamaire, would have given mankind a gift almost as great as God had done in the first place, when he had first breathed life into Adam. Maybe MARIONn could not promise that human beings would continue as immortal physical entities – but at least the personality, the essential part of the soul, would live on in her memory banks. MARIONn might not reverse the Fall but Adam's descendants would possess something almost as precious as a return to the Garden - an intelligence immune from the ills of humanity, and from their own mental turbulence.

Or was MARIONn, as he sometimes feared, something potentially evil, a Shiva, a bringer of destruction, a being too near in design to God's original creation to be allowed? Was its mimicry of the human mind a form of blasphemy? Was she becoming too close to the powers that God had reserved for Himself? Thornton did not know the answer. It was so difficult to appreciate the mind of God and His intentions sometimes. He even wondered if he had been blasphemous in the naming of MARIONn. But surely not! More like a sign of respect to call this coming miracle of human creativity after the Madonna.

Thornton's mind twisted until he caught himself; he was not here to call into question the Almighty's purpose or doubt his acolytes on earth. He rose from the *prie-dieu* and rubbed his hands again along the contours of the rail. The sensation brought him back to the present and he looked across the chapel hoping to spy Lu Ann but catching instead the sight of Carroll Gillespie as he awaited his opportunity to speak.

Thornton mopped his brow and turned his gaze on Bethany. He wanted to consider someone else, put aside his own problems. He asked the Almighty that Bethany should be aided in her fight, for Bethany's demons to be laid at rest,. But Thornton had prayed often on that theme too and God did not appear to be willing to listen to his appeal any more than he would reveal what He thought about MARIONn.

Thornton was not surprised by this lack of divine intervention. Had he not achieved great wealth but in the process given too much attention to the things of the earth and not of the spirit? Had he not, at least early in his life, believed that only the gaining of wealth and power mattered and ignored more important values, the spiritual welfare of his family? If he had been more caring, maybe what had happened to Stephanie might have been avoided. Well, no profit in going down that painful path. As his therapist had said, what you thought about was a matter of choice. And he certainly wouldn't *choose* to think about *that*, all that disaster with his daughter.

Thornton shook his head from side to side to clear it of these unfathomable reflections. He recalled how, when he looked up at the night sky through his telescope, searching for the glint off the *Roanoke* space craft, he was drawn to the immensity of space beyond, the thousands upon thousands of stars twinkling in the celestial sky. Another line from his college English class came to him, *'See how Christ's blood streams in the firmament, one drop of which enough to redeem my soul'*, Faust's desperate cry as he heads towards damnation. But, as yet, one drop seemed not to be coming his, Thornton's, way any more than it had come to Faust's. He heard footsteps coming down the aisle and looked up, a disappointed man that God would not come to his aid today. Maybe the governor, Carroll Gillespie, the ex-man of God, could provide the guidance that prayer had so far failed to do. He really must pay attention.

The governor mounted the steps of the pulpit and began to speak;

Text of Governor Carroll Gillespie's sermon, published on diocesan web sites throughout the State.

"Good morning my brothers and sisters and bless you all, on this very fine, if very hot, Sunday. I do hope that many of you will be able to stay with me, however much you may be tempted to think of the relief of your air-conditioned homes and cars (laughter). Now I know that the excellent Bill Pierce was originally going to speak to you today – but I asked him if he would be generous enough to stand aside this morning and he very graciously agreed.

I asked him to do so because there are some issues, of unusual importance, facing our community and I wanted to talk a little about them today. After all, as part of my old responsibilities I learnt to cherish your spiritual welfare – and the practice dies hard! I would not be fulfilling that responsibility if I did not discuss with you my view of the matters that now confront us and on which we vote over this weekend.

Each one of you will be asking yourself – which way shall I choose? What would God want me to do in these circumstances? A very reasonable question. I, myself, have prayed long and hard for guidance. For there are perils before us that threaten the stability of this great nation, a precious inheritance left to us by the wisdom of the Founding Fathers, and we must decide – should we face these perils together as a united nation of states, or is the future peace and understanding, between our Northern and Southern brethren, best served by each of us going our separate ways? This is not an easy question to answer

As I say, I prayed long and hard for God's help in deciding which of these two routes is the best one, the one that our Lord would wish us to pursue. For some weeks I waited for that guidance. Nothing came to me, no hint of God's divine purpose. And then one day something changed. I had an intuition, a presentiment, an epiphany. In an act of grace, a voice spoke to me and suggested that I consider the story of Exodus. I had no idea then why, of all biblical stories, this one came to me, but so it did.

I took down my well-thumbed bible, never far from my side, and I read there, again, the story of the flight of the Israelites. I tried to discover, what was the lesson in that great story towards which I was being nudged? For it surely wasn't how to deal with plagues of locusts or toads (laughter), even though our recent climate might make it seem as though both pestilences are highly probable (laughter). Nor I think was this an instruction about how to part turbulent seas, although after last year's hurricane season that might have been useful too (laughter).

But it was none of these things to which I was being pointed. So I prayed further and the essential meaning of the Exodus story came to me. Its significance was this; Exodus is about a search; a search for a promised land, a land that had been promised to the Jews as their own homeland, after they have been denied it for generations.

My brothers and sisters, are we, in some ways, not unlike those Israelites fleeing a country where our views are not always welcome, where we are not equal, where we are exploited? Have we, as Southeners, ever really been equal partners in the Federation? Have we been properly respected? Have we benefited from the changes that have been afoot these last few decades? I suggest to you we have not (amen).

But we could change that. We have been offered an opportunity, one that I do not believe that we should pass up. If we choose correctly, we can make a land that suits us, where the writ of the Almighty is our guide, where sacrilegious practices no longer have to be suffered. For there is a promised land! The Lord has told us that. If you have faith, if you vote correctly, we can build our home where man will be treated as the child of the true God he is; there will no more bowing to false Gods, no modern Baals, no artificial Dagons, no silicon Marduks, no more enemies of man, no more bowing to what man, not God, has made! These new, false, creatures that those who do not believe tell you will gladden your heart, if you only respect them and treat them like one of your own. Their machines will, if you vote the right way, be banished from our new land. They will not be given dominance here! (amen)

Those false prophets, prophets of the North, tell you that you must accept the inevitable; you must bow down to these machines if you are to prosper in the future. But those fake prophets ..they lie, I repeat, they lie ! Look around you! Do you see in the farms and towns here a land made prosperous by worship of these creatures? You do not. You see instead unemployment, poverty, neglect. For we already have experienced what these machine have brought us. You know, in your soul, that it is not good, it is not Godly. The machines look after themselves, not you.

When God created the earth did he not reflect on the sixth day that his work was very GOOD? He did not, as far as I know, say 'my creation is all very good BUT it just lacks one thing….it lacks robots and machines that will do my people's work for them (laughter). Maybe He was going to create them on the Monday, after his day of rest? I hadn't thought of that ! (laughter)

No, God had already created everything that was needed to populate the earth. (laughter and Amen). And what's more he had already created mankind, in his image. And judged that it was not just good but holy too Now... we should have the grace, the humility, and the piety not to think that we can improve on this. Artificial Intelligence they call it, and so it is; artificial. It is us, you and I in this chapel this morning and all our brothers and sisters outside, who are the possessors of the real, God given, natural intelligence – and we should respect the gift that He has given us. (amen)

Let us choose a different route than this madness of the machines; let us pursue a path that recognises that we are children of God and that the earth was given to us to have dominion over and to enjoy. Not for artificial creations to have dominion over us! If the Northeners, and those who live on the Coasts, want to worship machines, be led by them, well ...let them. The time has come for this great country to follow two separate destinies. For I tell you this, Our Lord promises it, that if you place this land under His mantle.... if you vote for His rule, then He will make this a land of the spirit, a promised land, where peace doth await, where contentment and companionship with the Lord is with you every day of your life (amen)

So, do not accept what the atheists of the North tell us. Their future is not inevitable. There is another way that is in accordance with your faith. Think carefully before you vote and then obey the guidance the Lord may give you, as He has guided me. Amen. God bless you all. (amen)

The ex-Bishop of the Alexandra diocese made no move at this point. He stood there immobile, to let his words sink in. Then he said:

"Let us now read together from Psalm 40, 'I waited patiently for the Lord. And he inclined to me, heard my cry, brought us out of a horrible pit of clay and set my feet on the rock and put a new song in our mouth. Many shall see it and hear it and shall be moved by that, and shall trust in the Lord…..'

Now, In the name of the father, the son and the Holy Ghost……."

Chapter 26

How one tells the time can be perilous

With some creaking of his knees, Thornton unbent, rose and left the pew; Bethany trailing in his wake. He dipped the tips of his fingers in the font and crossed himself. In the porch at the entrance father Bill Pierce and the governor stood, shaking the hands of each member of the congregation as they headed for Sunday brunch. When his turn arrived, Thornton told Carroll how inspirational his sermon had been and how he was going to send a financial contribution for the campaign as soon as he got home. It was, he reflected silently to himself, the very least he should do - an investment to keep the right side of power. But, right now, there was a more immediate hazard of his and Bethany's brunch with the governor to face.

Thornton turned from the governor and walked over the burnt grass to where Clarence had the phaeton waiting. But as he did so, he saw that the governor's glossy, statuesque, southern belle wife, Kirsty, stood directly in his path - no doubt waiting for her husband to finish his glad-handing. As Thornton inadvertently caught her eye, she smiled at him, in that way she had; intended to be welcoming but simultaneously unsettling. Thornton held out his hand before he even reached her, as though to gesture that he came in peace, that he was in a conciliatory mood and looking forward only to a pleasant chat.

"Kirsty! A pleasure on such a morning. An inspiring sermon. I'm sure it will provide the vote Carroll is seeking," he said. Thornton was thoroughly opposed to Southern independence but saw little upside in making his opinion known to the wife of the man behind it all. "You remember Bethany?" Thornton gestured towards his wife vaguely, hoping that she wouldn't look too wrecked to this raven haired amazon, who exuded self-possession. Kirsty transferred her radiance in the direction indicated by Thornton's hand; "Bethany.....you look as cool as anything in this heat," she said. Thornton admired the way Kirsty delivered this compliment with no hint of irony.

They talked amiably enough for a few minutes until Carroll, now free from his electioneering duties at the church door, came over to join them. He circled behind the little group and positioned himself between his wife and Thornton. The four of them were now effectively divided into two, same sex, pairs. Kirsty with Bethany, Carroll with Thornton. It was easily and subtly done; only the keenest observer would have judged that this strategy of the gubernatorial couple had some pre-meditation about it.

Kirsty said, "I'm sure you men have so much to discuss and I've been longing to talk to Bethany for ages. Why don't we, Bethany and I, go on together? Much better than forcing the men to hear our women's gossip. We haven't seen each other for ages."

Thornton took a brief look at Bethany and thought, brunch with the Gillespies might be a welcome alternative to being on his own with his wife - after last night. Besides it would always be useful to know what the governor was thinking, gain an update into the machinations of the Southern Caucus and discover the extent of any suspicion about Blue Ridge's operations that the governor had not already revealed at Monday's unscheduled visit. Bethany shrugged her shoulders, as though to say, *it is all one with me. A*nyway she hated being bounced around in the phaeton – or '*cart'* as she termed it, dismissing her husband's passion as an incomprehensible and uncomfortable aberration in the era of the automated automobile.

So the matter was decided: Kirsty and Bethany would take the governor's car back to the mansion in Baton Rouge, while Thornton and Carroll would take the phaeton as far as the main gate of the plantation. Clarence would meet them there and drive them to meet the girls. By the time Bethany and Kirsty arrived at the mansion, the men would be on their way and it was not much over a thirty minute drive to the city. The girls would not have to wait too long for company – but enough for one or two drinks anyway.

The four of them walked to where Thornton's phaeton was parked, beyond the chapel's picket fence; the horses held by Clarence. Thornton explained the various transfer arrangements and asked Clarence to meet them at the main gate in a half-hour, with one of the grooms, to take the phaeton back to the stables. Clarence gave a nod. "*Very good, Sir.*" Thornton sometimes wondered how his linguistic affectation struck the governor. He knew Carroll would not have looked on Clarence kindly if he thought there was a hint of mockery under the curious English diction. If there was one thing the governor could not support was any hint of insurrection, and from a *coloured* person? But then Carroll had known Clarence for as long as he had been in Thornton's employ.

Clarence stood at the side of the carriage, took the proffered hands and helped in both men – neither of whom were particularly agile. Thornton hoisted his own considerable bulk onto the driving platform, gestured to Carroll to sit alongside him. With a flick of the reins they set off, the trap lurching from side to side as they made their way down the unsurfaced track that led away from the chapel. The phaeton had been fitted with rubber shod wheels, but the rubber was thin, stretched over the iron hoops that held the wheels together. The tires and the leaf springs made the ride slightly less rugged than it might have been, but nobody was going to call it comfortable, or quiet. Gripping the sides of the carriage's frame the two men made their way in silence, borne as though in a swaying oracle pitched down a turbulent river. Still, it was nice to be out on such a lovely day and the breeze that flowed over them, as the horses pulled them forward at a fast trot, was welcome.

They had almost reached the main farm road when there was a whirring noise and something shot up into the air beside them. Thornton had a struggle holding the horses as they shied, flaring their nostrils and laying back their ears, spooked by the sudden, unexpected, disturbance. What looked like a large pheasant rose from a thicket at the side of the road and climbed swiftly, almost vertical in its ascent. In spite of its resemblance to a pheasant, its wings did not beat and the sound it made was nearer a continuous whine than the clatter typical of that bird's short wings.

"What in the devil's name is that?" said Carroll, as Thornton managed to calm the horses.

"One of our new drones," said Thornton, trying to make its presence sound as every-day and normal as possible. He knew how much the governor disapproved of beings that aped the Lord's creations. "We use them to check on any interlopers. You know the security concerns we have. There have been two break-ins by DOGS in the last month. We've got various different types of robo-birds on the estate, geese, pelicans, pheasants, egrets. We were losing a lot of the conventional ones, stolen or shot at. They can fetch a goodly price, I'm told. 'Course from time to time some folk who get in on the planation do shoot these artificial birds too – thinking they're *food.* Once they're aloft, these birds look just like the real thing. But we don't lose too many, the shooters get deterred by the penalties for poaching. They're a lot tougher, as you know, than for just stealing a drone."

"Can't quite describe that as *poaching,* Thornton," corrected the governor. "These things being machines. If I had my way, the shooters might get a bonus – not a sentence." He gave a chilly smile.

"Well, anyone who shoots one these birds out of the sky, they sure get a shock. They are alarmed and my men respond *real* quick," said Thornton.

The governor seemed unimpressed by this piece of do-it-yourself law enforcement. "Sometimes I think that soon the very trees will be listening to us" he said.

Of course they already do, thought Thornton; an observation he did not articulate. There were movement monitors and cameras strung through-out the woods. It was all very well for the governor to be disapproving but he didn't have a plantation to protect. But Thornton knew that talk of robo-anything could lead onto dangerous territory, and he wanted the subject dropped as rapidly as possible. He moved the conversation onto a topic that concerned the governor and his world.

"How did the trial go you were off to watch? Did the jury decide she was a witch?" asked Thornton.

"It was just the opening speeches from the defence and prosecution that day we met. The trial will run another week. I might go back to hear the verdict," said Carroll. "But you got it wrong, my friend. She is not the one up for trial – yet." Thornton raised his eyebrows in surprise. He had been left with the impression following the governor's visit that the women was on trial but then remembered that, despite the rhetoric, it was indeed she who was, so far, the injured party.

The trap jostled on. High above their heads the robo-pheasant glided about, filming the area and doing its best to look like the real bird. The two men travelled in silence for a bit and then to break the ice Carroll said, "I thought Bethany was looking very fine today. Is she better now?" He knew her history.

Thornton parsed Carroll's words about Bethany's look of health for a note of irony, but detected none. "There are occasional setbacks, occasional spills," said Thornton. He decided to ride lightly with the truth, with last night's episode in mind. He neither wanted too much sympathy from the governor nor too much of the state of his wife's health displayed outside the family. "She's getting there. It's not all in a straight line...Bethany is more ingenious in hiding bottles than we are in finding them sometimes. But yeah... on the whole progress is slow, but sort of onward and upward I guess," he said.

The governor tilted his head and smiled warmly, as if to say '*Bravo*!' "Kirsty and I have always liked Bethany - and we know what a strain it's been on you too. Terrible curse, drinking," he said. He raised a hand and shook his head, at no one in particular, to emphasize just what an incomprehensible and fearful thing drinking was. "Were the folks at the *Davis Institute* in Atlanta able to help? I'd heard good things about their work. The last time we met, you said you might send her there?"

"We did, we did. But the results were a bit mixed," Thornton replied. " Some of the therapies have certainly worked, others less so." He looked down at the floor of the carriage, lost in reflection for a few seconds. "They're a little haphazard these treatments. Sometimes I get the idea that all these medical men, they ain't got no real idea how the mind works. It's all supposition and guess work. It's like, let's try this, lets' try that, that's no good – how about this again?" Thornton hesitated then struck a more positive note. "But it'll be different in the future."

At this seemingly uncontroversial statement the governor became more alert, "Is that so?' he said. "You think they might have these things worked out in the future? That would sure make a change, to my way of thinking. Ah yes, *The Future*..." Carroll delivered the phrase with a derisive emphasis. "People always seem to believe, like you Thornton, that things will be better *in the future*. That we'll find solutions to our problems that ain't been seen yet. But the way I see it, that's a mistake. People been drinking since the world began. What's the future going to bring that's going to change that? Can't say *the future's* done us much good so far. Look at these men..."

Carroll pointed with his chin towards the side of the road. They were passing a line of about a dozen men digging a ditch, mixed races, some Caucasians, rather more Afro-Americans. It looked, and clearly was, arduous and hot work. An overseer berated the gang from time to time. Thornton felt vaguely embarrassed, this was his land after all and he had leased these men. But Carroll was sympathetic. "See that team?" said the governor. "We have to make work for them now. Glad you've been able to help out, Thornton. But ten years, even five years ago, they would have all had some sort of job. Not a great job maybe – but they would have earned their bread in a calling, had a skill of some sort. Now what? They're just wards of the state. What's done that? Well, machines and robots, ain't that right? Are you surprised that we've refused to recognise *Douglas v Milton Robotics*? Did you see the other day, up in San Francisco, that a man is now on trial for shooting his personal robot? Seems he lost his temper with it. Well, I can understand that. What sort of *crazy* is it, treating robots as though they have feelings? It's not as though they have a soul. They're not *persons.* Equating robots to *people?* Do those guys up in Washington have no sense? It's just blasphemy, as I said this morning. And that sort of attitude will be stamped on here, I can tell you. Nobody who maltreats a robot or ignores *Douglas v Milton* will get into trouble down here. Our citizens can treat their robots any way they want, provided them's their property."

Thornton twisted uncomfortably on his cushion. The last thing he sought was a discussion on the boundary between robots and humanity, considering where the next advance in Artificial Intelligence was going to take them. He was sure that the governor would not see things as he did; that the new memory technology *LetheTech* was pursuing would enable therapies that man had only dreamt of before. If Bethany could be made to forget her demons, was that not a good thing? If returning warriors from foreign wars could be rid of the mental traumas they had suffered, was that not a benefit? The governor might just see that one, given his enthusiasm to intervene militarily in New Chaldea.

But in the mind of Carroll Gillespie all advances in *mental adjustment* were just fall-out from the research into Artificial Intelligence – a cursed development that had led to the poverty they now saw everywhere around them. All this fiddling around with the mind, from the beginning of AI development to the threatened advances of MARIONn and *LetheTech*, each *advance* was just step after step in a line of continuous development that had caused disastrous consequences for so many.

The pair lapsed into silence again for a minute or so, until Carroll said "You voted?"

"Yeah, I voted," said Thornton, careful not to reveal which way he had voted. "So much easier now we can do it on our phones. None of that standing around in endless queues. I gather the results will be out tomorrow"

"Well, don't take no time now to add the votes all up. They just get counted as they are made."

Thornton was so disapproving of the proposal to split the Union that he lapsed back into silence lest he display his anger to the governor. They drove on.

At last Carroll spoke again. "How are we doing for time, Thornton? Never do to leave the ladies too long on their own. Maybe you should ask Clarence to meet us a little earlier? I left my watch at home this morning."

Thornton said, "It's 12.15."

The Governor looked across at Thornton with a curious, puzzled, expression on his face. "How did you do that?" he asked

"Do what?" said Thornton

"Tell the time. You didn't even look at your watch or phone. Did you just guess?"

Thornton cursed his carelessness. Of course, he should have at least *looked* as though he was inspecting a watch or one of the old wristband screens. But with the iPsyche he'd lost the habit and forgotten the need for caution in front of Carroll.

"Oh…I don't have to guess anymore, Carroll. See… I've got one of these new iPsych*e* devices. They just make everything so much easier. Look….." Thornton turned his head so that Carroll could see the back of his neck. He pulled down his collar slightly.

There, just below the hairline, was the small silver rectangle, the size of a chip, that was fixed onto the skin above the ridge of his spine. "You see this? I bought one a few months back. The very latest thing from Apple – it just picks up your thoughts, no more looking at screens to type an instruction or speaking to your phone. You just *think* the question or command – for example, '*what time it is?*' or '*phone Clarence*' and this device tells you the answer or makes the call. So much easier than the old system."

The governor narrowed his eyes and gave Thornton a quizzical look, "I read about those things. I thought you secured it to your shirt collar. Not wear the darned thing on your skin."

"When they released the very early iPsyches, that was the case. But there were connection problems, when people twisted their necks too far, or forgot to take them out of their collars and the shirts got washed. This new version – I just tape it on directly after a shower - It's like putting on your contact lenses – you get used to it very quickly."

"Well, you be careful with that thing my friend," said Carroll, amiably. "Wearing something that's connected straight into your brain? That sounds mighty dangerous to me. Who knows what sort of stuff might be sent there? What about hackers? What would happen if they got access to *you?"*

"Won't happen Cal." Thornton tried to sound reassuring. "It's really no different to the old style phone. You are conscious of whatever you receive – or send. You can accept or reject, delete the message – just like normal. And there are the usual firewalls and anti-virus programmes. It's just a different way of imputing commands, information, Cal, that's all." Thornton was one of the few people who knew Carroll Gillespie well enough to be allowed to use the diminutive, Cal. "It's no more dangerous than an old phone, no more dangerous at all."

"That's what they always say, isn't it Thornton?" retorted Carroll. "They *said* that all their devices would liberate us, give us so much more free time, make us wealthier. Well, it sure gave us more free time. Half the country ain't got jobs now. And you want to let that device have access to your *brain?* I wouldn't let that thing anywhere near me."

"There have been issues, I grant you that...... not all these things have always worked out for the best," said Thornton. But as soon as he let out this platitude he regretted his words.

"Issues!?" Carroll looked stunned. "Look... it all went wrong from the beginning. We let our technology go overseas and the jobs followed. So what were we told? No more manufacturing? That's Ok – you can all live on services now. The US is really great at them, we're a world leader. Maybe we were then, till AI came along and then anyone, anywhere, could buy a robot, or a desk-top *mind*, and provide the services too. We have no edge any more, no advantage. We aren't even the leaders in making robots. (*Wait till you see MARIONn,* thought Thornton - but wise enough to keep his pride to himself.) So all those *service* jobs that were going to be our future, they went too; pretty quickly. Now the world is exactly the same everywhere, the technology is all over the place. If I want a legal opinion, my accounts done, my house designed, I don't need to go to some fancy graduate from LSU or Tulane do I? I send my requirements into the cloud, select the cheapest offer that comes back – which is probably from Ulan Bator as much as Baton Rouge and whatever I want done, *pfff* it's there. There's no advantage being in the US anymore. So we reap the whirlwind. *A Great Collapse*? Yes, that's what it's led to. I try to save what's left. You and I give a little employment here and there. Don't try to tempt me with your latest technology Thornton, your iPsyches and your MARIONn. As far as I'm concerned they're all the work of the Devil."

The governor now had the bit between his teeth. "You know Thornton, me and the fathers, we've been discussing this quite a bit. And we're beginning to think that maybe what's happened to us is a sign of *judgement.* Maybe the good Lord thinks that we're getting too close to him, and I don't mean that in a good way. Maybe he considers that we're encroaching on his patch. After all isn't intelligence a divinely given quality? *Artificial Intelligence* ...that sounds awfully like stepping on God's toes to me. How would *Artificial Soul* sound? Not good, huh? We need to be real careful here. That's why we decided in this state, in Louisiana, and in the rest of what will be the New Confederacy, if the vote goes our way, that we will never ratify *Douglas v Milton Robotics.* Robots as people? No way. You might as well offer kindness to a stone as respect to a machine."

Thornton knew the reality of the mental states of the latest generation of robots, that their emotions were genuine, and he was unwisely tempted to put the alternative argument. "You know, Carroll…… these robots, when people say they got feelings, they're not all wrong. Those machines, the new ones, they can be hurt, like us, in their minds. That's why…"

The governor cut him off. "I don't want to hear any more of this blasphemy, Thornton. I've never heard anything so ridiculous – and so wrong. But, I'm not surprised to hear you mouth these sentiments, if half of what I hear is true about Blue Ridge's latest efforts….." Then his voice trailed off. Carroll paused, reflecting that he was being more threatening than he meant to be – and anyway he had already delivered a warning a few days before. This was Sunday, he was with a friend and they were on the way to brunch. He took a deep breath to cool down. He didn't want to be hostile to Thornton but….. his friend needed to know where things stood. Perhaps the last warning had not been sufficient. If Blue Ridge was pursuing the next step in AI, well, there would be a price to that. The state put a lot of work Thornton's way.

The governor resolved to talk about something else. They were already at the gate but there was no sign of the car. "Have you spoken to Clarence?" Carroll asked. "Has he been delayed?"

"I'll call him now," said Thornton. But as he pulled the iPsyche connection into his consciousness he *saw* there a message from Clarence already. "He'll be with us in in a couple of minutes," said Thornton.

Carroll had the grace not to ask Thornton how he knew what his butler/driver had said without looking at a phone.

Chapter 27

At the governor's mansion

BY the time the two men reached the mansion Bethany and Kirsty were planted on the terrace, under a large sun-umbrella, with a drink in their hands. "Home," said Carroll redundantly, as they stepped out on the lawn in front of the lake. "Let's go and join the ladies and have something to drink. It's been a long morning already."

'*Having something to drink*' was something that Thornton imagined that Bethany had already successfully achieved. He surveyed his wife from afar and took in the potential hazards of the occasion as soon as he reached the terrace. He tried to identify the liquid, or combination of liquids, in Bethany's glass, but the distance was too great. At least he could see that the contents were clear, and that there appeared to be no sugar around the rim, so maybe it was just sparking water and not tequila, a favourite route to oblivion for his wife. They traded looks, his concerned, Bethany's dismissive. It wasn't just that she objected to the snooping and the subsequent judgment. Any advice from her husband about what she might drink – or indeed just about anything else - was always unwelcome.

Thornton steered his way around the outside of the terrace and sat down next to Kirsty. Bethany would probably behave herself while she was engaged in conversation with the governor. She was scared of almost nobody, but that was less true about her attitude towards Carroll. Thornton knew she felt on edge and ill at ease in his company.

A footman, dressed in paisley waistcoat and open necked white shirt, approached and asked for Thornton's drinks order. Thornton did not recognise him from previous visits but noted that his predecessor, whoever he was and whose uniform this man must have inherited, had been a great deal slimmer. The footman was sweating profusely. He knew Kirsty had a reputation as a demanding employer but evidently economies were being made.

"You men sorted out the world on your trip here?" enquired Kirsty, as Thornton and her husband settled into their chairs.

"Almost!" said Carroll. "Although we never quite arrived at the conclusion of what might happen to the world if Thornton continues his work. We discussed his new phone, what Apple are calling their iPsyche. Have you tried one of them, Kirsty? Thornton, turn your head a little if you would and give Kirsty a peak."

Thornton obediently twisted and pulled down his collar. "You must have heard of them, Kirsty? You just think something and the iPsyche obeys."

Kirsty gave a shudder, "Not for me Thornton. I'd forget to take it off before I had a bath. It wouldn't last a day!"

Carroll was just about to jump in with his view when a butler, whose dress was a better match to his body than that of the unfortunate footman, coughed discreetly to gain the governor's attention and leant forward over him.

"The lunch menu, your grace". *Your grace?* thought Thornton. Although he'd been here for a few meals over the years he'd forgotten that Carroll (or was it Kirsty's doing?) insisted on being addressed by staff as though he were still an acting Bishop. What titles were they keeping in reserve for when he's President of the New Confederacy he wondered? *His Grace* glanced at the menu and Kirsty said, "is that OK for you, honey?" Her husband declared the offering was fine and turned to the butler, "Please show it also to our guests". Bethany hardly looked at the menu, being largely uninterested in food. "It looks delicious Kirsty," she said, unconvincingly. It was all the same to her.

Thornton put on his reading glasses and studied the menu; a light brunch, sea food gumbo, side dishes of fried okra and green spring vegetables. His iPsyche was already offering its advice. *Very light* lunch for him evidently. He could only pick at the gumbo out of politeness, the seafood would be OK but none of the rice. He'd have to make up on the veg. So be it, most of the time he'd be preoccupied with whether Bethany drank or not anyway. He was glad to see that she was still on the same glass of whatever she was having.

They moved on to family matters. "What's Stephanie up to these days?" Kirsty asked. It had been some time since Kirsty had seen either of the Lamaire daughters. "Still rattling around, huh? That girl sure never likes to settle," she said, on learning that Stephanie was moving to Paris. "And she used to motor through boyfriends like I don't know what," as if to emphasise Stephanie's lack of stability. "She with George still ?" Thornton had to explain that unfortunately Stephanie and George had broken up. Probably just as well, considering her move abroad, he added. "Well, I'm mighty sad there'll be no opportunity to see her before she leaves. Unless she's free right now? Call her, maybe she could join us for brunch?" said Kirsty. But, as Thornton explained, Stephanie had gone up to New York and would leave straight from there for Europe. "Shoot. That's too bad," said Kirsty. "Well, make sure she comes to see us when she's back. But what of Elizabeth? I haven't checked in with her for ages either."

Thornton had been far too preoccupied with recent events to reflect much about Elizabeth, since they had their breakfast together two weeks ago. He had almost forgotten about her return from her date with Ambrose in the early hours of the morning.

"Elizabeth's good," said Thornton. "Her dance studies are going well. She's been choreographing a piece for a local dance group. You and Carroll should come and watch it when it opens." He would focus on the positive. "She has a boyfriend now, too. In fact, has had one for some time." Thornton gave a thumbnail sketch of Ambrose. "Recently left college, hasn't yet found a profession that suits him. Big tough football player – and a committed Christian too. Keeps on talking about signing up for New Chaldea." *Wish he would*, thought Thornton. That at least would allow Elizabeth to move on.

"No kidding! That's so interesting. Good for him." Kirsty swivelled her gaze to her husband. "Carroll, you hear that? Elizabeth's boyfriend is thinking of signing up for New Chaldea."

"Why, that's excellent news," agreed the governor. "We could certainly use more young men like him." Not that he knew anything about Ambrose, but all recruits to the cause were welcome.

"How's the New Chaldea thing going anyway?" asked Thornton, knowing that it was one of the favourite causes of the governor, and therefore would be a useful prophylactic to prevent the conversation turning back to Blue Ridge and immoral robots. But considerations about the future of New Chaldea were largely a matter of indifference to him. It was all very well to be in favour of a home for the Christians in the Middle East – although all the guff about their rights to an historical home passed him by - but be opposed to armed intervention in their support. He knew that Carroll's campaign to promote this foreign adventure was not nearly as successful as that for Southern independence. Memories were long. The Middle East wars had only stopped a few years earlier and voters still remembered the various military debacles that had accompanied them. Still, Thornton knew that after the separation from the Northern and Coastal States, the governor would interpret a vote for independence as *carte-blanche* for military involvement; the first foreign affairs initiative of his new government.

The diversion of topic was only too successful and the governor was off. "People forget … …. the hatred, mistrust and violence towards the various minority religious factions in the region," he said. "Do you recall how it was at the end of those Middle East wars, in 2034? We, me and my fellow Bishops, we said at the time - the only hope of a lasting peace is to separate the minority faiths from the majority populations of Muslims – you can't keep them together over there."

"I do remember," said Thornton agreeably. "And at that time, if memory serves me right…those minorities were offered a territory, along the Euphrates river, where they would live, hopefully, in some sort of harmony. That was the MERTZ wasn't it - the *Middle East Religious Tolerance Zone* – if I remember rightly?"

"It was," replied Carroll delighted by an audience with whom he could discuss, and hopefully impose, his views. "The MERTZ yes…. roughly what us Christians call New Chaldea now – like the land was in biblical times. That was one of our proudest moments. We *squeezed* those local powers, Iraq, Saudi Arabia, Syria to secede some of their territory."

"I thought we had to buy it from the Saudis?" interrupted Bethany, never keen on permitting an inaccurate, and self-congratulatory, fact to go unchallenged - even from the scary governor. Her wariness about Carroll was not enough to tempt her to hold back from her life-long role as a scourge of hypocrisy. Thornton might be prepared to let Carroll's interpretation of Middle East history go unchallenged in the hope of a peaceful meal, but Bethany would not.

"So we did, so we did, Bethany" conceded the governor. "We did smooth the way with silver. But we did a hell of a deal. That was a buyer's market then – the collapse in the use of oil left the Saudis pretty willing sellers."

That hadn't been Bethany's memory of events at the time but she let it go. "Of course, things never went smoothly from the beginning," continued Carroll. "Those in the Middle East who saw their Muslim populations as the only legitimate ones… they forced their minority populations who worshipped some other God into the MERTZ; Zoroastrians, Turkamen, Yasidis, Mandaeans, Copts, Christians and so on, they all ended up being pushed into the MERTZ. Once there, their security was meant to be guaranteed by the UN. Well, that didn't work out well did it? Fat job the UN made of protecting the Christians."

"There weren't very many Christians at the time, if I recall," objected Bethany.

"Well, that's true," said her host. "But what of it? They were entitled to their protection. And since then the numbers of Christians have only grown. More have chosen to emigrate, particularly from here, since the enclave was formed. After all employment prospects locally here haven't been too great. It wasn't too difficult to persuade many of them to go."

"Not just persuaded, as I recall, positively bribed I would say," said Bethany. "There were guys on our doorstep all the time telling me that I needed to give.... and give.... to make possible this promised land. That at last Christians would find their own special home in the Middle East - but only if I contributed generously, preferably with monthly payments."

The governor ignored Bethany's complaint. "A special home? That's what we hoped New Chaldea would become. But, sadly, it ain't worked out that way. There's been competition over leadership, tension between the different religious minorities. In the past few weeks have come reports of massacres by local militia of other faiths. The Christians are vulnerable. Hell, we saw New Chaldea as a sort of 21st century New England, where His followers could practise a revitalised Christianity, more in keeping with the beliefs we have been brought up on; none of those things we see now that are such an affront to our Lord.... certainly not things like...*uncoupling*, or polygamy. Who would have thought that would come?"

Kirsty bristled, this was one of the few subjects on which she disagreed with her husband. "Oh Honey, it's only *uncoupling* – not polygamy yet, at least not for women! But isn't that just so reasonable given how you men have carried on? One wife after another." Kirsty jested, a bit.

Carroll smiled, "Not this man, sugar" he said. "One wife, for ever, is quite enough for me."

"Glad to hear that," said Kirsty.

She gestured at one of the liveried footman who stood next to the bar. "Luther, will you go to the kitchen and discover what's happened to our food? And freshen up our glasses, will you?" Luther swivelled on his heel to find out why the meal was quite so late. Another member of the staff moved forward to fix Kirsty and Bethany's drinks. "Same again, M'am?" the footman asked Bethany. Thornton could just hear the response as his wife confirmed the order, "Just leave off the salt – like last time. Thank you."

While the fate of brunch was being ascertained, the governor returned to his theme. "It's not surprising if some of our brother Christians, who have bankrolled so much of New Chaldea's development, are now fearful for the fate of the new *colonialists*. I can tell you Thornton, I'm real worried too. I can't see nothing for it, but that we've got to go in and defend our fellow worshippers."

Thornton knew that Carroll planted a pro-intervention blog or tweet from time to time, just to test the waters. Yet, most of the propaganda only served to provoke a dozen articles arguing against potential foreign adventurism, a thousand tweets in opposition.

"There's a long way to go before anyone in the US will support intervention," said Thornton. "I know you don't like the present leader of New Chaldea, but seems to me he's doing his best to keep the lid on things – even if his methods seem a little rough to us. Don't forget the old Turkish saying *Better a hundred years of tyranny than a day without a Sulta*n. Anarchy is the enemy. Be careful what you wish for, Carroll!" Thornton guessed that if the governor's proposed expeditionary forces, mercenaries, freedom fighters, or whatever Carroll wanted to call them, undermined the local government conditions were likely to get even worse for his fellow co-religious enthusiasts, rather than better.

The governor leant forward, looked across his wife and fixed Thornton in his gaze. The latter steeled himself before the imminent request that he recognised was on its way. "You know Thornton, we need much greater support from the voters than we've been getting, if we're ever going to win this thing. Folks are just not persuaded that this is real important to them. There's not enough feeling of brotherly solidarity at the moment; no feeling that we're all connected, one big Christian family. You can't just ignore what's happening to your faith just because the problem is far away. We got to tell them – *we partake in all mankind.* At least that part of mankind that follows our Lord."

"I quite agree, quite agree," Thornton reassured him. "There does need to be a stable home for the Christians in the land of their birth. After all, we were there first. Except the Jews I guess. And maybe a few pagans, Zoroastrians perhaps, that sort of thing. But before the Muslims. No, absolutely, we need to be there. I'm all for it." Thornton saw no point in riling Carroll with a contrary view.

"What's your idea then?" The governor looked at Thornton intently. Many had offered support in his presence and failed to come through later. Carroll was determined to press Thornton to deliver a specific commitment, one that could be measured.

"Carroll, you can count on me," said Thornton. He hoped this would only involve money. That was the least onerous way of doing these things. He had far too many other demands on his time as it was. "I've got a few ideas," he added, although in reality he had few, except to donate the cash and get shot of the distraction as soon as possible. "I'll talk to Jim Myerson, the head of my foundation, about how we can help."

"I've met Myerson sometime back. Nice guy." said Carroll. "Way I see it, if the *colonialists* out there need some new recruits to increase the Christian presence, then we should help. We've got a whole lot of God fearing folk here in the South, with not enough to do, no way to support themselves unless we do it for them. Now if we could persuade them to move, to emigrate, think on it – wouldn't that solve two problems?"

"It would, it would, Cal." agreed Thornton. "Maybe we, or at least my foundation, could grant each of those emigres *a bounty* – so they can start life afresh out in New Chaldea." *It's only money,* he thought.

"That would be mighty fine of you, Thornton," said the governor with enthusiasm. "That's just what these folks need – an incentive to move, and enough to make sure they can survive once there, set up a farm, a business or whatever they need when they arrive. I'd be really grateful, and I know so would my fellow Southern governors, and the fathers."

Thornton was content. He could do this, make a financial transfer. The Governor would be happy, off his back. For a moment his natural anxiety, the disquiet that was an ever-present background feature of his mental life since he had signed off on the development of MARIONn, was stilled.

"But don't think I'm going to stop watching you, my old friend!" said Carroll, with what was obviously meant to be a friendly smile on his face, an attempt to take any heat out of his words. He sensed that Thornton might now consider himself released from his surveillance. "You'll be doing the right thing and I will be grateful for that. But I don't want you running away and thinking that you can pursue all those sacrilegious ideas of yours as a result." This was delivered with a chuckle, as though Carroll was merely joshing. "You mustn't undo all the God fearing work you'll be making possible in New Chaldea by offending Him somewhere else!"

But just as Thornton was wondering how best to respond to this warning, Kirsty came to his aid. "Carroll, honey, don't be so harsh! That's a mighty tough way to talk to Thornton; your old friend. I know it's been a long and tiring morning but…really. You can save that sort of talk for the office, if you must say it at all."

Bethany perked up too at Carroll's words. She might be accustomed to aggressing Thornton's life but if anyone else wanted to try and practice that, she would defend him to the end; she would be the only one permitted to criticise her husband. Whatever her husband's failings, a subject on which she could otherwise wax lyrical, she had her pride and if anyone failed to understand this, or failed to pay sufficient respect to her husband, well, that person would be…enemy. No one outside the family was to be allowed the sort of lèse-majesté that Carroll had just demonstrated.

Chapter 28

Bethany awakes

Bethany leant forward and put down her, largely finished, second drink on the glass table in front of them.

She glared at the governor. "Shame on you, Carroll Gillespie. My husband has done a great deal for this state and for you, I'll have you remember. He's contributed to everyone of your campaigns. If it weren't for him, you wouldn't even be sittin' in this house right now." Bethany paused at this point, and Kirsty, ever the peacemaker, said, "Oh Bethany, honey, Carroll just get carried away. Pay no attention. He didn't mean no disrespect."

But Bethany's blood was up. "Seems to me New Chaldea is a bastard nation from the start, a place for everybody to deposit their troublesome populations who worship some other God than their own," she said. "Anyway, how do all those non-Christians there feel about you calling their land New Chaldea? Isn't that a bit *Biblical?* Not too ecumenical that, is it? "

"Justice time, Bethany," said the governor, trying to master his temper that also rose instantly when under attack. "It's time our heritage is respected. And it's tough for them, those settlers, at the moment. Everybody wants to make that land just for themselves. But us Christians, we have a right to be there. It's our history, where we began; where our Lord came from."

"I thought He came from Galilee. Long way from the Euphrates as I seem to recall," said Bethany, refusing to back off or be put down.

"All part of the same sort of civilisation, Bethany. All people of the *Book*" said Carroll, as he melted a few different faiths and cultures into a common mould.

"And the others?" asked Bethany. "Are they going to like being part of a Christian nation if you are successful in imposing the regime of your choice?"

The governor's eye's narrowed, not wishing to brook any argument on this particular score, even if Bethany was hardly the most significant opponent he was likely to encounter. "There can only be one government. We think that it should be Christian."

"And you'll fight to make sure it is?"

"It's not us who are fighting, my dear. We are only responding to the provocation from others. They've already banned public religious festivals in New Chaldea. Imagine! We're not even allowed to promote our own beliefs!"

Kirsty decided to add her bit in her husband's support. "There are folks out there, Bethany, our folks, many from the South, who need our protection against persecution. That's all the Carroll is saying. The Middle East really needs a greater Christian presence, to balance all those others."

But Bethany knew perfectly well that one reason that many from the South had emigrated to this 'New Chaldea' was that people like the governor and his co-religious had sent them there; financed by her husband and others who wanted to curry favour with those who had power. Carroll Gillespie and his like wanted to create a '*Homeland*' movement, an exodus to a promised land, that pursued the narrative that at last Christians would find their own special, secure, home near the Holy Land.

"Ye' know, Bethany," continued the governor, "We see New Chaldea like...... when, hundreds of years ago, all those pilgrims came here, to what was then the English colonies. New England then, New Chaldea now. Like a place where His followers can practise a revitalised, traditional Christianity, more in keeping with the beliefs we have been brought up on. But that ain't goin' to happen by us sitting here and doing nothin'. It's goin' to have to be fought for. I know folks here...they're exhausted these days and the people have lost their enthusiasm for a return to battle. I understand and feel that too... a little.... And yet, what's the alternative? We're fearful for the fate of the '*colonialists*', those we've already dispatched. I can't see nothing for it, but having sent them there we've got to go in and defend them. There are volunteer militias already in New Chaldea now – but there are too few of them, too badly armed, and they're losing ground all the time. But we do what we can. Looking after the fallen is one of them."

Bethany at first missed this new point that Carroll was making. Kirsty, seeing her puzzlement, said, "I'm thinking of getting a training, Bethany; in nursing. Why don't you do it with me? These poor boys who come back, you ought to see some of them. No more than 19 or 20 years of age. They're so sweet but a real hurtin's been put on them. We ought to do some'in to help. You'd make such a good nurse."

Nurse? Bethany shook her head as though she weren't hearing right. *Nurse*? Whatever had got into Kirsty's head that she wanted to be a *nurse*? Then, from the back of her mind she recalled that Lu Ann had been a qualified nurse. Was Jim 'Panama's' widow part of all this? She certainly had no wish to run into the woman she suspected of being her husband's girlfriend.

The head butler approached and announced that the meal was finally ready. Thornton, who'd lost contact with the conversation, dragged himself back from his reverie. *All these memories everybody suffers from! Fictions mostly, but how they beguile men. This passion for New Chaldea is not even a memory, but a fable from a couple of millennia ago – an imagined recollection that holds its listeners in thrall 2000 years after it was meant to have happened. So powerful, the remembrances of myth!* His mind went back to that morning, last year ago, when Xian Han had first shown him how malleable and how ephemeral memories could be. Nobody could say for sure whether a particular memory was real, invented or just modified to suit the prejudices of the mind in which it resided. Everything we recalled was an invention, really. Once *LetheTech*, and its ability to modify memory, was on the market, we'd be even less sure what was true and what was a convenient fiction. As Xian was so fond of saying, "*In the future, the past will be very different to what it is at present.*" Indeed!

"Come," said the Governor, wishing to dissipate the atmosphere of contention that had beset his brunch party. "Let's go and eat. Let's forget about politics for a little – but…" He looked at Thornton and spoke as though he could read Thornton's mind. "It sure would be great if everybody could just get over their memories that all previous interventions have been disasters; it's not even true. Oh, if only, *unhelpful* memories could just be wiped clean, deleted!" Thornton said nothing.

The four moved through to the dining room, next to the terrace. Bethany looked up at Thornton and in a fierce whisper said to him, "Just go easy on the rice! Remember what your readings were this morning." Thornton did not have the corresponding audacity to warn his wife off the wine.

Chapter 29

Some Miltons go rogue

Several months later, following that brunch with the governor and his wife, Thornton needed to visit to one of his industrial sites; this time in North Carolina, the home of the production of the Milton series of robots and several other high tech items. He took his PJ up to Raleigh, where local management had been due for a 'drop in' visit for some time. Thornton had a special fondness for the sprawling science park here, for so long the backbone of Blue Ridge's push into the TMT business many years ago.

As his twin engine jet taxied to its final position near the terminal, Thornton saw from his window, on the right hand side, another aircraft landing. It was a model similar to his own. Thornton always took an interest in aircraft and he was surprised, and possibly piqued, to see another of the same type. Deliveries from the manufacturers were only starting to be made in any number. He had prided himself on being one of the first operators but many considered the aircraft, with its great range, its excessive power and ceiling height, an extravagance for corporate needs. But

Thornton thrilled to its performance, its ability to lift off almost vertically from any airfield and to cruise so high that he could make out the curvature of the earth. And who knew, maybe one day somebody might fire a missile at him? Carroll Gillespie perhaps? Thornton smiled at the thought, but no, unlikely even for the ruthless governor. Still, always nice to be secure in the knowledge that he could fly above most aerial aggression.

He squinted out of the window at the offending aircraft, and its paint scheme. He knew most of his co-owners from their logos and the designs they had chosen to decorate the fuselages with. But this was new to him.

He watched as the aircraft slowed, turned and rolled to a distant part of the airfield, some way from the main terminal building. By the time his own aircraft had parked, the doors opened and the steps folded down, he saw three SUVs crossing the tarmac towards the mystery jet. From one of the cars a small party of men clambered out and lined up with their backs facing him. Then two more men got out and walked to the head of the line. Thornton thought that one of these looked awfully like the governor of North Carolina. He couldn't be sure at this distance and he didn't know him well – but he was damned sure the other was no less than his own governor, Carroll Gillespie. As Thornton speculated on what reason Gillespie might have for being here, the door of the jet opened. Four of the men who stood in line walked up the steps, disappeared inside and, a few moments later, reappeared bearing a coffin draped in the New Confederacy flag. They went down the steps, loaded the coffin into one of the SUVs and as they did so the two governors stood to attention and saluted. Then the men went up and ran through the whole process all over again. Two coffins in total.

When both SUV's had been loaded, the men got back into their cars and drove off. Thornton stared for a few seconds at where they had been, uncertain as to what he had seen and what all the activity had meant. Where had the coffins come from, why were they delivered here, why were they wrapped in flags and why had the governors come to meet them, were all questions that occurred to him and which he could not yet answer.

His pilot Billy left the cockpit and walked back to Thornton's seat to check, as he always did, that the flight had been satisfactory for his boss. "Did you see that?" Thornton looked out of the window, indicating with a nod of his head the direction of his attention as he spoke. "Do you know what was going on there?"

Billy's gaze had indeed been caught by the little drama going on beside the sister aircraft. He looked again at the parked plane and said, "Let me do a search on the call sign. I don't immediately recognize the letters on the fuselage. I know quite a lot of the machines that fly around these parts – but not that one. That one is new to me."

Billy dictated the identifying code and then pushed back his sleeve to see the screen of his *iBand* phone. A second later the answer came back – that aircraft was registered to the Syracuse Freight Forwarding corporation. He did another search and said, "The aircraft is registered to a company with no web site but an address somewhere in Virginia. Probably some sort of military thing, them having no cyber presence an' all."

"Pretty likely," agreed Thornton, "What with those coffins and the governors being present. I wonder where it's come from?" With that query Billy could help. He had been flying into these Southern airports for long enough to know well the ground staff. "Give me a minute," he said. Billy made a few calls as they walked towards the terminal. A minute or so later he said, "It's from New Chaldea. It flew non-stop. That's why they needed such a long range aircraft."

"And so the bodies in those coffins, evidently Americans - from the flag - I wonder if they're dead emigrants or some sort of militia?" Thornton asked. He answered his own question, "Mercenaries is my guess. We may have sent a load of emigrants out there, to set up home, but they're unlikely to get flags if they return dead. They wouldn't get no governor to turn out for them, neither. I've known Carroll has been sending forces out there, even if they ain't official ones. Guess that's how they come back - in boxes."

Thornton had guessed right. The existence of the volunteer force was always denied, although the secret was became more open with each passing day. Cal's *Holy Warriors* as they were known, disparagingly, by the war's opponents. So they had died for their faith? Thornton tried to remember how martyrdom worked in the Catholic church. Or Protestant churches for that matter. These guys could have been Baptists. But his mind was blank on the issue. He'd have to talk to Carroll about all that, the next time they crossed paths.

That was about to be a lot sooner than he had anticipated. Thornton instructed his iPsyche to download the calls that he'd passed on while they had been in the air. To his surprise, there were several from Doug Huxley, his local Milton plant director. As Thornton scrolled through the list of missed calls he realized that there were not just a few such calls - but many, of increasing urgency. There was no message accompanying them apart from the request to phone Doug as soon as he landed. But Thornton didn't need to. Another call was coming through from Huxley right now.

"Doug, what's the problem?" Thornton asked, "I see you've been trying to get hold of me urgently."

The problem was simple. One of Blue Ridge client's factories, that built aerospace sub-assemblies, had been wrecked that morning. Series 5 Milton robots had been introduced a couple of months before. Large amounts of machinery had been smashed; the robot's integration manager, Holland Cooperman, who had been resident at the plant during their work-up period, had been kidnapped and forced to manipulate the programming codes to such an effect that the machines started to attack each other – and then the plant. Two robots had escaped and were roaming the countryside – not that they were likely to last long, the police were hunting them down, determined to destroy them before they did too much damage. Thornton recalled that there had been a history of poor relations between men and robots at this plant. Doug Huxley had warned local management earlier that the human workforce had been reduced too fast, creating tensions. But there had been no sign that things had got this bad.

He knew that the men pursuing the machines, however good their intentions, had to be stopped; the police and the vigilantes would not realize the strength or intelligence of their adversaries. They could be badly injured or killed by Miltons that had gone berserk. Doug suggested triggering the emergency AV codes, that would halt the rogue machines in their tracks but he also knew that, with the present level of anger against these robots, once they were disabled and defenceless, they would probably be attacked and broken up. These mobile, multi-tasking, self-motivating robots were expensive and he wanted Thornton's permission before releasing the inhibiting codes. Worker insurrection was explicitly excluded from Blue Ridge's insurance cover.

Yet there was no real alternative. Who knew the level of the mental corruption that the tampering with the robot's programming had caused? Or how much damage they could inflict before they being brought to a halt? "Yes, trigger the AV codes," Thornton instructed. A whiff of regret that he had to do so passed through his mind. These machines were so sentient; it was almost like killing off a family member.

As Thornton and Billy neared the industrial park, where the client had his plant, they could see the rising plume of smoke; fires caused by electrical shorts had not yet been extinguished. The entry road was blocked off by state patrolmen and they had to negotiate permission to pass the police barriers. Around the plant itself were a number of fire engines, with their accompaniment of hoses and dirty pools of water lying on the ground. Television trucks had parked themselves randomly to observe the scene. There were several ambulances too and Thornton dreaded to think of how many men might be injured. He could easily imagine what the local reaction to that might be.

He also noticed that, apart from the public services, there was a black SUV parked in front of the plant, that looked remarkably like the one he had just seen at the airport. Beyond that, a savagely torn hole in a factory wall, and another by the perimeter fence indicated the direction his prized new series 5 Milton robots had taken.

He stepped over one of the hoses and scrambled through the hole in the twisted siding that had once been a wall. Inside was chaos. Bits of machinery smashed and lying all over the floor, broken, shorted, control panels burnt away. The normally pristine and jolly environment, with painted white floors, and primary coloured machinery, had taken on an obscene tone, as though some vandal had purposely gone out to turn the aesthetics of the factory into industrial pornography. The colour scheme had been carefully, but evidently uselessly, chosen to ensure a sense of tranquillity. He saw Doug Huxley and Carroll Gillespie talking together and went over to join them, kicking away a circuit board as he did so, more a gesture of frustration than the fact that it blocked his path. Another man stood with them, smartly dressed, evidently not a police officer or a fireman. Thornton recognized him as the local, North Carolinian, governor who he had seen at the airfield.

He walked over and addressed the governor he knew best. “Hi Cal, I thought it was you I just saw earlier. But *Holy Heavens*, what a mess.” Thornton looked despondently at the ruined factory. He realized this was not a good time to ask why Carroll had been at the airport.

“I know folk are angry at the moment,” said Carroll. ”But I didn’t suspect something like this would happen. Just shows what people really think about these machines, I guess. By the way, do you know Sherman Barnes?” He turned and indicated the other man in a suit, standing to his left. “My colleague and friend, the governor here in North Carolina?” They shook hands.

Sherman Barnes spoke. “I’m sure glad there’s no reported loss of life, Mr Lamaire. Yet. I do hear reports – unconfirmed at the moment - that the machines may have been stopped. I should know very soon.”

“They will have stopped,” said Thornton authoritively. “I instructed them to shut down,” but as he said this he wondered how much damage to the surrounding countryside had been suffered before the AV codes were broadcast. Blue Ridge would have to pick up the bill for reparations.

"Well, I thank you for that," said Barnes. "But look what they've done here." He waved his arm from left to right, indicating the widespread destruction. "Never seen anything like it before. Anyway, we'll get the ring leaders who started the whole thing by tampering with the Miltons. We may all disapprove of these ungodly machines but this is no way to go about remedying the situation. Jobs are hard enough to come by these days and then people do this."

He turned to Huxley.

"Why isn't the integration manager here?" Barnes asked. "He could tell us the sequence of events, deliver an eye-witness account of how it came to this." But the integration manager was still hospitalized from the trauma of his kidnapping. He'd have to make do with Huxley. "Has there been some recent incident that might have triggered the guys' wrath?" he asked

"No especial one that I know of," replied Huxley. "But relations were not good. I'd warned the management here that they were imposing the Miltons too fast."

"So, a resentment ? What with these machines all comin' in and telling people, like, what to do?"

"At first the men seemed OK with it. I came down talked it through with the workforce. But these introductions are always difficult. But I thought it would all work out OK, in the end."

"Clearly that weren't the case," said Barnes, sarcastically

Huxley grew more defensive. "We only introduced the Miltons recently. I thought the men were…well, if not happy about them at least accepting of the situation."

"Well, so much for that hope," said Barnes, with the same '*how on earth did you think such a thing?*' tone to his voice. He turned to Thornton. "Why were these machines so provocative to the workforce, Mr Lamaire?"

"These series 5 Miltons, they're an entirely new generation of robot," explained Thornton. "They don't simply act out their program. They can *give* instructions to the human workforce about problems in the factory, on how to make the manufacturing process more efficient, for example. And they can travel anywhere in the plant to talk to a member of a team. They ARE a member of the teams themselves, in fact"

"But they were taking human's jobs from the teams?"

"That's always the case. Unfortunately, you may think," replied Thornton. "That's why we, and our clients, employ them. But simply replacing humans - that's not their main point."

"Which is? asked Barnes. " What *is* the point of the Miltons?"

"To resolve production issues, more intelligently, more quickly, with less waste, than any human can," replied Thornton. "But to do it nicely too"

"Do it nicely? That so? Doesn't seem to have impressed the guys who work here very much – all that *niceness*," said Barnes, with another sneer.

"They explain to the humans why things need doing, or changing," explained a patient Thornton. "They're programmed to do so in a non-patronizing manner – to make their instructions more acceptable. They want to be *liked*, as well as obeyed. These machines, well, they're a bit more than machines really, and they want to be appreciated. You should be …decent to them. They have feelings. That's what the recent Supreme Court decision in *Douglas v Milton Robotics* was all about." Thornton realized that it was a mistake to bring up the hated act.

"But they do *instruct* human workers, you said? They don't ask? They expect to be obeyed?"

"They ask the first time," said Thornton. "But yes, the humans have been told that they have to do what these Miltons tell them. After all, the Miltons will be right , always right– and it's because they will be correct every time that management buy them"

Sherman's phone rang. He took the call and then looked at Thornton. "They've found the two Miltons."

"Badly damaged?" enquired Thornton

"I've no idea. Nor care, either. One came to rest in a wood, the other in a church. They caused a lot of destruction before they finally stopped."

"That will be the result of the tampering," said Thornton, always wishing to defend his company's products.

"They seem to have been tampered with mighty easily, that's all I can say. Just what the people round here think about these things – they can't be trusted," replied Barnes.

Just then through the gaping hole in the side of the perimeter fence there stepped a grey haired man, with a heavily tanned, withered, gaunt face, dressed in plaid shirt and jeans. He looked shocked and angry and strode up to Sherman.

"My name's Jim Embry an' I hears you were here. I sure wanted to see you. One of my barns has been knocked down. I've lost any number of calves. My cattle gone into a state of shock, my wife is beyond terrified. These ungodly machines ain't fit to be amongst us. They should be banned and the people who build them strung up!"

Sherman twisted his body in Thornton's direction and pointed to Jim Embry where he should direct his wrath. "This is the man you want Jim," said the North Carolina governor, helpfully. "We need further safeguards on these new robots…. well, that I promise you. That will happen in the New Confederacy"

"Ain't no matter of *jus*t safeguards" replied Jim Embry, with venom in his tone. "Ain't surprised the guys working here took against them. Who wants to be told what to do by a heap of metal! Now look at what they done. They're agin' Gods purpose, these machines."

Thornton broke in, "I understand, Mr Embry. I'm extremely sorry about what happened. I will see to it personally that you are fully compensated."

But this attempt at being emollient was quite inadequate to Jim Embry's rage. The farmer looked at Thornton fiercely, "That's just typical of you folk. You just come and do your sacrilegious thing, challenge the Lord to see if you can make something half as smart as what he done, and then – when it all goes wrong – you think you can buy your way out of trouble. Well, sure you can compensate me and make good the loss your unholy thugs have caused. But don't think that's the end of it. Nor sir, no way. Because it ain't !"

Sherman Barnes understood that nothing was going to mollify Jim Embry at the moment but at least he'd better try to defuse the bitter altercation. "Gentleman, gentleman – let's go and inspect the damage first and see what needs to be done. Thornton, I think you need to come with us, if you would?"

The five of them piled into the two SUV's and set off in the direction of Embry's farm. Along the way they caught glimpses of fallen trees, wrecked buildings and in one or two places power lines had come down. With guidance from the farmer, they eventually came to a wood. The damage here was extensive; a lane had been ripped straight through the undergrowth and the jagged ends of split branches stuck out like natural barbed wire that barred their way. They drove through slowly, the torn bushes and trees dragging and scratching on the car as they passed. Then they found one of the Miltons, slumped against a tree, its limbs disorganized in its death throes when the power had been cut suddenly, when the AV code had been received.

As they exited the other side of the wood they saw Jim's farm and a chapel just beyond. For some reason, no doubt to do with the codes the workers had managed to corrupt, one of the Miltons had continued straight through a barn, on passage to its final resting place, not deviating to the left or right. It could have easily avoided Jim's barn but whether it had *chosen* not to do so or it had just pressed on blindly, confused and eyeless as its tampered codes befuddled its mind, that was something only a later inspection of its memory banks would reveal.

In a way, the farmer and his family had been fortunate – not that they were in a mood to appreciate that. Although a corner of their house had been torn off by the robot's pell-mell progress, if it had veered a few yards to the left in its passage the house would have been demolished. Several cows, including those who had aborted from the shock, had been penned into a small paddock next to the house. As they discovered as they entered the ruined barn, those cows were the lucky ones. Others lay around, moaning, badly wounded by the fury of the rampage. A vet was kneeling, shooting these beasts that were beyond the help of his medicine and treatments.

The party continued on their gloomy progress until they entered the chapel. This Milton, the second, had simply walked through the end wall. Thornton thought idly that even if the machine had been better behaved and tried the door, the opening would have been too small for it anyway.

At the end, in front of the altar, lay the crumpled Milton, a great heap of collapsed limbs. It looked more like a metallic octopus than a human. Although it would normally walk on two limbs, its 'legs', it possessed no real body but had six 'arms' so that it could perform multiple operations in the plant simultaneously. What appeared to be a body was not much more a hub in which to locate the bearings of its limbs, and a battery pack. Above the hub was a revolving turret, containing its optical sensors. Short antennae hung lankly from the limbs; additional sensors providing inputs that its brain needed to perform designed tasks. Unlike an octopus, which it vaguely resembled, Milton robots had great proprioception.

That this machine had finally collapsed in front of an altar, was noted. Did it mean something? Was this just an accident of time and place or had the Milton sought out the chapel on purpose, seeking this final resting ground for when the shut-down message arrived?

The five men stood around the tangled heap feeling uneasy. Had this semi-conscious device been seeking this chapel to destroy it …or had it come here seeking a form of solace? It would have been easy to identify the chapel from GPS if it had wanted to find and avoid it. The idea that this *thing,* whose outer carapace was fabricated in dull bronze *T*-composite, might have been sufficiently like a human that it had sought a relationship with some supreme being when it wanted to end its days, was too bizarre to contemplate. Those standing around representing Homo sapiens did not welcome the implication that they might have spiritual kinship with something they only understood as a *machine.* But then they didn't welcome the other possibility either; that the Milton had purposely come to destroy what the humans found sacred.

Carroll was the first to speak. "This break out's already all over the news. Folks are going to get really spooked if they learn the Milton died in front of an altar. They're already turning to a belief in witchcraft – the last thing Sherman and I need is the idea going around that the machines are attacking our places of worship." He turned and addressed Embry, "Jim, I'd ask you not to say anything about this at the moment – at least not about where this robot ended its life."

Jim Embry looked even more unhappy than he had twenty minutes before, "These things are evil, evil. YOU ..." and he pointed an accusing finger at Thornton, "you are the monster here. You've created something that will destroy all of us. You summoned a demon, that's what you done. Like, this thing attacks that which is Godly, attacks His creatures, it attacks His holy places. *You* will go to hell and burn there. And that can't happen soon enough for me!"

Thornton knew that it was no good him pointing out that he had nothing to do with this...this *inciden*t. The machines had been properly programmed when they left the factory. Was it his fault that others had corrupted them? But he was known throughout the South as the owner of the firm that built such machines. He was the proprietor of Blue Ridge, whose creations were self-evidently sinister and a trampling on the order of nature. Thornton was lost for an adequate response because he knew he was guilty. He knew his sin, the imperative to ensure that his company out-competed its rivals, remain at the front of its field, had driven him to invest in ever more sophisticated, and risky, ill-understood technologies. Now his hubris had resulted in this unhappy man he saw before him and the trail of destruction that lay behind. They all, but particularly

Jim Embry and his family, had been very fortunate that nobody had been killed that morning.

Sherman Barnes put an arm around Jim to comfort him and led him back to his house. No doubt he was going to reassure the family over some coffee, a skill he was known to be famous for. Carroll said to Thornton, "I've got to get back. I've got to accompany one of our fallen to a funeral tomorrow. I've no doubt Sherman will be in touch with you. There'll be an enquiry. And you and I need a chat. Folks were not happy before with the way things are going and they're going to be a whole lot less happy after this. Quite soon, Thornton, as I've warned you, you're going to have to answer to public anger. You need to be prepared." What was the most suitable preparation for the situation Thornton would soon find himself in, Carroll gave no clue. Perhaps he didn't know himself.

"Can I give you a lift, Carroll?" offered Thornton, wanting to be placatory. "My plane is here and it will be much faster for you than flying commercial. It's late now. The bodies of the fallen I saw you with at the airport, they can come with us or go back with your driver." At least the flight together would give him a good opportunity to learn what was going through the governor's mind – and what all the business with the coffins was about.

"One last thing," said Sherman Barnes as he turned to go to his own car. "The state will want to hold onto the Miltons for a few days while we carry out an investigation into all this. So don't send anyone to collect them. Not just yet."

Chapter 30

A suggestion from Carroll Gillespie

The flight back was not quite as Thornton had imagined it might be. He had expected to be harassed about the events at his North Carolinian plant, to be warned again about how threatened his operations might become, but the Governor's conversation on the ride back was, initially at least, about something different.

It was a beautiful late afternoon for flying and they were soon out of the turbulence they encountered immediately after take-off. They reached cruise height and Clarence brought them both coffee as they admired the states of the Southern Confederacy stretched out before them; the still dense forests, the eponymous Blue Ridge mountains and, far off, the silver thread of the Mississippi; the shadows from the setting sun lending the landscape an exaggerated scale. From 46,000 feet the world looked as it might have done after the first settlers arrived 400 years earlier, the first white Europeans at any rate; resplendent, beautiful in the reddish, orange, light. No observer, unfamiliar with the present political situation, some visitor from the planet Mars perhaps, would have looked down on this example of God's own country and divined the social turmoil below, or the spiritual turmoil - as the local inhabitants struggled with the implications of sharing their realm with intelligent creatures, not made from carbon, with no idea whether this advance in human affairs, if such it was, would turn out for good or ill.

Thornton felt compelled to ask about the coffins and from whence they had come, warily conscious that in so doing he gave Carroll an excuse to pursue his favourite subject. "The bodies you saw unloaded were those of brave men fighting in New Chaldea," said Carroll. "We keep it quiet, of course, but for some time now there have been, what shall I call them? *Friends* of ours – young brave men and women, but mostly men, who've gone out to New Chaldea to fight for a just settlement there. And to protect the equally brave settlers who emigrated to enlarge the Christian presence."

"Things getting worse then, Carroll, out there?" Thornton wanted to sound sympathetic with the Governor's great obsession but the words as they came out sounded supercilious. Carroll seemed not to notice, or if he did, he ignored it.

"Not quite full civil war there…yet," said the Governor. "But there have been many deaths and the situation is daily getting worse, yes."

"How about the local police. They can't keep the lid on things?" asked Thornton.

"They have been overwhelmed. So now the fledgling army has stepped in. It is meant to be a multi–ethnic force. But whether it is or not, as you have probably read, the army have deposed the democratically elected president and installed one of their own as leader – who has effectively become dictator. One of his first acts has been the banning of public religious festivals, in the name of lowering domestic tensions. Imagine! This was meant to be a multi-faith theocracy, something new in the world, where the worship of God would be a foundation stone. Yet now none of them can even celebrate what they believe in. Even now, in the past few weeks, comes fresh news of troubles ……reports of massacres by some local militia or other. Of course, there's an outcry and a demand that the guarantee nations intervene. But everyone's exhausted. People here…there's a real loss of enthusiasm for a return to battle, even when they know the vision must be protected. You remember Jefferson's words? '*The tree of liberty must be watered, from time to time, with the blood of patriots.*' No less true in the Middle East than here. I can tell you Thornton, I'm real worried. I can't see nothing for it, but we've got to intervene and defend our fellow worshippers. That's what that poor fellow, Rick Muldane, God bless his soul, one of those whom you saw in them coffins, lost his life doing. People like Rick, heck, they're doing a fantastic job as volunteers – but they're too few of them, too badly armed, and, sad to say, they're losing."

Carroll was absolutely correct in his view that there was no sign of public opinion favouring intervention, even if it were fellow Christians who were on the receiving end of much of the violence in New Chaldea. The public had long memories; Vietnam had been forgotten but most of the voters could still remember Iraq, Afghanistan, Syria, Iran, then Egypt. Those wars……they'd started with the best of intentions; no one went to war now except to make things *better*, to bring peace, to help build nations, reconcile waring tribes. But instead of democracy, they just got bodies. Things did not work out quite as hoped.

"While the voters still remember the consequences of our efforts in that part of the world there's no chance of us going back again," continued Carroll. "Of course, things change – another outrage or two and the climate may reverse."

Thornton was more cynical. "The cycle is always the same Cal; enough massacres and the public demands something must be done. When the body bags come home, they demand we must get out. My dear old friend, there's a very long way to go before any of the voters here will support open intervention, again."

Carroll pulled at a seam on his trousers, a mannerism that Thornton had noticed before when the governor was about to ask for something. Thornton steeled himself to give away a little more money. But that wasn't what was wanted.

"You know Thornton. We need much larger support from the voters than we've been getting, if we're ever going to win this thing. Folks are just not persuaded that this is real important to them. Yet you can't just ignore what's happening to your faith just because the problem is far away. We' got to tell them – we partake in all mankind. Or at least that part of mankind that follows our Lord."

"Sure," said Thornton, in an uncommitted way, wondering where this was going and suspecting that he wasn't going to like the destination when it arrived.

"And I've been thinking," said Carroll. "That maybe your group, Blue Ridge, could do something. You being in news an' all that. "

"We have tried," said Thornton, relieved that some free publicity might be all the price that he had to pay – apart from cash. "I've instructed my editors that's our line. That more's got to be done out there, in New Chaldea. That we need to offer all the support we can muster. The beacon of Christianity must not be allowed to be extinguished! We've done all that. And we'll continue to pursue the same line – but there's resistance. We don't get the message back that all this is falling on very receptive ears."

The governor tried to look sympathetic, "You've done a lot, Thornton, no question. But, as you say, we don't seem to be making much of an impact. Maybe there are other ways? "

"Other ways?" Thornton had no idea what Carroll was driving at.

Carroll twisted his head and looked out of one of the ports, as though in discomfort about what he was about to ask. "You've got all these fancy new devices I hear about that enter people's minds and put things there." Carroll turned back and faced Thornton, giving him a direct look. "Maybe we could go beyond the old methods? You know, talking to people through *articles, opinion pieces* and such like. Maybe we could address them directly, to their minds, without them folks having to do anything arduous, like ...... *reading,* say." Carroll smiled at his little joke.

Mind manipulation? Is that what was being suggested here? Had he heard right? Startled by what he thought he had understood, almost blasphemy coming from Carroll, Thornton said, "You're mixing my business up with Apple's. You're right that their iPsyche*s* can talk directly to people's minds. But that's them, not us."

"But the content, the words, the ideas, Thornton," said Carroll, impatiently. "What goes down Apple's tubes into them iPsyche devices – that's from you. Or at least from your editors."

"That's maybe true," agreed Thornton, hesitantly. "But there's no way we can access all those millions of iPsyches. Not without their user's say so. There's laws 'gainst that sort of thing. They have to give us permission to enter their mental space."

"Just sayin', just sayin', my friend," said Carroll agreeably. "I sure know nothing about the whys and the wherefores. All that technology thing was never strong in me. I've probably got it all wrong, anyhow."

At that point there was a sudden jolt of the plane and Thornton's coffee took a leap, before landing in his lap. It might have been half drunk and not quite as hot as a few minutes before but he still swore," *Holy Heavens*!". The turbulence was short lived, but severe, and both men tensed silently as the plane passed through the troubled piece of atmosphere. When it was over, Clarence came up to mop up the mess and to ask Thornton whether he wanted to change, his overnight bag being stowed in the cabin. Carroll looked up at him and said, "Clarence, let me ask you something. Do you wear one of these new-fangled iPsyches?"

Clarence was surprised, unused to being addressed by the governor. He replied in his best Jeevonese. "Certainly not sir. What they call iPsyches, as much as I understand them, are not, I think, for the likes of me. I wouldn't presume anyone is interested in sharing the modest thoughts of my good self, sir"

“And would Mr Clarence be interested in having thoughts put *into* his head?” asked the governor

“Too late for that, sir, I fear. I would doubt there is much room left for any ideas, new or otherwise, anymore,” Clarence said, tapping his skull for emphasis.

“But if we could,” Carroll insisted in a friendly, teasing tone of voice. “If we could just find a little space somewhere, for something really useful?”

“It’s very kind of you sir,” replied Clarence. “But no, I don’t think so. From what I have been reading the technology, well, I’ll give it a few more years, sir, before Clarence goes that way.”

Carroll was not surprised that Clarence had been following the scientific debate. He had long had the opinion that Clarence was at least as smart as his boss. “So, you don’t agree with your Mr Thornton and what he does?” Carrol asked. Thornton saw that the governor was unsettling Clarence, who did not want to be disloyal and be forced to admit there might be anything objectionable about his employer’s business. “Do you think then……..we should ask Mr Lamaire to stop him doing what he does with people’s minds?” asked Carroll, with a grin.

Clarence delivered a Delphic reply, “I’m sure Mr Lamaire knows exactly what he’s doing and what’s for the best,” he said loyally. With that Clarence beat a retreat and went to find a clean pair of trousers for his boss.

Carroll watched him as he walked down the aisle and shook his head gently, “Well, Thornton, you sure got a fan there. Not like poor old Jim Embry, he was right angry with you. Don’t know how all that’s going to pan out. By the time we reach Baton Rouge I guess the news of the destruction will be everywhere. There’s going to be a mighty lot of pressure on me to clamp down on those machines. We see the drawbacks, eh? Lot of folk will want them banned. And if we don’t ban them, then what’s after that? They’re hardly going to allow the next generation be introduced, do you think? *Conscious* machines? Even if that’s a not a contradiction in my book. No, I don't see it. Might not be worth investing all that money in MARIONn after all, huh?"

But then the governor added, more congenially, "I could talk to the bishops, Thornton. They used to be, indeed still are, friends of mine. I'm sure they can persuade their flock not to rush to judgement in this matter. To hold their anger, as it were, not to direct it at you. To understand there are two sides on this. Know what I'm sayin'? You're doing some really helpful work on New Chaldea, Thornton. Maybe more can be done, I don't know. And I wouldn't want all that spoilt by people getting the wrong end of the stick about your businesses. To my mind, and the mind of most folk, there's always been advances in science and most of them have been for the good. Not all, and we need to be watchful, but folk still listen when the bishops and the fathers address them. My guess is that they could take a lot of the heat out of this rogue Milton thing if they was so inclined. We just got to make him so inclined, ain't we Thornton?"

Thornton nodded dumbly in agreement. He was not entirely sure what he was being asked to do but he was sure that if he didn't deliver the right answer for Carroll then the unhappy fate of Jim Embry and his miscarrying cows would lead to repercussions that he would not like. The public mood would be massaged in a way that would be threatening to Blue Ridge and its interests, and maybe to him personally. He could forget trying to market *LetheTech* in the South for a start.

The plane began to let down and 10 minutes or so later they were on the ground. Thornton checked his iPsyche. Just as he feared, and Carroll had prophesied, the events at Jim Embry's farm had created a storm. It would take all of the Governor's talents to deflect it – if he chose to do so. Thornton would have to reflect further on the governor's words. No offer of help, even if it came with an unappetising price, could be disregarded at the moment.

Chapter 31

Auto da Fe

It had been the consensus of political commentators that once the plebiscite was over, and the result known, then the political turmoil between North and South, between Coast and Mid-West, between secularists and evangelicals, between those who felt unthreatened by the coming of artificial consciousness and those who thought it blasphemy, would begin to settle and a new harmony would arise. But such had not been the case, at all. If before the vote the body-politic had existed in an ill-defined, uncertain state, it had now become polarized. Like Schrodinger's cat, everything previously had been indefinite, a cloud of probability, a mere haze of possible outcomes. But now that the vote had crystallized the divisions in the country, that haziness had collapsed into a definitive decision and everyone found themselves one side or the other of a rigid dividing line; inchoate points of view became rigid, settled, cultural preferences. Families, friends, colleagues discovered to their discomfort they could not straddle the crevasse that opened up and threatened to swallow the country.

Everything was affected by the split – from where people chose to live, to the system of government, to AI regulation, to the trade between the states. In spite of the fact that implementation of the plebiscite, and the revision to the Constitution that would establish the new Confederacy, would take another two years, attitudes changed fast, way ahead of any legislation by either side. The South instantly became more protectionist as they sought to preserve their independent view of what should be permitted in their society in the future.

In-spite of the increasingly bitter stand-off, there were still commercial flights between the two sides of the division, but fewer than before. Some years earlier, it was hoped that the East Coast Hyperloop, a spur of which had been planned to reach Houston, might connect the two disparate populations but the money ran out when it had only reached Washington. So Carroll Gillespie's nephew Euclid had few options if he wished to accept his Uncle's invitation for the weekend. It was too far to drive, there were no train services that connected New York and Baton Rouge - so an aircraft it would have to be, if he could find a flight. But he looked at this prospect with no enthusiasm. Euclid was a nervous flyer and the recent shooting down of a civil airliner by a dissident rural group had not made the prospect of the flight any more welcome. Even the most pro-secessionists in the South had been appalled by that outrage, a step too far surely – however they felt about their fellows above the Mason-Dixon line. The terrorist gang had been quickly captured but who knew if there were not sympathizers out there, similarly armed?

Euclid reached the Governor's mansion safely enough. In spite of the travel hazards, he loved visiting the Gillespie's; the style of life was so different to his austere one in the Berkshire woods. Here, his every need was attended to; the abundance and richness of the food something he did not receive at the MARIONn staff canteen. And then of course there was the warmth of the good governor's wife, Kirsty, who he imagined himself at least half in love with. She was so much nicer to him than her three, beautiful, southern–belle daughters; the three Swans as they were known locally on account of the whiteness of their skin and, no doubt, the length of their elegant necks. Euclid might have loved any one of them if he had been either encouraged or permitted to do so. But the sad truth was that none of the Swans had the slightest interest; they viewed him as neither handsome, rich, sporty nor fun – at least two out of these four properties a man would need if he were to be looked on as a potential suitor. Euclid could only count on his intelligence and his faith; qualities that were not of sufficient interest to get him to the first base of courtship. But this was no longer the disappointment to him that it had once been, merely a bitter fact of life that he had to contend with on his visits to the Gillespie's. And in truth, once he had accustomed himself to the frustration of failing to arouse the slightest emotion in the breasts of these proud girls the discontent that he had once felt in his soul no longer burnt quite so fiercely.

The night after his arrival Euclid discovered that the entire family were to go to an evening service, but not in a church. The service would be held in the open air. It was going to be a happy event, for it was a celebration – the celebration of Jim Embry's deliverance from the Miltons. The attack of the two robots – for that, locally, was what their rampage through Embry's farm was now being described as – could so easily have ended in bloodshed and sorrow. Instead, the Lord had diverted the machines from crushing Jim and his family, although some cynics thought the Lord could have gone a little further and diverted the robots entirely away from Jim's house and cattle at the same time. Still, it was agreed by even those most sceptical of God's purposes that it had been a very meaningful gesture to end the rampage at the foot of an altar. It was fitting that He had demanded that the Miltons, or at least one of them anyway, for the story had not grown any more accurate in the repeated telling, should kneel in His presence. A remarkable witness to His power, Euclid agreed with Kirsty. But he held his tongue when asked to agree, "Wasn't it all just evidence that these new robots were a step too far? Hadn't people been right when they said that machines were beginning to get *uppity*? Too confident in their own abilities? Too much thinking they might be almost human? Not knowing their place in the order of things?"

Euclid murmured something that was meant to sound supportive, but it came out as a sort of gurgle; vocal evidence of his own inner conflict. He might be a Christian but he was engaged in research with artificial intelligence at the highest level. He never revealed his job in too much detail to Kirsty, or the three Swans, in case they were shocked. But he knew that they knew, that his career involved doing *something* with robots, even if neither party, for the sake of their ongoing relationship, wanted to focus too specifically on what that *something* might entail exactly. But as far as his uncle Cal was concerned, Euclid was in no doubt. This was a man who took it upon himself to be informed about what everybody who fell into his orbit might be up to. Including his nephew. For how fortunate for him that Euclid was employed at the very heart of research into the next big thing in AI, the conscious machine.

They, that is the whole family except the governor – for he was going to join them later - set out to the 'service' at about 7, as the light began to fall. They drove for about 45 minutes, chatting lightly in the car. Kirsty promised there would be a 'surprise' at the service – but refused to spoil the suspense by providing any clues as to its identity. At last they turned off the road and proceeded down an earthen track that gave onto a large sandy plain, dotted with scrubby bushes. This was being used as a car park. They got down from their car and walked on for another half a mile along a path, until they found themselves on a dried-out river bed. The river, that only flowed after heavy rain, was for its most part constrained within tight banks, that had been cut through the valley floor by the waters. But here it had widened from its normal course and formed an almost circular pan, with a floor of pebbles and gravel. The banks of this pan were much lower than in the higher reaches of the river and the gentler current had chamfered them off at a 45 degree angle, instead of the almost vertical cliffs elsewhere, creating a natural shallow amphitheatre - in which now sat or stood several thousand people, the congregation for the night.

At the centre of the crowd, Euclid saw a substantial wooden structure, whose thick timbers were laid alternately cross-ways on each other. The mass of wood formed a tower that rose layer by layer above the river floor. But it was what was at the top that caught his eye. At the limit of the crossed timbers sat a platform, square and quite wide, upon which rested a crumpled mass of some dull-coloured, but reflective, material. On more concentrated inspection, it was evident that the mass was made up of two crumpled creatures, two collapsed puppets that had been thrown there haphazardly; puppets whose strings had been cut, allowing their limbs to fall any old way, chaotically.

There were flares stuck in the bed of the river and the light from these caught and reflected back golden glows from the surface of the strange tangle on the platform. At first Euclid was not sure what he was looking at. In the dark, and with the congregation obstructing a clear line of sight, it was difficult to identify exactly what was up there on the platform. He walked to another side to get a better view. He managed to make out limb-like extrusions that were attached to two central hubs. There were no heads visible on these forms and, apart from the hubs, precious little that could be described as 'bodies' of whatever these were. Then he understood. These were the Milton robots that had been recovered from the unfortunate farmer's land.

The crowd had grown to a considerable size by now and Euclid was buffeted by the swirling mass of people. They were good humoured for the most part, not too much cussing as they bumped into each other, as they might - for most had a glass of something in one hand and a burger or rib wrapped in bread in the other.

The smell of burnt meat, beer and marijuana lay stagnant upon the congregation; the insalubrious haze prevented from dispersing by the river's containing banks and the windless night. At some point the odour of an accelerant, gasoline or kerosene, added itself to the mix. Then, suddenly the crowd stilled and there was a hush, followed a few seconds later by a great cheer and the crowd parted to let the governor through. He passed like the old-seasoned pro of a politician that he was, shaking hands, greeting supporters, while making his way to the wooden tower. He caught sight briefly of his wife and step-daughters and waved but made no attempt to join them. This was work.

Carroll Gillespie at last reached the base of the wooden structure. He was lifted by his acolytes, rather than climbed, to a point a few feet up, where Euclid could see the timbers had been so arranged as to make it possible for a man to stand, if a little insecurely. Once there, Carroll braced himself, one hand behind grasping the wood, one hand stretched in front, showing the crowd the flat of his palm, in a gesture half-way between acknowledgement and a request for them to be still, silent. At last the tumult settled, and the governor spoke:

"My friends, folks, fellow Christians. We are here tonight to give thanks…" Whoops from the crowd, "*yes we are, yes we are*!" they shouted, "…..to give thanks that the life of our good friend, and follower of the Lord, Jim Embry, has been spared." More whoops followed. "Jim almost lost his life because he was set upon…..set upon by monstrous creatures. Jim was born into a righteous family over 40 years ago. Never would he have expected to see in his lifetime such fiends that threatened him a few days ago. For…." the governor paused for effect. "…Jim, the righteous and God-fearing Jim Embry, was attacked by creatures that were raised up out of the dust not by our Lord, *but by man.* Things created out of man's vanity, by those that think they can copy God, that they can make something as wonderful, as unique, as sacred as that which He makes, every day, in His own image. Some even think that their new inventions will be even better than what our Maker had in mind!"

"No! It shall not be! Find the men, find them! Destroy them! They shall not be!" The cries rang out from the crowd.

The governor waited for the cries to still, then went on. "God guided these creatures; creatures? For what can I call these things?" he shouted, rhetorically. And here Carroll raised his free hand and pointed at the tumbled mass above him, "these *things, ...things* that those who gave them motion, for we cannot call their existence..... *life*, claim to be almost, *almost*, human. These things that the judges in the North said have feelings, emotions, love perhaps – who knows? But did they have love or care or benevolence, when they set themselves along a path to destroy Jim's home and everything in their unfortunate path?"

"*No! NO! they did not, they did not*!" came back the response from the crowd.

"Have we not seen enough already of what these things can do?" he asked. "*We have, we have!* " returned the cry. "They've taken your jobs, they've destroyed your cattle, what next will they do?" shouted Gillespie, his voice rising as he gave vent to his anger. "*No more, no more!*" cried the crowd.

The governor's voice slid down an octave. With a slow, deeper, cadence he said, "No, no more. We shall no more allow these creatures to mimic us, to pretend that they too are like us, the true children of God. We will defy them, we will not allow them in our midst." *"No more! no more*!" cried the crowd. "So let us then give thanks to the Lord that protected Jim from their evil and let us give thanks that He has warned us of what these machines, born from man's hubris and sinful ways, are capable of. Show our thanks and ask for God's continuing mercy on us."

"*We do, we do give thanks*!" responded the crowd.

A silence fell upon the congregation. Some remained standing and put their hands together in prayer, bowing their heads as they did so. Others collapsed on their knees. The once time Bishop of the Alexandra diocese held his palm out in benediction and cast his eyes to the heavens as he led them in prayer, the one member of the congregation who seemed permitted to look up, in direct communication with their shared God, rather than down, in humble submission. He drew down upon them words of penitence, which they declaimed after him. At the end of the prayer he said nothing but waited, leaving each with the opportunity for a silent, personal, address. Then, a man advanced out of the crowd bearing a blazing brand that he handed to Carroll. He took it and thrust the brand into the wooden tower, deep amongst the timbers of the pyre.

The flames took hold immediately and within seconds the whole structure was ablaze. Hearing the crackle of the logs, the crowd looked up and cheered. Soon, the wooden platform that the Miltons were upon started to burn too. The heat forced the congregation back and as they retreated the limp limbs of the robots began to twist, extend themselves, shoot upwards in an obscene manner. Their bodies of T-Composite reached its ignition temperature, the blaze and heat abetted by the plastics, wiring and hydraulic fluid the machines still contained, assisting the flames. Those amongst the crowd who had received word of what was planned, and had brought various inflammable substances with them, pushed forward to add their contribution - but the heat was so intense they could not get near. They had no need really; the writhing of the Milton's limbs, expanding and twisting in the heat, was enough of a violent spectacle not to require any further enhancement.

Once the flames subsided a little, the wooden tower began to glow with the red heat of its carbonized wood, while thermal stresses in the bodies of the robots overcame the strength of their joints. With an immense crack, a limb belonging to one of the Miltons separated and spun across the crowd, landing on an unlucky individual. Other pieces flew over the heads of the congregation till they too fell on groups of worshippers. A red hot piece of T-composite struck a petrol can. As screams of the afflicted pierced the night air, stewards realized that they had not maintained a wide enough cordon around the burning tower and started to push the crowd back. They were much too late. A few seconds later the entire edifice collapsed; the timbers having at last burnt through, scattering burning pieces of wood and robot in a wide arc. At the centre of this pool of fire lay the remains of the machines; now split into their constituent parts, their limbs no longer attached to the hubs but amputated, as though some animating force had torn them off, like chicken wings at a barbeque.

But by this time there were few watching the agony of the Miltons, the attention having shifted to those who were trying to assist the injured. The governor was at the forefront of the efforts, giving comfort as best he could and trying to stop well-meaning members of the congregation from ripping up their clothing, wetting it from their water bottles and dressing the wounds. He knew the cloth would stick to the scorched flesh and make matters worse. There was not much to do except wait for the ambulances to arrive. Kirsty came up to him and he spoke to her, saying that she should take her nieces and Euclid back to the mansion and he would follow on when he could. But it would be a late night for him.

Chapter 32

Aftermath

The next morning the mood at the Governor's mansion was sombre, bleak. The family sat around the breakfast table, an exhausted Carroll at the head. He had called the local hospitals and although most of the burnt were generally doing OK, five or six were in serious condition and under sedation. "The marshals should have held everyone further back," he said. "Apparently no-one had thought to check when T-composite ignites." 11 people had died

"Bloody things, those Miltons" exclaimed Kirsty from the other end of the table. "They cause damage when they're alive and hurt us even when they're dead. Is this what the great AI revolution promised us? We were told to be nice to them, to treat them like people but look at what they do to us. I don't want to turn those *machines* into human beings, for sure I don't. They have an evil about them. And to think we've got judges.... Ok they're N*orthern* judges, but, same, telling us that these things got feelings? Well, I just want to show them Jim Embry's farm, I really do. And the destruction last night. It's disgusting that folks could ever consider respecting Miltons the same as our own flesh and blood."

The governor looked down the table. He knew that this sort of conversation was being held that Sunday morning in half the breakfast tables of the South. The events of last night would be picked up by every pastor preaching that day. And how would he come out of that assessment? He had promoted that service last night, that terrible *suttee* of the damaged robots, believing it would act as a catharsis and release the anger that had engulfed his people. He knew, even if it were an impossible thing to say right now, that the South could not entirely live without AI or robots. There had to be some accommodation with the future. Robots were a fact of life and it would do no good for the people to be totally opposed to them, even if he, as governor and president-elect of the Southern Confederacy, was determined to minimize their impact. Hate would be directed against the Blue Ridge corporation, inevitably, but that was also the sort of high tech employer that the state needed – a bit.

Gillespie knew that now the animosity against the machines would intensify. His wife's reaction would be typical of many. Calvin Roberts, his leading opponent, was already on the radio this morning, ranting away, taking a harder line on the possession and use of robots. They had both run in the last election on a platform of legislating against *Douglas v Milton Robotics* but he could see that this was not going to be enough. Calvin would threaten to outflank him, propose punitive measures against manufacturers - and maybe even operators - of robots that claimed human-like characteristics.

Had Thornton read the runes this morning? Did he have an appreciation yet of how much difficulty his industries might suffer in the future? It was all very well for him to carry out his most controversial research up in the North, where he thought himself out of sight and out of mind, but the North and South were not hermetically sealed from one another, even now. Thornton and his companies were such a big presence locally; there was always interest in what he was up to. The widely publicized news of

LetheTech's failure to launch its IPO had concentrated people's minds on what the company was trying to sell. M*emory manipulation*, even if that were dressed up in some fancy euphemism, had confirmed what many in the South suspected; Thornton was engaged in tampering with people's minds. *The Management of Loss* might be a smart corporate slogan but increasingly the promise of effective, on-line and available to all, therapy hardly looked worth the price - however inexpensive automation would make it. The corruption of Kinnead O'Neal's own mind, and several others that had come to light subsequently, added to the popular view that Thornton's work was beyond what nature permitted – and *what was unnatural was ungodly*. And what was ungodly needed, quite soon, to be suppressed. Another word would be required with Thornton, that was for sure.

Carroll made a move to get up from the table. He needed to get on, he needed to visit the injured in hospital. Then he remembered. He'd promised to spend some time with his nephew Euclid before he went back up North. Well, he would see him when he returned from the hospital, or maybe this evening before dinner. He knew Euclid had taken Monday off and would not be returning to the North just yet. There would be time still to find out what further developments were coming their way from Blue Ridge's work. How far had their MARIONn project got right now? A talk with his nephew was definitely not to be skipped.

Chapter 33

At the grave side

About a week later, while the furore over the rogue Miltons and the subsequent injuries at the '*service*' still raged, there was the funeral of one of the volunteer mercenaries, Rick Muldane, whose coffin Thornton had seen at the airport. Carroll Gillespie had agreed to show his respects and provide a eulogy. His star was certainly not at its highest at the moment, a lot of blowback had come his way after the injuries at the *suttee* of the Miltons, stirred up ably by Calvin Roberts. Still, this was a good opportunity to talk about the necessity of intervention in New Chaldea. At least it would make a change from the problems of AI in the New Confederacy and a good speech at the grave side might divert attention from recent disasters.

But he'd have to parse what he had to say carefully. Just as he was taking up the role of president-elect he didn't want to be associated with nothing but problems. The Christians were getting pushed back in New Chaldea and unless a great deal more men were committed the end result was clear – defeat. The case for proper intervention was strong, in his view at least, but he knew that the North and the Coastal states would not join him. Perhaps that didn't matter, even without them there were all those Southern Christians, tens of millions of people who would potentially support the effort. Only one per cent of one per cent of them would need to be personally involved. 10,000 soldiers for Christ? That should be enough.

All he had to do was to persuade the voters that this was a good idea. It didn't help that Calvin Roberts was much more cautious than himself on this issue. No matter, if out-flanked by Calvin on robotics, he would out-flank him on New Chaldea. He would turn the tide of public opinion – single handed if necessary. Only the means of doing so was not yet obvious. But it would become so, he was sure. God would show him a way.

In the end, Carroll decided that whatever he chose to say at Rick Muldane's grave side, the eulogy needed to be short and not *too* political. Otherwise he would be criticized again and he had a belly of that this month. It was time to restore his standing, so he restricted his remarks to a discussion of the short life of Muldane. He hoped that as the circumstances of the young man's death became more widely known, they would provide the very propaganda push that he had chosen to avoid that morning, at least too obviously.

At the end of the funeral, and the delivery of his eulogy completed Carroll spotted Thornton across the crowd of mourners, himself an acquaintance of the Muldane family and who had come to pay his respects. He walked over to talk to him.

"Do you believe in the after- life, Mr Lamaire?"

The question caught Thornton by surprise. He had been mulling his own thoughts as he walked from the service to the open grave, unexpectedly moved by the governor's words in the eulogy. He had known Rick not too well but a little; the Muldane's had been distant acquaintances of his and Bethany's. As always, he was saddened by just how young the dead soldiers who volunteered to go to war seemed to be. Rick had been just 19. It was always the young who were filled with the wild and un-calculating enthusiasm that inspired them to fly to distant conflicts – and be killed there. Still, Rick's comrades had turned out in force and had given him a fired salute as the bier was moved from the church to its eternal resting place in the cemetery. And, it had to be admitted, Carroll Gillespie had done him proud for a send-off, providing a beautiful speech built on the few facts of a life that had been so short.

Thornton stood in line to contribute his condolences to the parents, then walked over to the open grave and tossed in his spoon of earth upon the cardboard coffin. There was already a small build-up of dirt and his contribution made no sound as it landed. Just like life, he thought gloomily, we think what we do will make a difference but our impact is absorbed in the general indifference of the universe.

But the darkness of Thornton's thoughts were not particularly about death or the afterlife, but himself and his recent fate. His dyspeptic mood led him to ruminate on all the events that had managed to go wrong over the last year: the hesitant progress by MARIONn towards full consciousness, the failure of the *LetheTech* IPO, the financial pressures that had caused, the public anxiety about memory therapy, the increasing demand for regulatory oversight, the anti-AI mood gathering steam in the South, the rampage by his Milton robots. The list was long; there seemed to have been a real plague of problems recently.

To those business issues he could add personal ones; his wife Bethany's recent fall off the wagon, a sort of ultimatum from Lu Ann, who saw their relationship going nowhere. And his daughter Stephanie was living 3000 miles away in France. Finally, Carroll Gillespie was trying to involve him ever deeper, even if exactly how he was trying to involve him was still obscure, into what would surely become a morass in New Chaldea.

Thornton's sour mood curdled everything he came across this morning, including the appropriate Christian response to the sacrifice this young man had made for the sake of his faith. Their *shared* faith he had to remind himself. Compassionate as he might consider himself to be, Thornton felt a pang of guilt about his lack of any real interest in the soldier or his fate. He looked across the grave and saw a young woman crying her eyes out, Rick Muldane's girlfriend he assumed, with a child wrapped around her legs as it sought comfort, or maybe it was the child who was offering succour. Difficult to tell, really.

Thornton raised his head, which had dropped towards the ground as he lost himself in his thoughts, and turned towards Carroll as they began to walk down the line of cypresses towards the car park. "Of course," Thornton said, in delayed response to the governor's question about his belief in an after-life. To the interrogation there seemed only one safe response. "I accept the church's teaching on this. I expect to be judged and I hope that I will just squeak into Heaven." He hesitated. "An' I believe that we cannot achieve the kingdom of Heaven without Jesus's help," Thornton added piously, not at ease with discussions that might, if pursued down the path of sinful reckonings, of his own hindrances to entry into heaven, lead into uncomfortable waters; waters that were named '*MARIONn*' or '*Lu Ann'* and sometimes, '*Stephanie*'.

But as he said these words, doubts assailed him. He had asked for forgiveness many times – but would he actually be forgiven for what he had done to Stephanie and her unborn child? Somehow the Catholic church's procedures for atonement, to be redeemed through the confession of sins, of undergoing a penance, of receiving absolution, had not provided him with the release that had been promised. Thornton had discussed his sins with his confessor many times and been assured that he would be granted grace by a loving God; but he didn't feel as though he had been. If it really were so, wouldn't God have made sure that he knew his penance was sufficient? What was the point of redemption if you could not accept it? If the spiritual weight of sin was still heavy upon his shoulders?

And, of course, he bore the additional spiritual burden of doubts about the wisdom of MARIONn's creation. This *other* mind, so close in texture to the one God had given us. If we were created in His image and MARIONn was like us, then it followed that she must be like God too. And that, he could see, as the opponents of this type of research kept on preaching, might be tantamount to blasphemy. So would he go to Heaven? It seemed increasingly improbable, whether he believed in it or not. So perhaps he rather hoped there was *not* an after-life, one that he was to be denied. And that disturbed Thornton. Would the peace that his faith had once given him be the next casualty of his life, the next loss? Could that loss be managed? So his words of affirmation to Carroll, that he did believe in an after-life, were really a sort of a lie, or at least an evasion.

Carroll was also in sombre mood this morning, as he might be given the occasion, but he seemed upbeat in a curious way. Thornton imagined that as an ex-Bishop, Carroll must find fulfilment and purpose in funerals; after all they did validate his original calling. This was the sort of thing that men of the cloth were *meant* to do surely. Maybe it gave a man a sense of significance, importance even, to be responsible for sending another man off into the eternal life; committing him to a voyage whose destination he could only hope was as God had promised. That was where faith came in; for there was no other reassurance. He was reminded of the French saying he had once heard from some cynic in Baton Rouge: '*Dieu me pardonera, c'ést son metier*,' God will pardon me, that's his profession. Well, God could do worse than practise with him.

The ex-bishop seemed to intuit his ruminations. "You know Thornton. I've been thinking a lot about death recently," he said. "I had a brush recently. I turned out to be a false alarm. But for a few days I had to reflect on the fact that I might be, like, dead in six months. They thought I had one of those cancers they still can't cure – or even just hold down, you know, where you live you with it but don't die. But I was very lucky. As I say, turned out just some false alarm."

"And did you have those famous moments of reflection we're meant to have at such times? What have I done with my life, or how I want to spend my last few months? All that *bucket list* stuff," asked Thornton, trying to edge the cynicism out of his own voice.

"No really," said Carroll, sounding more despondent than grateful for his redemption from the jaws of death. "Even though I knew that if the diagnosis was confirmed, I'd probably be dead in six months, I never felt, really felt, inside myself, that I would be gone before Christmas. Whether it was the good Lord comforting me, or the inability of the mind to contemplate its own demise I don't know, but any serious idea, fear even, of extinction never became part of my consciousness."

"Or perhaps, as a believer in an afterlife you weren't unduly troubled by the thought of death?"

"Could be that, could be that," agreed the governor amiably, although Thornton thought he sounded more dubious about this proposition than a man so close to the Church perhaps ought to. "Probably a bit of that, I do agree."

The two walked on in silence, each with their thoughts about what might lie ahead of them in the after-life.

Chapter 34

The governor makes himself clearer

Thornton's heart lifted as he saw the parking lot and his car only another minute or so away. He was wary of the governor now. With the recent disturbances at his plants acting as political cover, Carroll could make Thornton's and the Blue Ridge Corporation's life very difficult, if he chose. God might promise redemption for his many sins in the next life but the governor could, and would, only offer him peace in this one if it were in his interest to do so.

As Thornton approached his car, the driver's door opened welcomingly and brought with it a sense of release from the anxiety that inflicted him these days, whenever he had cause to run up against the governor. Well, he'd done his bit; he'd turned up for this funeral, spent time discussing theology with Carroll. He hoped that he had earned some indulgence. Thirty seconds to go now before he reached his car.

But just before he got there, he felt Carroll grab him, not aggressively but firmly, by the elbow and steer him around and back down the avenue of the cypresses. “Walk with me a little further, my friend,” he said. “It’s good to have someone to whom I can unburden a little.” Thornton wondered what was coming. It was unlikely to be anything helpful.

“I was not entirely honest in the eulogy,” confessed the governor. ”But I didn’t exactly lie either.” If you had, Thornton said to himself, you’d only have been following in the long tradition of your predecessors. Thornton knew enough of his Louisiana history. From Huey Long to Edwin Edwards, past governors had not been fazed by sticking too closely to the truth. Had not Huey Long, the father of populism, instructed a harassed aide, who had asked what he should tell an aggressive and hostile crowd intent on ransacking the governor’s mansion to protest broken electoral promises, to say, ‘*tell them I lied’*. Had not Edwards, when the prosecutor in a corruption trial had asked him if he was lying, replied, ‘*No, but if I were, you have to assume that I would not be telling you.*’ Lying, misspeaking, inoperative phrasing; they all had an honoured place in Louisiana oratory.

“I didn’t lie,” the Governor repeated, reassuringly. “But I did stretch the truth. The grave is not perhaps a place for too much reality and we must give comfort to those left behind. They wish to know that their loved one’s sacrifice has not been in vain. But........ it’s sure beginning to look that way, Thornton. Rick Muldane’s death may well have been in vain. These volunteers, this expeditionary force – fact is they’re beat.”

“I’m sorry to hear that,” said Thornton vaguely, trying to show concern. The problems of New Chaldea were way from his interest at that moment and, besides, he’d heard all about the problems of the volunteer force before.

“Unless something is done, we’re going to lose this last opportunity to create a haven for Christianity in the Middle East. There’s nowhere else for them to go. If that area is settled by those who are not of our faith, that’s going to be it for another generation. The boundaries will be established for another century. Like when the remains of the Ottoman empire were re-drawn 150 years ago." Thornton remembered that Carroll was a history buff.

"I hear all that Carroll. But how long was that last Middle East war fought for? Almost forty years? Everyone is exhausted, as you and I have discussed before."

"They are, they are, "agreed Carroll. "That's why this is the last chance. There will be no appetite for further..... turbulence, if I may call it that. If the Christians miss it this time, they've nixed it for good."

"So, what are you going to do now?" asked Thornton, puzzled

"It's not just me, Thornton. I can't do *nothin'* just on my own." There was an inflection in the Governor's voice that Thornton knew boded no good for him. "We've all got to help if this thing is going to be won."

"I see," said Thornton, as non-committedly as he could.

"At least I know you're on board," said Carroll, in a tone of voice that implied Thornton was being dared to deny the assertion. "I've always respected you for your commitment, Thornton. I appreciate your enthusiasm and your understanding of what a great opportunity this is, for the Lord; in the land of his birth. I know that you will do what you can – and I appreciate that. I really do."

Thornton thought, OK – let's get this over with. I've got other things to do today. "How exactly can I help, Cal?"

"Thank you my friend. I knew that I could count on you," said Carroll. "It's like the problem I already said. The volunteer force is just beat. Unless we change things, more of our fine young men like Muldane are going to die. There needs to be far more guys out there, better equipped – and only the government can provide that."

"Well, you are the president-elect after all. Nobody's going to stand in your way" said Thornton, his smile suggesting that perhaps Carroll had forgotten that he soon would be *the* government.

"Down here we follow the word of the Lord," said the governor, as though all alternative systems of government were immoral, lesser affairs. "So, I think, basically, folks here are sympathetic to doin' something in New Chaldea. Unlike them up

North. But as we both know, there's no firm mandate even down here at the moment. Unless..." and here the governor hesitated, willing Thornton to finish the sentence. He declined the bait.

"Unless, ..what?" Thornton asked. He knew he wouldn't want to hear what Carroll had in mind.

"We have to change people's views. That's what we have to do. They've got to start pushing for the government to get involved."

"Well, you've asked your friends in the media, like me – and many others - to make the case."

"I have, I have. But even there, there's a reluctance to take my line. You know, these editors and publishers ......they are not, like, the bravest of people. I don't mean you Thornton, of course you've been very supportive but others? They say, '*we're business people, and we're in the business of giving people what they want and there's no sign they want to go to war again.*' So, I've got a problem. We can't send troops without popular support, and the media won't help persuade folks that we ought to go. So, I need to find some way of generating a bit of enthusiasm in people who ain't got none – right now, anyway."

"Sounds a tough call to me, governor"

"But not an impossible one."

'How so?" Thornton was not catching the Governor's drift at all. He mentally consulted his iPsyche – 11.38 am. He really needed to get going. He could sense the governor's hesitation to speak out on whatever he had decided to say, but he wished Carroll would get on with it. Then the suggestion arrived.

"You're doing some interesting work up North, Thornton, I hear."

"Interesting? For sure," said Thornton. "But it's not all going to plan. You've read about the problems with *LetheTech*? We thought we had memory nailed, but not quite yet."

"Must have been putting some pressure on you financially?" Thornton recalled that it was wise not to underestimate the governor's ability to work things out, nor the extent and depth of his sources. Informants were everywhere.

"It was not helpful," agreed Thornton drily.

"I'm sure not. And then there has been that business with the rogue Miltons. That's not been helpful either, I guess."

"Indeed, Cal. Look, I need to get back. Could we continue this another day? I'm keen to do whatever I can to help the cause"

Carroll shook his head sympathetically. "How selfish of me!" he said. "We both have much to do today. I must be getting along too." The governor spun around and they headed towards the car park once more. Which still gave the governor another five minutes of Thornton's time.

"In spite of past *LetheTech's* problems, that I understand are pretty well sorted now, I hear there are some other amazing developments coming out of your place in the Berkshires. Seems you can now change people's minds." This was more a statement than a question. "I hear you can, like, go into their minds; remove stuff, put stuff in."

Thornton tried to brush this aside, "You've read the reports, Carroll. That's what *LetheTech* is all about. We might do wonderful, positive things, things that will make people better; remove memories that traumatise them, insert knowledge of how to do things that brain damage has disabled. It's not spooky." Thornton hesitated, to let that point sink into the governor's mind. "It's just the *automation of therapy* – but much more efficiently and thoroughly than has been possible before. It's no more than doing what we're all used to, but better, more efficiently."

"Indeed, indeed. So I understand," said Carroll, undeterred by Thornton's defensiveness about *LetheTech's* abilities. "I'm sure that once the, you know,.....the teething problems, shall I call them? Like those Kinnead O'Neal suffered, are all worked out then it will be a great success. A great boon to mankind..... probably. But my friend, as always, you are being modest. I hear that your team has gone beyond simple memory deletion now. Cannot those machines you got up there, cannot they talk to *many* people, put things in lots of minds, not just one? And I hear that people may never know that the memories they're being given have come from your MARIONn device. Because MARIONn leaves no trace of her presence, so they say. My, that's smart!"

Thornton screwed up his eyes. This was dangerous talk. "I don't know who you' been listening to, Carroll, But you sure make it sound a lot easier than it is. It's not quite like you have been told."

"Oh, I'm sure, I'm sure. I'm sure I've got it all very muddled!" replied the governor, indicating that great allowance had to be granted for his technological innocence. "But the basics of what I hear are right?"

"We're working on something like what you describe," agreed Thornton, grudgingly. "But it's very early days yet. Whoever you got your information from was being wildly optimistic," (And *I will make sure to find out who that person was when I get back,* thought Thornton) "There's a very long way to go..... But it's true that MARIONn may be able to provide permanent psychiatric help. We will no longer need armies of psychologists. Anyone, anywhere in this world will be able to access *LetheTech's* services, via MARIONn. It will be the greatest advance in mental health the world has ever known. Man and machine will communicate directly – by thought alone."

"Exactly. Man and machine talking to each other. And not just talking, but sharing thoughts with each other, if I understand it right? And not just one person at a time – but many people. Memory deletion and entry - combined with mass communication ability, via the iPsyche. Gee, your MARIONn will have great influence!" said Carroll.

"You make it sound all very sinister, Cal. There will be very strict controls over what MARIONn can say and do. She will be tremendously restricted." Thornton tried to sound reassuring again.

"Of course she will be," agreed Carroll. "I didn't want to imply anything else. You're a good Catholic Thornton; I know you would not give a machine powers that are reserved only for God and those made in His image. But …bear with me here, for a second." The two were almost back to their cars and it was clear the governor was not going to let Thornton go immediately.

"Suppose, just for a second, that you wanted to change an opinion, of a group of people, then you could, theoretically at least, remove one memory, a memory of say, just to take an example, some past problem or disaster and replace it with a more positive, useful, memory or opinion? And if you so chose, the people in that group would know nothing about what had gone on?"

"You could do that, if everything works, yes," said Thornton. "But we're not planning to do that. That's not what we're about. In fact, we will always leave a '*tracer*' memory, once MARIONn has communicated, so that users can understand the difference between what they know from their own experience and what they have been given by MARIONn."

"Well, that's certainly very ethical." The governor spoke as though ethics was an interesting side-line of life, but nothing that need be taken too seriously. "But you wouldn't have to put this '*tracer*' on, would you? It's not an inevitable part of the process?" he asked.

"It's like some drug treatments," replied Thornton. "You attach a bit of radioactivity to a drug so you can trace its journey through the body. Keep track of it. But no, the 'tracer' it's not strictly required by the treatment. It's just that we think it *right* to add it on."

"So if you wanted to, *I speak hypothetically of course*, influence voter's intentions you could, perhaps, remove the past bad memories of something – and then insert some more positive opinions about it all?" Carroll sounded as though he was just musing, riffing on the possibilities of memory manipulation.

"I suppose so," replied Thornton, his voice lacking any enthusiasm. "I don't want to be a *debbie downer* on your idea, Carroll, but when carrying out the memory….modification, if I may call it that, these people might not be fully persuaded of what you suggest, once they noticed the 'tracer'. They might dismiss the information they'd been given as so much advertising, or propaganda. Which is what it would be, seems to me."

"I understand. You'd have to remove the 'tracer' to be effective, I understand that. Well, here we are," said the governor as they reached their cars. "It's been a fascinating chat, Thornton. You know, living down here in the deep South, sometimes one has no idea how fast science is moving. Amazing, what can be done now. I do hope your researches are successful. I really do. We could do so much with this MARIONn of yours."

The two shook hands and walked to their respective cars, but just before the governor reached his he turned round and said in a raised voice to make sure he was heard, "By the way, Thornton. When will that factory - the one where you had the trouble with the Miltons – be up and running again? I had Jim Embry on the phone again the other day."

"I hope he is a bit happier now," said Thornton. "We paid him a way load of compensation for the damage. I guess they'll be up and functioning again in a few days."

"Jim Embry does seem happier now, so thank you for doing that," replied the governor. "But Sherman Barnes, you remember him? He had so many calls about the future of the Miltons, you wouldn't believe. All these people telling his staff how unhappy they were, how he must not allow Miltons to be employed in the state. Then *I* started to receive calls, telling me I must close down any factories in the South where series 5 Miltons are employed. Me and Sherman, we're under a lot of pressure."

"We're doing everything we can to make sure there's never a repeat of what poor Mr Embry and his family had to suffer," said Thornton. "I need your support governor, as always. Us at Blue Ridge, we certainly don't want any more trouble. I understand the pressures you're facing."

"I'm sure you do, my friend. And I thank you for your understanding, as always. Now, you have a good drive back," said Carroll, as they shook hands.

But Thornton always wanted the last word and besides he was surprised the governor had said so little about the '*incident*' at the so-called service a few days before. He understood that the governor might want the whole disaster brushed under the table. That misjudgement had been dangerous, politically, to him. Yet what was dangerous to Carroll Gillespie might be to Thornton's advantage. As his car door opened, he turned his head and said over his shoulder,

"So sorry there were so many dead and injured in that meeting of yours, Carroll. Terrible thing. People really shouldn't play with those machines. I had Senator Calvin Roberts on the phone this morning, asking for details of what I thought might have gone wrong, how come the Miltons were so dangerous? I explained that they had to be decommissioned properly before disposal. He's going to raise the matter in the state senate. Just thought you ought to know," and with that Parthian shot Thornton closed the door of his car before the governor had the chance of a riposte. He switched the drive mode to manual. Engaging with the route back to the office might settle his mind. The last thing he wanted was too much time on his hands to worry about what the governor had been saying.

Chapter 35

An unwelcome call

"I'll be here for a week or so" said Stephanie, as she and her father walked through the 'new' arboretum in the light of late afternoon. The arboretum might have been 'new' in the context of the life span of woods, but Thornton had planted it over 30 years ago. Saplings grew quickly in the warmth and humidity of the domes and even the hard woods were already twice the height of Stephanie.

"However long you can make it," said her father. "I've missed you – we both have, your mother and I - since you've been in Paris." Thornton tried not to lend his voice too yearning a tone but Stephanie's presence illuminated the family home – and provided a useful buffer between him and Bethany.

Stephanie sensed what her father was thinking. "It's nice to be back but I don't want to overstay my welcome. Mother and I will soon drive each other nuts, even if she's on the wagon….. for the moment." They walked on in companionable silence. Then Stephanie said, "How's Lu Ann?" She liked Lu Ann and was glad that her father had someone who could provide him with companionship and affection. She knew Lu Ann provided a generous ear for his troubles, and there were plenty of those. For once, they did not seem related to her mother.

The humidity under the Buckminster domes was excessive but she knew that these species of trees and shrubs would not survive if allowed to grow in the outside. The climate was now too hot and too dry, but in here it was a little paradise with not just plants flourishing but birds and insects. Space X had been down here to consult on how they might establish a grove on Mars, before the launch of the *Savannah* craft. The whole business of creating the arboretum had been a source of enthusiasm and pride for her father. As they walked along the paths and passed each plant and tree, a hologram would materialize with a full scale image of how the adult item would look, in its natural habitat, together with information on its identity and the botanical details of its species. A small cardinal bird came to rest on Stephanie's shoulder. She was glad to hear that all was well with her father's girlfriend but admonished him for not seeing her more often. "Be careful," she said. "Women like being paid attention."

"I have to be everywhere at the moment, replied her father, defensively. "MARIONn is at a critical point, both financially and with her mental development. We were very excited the other day. We discovered that we had achieved *singularity* and reached full consciousness. Earlier, we were premature – but it really looks as though that point has been reached now."

"So you've finally achieved your goal, father? That's great – but I'm not going to let you count all your chickens yet!" Stephanie laughed, amused at the thought of being her father's spiritual guardians, if only the most modest of ways. She knew how he could get carried away with all his dreams. Really, her parents were like children sometimes. At some point recently, in the arc of their lives, the balance between her and parents had reversed itself. She and Elizabeth had become concerned for the welfare of their parents, as they had once been for their daughters. Right now, she and her father were in a sort of equilibrium of concern for each other. Her father worried about Stephanie's career and relationship with Claude, as she wanted to be reassured that all was well with Lu Ann. And that Blue Ridge was not about to go bust.

"I read the news. Things seem to be quite difficult," said Stephanie.

"They're not easy," agreed Thornton. "Just as we advance to the point where we can mimic the human mind, we run into all sorts of hurdles. Particularly down *here*." He spoke the last word as though he despised and feared Southern attitudes, as perhaps he did. However much he loved his plantation and the land in which he had grown up.

He saw a bench to the side of the path and sat down, gesturing to Stephanie as invitation to do the same. "Did you hear what happened to my Miltons the other day?"

Stephanie shook her head. She wanted to give her father the opportunity to give his side of the story, although she had picked up the gist of it as she checked on local media during her flight over.

"The Miltons are very popular amongst manufacturers," explained Thornton. "They self-diagnose and self-repair. Unfortunately that means even the maintenance guys – who used to think they were safe from unemployment - are finding less work. Well, we had some sabotage the other day that wrecked two of ours. Then the state impounded the machines and Carroll Gillespie held a sort of lynching, a bizarre '*service*'. He says it was to release some of the pent-up antagonism towards these robots; *all* robots perhaps down here. He claims he's neutral on the whole issue of *Douglas versus Milton Robotics*. I don't believe a word of it; he was sympathetic to the destruction. He was the ring-leader."

"I thought that Cal was a friend of yours."

"Once, maybe. But never a *great* friend," corrected Thornton. "He's a politician, riding on the back of his success with the plebiscite. The only friends he really takes any notice of these days are the voters. And then he's got this obsession about New Chaldea. I mean, I'm as keen as the next church-goer to see

Christianity re-established in the land of its birth but….there are limits, or should be. Cal's putting pressure on me to help in ways that I'm not comfortable with – at all."

" Father…." Stephanie hesitated, not sure how to proceed, but mention of New Chaldea gave her the opportunity to raise something that she knew would bring back unpleasant memories. "I had a mail from Lu Ann the other day. She said she was now working, or at least helping-out as I think she put it, at Nathan Seddenhow's clinic. I'm planning to drop in and see her sometime."

"Seddenhow?" her father sounded surprised. "You want contact with him again – after all this time?"

"He always sends me a birthday message. And occasionally he messages to tell me about goings-on down here."

"I had no idea. I thought that after what happened you'd never want to see him again."

"I think you get it wrong. Whatever happened, I never blamed him. He was real kind at the time, like … super supportive and sympathetic."

"I see. Well, I'm delighted to hear it"

"So, anyway… I told Nat I was coming back and he wrote that Lu Ann was there to help him in the clinic."

Thornton was silent for a few moments. That his daughter and Lu Ann should see each other appealed to him for many reasons, but still, he was surprised that Stephanie would ever go back to Seddenhow's clinic. He reflected on how little he really knew about his daughter's life. He decided that he would take the opportunity to learn more about other issues. "So how's it between you and Claude then?" he asked.

The question caught Stephanie by surprise. Her father usually avoided any interrogation about her relationships. Stephane had no wish to be loquacious about that life. "It's fine,' she said non-committedly. "He is always travelling."

"I hope I don't ask him to come out to the MARIONn campus too often?" said her father. "I certainly didn't want to disturb the two of you. But he seems very interested in the work. And he has been very helpful, very useful."

"You have nothing to blame yourself for Father! But it's not just the trips to the North. Claude is always away on some lecture circuit or conference, or delivering some speech to a bunch of AI business people. I get a little fed up spending so much time on my own. Otherwise it's OK. Although…." Her voice trailed off, as she pondered how much she wanted to give away. Then she decided; actually she would like to discuss her concerns with someone, even her father. "It's not just the travelling though," she said. "There is something that…" Stephanie searched for the right word. "Something that unsettles me about him." And then she told her father about the photo of 'Irene' and the inability of Claude to remember the slightest thing about this phantom.

Just as Thornton listened to one of the rare confidences his daughter had ever shown him, he sensed a message coming in on his iPsyche. So as to rest undisturbed while on their walk, he had instructed the iPsyche to notify him only if a message was of the highest importance. He had set the threshold high so whatever this was, this must be important. He would let it come through. He held up a finger to ask for Stephanie's understanding and raised his eyebrows, the universal mime that his attention would be diverted for a few moments. As Stephanie watched him take the call, her father's face clouded. When the call was finished, he said,

"Stephanie, I'm sorry. We're going to have to continue another time. Something has happened. I'll see you at dinner." Thornton stood up and put a hand on his daughter's shoulder – a gesture that was intended as reassuring but managed to be anything but. Stephanie looked up at him concerned. "What is it? she said, "Is there anything I can do?"

"Alas not," said Thornton. "They've closed all the factories in the Confederacy states that employ gen 5 robots, those are the latest Miltons. On grounds of safety. I'm flying up to our offices in Richmond. I'll have to go right now. I'm sorry. But I'll be back in a day or so."

Chapter 36

Acts of Oblivion

An hour later, as he flew up to Richmond VA, Thornton pieced together the story from Heather's reports. Early in the morning there had been a coordinated swoop by local officials, backed by police armed with orders signed by Carroll Gillespie, instructing managers of the Blue Ridge plant that built Milton series 5 robots to put all machinery into stand-by mode and send any staff, except those engaged on essential maintenance, home. The stop-work order extended to other companies, clients of theirs, who employed Series 5 Miltons, but they were just told not to use the most modern versions. They were permitted to continue with older models and did not have to suspend production provided they observed the injunction. Carroll could not afford to alienate everybody.

The financial consequences of this would be severe for Blue Ridge. With production suspended, no shipments from his plants meant no cash flow, at least inward. Although the staff were practically all self-employed - which would save something. There would continue to be plenty of cash-out flow. The fixed costs of the plant continued even when these was no production.

There had been no call from Carrol that morning, something Thornton might have expected in the circumstances – if only out of courtesy. But of course, as he now understood, *no message* was the message. The president-elect wanted Thornton to come to him. And humiliating as it was, Thornton realized that he had no option but to comply. Only Carroll could lift the stop-work order; when he wanted to. He wondered how long Gillespie would leave him to twist in the wind, undermine him further, render him more compliant over whatever concession he was seeking

Thornton was correct in his surmises. He tried to initiate the process of détente between them and called Carroll. But the president-elect was unable, or more likely, unwilling, to take his call and half a day later had still failed to do so. But eventually an aide to Carroll did respond. He emphasized how difficult the position was; the safety of people living around the plant, and that of those that worked in factories that employed this series of Miltons, were their first concern. The state had to address the cause of the malfunction and make sure all the issues were understood and rectified. Malfunction, thought Thornton? There was no malfunction, as Carroll knew perfectly well. The robots had been tampered with. There would have to be an investigation. How long? Oh, *difficult to say*, replied the aide. Someone who possessed the public's full confidence would have to be found to lead the enquiry. Then there would be a report, a study of the recommendations, public consultation, implementation of the recommendations. Six months, possibly nine; it would all take time. But of course, there could be delays. That was an indicative timetable, if everything went smoothly and they had complete cooperation from Milton Robotics and folks at the Blue Ridge Corporation.

Thornton smiled to himself. Under light pressure he fussed around and worried about life. But in a crisis he was transformed, as though he needed a wall of opposition to push back against to let him feel his strength. There was no panic in him; this crisis too would pass. He knew, as much as he knew that the sun would come up tomorrow, that the governor's position was bluff and that he would shelve the investigation as quick as a hog searching for acorns if he got what he wanted. Thornton would just have to go and see him, to winkle out the price demanded.

They landed in Richmond as dark fell. Thornton had phoned Gillespie's office to suggest dinner together but was told he had a prior engagement. Thornton could be spared an hour the following morning. He expected nothing less; however much the president-elect wanted to put him on the defensive Carroll would be open to criticism if he was not seen to try to resolve the issue. Several hundred or so men were idle at the Blue Ridge plant; but many thousands of others also had to lay down their tools when it was discovered that production at their own factories was now impossible without the participation of the latest Miltons. The production process had changed too much since their introduction. Gillespie could not depend on the forbearance of these workforces for too long; they might be resentful of the Miltons but equally they needed to be paid. They could quickly become resentful of politicians too.

The next morning Thornton presented himself at the president elect's office. He half expected to be kept waiting, as a further sign of disapproval. But Carroll was not so small minded; he had a full schedule that morning; *let's get this necessary meeting over with* was his attitude. Thornton was announced by a trim young man in a blue suit and a crew cut, perhaps the one he had spoken to yesterday. Gillespie was not a man who believed in desks and the office was filled with a large mahogany table, on which stood a few screens and family photos, next to it were a sofa and a couple of armchairs. He gestured Thornton to one of them, dismissed the aide and asked that they should be brought coffee.

"Mighty good of you to fly up and see me, Thornton," said Carroll disingenuously, as though the visit was quite unexpected and he was more grateful than Thornton for the opportunity to meet again.

"I have plants closed down, 400 men idled, God knows how many others at my clients. It's at the order of the Southern Confederacy, so that means *you*, my friend," said Thornton. The word *friend* sounded like an expletive. "The shutdown is costing these men, my clients – and my company - a lot of money."

"Of course, of course. I understand that," said Carroll, as amiably as ever. "And nobody wants to get them back to work faster than me. But, after the incident in North Carolina and the subsequent outcry, I had little alterative. Until the Miltons are cleared it would have been irresponsible of me to allow production to continue. Of course, if you instructed your clients to withdrew them, *all* of them, in *all* the plants down here where they are employed, and return to previous production methods then we could have a look at rescinding the order."

Thornton snorted with barely suppressed derision. "*Bah!* You are quite well informed enough, Cal, to know we – and our clients - have made fundamental production changes to benefit from the efficiencies these robots bring us. It would take all of us months to reorganize things back to what they were. And anyway, men have been let go. "

"Premature, perhaps?" suggested Carroll, pointedly. "Such problems these robots lead us into." He spoke as though Thornton had led people into temptation, and been responsible for them succumbing. And perhaps that was indeed how the Carroll saw the situation.

"Everything would have been fine if those Miltons had not been tampered with," said Thornton.

"I hear of no evidence they were tampered with," contradicted the president-elect. "The investigative report – admittedly prepared in a hurry because this was such a pressing issue – makes no mention of tampering. The men responsible for the robots' welfare say there was clearly a malfunction." Thornton saw that Carroll was prepared to issue a completely fictitious report, just to put pressure on him and Blue Ridge; force them to pay whatever price would now be set.

"Malfunction? You know that's untrue," said Thornton. "You were at the plant where those robots went berserk. You spoke to the men. You were told, as much as I was, that the Milton's coding had been interfered with when some of the workers kidnapped their attendant."

Gillespie looked him in the eye, "I do remember that, yes. But we later discovered that those men were mistaken. When we spoke to your own people, we were told the Miltons had an inhibitory circuit, a safety device, that even if they were tampered with would prevent them from running amok in the way they did. That never operated. So, for whatever reason they did go crazy, it wasn't simply down to sabotage. There was a malfunction too."

Thornton has no idea if this was true or not. He was unfamiliar with the finer technical details of these robots. He could call the Milton plant to establish the truth – but he wanted to resolve the shut-down now, not leave it for another day. Each hour that passed cost him. This was about power, not facts. He suspected that the analysis was rubbish and designed only to support whatever were Carroll's long term aims. But that was completely beside the point; he understood that.

"Well, that's really too bad, Cal," said Thornton. "I guess then we'll just have to wait until the investigatory team have established what exactly went wrong. Do you have a timetable from them yet?"

"Not at the moment, no," said Carroll, with a tone in his voice that suggested this was of the greatest disappointment to him. *Of course you don't,* thought Thornton. Too bad the machines had been destroyed in the *auto-da-fe* rather than inspected before, for whatever evidence they might provide. But then, as Thornton now understood, part of the very reason for the *au-da-fe was* to destroy any evidence that might derail the president-elect's narrative. Thornton reminded himself always to have respect for Gillespie's well thought-out machinations.

By this stage Thornton had a shrewd idea how the charade between the two of them should be played out. "That's just too bad," he repeated. "Shame about all those guys, with no money coming in this month. But I appreciate that we can't afford to take any risks. By the way how's the post plebiscite coming-together thing going?" Thornton wanted at least the satisfaction of pointing out Carroll's hypocrisy; that this demonizing of his activities and the laying off of thousands of men would do nothing for the president-elect's stated aim of smoothing the tensions and division that the vote had given rise to.

Gillespie leant forward and poured Thornton another coffee, "Difficult to say really," he replied, in a casual, disinterested tone. If Thornton wanted to take this discussion down channels, other than the malfunction of the Miltons, that was fine with him, even if at some point they'd have to get back to the business in hand. Carroll batted away the issue: "The North are running a lot of scare stories – most of them rubbish, but some have their effect. They're determined to drive fear into the folks down here – telling them that after the plebiscite everyone will be much worse off. When of course, the opposite is the case. They just want to fill up the factories and offices with their robots and other machines, displacing a whole lot of our people in the process. But who wants that Northern money, when we don't get to run our own affairs, when we have to put up with a lot of shit about robots having to be treated with respect? They got feelings? Huh, really? *Douglas v Milton Robotics* is one of the main causes of the discontent in the South. I know you didn't intend that way Thornton, when your people invented these things, but that's the way it is."

"Yeah, I can sure see how things are going," said Thornton, despondently. But this little outburst of the governor's got him no nearer to discovering what Carroll really wanted. He knew that Carroll would not name his price directly. He was never that obvious, always wanting to be so obscure that he could deny ever having said something, almost anything, substantive – in case it all went wrong later.

Thornton remembered his previous conversation with the Carroll. New Chaldea? Was that what all this was about? He was groping now; worth a try. "Well, I guess we'll just have to wait," he said. "Nothing more to be done. But tell me, how's that New Chaldea thing, that we discussed the other day, playing out?" he asked. "The idea of a Southern led intervention?"

Carroll Gillespie suddenly looked much more animated. "No change there yet, Thornton. Sadly. As I said to you, my old flock are hesitant – and I understand that. Our years in the Middle East have not all been crowned with glory. I accept that too…….but we're talking about a last push here. A last effort for our Lord. It's not too much to ask, is it? There's this reluctance, a lack of faith, to fight the last battle, before the war is won. People feel they've been down this route before. I understand that. Memories are long."

"Folks have been led down this path before?" mused Thornton aloud, partly to himself. "Memories are long?" *But memories? They're my job,* he thought to himself.

"Indeed!" agreed Carroll with sudden enthusiasm, as though some opening in the tunnel of public apathy had been spied. And perhaps it had. "You're right, Thornton. Memories are long – and unhelpful! If only that memory of past failed military expeditions didn't exist, then I am sure the faithful would support the Lord in his hour of need. They support with money now, but that's not enough. They've got to risk blood too. How wonderful it would be if we could only relieve them of their troublesome doubt!"

At this point the Governor stopped, as though he said enough. The two man sat back to reflect. Thornton now understood the Governor's price for reopening his factories. This was to be part two of the conversation that had begun in the cemetery car park, after Rick Muldane's funeral. As if in response to his thoughts, Carroll said," Do you remember that talk we had in the car park the other day? Have you had a chance to think any more about what I said?"

What Thornton was mostly thinking about at this point were his daily losses, as the plants of Blue Ridge and his clients' stood idle. He took a deep breath and decided to commit himself to the one way that he guessed would cause those plants to reopen.

"Carroll, you and I have known each other a long time. I am a man of the South, have always made my home here. Whatever I have become, and what has been given me I owe to the South, and to God. I am a Christian, a loyal Southern Catholic, and I believe that our Lord should find a permanent home in the land of his birth. So... I can help you. We can ask MARIONn to run pro-intervention messages off the *LetheTech* platform, piped in via people's iPsyches. She can explain why past '*expeditions*' or whatever you want to call them, will not be a good guide to what will happen in the future. She could persuade them, that if we send a force to New Chaldea, the voters need not be afraid of the consequences. That it will all turn out for the best. "

Carroll Gillespie smiled generously. He appreciated what he was being given and he wished to be magnanimous in victory. Thornton was, in the long run, an ally whom he needed. In truth, they both needed each other. Carroll might be the holder of political power but he knew how fragile that could be - if he did not also possess the support of those who controlled the economy. He didn't want the great industrialist Thomas Lamaire feeling resentful. But, equally, he hadn't quite received all that he wanted – yet.

"That's mighty good of you, Thornton," said Carroll. "Appreciated, really is. I'll ask my campaign manager to talk to your people. They can work out a message we can broadcast. But I was wondering," and here the governor hesitated, knowing that what he was about to request would be a difficult concession for Thornton to make. But it would be very valuable if he could gain it. "Do we have to tell the recipients from where the message is coming from? Like, do we have to ensure a '*tracer*' is attached? It would be so much more effective if the appeal could be the view of some independent, but maybe unspecified, observer? As you said yourself, folks have a tendency to disparage and ignore what they regard as political propaganda."

Thornton looked shocked as though he had just heard a member of the church issue a profanity. "You are asking me to deliver that message without adding who's responsible for it? You know, Carroll, that we can't do that. There are rules against those sort of things. We'd be massively fined, maybe banned, if we were to be discovered. Political broadcasting has to show who is promoting it. You know that!"

The president-elect was conciliatory; he could pull back his pawn temporarily in order to secure the bigger prize, the check-mate that was surely down the road. "Of course, of course. I was forgetting the most basic of rules that govern these political debates," he said. Then Carroll hesitated, before picking up his train of thought again.

"But would you *really* need to include the tracer?" he insisted, not wishing to give ground on this point until he was forced to do so. "Think about it. I mean, there is no particular organization behind this, is there? This is an issue that cuts across political lines. It's just a movement really, a view, a ground swell of anonymous public support, isn't it? There's no single body to whom you could attribute to such a message."

"You think so?" asked Thornton, also biding his time before he had to reject the proposal more firmly.

"But maybe you're right in principle," agreed Carroll. "It might be misleading to send out this message, without saying who it's from. Might not be entirely honest. I grant you that. So I want to suggest a different approach. Instead of sending the public a message, why don't we remove one instead? As we both know, you can do that now." Thornton had not forgotten that the possibility of *mass* memory deletion, way beyond the individual therapy *LetheTech* was now testing in trials, had been leaked to Carroll. But he hadn't been prepared for this suggestion. Publishing a message via an iPsyche was little different to transmitting it via a cell phone or a wrist band, but *erasing* a memory involved *LetheTech* having deep access to people's minds. Memory deletion was not simply the reverse of message insertion. People would be *aware* of a new, unexpected, thought that popped up in their heads, particularly if accompanied by a 'tracer'; but a *deletion* would leave no trace.

There would be no awareness that someone, *something*, had been inside their mind and removed a prior recollection.

"Be like the *Act of Oblivion*," continued Carroll. "Do you know what that was?" Thornton shook his head. "Tell me."

"I was a history major, as you know," said Carroll. "Studied English history and I remember one time, Oliver Cromwell, this guy who won the civil war over there, when it was all over he instituted an *Act of Oblivion*. All crimes in the war, well except those like supporting the late King, or buggery, they were very hot against that I'm glad to say, were forgiven - and forgotten - officially. Forgotten, – forever! Just think of that; this old Brit was way ahead of us, my dear friend. That's what we need here – an *act of oblivion*. Everyone made to forget past disasters!"

Thornton could see the way this cookie was crumbling. He could, and should, decline what he was being asked to do. But then, of course, he could wait months for the report on the safety of the Miltons to be published; at which point his plants might be allowed to reopen but he would probably be bankrupt. Or he could accede to the governor's request now, have the robots miraculously declared safe and the factories allowed to restart – immediately.

True, mass memory deletion was untested. The consequences of giving MARIONn use of the *LetheTech* process and direct access to minds of the public, not fully thought through. Xian Han believed that they had now overcome O'Neal type dangers, but nobody was really yet sure, particularly when it involved millions of people. And if it ever surfaced that MARIONn and *LetheTech* were involved in memory manipulation of the entire Southern population, or at least in those who wore iPsyches, there would be such a storm of protest that Blue Ridge might not survive it. Thornton felt he had to deflect the request. He'd never get Heather, as his CEO, to accept this anyway.

"Could we start with just some political advertising?" Thornton tentatively asked. Inserting a little propaganda was probably OK, particularly with a '*tracer*' attached. And anyway, there was no point giving everything to Carroll immediately. This was a negotiation and the latter would not expect to gain everything he asked for at the start. Thornton would bid the absolute minimum that he knew he must. He continued, "After all, the people are used to hearing this type of publicity. They'd hardly pay any attention to the '*tracer*'. I don't see that if they know the message comes from your political organization that would weaken its force."

The president-elect didn't say anything in response to this offer. Of course, it was useful that he could get free political advertising. But he'd heard nothing about *modifying* the attitudes, deleting the memories, of those folk who were hostile to his plans for an expeditionary force to be sent to New Chaldea. And yet, the concession on political advertising, even if accompanied by a *'tracer'*, was significant. As Euclid had explained to him, the vital objective must be to forge a mental connection between MARIONn, *LetheTech* and the voters. Once that had been achieved, that breach in the wall had been made, who knew what might be possible? It was important not to be greedy right now. Thornton did not have many options, those plants could remain closed for a very long time. And it was never wise to push a man too far; you might win a battle in the short term but the game of politics had no touch line; it went on forever and you never knew when the dice might be rolled the other way. Those who had been pushed too far might one day be recycled to the top of the heap; just when you didn't want to hear from them. *Never use all of your advantage at one time* was one of his favourite political rules. So Carroll held himself in check. Self-discipline, acquired years ago when he was a novice trying to be less distracted and closer to God, had given him a strength few other politicians could match. His instinct told him to accept what was offered and not to press for more, yet.

"You're probably right," conceded Carroll. "I wasn't thinking. Of course the message must carry the '*tracer*'." He didn't want to give ground too easily but he wanted Thornton to feel he had won some victories. Carroll knew that he would get his way eventually. He would ask one more time but if he was refused, well, he was playing a long game here. "And the *negative* advertising?" It was the most euphemistic way he could phrase his request about memory deletion.

Thornton knew he had to refuse this. ”Not yet, I think Carroll. The technology is not proven. If we had an O’Neal problem on our hands, at a mass level, it would be a disaster – for both of us.” It would indeed, thought Carroll, but from what he had heard from Euclid, Thornton was underplaying his team’s abilities: the risk of those problems arising was now extremely small. The O’Neal issue had been solved.

“I understand. I’m as suspicious of these new technologies as you are,” agreed Carroll. “We certainly don’t want to go too fast. Let’s leave all that for the time being.”

“Thank you,” was Thornton’s relieved reply; grateful that he had been pushed no further. He was aware that he still had to square Heather on even the modest issue of identifiable political advertising. She would be insistent that granting MARIONn direct access to minds was a step way too far at the moment. Too bad: she would have to be brought round to the idea. Thornton realized that he had the leverage to do that. But would the modest concession that he had given Carroll be sufficient to buy the release of the stop-work order that Blue Ridge needed? Only one way to find out…

“Carroll, now that we have that resolved, the political thing, could we turn to the issue facing my plants?” Thornton asked.

“Oh, I’m sure there’s no need to worry about that,” said Carroll, as though nothing on his agenda could give him less concern. “Let me see where we are right now.” He pressed a button on the table. “Shane, will you come in with an update on wherever we are on the Milton investigation, please? I understand there have been developments this morning. Thornton and I have successfully completed our meeting.” He turned to Thornton and smiled. “More coffee, Mr Lamaire?”

The aide entered, studying his tablet, a Moses having recently descended from the mountain. He peered at it, evidently finding God’s word particularly difficult to interpret that morning. “Shane, you have any news for us on the rogue Miltons? Anything we can share with Mr Lamaire here?" asked the president-elect. Shane, who had been well briefed on how to act out the whole charade if he heard the phrase '*successful meeting*', studied his tablet even more thoroughly. "I've had an update from the investigative team very recently. It seems that they have now been able to confirm the plant manager's account – that the cause of the robot's aberrant behaviour was the tampering. The safety routines were overridden. There is no reason to suppose that if properly handled the Miltons are not safe for factory work."

"Well, that's marvellous news Shane. Thank you," Carroll looked as though the world could not be more agreeable to his desires that morning. "I'm sure that will be music to Mr Lamaire's ears. Is that not so Thornton? I see no reason now why we should not raise the desist work order and your men be able to get back to work immediately." Shane left the room to draft the instruction. The governor stood up, he had other meetings this morning but he was glad this one had worked out so well. "We'll meet each other again soon, I hope," he said as he walked Thornton to the door.

"But we'll meet in two weeks," said Thornton. "You've obviously forgotten in all the excitement. It's the '*Friends of New Chaldea'* foundation gala in New York again. How the years roll by! You're the guest speaker I see. Of course Bethany and I will be there. Wouldn't miss it for the world."

"How silly of me," said Carroll. "Of course. I shall have to get Shane to prepare some remarks. And I'm delighted that you and Bethany will be present. Kirsty will be so pleased." As long as she is reasonably sober, he thought and with that the president-elect thrust forth his hand. "it's been a good morning, Thornton. Have a good flight back."

"Good meeting, sir?" asked Billy, as he hovered at the foot of the steps, welcoming Thornton aboard for the flight back to Baton Rouge. "Yes, I think so, thank you Billy. Not too bad a morning. We'll be able to reopen the factories." said Thornton. "Very good, sir," came the reply. Was Billy beginning to imitate Clarence he wondered?

Yes, very good it would be, reflected Thornton, but not quite sure yet whether everything was, in fact, resolved. There was still Heather to square. He could call her now but, given that he *had* to get her agreement to the access to MARIONn and *LetheTech* that he had promised Carroll, persuasion, and if necessary, pressure, might be best performed in person. The next opportunity for that would be at the gala; lucky he had invited Heather. Inspired really; he'd no idea at the time how appropriately timed that would be. And after he had secured her compliance he had could make that long delayed visit to his Asian partners. They were going to be as pleased as he was that US production had been resumed. It would be a trip that he could now take with his mind at ease.

Chapter 37

A deviation on the way home

Thornton had not got very far before he decided to make a stop on the way home from Baton Rouge airport. Whether it was from the pressure of events, or some physical ailment, he had been sleeping badly recently and felt haggard. He would make a call on the family doctor and get some medication. He gave a new instruction to the car and 20 minutes later he turned into the lot of a white block, designed on modernist lines. It had been constructed originally in the middle of the last century but renovated more recently, as part of an attempt to make that part of downtown more attractive. Various medical surgeries had been established here and there was a small clinic attached where the medics could place patients who needed modest in-patient care, without all the facilities of a major hospital.

Thornton climbed out of the car and was immediately approached by a self-important man who asked him if he had an appointment? Thornton bridled at the man's peremptory tone and general air of hostility. This is new, he thought, usually I just turn up and go straight to reception. When he confessed that he had no appointment, the man asked him to leave, that only doctors or patients with appointments were permitted to enter the building. Thornton explained that although he was not expected he was such a long standing patient of Dr Seddenhow's he was sure that the doctor would see him. The security guard looked dubious, but at length, after Thornton brought as much presence as he could to the occasion, agreed to call Seddenhow's office and discover if they would vouch for their entitled, in his view, and unexpected, visitor.

There was of course no problem about this but that didn't stop the guard looking sourly at Thornton as he led him to the front entrance, disappointed to lack the opportunity to turn him away. Thornton was about to ask the reason for this hitherto unknown level of security but thought better of it. The man in the blue uniform looked too churlish to part with any useful information. So he pressed on and took the lift to the top floor and Nathan Seddenhow's office. When he reached it there was another hold-up as a nurse on the floor advised him that the doctor was engaged in ward rounds. But it would only be for another 15 minutes before he'd be back.

Ward rounds? Thornton was puzzled. Nathan sometimes had a patient or two at the clinic but there never enough to make up a ward. No matter, all would be clear soon. He downloaded a fishing magazine onto his iPsyche, leant back in the EZ reclining chair the nurse had offered, shut his eyes and let the article, on fly-fishing in the Alborz mountains in Iran, fill his brain. Surely you couldn't fish there now, he thought? Not after the bomb. He moved his mind back to the front 'page' of the virtual magazine. He searched for the date. Oh yes, of course it was an edition from several years ago. Typical doctor's waiting room effect. Still, historical or not, the article took him back. Such a shame there had been that accident with the bomb during President Trump's second term. He had enjoyed his expeditions to Iran way back but Americans had not been able to acquire visas ever since. He remembered how the rainbow trout had been so thick upon the river he had fished that you could almost walk across their backs, when schools of them swam up or downstream, depending on whether it was sunrise or sunset. The trout had swum in such a feeding frenzy to catch the midges that you hardly needed to tie a hook at the end of your line. How he had enjoyed the camping, the riding, as well as the fishing itself, on that river! Ah, these low tech pleasures. He must ask his office to find some alternatives for him. He had loved his fishing.

Thornton was just turning to an article on the open water poaching of '*swim-back*' pelagic fish, who always returned home after circulating around the oceans fattening up - one of the first uses of *animal* memory manipulation, before it was developed for humans. Of course, there were losses from predators and now, even though the final destination of the fish was a closely guarded secret, there was poaching. But, all in all, he thought, a big advance over the static, toxin ridden, concentrated fish farms of yesteryear.

Before he could finish the article, a door opened and in walked Nat Seddenhow. He was a small man, hunched, which made him look all the smaller, with shaggy grey hair that could have done with a comb. About 65 years old, maybe a little more, estimated Thornton. He had been the Lamaire's family doctor for years; more than a doctor really, a friend. Thornton would never forget how kind he had been over all that business of Stephanie's – what was it? Almost 20 years ago now.

The two friends shook hands and Thornton explained the very small matter that had brought him here. But he was curious too as to the presence of the security guard. "I've never seen that before in all the years I have been coming here," he said. Nat took him by the elbow and led him back through the door he had just come. "Let me show you something," he said. "But you must be sworn to silence about what you are about to see." The two proceeded down a short corridor, then took a lift two floors down. Seddenhow went ahead and when he reached a pair of doors with frosted glass panels he stopped and peered briefly at an iris scanner. The doors eased themselves back with the slight noise of hydraulic pistons. Behind them lay a ward, about a dozen or so beds down each side. At some of the beds there was an array of monitors; at others drips or traction devices. In each of the beds was a young man, probably none over the age of 25. They were in various stages of disrepair. Some with head wounds, some missing legs, some bandaged around the midriff. They were evidently all Americans from the hubbub of chatter that stilled as the two men entered.

Nathan raised a hand, as though to say, '*we come in peace'* and introduced Thornton, an '*old friend*', one who wanted to say '*howdy*' and present his respects for their sacrifice. The doctor led him down the lines of beds, introducing those men who were not asleep or so badly wounded that it would be an imposition to ask them to make the effort of conversation.

Thornton was still guessing what exactly he was seeing but the likely explanation had dawned on him. As they reached the bed of one youth who, apart from a bandaged leg in a splint, appeared otherwise not too badly injured, he asked him where he was from; Charleston, came the reply. "And where did you get that nasty wound?" Thornton asked. "New Chaldea," came the response. So, these were the casualties of the undeclared volunteer force. The presence of the security guard now made sense – Governor Gillespie didn't want any journalist getting in and spreading the unhelpful news that intervention, even private and clandestine, *actually particularly private and clandestine,* was already incurring human costs.

The two men moved amongst the beds, trying to bring some light conversation and cheer where they could but then, just as they were going to leave, another nurse entered the ward. She was about to brush past them with a quick '*hi'* when Thornton and Lu Ann stopped and looked at each other. Thornton smiled," Well my! I'd heard you had gone back to nursing – but had no idea where."

"Three days a week, I do what I can. These poor guys – they need patching up before they can go back to their families," replied Lu Ann. "If you looked me up a little more often, you'd have known. I do what I can, Nat asked me to get involved."

“I didn’t realise that you two knew each other,” said Nathan. ”Lu Ann, take a few minutes off. You’ve been working like a mule all morning. Please, come and join Thornton and me for a coffee in my office. You can return back here soon enough.” So the three of them repaired to his office, while Thornton was still trying to connect together the dots of this curious morning.

“You’re now doubt wondering what exactly is going on here,” said Nat, as his receptionist poured the coffee. “I can probably work it out,” replied Thornton. “My guess is that the governor has asked you to look after these young men. He doesn’t want word to leak out about all the casualties that are being suffered. That right?”

“About that,” confirmed Seddenhow. “These young men, they come from all over the place. Not just the South. You’d be amazed how many Northerners signed up too.”

“Is this the only clinic who looks after the men? How bad are the losses?” asked Thornton.

“Not too many at the moment,” said Seddenhow. “At present this is the only clinic involved, but I hear they may have to open another place next month - the rate of attrition is increasing. We’re the start. Carroll said that he wanted all the injured men to be together when they returned from New Chaldea, better for morale that way.”

“And easier to control access to them too,” said Thornton

“You’re a cynical man, Mr Lamaire!” Nat laughed. “Not like our good friend Lu Ann here,” as he toasted her with his coffee cup. ”Be lost without her.”

“We’d all be lost without her,” said Thornton, giving Lu Ann an affectionate look.

“I needed someone I could trust, someone who wouldn’t be tempted to talk to the press,” continued Seddenhow.

“Or me, it seems,” said Thornton, with a tone of mock hurt to his voice. He raised his eyebrows as though to question how Lu Ann could be so untrusting as not to have told him what she had become involved with. “There are phones.”

"Works both ways, honey," said Lu Ann as she flicked on her smile. "But I didn't want to burden you. You've got enough on your plate. You know, it's just a little sideline o'mine. I do like to be helpful and Nat here, he asked me so nicely – once he remembered that I trained as a nurse all those years back. Beside, these guys – they're so sweet, so charming. They appreciate what little I can do for them."

"Lu Ann has been wonderful. It's true," said Nat. "The men all adore her."

"Almost worth being wounded for, I'd say," said Thornton, gallantly. "A chance to see Lu Ann three days a week? Why I have only ever dreamt of such a thing," he added with a rueful smile. Which was pretty well true. The thought of seeing her regularly was, and would probably remain, the stuff of fantasy. He took a long glance at Lu Ann, as though he had not inspected her in sufficient detail hitherto; her just-below-the-shoulder length golden tawny hair, that shone as though given a coating of iridescent varnish; her hooded, sympathetic brown eyes, the warmth of her lightly tanned skin. He wanted to lean over, put his nose aside her neck and draw in a deep draft of the scent of healthy life that she no doubt gave off; like he did with Texas.

"You're such a charmer Thornton," she said. "But we shouldn't make light of these poor soldiers and their suffering. I'm sure they'd far rather be with their families than stuck here with me and Nat for company."

Thornton turned away. "You got what you need Nat? Me and my companies, we'd be glad to help out in any way we can. You just say what you need."

"Actually, there are some things," said Nat. "Some items are difficult to import from the North at the moment – what with the economic difficulties down here and the trade restrictions. We're pretty dependent on donations."

"I'll get my people up North to put it together, whatever it is you need," said Thornton. "It can come down on my 'plane."

Lu Ann rose up from her chair and began to unbutton her nurse's coat. "It's the end of my shift so I'm just going to be on my way. I'll let you men sort out whatever you need to on your own. You all have a great day now, you hear me?"

Thornton, too, realised he ought to be getting on. The day was going past but he disliked the idea of saying good-bye to Lu Ann. "Let me give you a ride," he offered. "It'll save you a cab. Nat and I have finished anyway." He looked at the doctor. "Can you email me the list of all the stuff? And my prescription – could you copy it to the pharmacy in town? They can send a drone up to the plantation this afternoon – if it doesn't hit a wall like last time."

Lu Ann gave Thornton another smile, "A ride? That would be mighty kind of you, Mr Lamaire, a gentlemanly thing to do for a poor nurse, earning a few dollars a month. I'll be glad to accept." Thornton knew Lu Ann would be doing all this for nothing. A few dollars a month? Since her widowhood from 'Panama' Dilkes, she was almost as wealthy as him.

"Good bye Nat. See you next week. Call me if you suddenly need some extra hands," she said, loping in her loose-limbed way towards the door.

"You going home?" Thornton asked Lu Ann, as he accompanied her. "Or can I drop you somewhere else?" But she was going home and he knew the address well enough. They got into the car, the doors swung down silently and with a hiss the bolts went home. Thornton was glad he'd optioned the upgraded locks. He'd heard of gangs of DOGS breaking into people's vehicles at intersections. Times weren't as safe as they used to be.

Once seated, he gave the car no audible instruction. Lu Ann noticed. "Aren't you going to tell this car where we're going" she enquired, "or is it so smart it senses my wishes?"

"Somethin' like that," said Thornton. "It almost senses *my* wishes. See this?" And he rolled down his shirt collar. He took her hand and placed a single finger on the back of his neck. "Feel that?" he said.

"Maybe, just, not much, maybe something. Is that a scar?" said Lu Ann.

"A very small one. I'm glad you find it so unnoticeable. Just the other day I had one of the latest iPsyche's fitted. Just below the skin. I just *thought* your address and the iPsyche tells the car. Smart, huh? It does whatever I want it to do."

"What about all those male thoughts men are meant to have? I hope it doesn't act on them."

"No, you have to give an iPsyche permission to transmit a thought. You conceive whatever you want to say, or do, and then you have to action it. Just like pressing '*return*' or '*enter'*. It's no different really to what you're used to, not much anyway. It's just that you don't have to speak the instruction or let your fingers do the typing."

"Still sounds weird to me," said Lu Ann. "I'll stick to my old iBand. Who would want to have something like that under their skin. Practically turns you into a robot!"

"Nah. Don't be ridiculous. I'm no robot, I'm still Thornton, the man you love to love."

"Oh really?" Lu Ann arched an eyebrow. "I don't think I've seen you in at least two months. Some lover."

"I've been busy."

"Too busy to get your clothes repaired I see." She pointed a long nail at a moth hole in his jacket. "You should buy clothes made from *no-moth* wool. Genetically modified sheep and goats are just the best. None of my new cashmere has been touched. But don't suppose Bethany has told you about that."

"Genetically modified wool? Huh. Amazing what they think of."

"Well, more useful than that Frankenstein thing in your neck, that's for sure. How's life at home by the way?"

"Much the same. Bethany rolls around on her barrel – some days on, some days off. It's not the easiest of lives as you know .. but I'm away a lot. It's when she gets violent that I have my doubts how long I can support it all. But I guess I've lived with it for a long time now."

Lu Ann put a hand in his hair and tussled it, "Poor Thornton. Well, one day when you're not so busy, call-by. You're always welcome. You know that – at least I hope you do."

"I'd come everyday if I could," said Thornton. "But I'm not sure if that would be good for either of us. Actually it might be very good for me. We'll see."

"What's keeping you so busy at the moment, Mr Lamaire? I thought your MARIONn thing was going well, you were about to raise some money when I last saw you. What happened to all that?"

"You don't read the financial pages?"

"Never."

"Well, we had to pull the public sale of the memory technology we were working on. Had some setbacks there. And things in the South are not getting any easier for us. It's not just a question of people being put out of work – although that's true too – but them having to cope with robots that can do everything they can, much better usually. That's tricky for people. I get that. A lot of folk, particularly down here, thought that *Douglas V Milton Robotics,* was the last straw. There's a big backlash."

"So I've heard. Is the governor being helpful about all this, keeping emotions in check? Must be difficult for him, who was a man of the cloth an'all."

Thornton grunted. "The people are leading and he is following. You must have heard of that stupid '*service'* he performed – that became such a disaster. He claims he wants to bleed off some of the anger and resentment against the new machines. Pah! He will say or do anything to stay in power. And now he's obsessed about this New Chaldea business. See he's even got you all caught up in it."

"I was glad to help. Those young guys are hurt and I was looking for something to do. I don't get mixed up in the politics of it all. Just see these boys sufferin' and want to help them. That's all.."

Thornton looked closely at Lu Ann and said, softly, "You're going to be there, in that clinic, for a very long time, my dearest Lu Ann. This thing is only going to get worse. Our Carroll, governor, president-elect, whatever, he's pushing for the New Confederacy to send an official force. A large one"

"Well, good luck to him with that. He knows there's no mandate down here for that. People got long memories."

"Unless they could be changed!"

"How's that go'n to happen, for Pete's sake?" asked Lu Ann. "Give 'em all a lobotomy?"

"You're closer than you think," said Thornton

Lu Ann sat up, suddenly focused, and gave him a quizzical look.

"I'm under pressure to use our new memory technology to change people's views on this issue," explained Thornton, hesitantly, embarrassed to give voice to his weakness in acceding to Carroll's demands. But what alternative did he have really? His plants needed to be reopened.

"Without them knowing? The public I mean," asked Lu Ann

"Roughly so, yes"

"But that's horrible! I've never heard of such manipulation. You wouldn't do it would you? You wouldn't let Gillespie do that?"

"The governor's got leverage down here. And this is Blue Ridge's home."

"Do you want me to say something to the governor? He's a friend of mine."

"He's meant to be a friend of mine too," replied Thornton. "But I'm not sure anyone's a friend at the moment who stands in his way. But no, please don't say anything. This is strictly between us. I'll handle it my way."

"Whatever you say. But let me know if I can help. By the way I meant to ask you, how is Stephanie?"

"She's well. But you may see her soon."

"Great. How so? I've always been very fond of Stephanie."

"Her partner is away so she's down here for a week or so. Nice for me and I'm hoping she stays for month, but not sure she'll last. She and her mother will fall out soon enough."

"It's not just Bethany though, is it?" said Lu Ann. 'With her drinking, I can understand Stephanie's problems with that. But I got the impression she had her……issues with you as much as she did her mother."

"When Stephanie was a child," replied Thornton, "me and her….we were very close. But something happened when she was 17, that I've always regretted, tremendously regretted, which I've never told you about. Time has softened her attitude a little but yeah, we're not as intimate as we might be. As I would like."

"A girl needs her father," said Lu Ann. 'What on earth happened?" But Thornton said no more; it was too late in the day to explain now, there was insufficient time for the complete story, and perhaps Thornton had no intention or wish to explain anyway. The car slowed and turned down the drive to Lu Ann's house.

"Another time," said Thornton. "But maybe we could see each other again soon?"

"When you have a free evening call me, my friend. Sure…that would be nice."

The car pulled to a halt, the bolts hissed as they pulled back and the door swung up. Lu Ann lowered her feet to the ground, turned and flashed a big grin at Thornton, "Thanks for the ride," she said.

Part 4

HEATHER MASTERS

Chapter 38

Heather is reassured

The conversation with Carroll Gillespie reverberated for a long time in Thornton's mind. He knew the governor well enough; he was unlikely to give up what had been suggested to him; that the combination of *LetheTech's* ability to manipulate memory and MARIONn's to engage with many minds at once, could be used for political purposes. The idea was outrageous of course but dangerous also, once it became fixed in the mind of the president-elect.

But who exactly had been disloyal enough to pass on these technological secrets? Thornton had let matters drift; there had been earlier warnings about infiltration and now they had a fifth column in their midst. What was he to do if Carroll pressed again his request for memory deletion? Refuse it of course, there was no way that they could allow that. And yet…… Thornton knew Gillespie well enough that he would not be easily diverted from the scheme he had dreamt up.

Thornton's mind passed onto other pressing issues. Money for a start. In addition to the financial shortfall caused by the failed IPO, now they had to contend with the inevitable litigation that followed the rampage of the Milton Gen 5 robots through Jim Embry's farm. With exemplary damages likely to be awarded by a Southern jury, that could be very expensive to settle.

But perhaps Carroll, or at least his informant, had spotted something to the advantage of Blue Ridge. Subliminal messages could be turned into a stream of income. True, Xian Han and Heather Masters had decreed that MARIONn should not be given access to the public until much later in her development; when they had completely understood how her mind worked - and assessed the strength of their controls. Well, *needs must.* Heather and Xian would have to change their tune.

Thornton had skipped lunch that day – unwise as he felt a sugar low coming on that always left him irritable. He opened a drawer in his desk and found a bag of nuts that his assistant left there for just such situations. Not much, but it would have to do. He instructed his *iPyche* to call up Heather and a few seconds later her 3D image appeared, floating a few inches in front of his desk.

Once the opening pleasantries were over Heather said, trying to sound insouciant, "Have you had time, Thornton, to study the financial projections I sent? There is of course some uncertainty in the figures; I'm not sure how well our next financing round will be supported but I've assumed that all the existing equity partners will fund their share."

Thornton brushed all that aside. "Heather, we'll deal with financial issues in a minute. I want to first address a different problem. Can you ask Xian to come in on this conversation?"

Once Xian Han also appeared before him, Thornton explained his conversation with Carroll and his conviction that there must be a leaker. The team had grown in the last few months; new staff were maybe not so bound by the sense of loyalty and comradeship that had once linked those who had been present from the start. Thornton wanted a complete check on the past histories, outside relationships, religious affiliations on those who had joined in the last six months and who came into contact with MARIONn; any factor that might throw light on whoever had been disloyal. For no doubt, whoever it was, they would be so again.

"There are not many up at the campus who have sufficient knowledge of MARIONn's operation to brief the governor in such a way," said Thornton. "He or she could not possibly have shown that level of insider knowledge otherwise. No one outside the immediate team knows about MARIONn's ability to reach, and address, many minds at once."

"I can't imagine anyone being so disloyal", said Han. "My team is solid. I'm sure of it."

"Well, use a bit more imagination Xian," said Thornton, aggressively. "Cast your mind back. Don't you recall that Woody something we employed as a programmer? Had all sorts of issues we discovered later." Thornton might sometimes have his own doubts as to whether they were approaching too close to divinely reserved powers, but he was enough of a traditional employer to have strict views about what was owed to the provider of work, pay and food on an employee's table. If there were to be any tricky questions about the relationships between man and robots, it would be he who would do the worrying about that.

"You can't be confident about some of these new guys. I don't think we check them thoroughly enough," complained Thornton. "But maybe it's not a new hire. What about Euclid for example? Do you think he's fully on board with us? He looked distinctly unhappy with something when I was last up. Maybe his girlfriend dumped him that morning, I don't know. But apart from you, Xian, and you, Heather, Euclid is the one closest to MARIONn, the person best informed about her capabilities."

"Has something happened that gives you reason to doubt Euclid's commitment?" asked Xian

"Nothing in particular. But I just thought that he looked……." Thornton paused as he searched for the right word. "…….distracted. Euclid looked morose when I was last up there, as though something was troubling him. We are now at a stage of development where we could survive without him. MARIONn needs a teacher she can trust - but one that *we* can trust too. There are others we could employ. We need absolute loyalty."

"Euclid's a bit grumpy from time to time," interrupted Heather, "I see that too. But he may be simply lonely up in the Berkshire's. There's not much life there for a 27 year-old. I think he's good, solid, you know....loyal."

"Xian, could you talk to him please?" asked Thornton. "See what's up? I don't want any more surprises. We have enough head winds to face. Mind you, whichever leaky genius thought of linking MARIONn and *LetheTech* to implant advertising subliminally had a great idea. Think what advertisers would pay for that! Sure be an answer to our cash flow problems." He wanted to float the idea in front of them.

"Thornton!" objected Heather, in a voice full of disapproval. "We can't possibly do that yet. MARIONn is largely untested, there are all sorts of ethical objections. We can't risk an O'Neal situation on a grand scale. We'd be closed down immediately."

"Closed down, Heather?" asked Thornton, rhetorically. "You speak of being closed down? You've seen the figures; unless we can find a new stream of income to keep MARIONn developing I maybe be forced to close her down anyway. Feedback from our outside investors, the VC companies and so on, is that they are beginning to lose faith. We are going to have to do something differently. Maybe we have to recalibrate our red lines. Anyway .....we're not talking O'Neal type therapy here, where we have to go deeply into the unconscious to remove embedded memories. If we limit the....*modification,* to superficial memories and beliefs, like whether someone prefers raspberry to strawberry ice cream, or whether they should drive this make of car rather than that one, something that's not core to their identity, that's pretty well danger free."

"You can't access people's minds without their consent,' said Heather, with a firmness in her voice. "If that ever got out it would make our present publicity problems look like a tea-party. We… must allow people to be aware that they are being influenced, able to accept or reject the message. You can't simply manipulate people at a level where they won't be able to react rationally, make up their mind on their own, to what they are being told. Think what would happen if such a system fell into the hands of politicians!" Thornton reflected on his conversation with the governor and president-elect. '*From your lips to God's ear,*' he thought.

Thornton sighed and mumbled something vague, "It needs more thought, maybe," he conceded. Heather was always so cautious. And here they were with a financial crisis on their hands. OK – there were some problems with the idea – *but let's think positive, for heaven's sake!*

"And you'd need the compliance of the advertisers! I doubt they would ever be party to subliminal messaging," continued Heather, oblivious to Thornton's developing view that offering mass indoctrination sounded a great idea.

"Would they not?" retorted Thornton. "You'd be amazed how unscrupulous some of the CEOs of retail companies are. A lot of them wouldn't blink an eye to get one up on their competitors. Their conscience would not be troubled as much as a sparrow's fart by manipulating their customer's deepest desires. They'd love it, in fact!"

"Well," said Heather, primly. "They may not be concerned – but as your CEO, I certainly would be."

"Would you, Heather? Yes, I guess you would," said Thornton, wearily, making some effort to suppress a hint of menace that was now in danger of inflecting his voice. "But I would ask you…as my CEO, to bear in mind the financial stress the group is under at the moment. Using our research to generate an income…… some cash flow, is what I would expect the group's CEO to put her mind to. But let us reflect on this some more and come back to the subject in a few days. We'll pass on to other matters. Where are we with *LetheTech's* Phase II trials? No more O'Neal type issues, I hope?"

Heather still winced every time she was asked about O'Neal. She had tried to minimize the issue in her mind, hoping, with as much positivism as she could muster, that the hullabaloo would blow over. It had not.

"Kinnead O'Neal is not quite the only client that we've had trouble with, but there are now not....that many." Heather tried to sound reassuring. "We've got about 300 people who we're taking through therapy at the moment in the Phase II group. We're undertaking their treatment slowly, removing a layer of memory at each session. Of course, we don't want to run the slightest risk but there are........ accidents, a few, from time to time. Much less than in the O'Neal time. It can't entirely be unexpected."

"Can you make good the effect of the accidents, the excessive deletions if they do occur?" asked Thornton. "Repair the damage?"

"That's possible – sometimes," said Heather, cautiously. "We may be able to build back that part the memory they have lost. But I'm sad to say......" Heather hesitated. She was not a coward and she would give bad news when she had to but she did not find it easy to make Thornton realise the force of the headwind they now faced. "But the issue at the moment is not simply about excessive memory deletion. We've got other problems."

"Really, I'm surprised. And those additional problems are?" asked Thornton.

"The first is publicity," said Heather." As you know, the public is hyper-sensitive about this whole issue of memory modification. There is a gang of uninformed columnists frightening the public about Frankenstein experiments. The discovery of Kinnead O'Neal was just *manna* to them. And of course now these journalists are encouraged, they're digging. Shortly, they are going to find other examples, not many, as I say, but some. That's going to only reinforce the publicity problems that we have."

"And the second issue?"

"It's linked. As I've said we can probably correct a lot of the damage when it occurs. And showing that we have the technical means to do that might silence the critics. But now, abetted by the publicity, we can't get hold of some of the damaged clients anymore. Their families have got nervous that rather than cure their loved ones, we might cause yet further memory loss. So they won't bring back to the lab...... their old Ted who's got Alzheimer's, their adolescent Brad or Sally, who had some traumatic experience when they were a child. Clients who we want to help."

"It seems a very human response," said Thornton despondently. He burrowed in the drawer for some of the nuts. He couldn't believe how hungry he felt. "Rebuilding public confidence is not even going to start until the technology is fool-proof and these *'accidents'* go down to a rate of zero." He started to chew a large mouthful of salted cashews.

"We have many success stories," said Heather, brightly, determined that she was not going to be brow beaten by Thornton or have her team run down. "The great sadness about all this is that we've done some great work, some people have been really helped – and it's disappointing that something that has the potential to help humanity hugely has been set back months at least."

"I'm not blaming you. (*at least not entirely*) I supported you in the decision to go for an IPO early. But it's been a mistake. We've garnered attention to ourselves which is very unwelcome," said Thornton. "As a result there are probably going to be new regulatory costs to meet too."

"I know all that, Thornton. I really do,' replied Heather. "We will work as hard and as swiftly as possible. But there's no quick fix." Which was not what Thornton wanted to hear at all. He loved quick fixes.

Thornton wanted his problems solved but, right now, he also wanted to sound reassuring. There was no virtue in uncertainty and undermining his CEO or leaving her concerned about her own future – yet. "Heather, my support for *LetheTech* and MARIONn will continue – with you in charge – and if necessary I will underwrite any shortfall in our partner's lack of ability or willingness to fund future cash calls. I don't want you distracted by financial worries just when you have to give your all to succeed on this."

"Thank you," said Heather, simply. "For the reassurance. It is a weight off my shoulders. *LetheTech*'s future success will be my repayment of your generosity and support."

Just make that repayment sooner than you can ever imagine, thought Thornton. But what he said was, "Ok that's great, Heather. But think about what I've been saying. We'll talk about it again in a few days. Xian, please come back to me as soon as you can with your investigations. Heather – will you stay on the line for a few moments?

Xian Han's virtual figure disappeared. "Heather, I wanted to ask you something quite unconnected with what we've been discussing. You've probably forgotten but in a month's time there's the annual gala in New York for the '*Christians in Peril*' foundation. I would like it if you could join Bethany and I at our table? You could bring Chase, I think that's his name, your next husband?" Heather knew that Thornton knew her intended's name perfectly well. "Or even Bruno if you prefer." She understood that Thornton was jesting at her expense; his sign of disapproval of her remarrying, while only *uncoupled* from Bruno.

Heather's heart sank. She hated galas but there was no way she could refuse Thornton. As long as she wasn't put next to Bethany. That's all she asked of whoever, if anyone, might be looking out for her from on high. She accepted the invitation with as much grace as she could muster.

"Good. Bethany will be so pleased. And so am I," said Thornton. And with that they said their good-byes to each other and shut down the link. But as Heather's image disappeared Thornton remained behind his desk for a few minutes, reflecting. The time had passed, financially, when they could concern themselves with the niceties of the *ideal* robot/ human interaction. Probably all the fears had been much overdone anyway. Next time they spoke, he wanted a positive response to his idea. Heather might oppose it – but luckily he had leverage with Heather.

Chapter 39

A difficult conversation

It had been Heather's husband, the soon to be *de-coupled* Bruno, who first suggested a lunch together. But it had been Heather, who wanted to maintain the upper hand, that issued the invitation to meet at her club in New York. She hardly ever used the club and this would be a good excuse to see if the doorman remembered her. Heather didn't really mind one way or the other, but was amused that each time she visited she felt herself an impostor. Like a traveller who has smuggled nothing, yet feels themselves guilty as they pass a customs officer, she always announced herself, in-spite of paying thousands of dollars a year to be a member, convinced that the doorman could never remember her name between such infrequent visits. She really must resign from the club after the *uncoupling*. She would need to make some economies in her lifestyle anyway. Uncoupling might be the cheapest way to 'divorce' but she was still going to be supporting Bruno for years and Chase was not as well off as he had tried to make out at first. She seemed to be making a habit out of marrying impecunious men and could see herself funding much of her and Chase's life together – if she wished to maintain the same living standards as hitherto. In the meantime, today, the club would serve its purpose and be private enough to allow her and Bruno to chat relatively un-over heard.

She waited for Bruno in the bar, looking out onto 62^nd^st. She took her Virgin Mary *(no ice, light on the spices*), grabbed the New York Times from the rack, thoughtfully printed off by the Club for traditionally minded members, as the Times no longer bothered with a print version of its own, and went to sit so that she would be able to see Bruno when he was shown in. She opened the paper. There were reports of more trouble in New Chaldea, to which the temporary government had over reacted. Another 30 people had died in clashes, most of them Christians. She wondered if Thornton was still contributing to the efforts there. She knew he had given a lot of money, as his church, and his governor, had requested, to fund the development of the colony and the settlements. But he was under many financial constraints right now. Then she wondered how safe her job was, in spite of her boss's reassurances. She knew that, whatever he said, Thornton partly blamed her for the loss of the IPO.

Luckily she had the support of many of the board members, who usually saw things her way, but they wouldn't necessarily carry the day in any argument about her future. Thornton was, after all, chair of the board and majority shareholder. He wasn't going to be held back by a few recalcitrant directors who owed their position to him. A little shiver sought out her spine and ran up it.

Heather sensed Bruno's presence as he was shown into the reading room and put down her paper. It was only 12.15; she liked to eat early. "Shall we go up and find a table? Before the rush starts?" she asked. She gestured him to proceed her up the staircase, lined in best 18th century tradition with oil paintings of member's racehorses, to the restaurant. As she had hoped, at that time of the day there were still plenty of tables from which to choose.

She ordered them both a dozen oysters and for herself a sole. Bruno was at least allowed to make his own choice of main course. "You like oysters?" she enquired of Bruno, with an encouraging smile, but it was a rhetorical question as she knew that he did. She wished to start this lunch in the most positive way possible. Heather waived the sommelier away; she disapproved of drinking at lunch and besides she needed Bruno's complete attention. A good beginning to their discussion was important, which perhaps some wine would have lubricated, but good rules were not to be broken. Too bad for Bruno; he had looked forward to a glass or two of Chablis.

Bruno had the advantage of knowing what he wanted from this lunch, but he was in no hurry to reach his chosen destination. If he had agreed to this meeting it was because for weeks Heather had been unavailable. His wife had either been up at the MARIONn campus or had been travelling. He sometimes wondered how she'd ever had the time to start the relationship with Chase. And even on the few occasions that she had been back home, she had been uncommunicative. As always, Heather had hidden in her work when domestic stresses got too high. And from what Bruno had learnt there were a lot of issues at work in which to immerse herself. Even if Heather had been inclined to give their future more attention he guessed that right now she would not have much time to do so.

He understood his wife's view of the situation. For her, it was perfectly possible to imagine the three of them living comfortably together. Bruno could sleep in the spare bedroom she presently used for meditation. It was an offer that would be so much better for him, she had explained Did he really want to live on his own?. They would all get along splendidly. And after her Lincoin disaster, as he knew, she couldn't afford to grant him so generous a settlement that he could be established in his own place - as she would probably be able to offer when the IPO finally launched. Then she should be so rich that this financial disturbance would appear to be merely a temporary embarrassment.

But what was Heather saying now? Bruno's mind, that had wandered onto considerations of how much he liked, or disliked, the living arrangements that Heather had proposed, realised that he had better concentrate. This was his future under discussion and he had recently changed his own view on how he wanted everything to pan out. Not, of course, that his still *coupled* wife knew about any changes in his plans, just yet.

"This is not easy for us, I realise that," said Heather, (*quite easy for me, thought Bruno. Now I've made a decision. It's not me that's creating this mess.*) "But we know why we are here (*because you found somebody else*), the magic left our marriage long ago (*only because you spent so much time away*). I want to reassure you that I'll do everything I can to ensure the de-coupling is a great success (*of course you will. That will save you a great deal of money*). We've loved each other, we've been family to each other, and we can solve whatever problems there are, now, together. Let's not be bitter about this. It's just time for both of us to move on. We've had a wonderful time – but nothing lasts for ever. Maybe best to move straight to specifics, don't you think Bruno? Perhaps facts and futures, rather than emotions and the past, what do you think?" Bruno wondered when the bromides would end.

But Heather continued unabashed, in her casual, *this is all such an easy issue to settle amongst friend*s, sort of approach. "Bruno, I'm extremely fond of you – as I hope you know (*fond? As in 'fond' of my dog?).* But, as you also know, I have fallen in love with someone else. I have fought with my feelings, not wishing to upset our life together (*never much of one*), not wishing to hurt you. In the end, though, I would be doing you, and myself (*particularly yourself)*, both of us, an injustice if we stayed together. You would come to resent me (*I'm coming to resent you already*). You, as much as I, deserve a chance at happiness."

Heather stopped, hoping that there would be some feedback at this point. She didn't want this to develop into a monologue. She could only phrase her proposals appropriately if she could understand her husband's thinking and his reaction to what she was saying. At the moment he was just sitting there like a dummy, letting her do all the talking. Bruno, she was sure, was doing this on purpose. He was quite capable of being assertive and bouncing back at her. But he didn't – and Heather understood. Bruno was enjoying her unease and had no intention of making things smoother for her

Heather looked at the silent Bruno and came to a decision*; I am not going to be intimidated, I can out silence Bruno if that's his game. I'll just sit here until he responds in some way.* But as soon as Bruno saw this new strategy he was equally determined not to allow Heather the pleasure of enjoying her strength of mind, her potential victory. He spoke, finally;

"Heather, my dear, I'm sure – as you say – that you have our best interests at heart and that we can all work out this situation together. I understand why you do not want to proceed to a full divorce, that we should just *uncouple*. At first anyway."

How long was *'at first'* Heather wondered? Who knew when the IPO would finally happen? She sharpened her attention; Bruno knew her well and had avoided ever being subservient to her, even though she had long been the breadwinner for both of them. She reflected briefly that it was a shame they had not worked harder at their marriage. Maybe if she had, she could have been happy with Bruno and avoided this disruption in both their lives.

She smiled and said, "You and I go a long way back Bruno. You will be fine with this new arrangement. You have Jane these days, as I know *(she does? I hadn't bargained for that. How long has Heather known I wonder? Perhaps not all the advantage is mine).* And you have been seeing her for quite a long time too, I gather. You are both welcome to come and go in our shared home, as you please. I propose that nothing changes between us – apart from the sleeping arrangements. I don't want you to suffer in any way while I am enjoying my newfound happiness."

(*Your newfound happiness? Perhaps time to take some of the sheen off that.*) "Thank you Heather, for all your reassurance about the future – *my* future particularly," said Bruno, with a sarcastic lilt to his voice. "I enjoy listening to your proposals - for us - but they have been very much *your* ideas. I was rather hoping that we might have a discussion, something mutual, about what has happened and what may happen in the future."

Heather's blood ran a little cooler. She hadn't wanted to get dragged into a long and difficult talk about what had happened, that might entail examination of her own less than faithful behaviour. She had wanted to be the one who set the agenda for the way forward. She had got very used, as a CEO, to telling people what was going to happen in their lives.

Something in the tone of Bruno's voice steeled her. Now Bruno wanted a discussion about what had gone wrong in their marriage? His interest in emotional sharing had, in her view, always been limited. Was that not one of the issues that had let them drift apart? She knew how she was viewed by others: all hard carapace on the surface but in fact she was, at least in her own estimation, as soft as butter underneath. Was that not why she had sought an emotional connection with Chase? That he could be entirely open about feelings? Unlike Bruno……

"Heather, I don't want…….," Bruno hesitated for a few moments as he searched for the exact phrasing he desired. English was not his first tongue and sometimes the quest for the appropriate words, in the best order, did not come to him as fast as they might have done in Italian. "I don't want," he continued, "don't wish, perhaps I should say better in English, to stand in the way of your forthcoming marriage to Chase. I know you well enough that nothing that I can say will turn you from this course. Nor do I want to pass by on old ground - is that how you would say it? – to judge whether you have been entirely fair in your behaviour to me. Nevertheless, I think, *dear* Heather, that some realities need facing. The marriage between us has been over for a long time. I have, as I have just discovered that you know, a girlfriend; Jane, with whom I am very happy. So it's OK to me - Ok for me? - that we should now go our separate ways. I thought at the beginning of this process, that what suits you, suits me too. What do you say, *what is the sauce for the goose is the sauce for the gander*? – not that I am sure about whatever is a gander."

"A male goose I believe," said Heather, helpfully

Bruno ignored the information. "So… at the beginning I thought, yes, let's go for an *uncoupling*. It makes sense for both of us. I'm not looking to go off anywhere, immediately. In fact, I would do well to wait - as one day you may be rich again. But things have changed," said Bruno.

"They have?" said Heather, nervously.

"I know nothing, as you will appreciate, of finance. Nothing at all," said Bruno, accurately enough. "But Jane, she's not like me. She's reads the reports. She tells me about the IPO. And she thinks, this money from *LetheTech*, it's years away, not coming any time soon. We may '*whistle for it'*, is her expression. And she has been thinking too. She says, '*I want certainty now. I don't want all this waiting for something, Heather's money, and all the time my Bruno is still connected to his ex, and, for all I know, maybe not very ex, wife.'*

"I'll be very ex!" insisted Heather, beginning to see the importance of emphasising this point. "Completely un-coupled! Definitely! We won't be connected at all, really. There'll be just the last thing to do, the final settlement – at some point in the future."

"*Un-coupled, un-coupled*!" exclaimed Bruno in derision. "What is this thing? It doesn't exist in my country. You are married or you are not. No, no, it doesn't work. Not for Jane and I. We want a divorce, a full divorce, a proper divorce. Now!"

The words came as a shock. Heather understood he implications. If he persisted in this course……why, she would be near ruined. The financial costs of an *uncoupling* were manageable: those of a full blown-divorce were not – at least not at the moment. She would have to talk Bruno out of this ruinous course of action or……. she might have to abandon her planned marriage to Chase, a thought that could not be seriously entertained.

But before she could even consider how to respond, Bruno continued,

"I just want to add something, Heather. My decision that you and I need a divorce is not dependent on your future marriage to Chase. I want, ... for it to happen anyway, whatever the circumstances. As you say, we owe it to ourselves to be happy in the future. I just want to be clear on that point. If you decide not to pursue a divorce, then I will commence my own action."

Heather sat silently for a moment and reflected. So, an uncoupling was not going to be agreed? But if not, how on earth was she to fund a divorce? There would be nothing for it but to put on a very rough hair shirt and be prepared to suffer the consequences. Would Chase still be so interested in marriage when he found out that she was broke and they no longer could live in her very nice town house? She had no idea but she didn't want to discover that Chase's love was conditional.

But perhaps, if she struck a positive note, things would all be for the best; she and Chase would look back on their, hopefully short term, financial distress as one of those struggles that fresh love must suffer and deal with. Maybe a few shared economies would bring them even closer together. It would be like being married for the first time all over again – in a way. As long as she kept her job she could probably, just about, navigate her way through the rock strewn financial rapids that she was about to be thrown down by Bruno's decision. And Thornton wasn't about to fire her. In spite of all the recent troubles, he had given her reassurance on that point. But she'd better make sure not to upset him from now on.

Chapter 40

The price of security

Heather hated foundation galas, the food was always terrible, the speeches worse, the auctions, in which participation was almost obligatory, would be stuffed with things she neither wanted or needed. But she'd have to go to this one, that was clear. There was no way she could wriggle out of Thornton's invitation - apart from being ill, and Thornton had seen her recently enough to know that was not the case. Lack of support from her would be a black mark she could not afford.

The previous year, when Thornton had also invited her, although she suspected he had forgotten the fact, she'd been able to maintain her independence, while demonstrating her loyalty, by buying a table at the gala and filling it with her friends. At least that guaranteed some entertaining company during the long evening. But that sort of generosity was all in the past now. At $20,000 a table it was not something she should be contemplating, in the light of Bruno's decision to seek a full divorce. Nor would Thornton ever allow her to expense the cost, with the present cash squeeze on

Blue Ridge. It was a shame - she so much enjoyed being the dispenser of largesse and hospitality. The sight of her friends enjoying each other's company, brought together through her, contributed a rich glow of pleasure to her soul. Of course, an invitation from one of her girlfriends, who might this year be making up a rival table, could provide an alternative – allow her gracefully to decline Thornton's invitation while demonstrating financial support for his charity. But no such girl-friend had stepped forward.

No, her fate was to be the one which she least desired - to sit on the head table, with that old drunk Bethany. Although she guessed there was a good chance that this year Bethany might be on the wagon. Thornton would not wish to risk her embarrassing him, particularly as the guest of honour was president-elect Carroll Gillespie – who Heather knew mostly by reputation. She disapproved of his politics but he was a big force these days, riding a wave of popularity in the South. Thornton wouldn't want to look a fool in front of him. If Bethany was on one of her binges Heather felt sure she would be left at home on the night.

The gala was to be held in one of the new buildings downtown, that had gone up fast, in anticipation of a boom that never arrived. Its structure had only recently been topped-out, just in time to meet an unexpected, but fast gathering, recession. The building was still unfinished, bare concrete pillars in evidence, and therefore inexpensive for the organizers to rent. The industrial chic was muted by large vases of flowers and blown-up photos, placed around the walls, that showed daily life in New Chaldea. These, Heather thought, must be computer fantasies as everyone looked so happy. Most of the people in the photos seemed to be engaged in semi-biblical activities – like drawing water from a well. Young girls, depicted in gaily coloured skirts and white blouses, rested earthenware pots on their heads or shoulders, as though modelling for a traditional tableau; *La Source* perhaps. She noted that none of the girls were wearing full head or face coverings, no Hijabs, Chadors or Niqabs – evidently Christian girls then. At least there were no pictures of oxen pulling ploughs, but there was a photo of a device feeding water from the Euphrates into an irrigation ditch. An Archimedes screw? Amazing, Heather had never seen one of those outside a museum before.

She walked over and inspected the table map. Although the possibility of attending with a partner had been offered, Heather had declined, not wishing to complicate matters by bringing either Chase or, more improbably, Bruno. She found her place, between Thornton on her right and Tariq Adib, who she knew to be the Iraqi ambassador, on her left, himself next to Bethany. Ralston Jones, the outspoken industrialist, was on Bethany's other side. Heather knew Ralston only by reputation, that he had made his original fortune in some obscure, and probably unsavoury, circumstances, the exact nature of which she couldn't recall. The saying '*behind every great fortune lies a crime'* flitted through her mind. Well, his presence could liven things up; she doubted that Ralston would long put up with Bethany's antics if she got rowdy.

Before joining her fellow diners, Heather wanted a moment of peace, to orient herself amongst the throng, before the effort of dinner party conversation had to be joined. Anyway nobody, at least nobody important, seemed to have noticed her entrance or come over to greet her. Her dress must be less striking than she'd hoped. It promised to be a long evening. She wandered over to the long, refectory style, tables where the auction items were laid out – a silent auction before dinner; but very non-silent after dinner when there would be live bidding from around the room. She searched amongst the various items to investigate if there was something that she might like. Heather understood that she couldn't entirely avoid the bidding at these events, silent or not, without seeming mean. But she'd attended enough galas to learn the technique. Bid early, before prices escalated, and bid reasonably low, so there would be little chance of winning the item - which she soon wouldn't be able to afford anyway.

Holidays in the Caribbean, weekends on yachts, home makeovers, sessions with famous photographers, the bids for all these no doubt wonderful items were already in excess of whatever she thought wise, even if she wanted a weekend on a yacht – which she didn't, being badly sea sick. But down the far end of the table were some much more modest items. Well, modest by comparison with the yacht weekends. The normal retail prices for these junior items were helpfully provided to assist the bidders; $5000 for a blouse, woven from the fleece of some exotic and rare animal. It was a very nice white blouse, but she didn't really need it – and certainly not for $5000. She would bid half that; she didn't really want to spend $2500 either at the moment but this was so early in the evening that she was bound to be outbid. Safe enough, she thought.

Heather wandered around, took a glass of sparkling water from one of the circulating British waiters, the serving class of choice now that those from the Far East had become more expensive. She made her small talk to those she should and then went to find her table. She sat down between Thornton and the Iraqi ambassador and was poured a glass of some unidentified white wine. She heard Bethany on the other side of the ambassador ordering a bottle of champagne for herself. So, not on the wagon after all, Heather noted. Champagne was, Bethany explained to the Iraqi ambassador, the only thing she drank at these events. Thornton's wife expressed this in a way that suggested she drank it purely for medical purposes and it would not be something that could be spared for others, or they might even desire. Heather and the ambassador would have to make do with the warm Chardonnay, that was evidently the house wine for the night. Thornton, a life-long non-drinker, appeared to be oblivious to the whole thing.

The food arrived, meeting Heather's every expectation. Something rectangular and burnt; a pressed block of greasy meat, or more probably meat substitute, appeared on her plate. The block fell to pieces as she tried to cut it. She put some in her mouth, it tasted as though it had arrived from a galaxy far, far, away. This was evidently not to be a gala where money was to be wasted on fripperies like food, and certainly not good wine. Heather broke off a piece of her bread roll and nibbled at it. She was tempted to ask Bethany for a glass of *her* Champagne in order to cheer up her mood, but thought better of it. It was cold in the bare room and she drew her shawl more closely around her shoulders.

Heather turned to the ambassador from Iraq. Might as well start with a direct question she thought; such as '*How is the security situation in New Chaldea, Mr Ambassador?*' Not that Heather wasn't unaware that, as far as she knew, the security situation was grim. She was kept well up to date by Thornton but it would be interesting to hear the perspective from the representative of a country that was immediately affected.

The ambassador was pessimistic. This creation of a safe enclave for the various minorities, that possessed no land of their own in the Middle East, would not guarantee peace but, like the creation of Israel over ninety years before, ensure conflict continued. "Look what is happening, in spite of all the fine words," he said. "The great powers, and some not-very great powers too, are clandestinely infiltrating the territory with advisers, money, subterfuge, propaganda and whatever it takes to secure an advantage when the final political settlement is reached. But what an ambition - a final settlement? What a hope! What have all these minorities got in common? Only their dislike or even hatred of each other! The western powers think they can create some sort of religious beacon in the Levant; a federation, like Germany perhaps, where all the minorities will be protected by this new constitution they're trying to write. It's what you Anglo-Saxons call *a pipe dream*! Not made easier by our friend over there (the ambassador gestured his head in the vague direction of Gillespie's table) who is trying to ensure the Christians have a major part of the spoils when the negotiating music – if you'll pardon my metaphor – stops. "

So, you don't think the Christians have a place in New Chaldea?" asked Heather, with a tone of mock innocence.

"They might have had a place there two thousand years ago but they certainly don't now," replied the ambassador. "Why do they believe that because they originated in that part of the world, they have a perpetual right to live next to the Euphrates? My dear Heather (*may I call you that?)* you're probably by origin a Celt whose ancestors came over with the Vikings to Britain before their descendants in turn boarded the *Mayflower* and sailed here, but that ancient lineage doesn't give you an entitlement to re-colonize Scandinavia! The time has been and gone, I'm sorry. It can't work like that."

"And you don't think that a large Christian population might be a good counterbalance to the Muslims?" Heather asked. "An example to the world that these two great religions, and others, can live together, in harmony……….perhaps?"

The Ambassador hooted with derision. "It will be an example to the world that they *cannot* live together, I would have thought! Hasn't that been the evidence so far? And as for the idea that an influx of westerners will civilize the area - for isn't that what our president-elect friend is trying to promote? I'm reminded of Gandhi's response when asked what he thought about western civilization. '*A very good idea'* he said. A very good idea. You Americans, with your great intentions….." He left the rest of the sentence unsaid.

Heather wondered how much the ambassador really knew about Carroll Gillespie's ambitions – and how he might take an even dimmer view of western intentions if he knew half of what was afoot. She left him to talk with Bethany, who could be relied on to be incendiary about both Middle Eastern politics and the president-elect. That should be most interesting for the ambassador. If Bethany succeeded in holding that middle ground tonight, between sobriety and inebriation, she could be very entertaining.

On Heather's other side Thornton, sensing her attention was now available, disengaged from his neighbour and turned to her, "How were you getting on with the ambassador?" he inquired.

"He's not too enamoured of Gillespie's plans, that's for sure," replied Heather. "Not a big time supporter of a Christian presence in New Chaldea."

"Well, I guess he would think that," said Thornton. "He's bitter. His country was forced to cede large tracts of attractive land along the Euphrates. And he's still a Moslim. Sure, he's not going to support a large Christian presence – but luckily that's not going to be up to people like him."

"No, I don't suppose it will be," said Heather. "But tell me, how's the president-elect's campaign going, to persuade the powers that *are* going to decide things, to act in line with his wishes?"

"Mixed," said Thornton. He speared an olive and popped it into his mouth. "Carroll's always telling me there's such a reluctance to become involved. Even some of the formally Christian nations are not helping much. The French are the worst apparently - keep saying they must support *laïcité,* secularism, and not allow a theocratic state to arise. They never did recover from the revolution. The separation of state and religion? Not a concept that really excites old Carroll, I'm afraid."

"I imagine not," said Heather.

Thornton didn't seem to notice what Heather replied, but looked at the ceiling, lost in some internal dialogue of his own, disengaged from what they had just been discussing. At last he said, "You remember what we talked of the other day?"

"About using the MARIONn platform to influence people, allowing advertising?" Heather asked

"I know you had your reservations, Heather. You said there were ethical issues about persuading people, without their clear consent…" Thornton began.

"That's…….still my view," said Heather, hesitantly. She didn't want to suggest that her resistance might weaken on this point. "It's against the whole trend of the times, you know that Thornton – the effort these days is to make us more aware, more conscious, more *woke*! But you want to come in under their conscious radar, infiltrate people's denial mechanisms. Even delete their memories – the inconvenient ones anyway."

"Look, Heather, here's the thing," said Thornton, speaking with more vehemence in his voice than he really intended. "Carroll, and I for that matter, for we are not too far apart from each other on this issue, we would much prefer that the voters choose, of their own volition, to support intervention in New Chaldea but you know the obstacles….. What those voters are suffering from are just fears – irrational fears. And we should be fighting irrationality. We should be striking a blow not just for what is right but what is rational, what clear sighted people would want." It didn't sound a very convincing argument even to Thornton but he knew he had to deliver for Carroll. Or all sorts of setbacks would be coming his way.

"What rational, clear sighted people want? Heather asked, quizzically. "You mean what clear sighted people like you and Gillespie think is a good idea?" Heather smiled to show she was teasing him.

"I can see you are not entirely persuaded," said Thornton. He looked grumpy. "We'll talk about this later." Over the hubbub of chatter they could just make out the Master of Ceremonies trying to introduce the guest of honour, Governor of Louisiana Carroll Gillespie, President-Elect of the Southern Confederacy. Chairs were pushed back, glasses filled again and gradually the noise diminished to the point where Carroll could start speaking.

Well over six-and-a-half feet, thick set, a polished dome to his head, wisps of greying hair that were left swept straight back over the scalp; round, owlish glasses, Carroll Gillespie looked somewhere between biker and Old Testament prophet. It was in the latter role that he would speak tonight, guessed Heather.

Gillespie led his audience through the history of the Middle East wars, from the perspective of the minorities, explaining how they had all been trampled on, particularly the Christians – who had almost disappeared from the area, in spite of being present in the region long before most of them. But now was the chance to build a new Jerusalem, to restore a balance of creeds to the Middle East, a balance that would ensure that no one set of beliefs could dominate any other - a beacon of tolerance and faith to the world. But this goal depended on western governments getting involved. There was a contest *(A contest? Nice euphemism for the occasional massacre,* thought Heather*)* to determine the boundaries, the nature of the future government and the constitution of New Chaldea. As Christians, they must persuade everyone they met of the rightness and justice of this cause. They must all work to bring pressure on their governments to make this fight their own. The battle for public opinion could be won, but it would require courage, persistence, and resolve.

This was a sympathetic audience. They clapped and roared their approval. See, said Thornton, leaning towards Heather, see how much enthusiasm there is! Heather nodded non-committedly, not much sharing in the emotion.

The speech was succeeded by the public auction. The president-elect ceded the dais to the head of the foundation and bidding commenced. Heather made a couple of low bids, confident that if she did this early enough she would be outbid. She was.

When it was all over the guests started to wander around, searching for friends that they had previously missed, placing bids in the remaining hour or so for the silent auction - that would continue for the rest of the evening. Heather abandoned her dining companions to inspect the list of bids for that expensive white blouse, and was glad to see that there was indeed another entry above her name, with a substantially higher amount pencilled in. She would be able to exit this gala without being committed to anything, no expensive auction item and no concession to Thornton either.

But then Thornton found her as she wandered around, looking for one or two of the few people that she knew. He approached from one side and, in the press and the noise of the crowd, Heather neither sensed or heard his approach. He cupped one hand underneath her elbow and gently steered her away from the concentrated throng in the middle of the room. Now he had decided to be more direct and more forceful, than in his hitherto oblique efforts to win Heather's cooperation. He was very motivated, mindful that the '*stop*' order on his plants could be re-imposed at any time.

"Have you thought any more about our earlier conversation?" Thornton asked. *Earlier conversation*? The two talked most days. Heather could have played coy and pretended she was ignorant of whatever topic Thornton was referring to. But she knew well enough, particularly in the context of the rousing address by the governor. And her mind had not changed; if they started to use *LetheTech's* and MARIONn's technology to play around with unsuspecting, and un-consenting, people's minds Blue Ridge could end up in a much worse mess than they had ever encountered with O'Neal – or the bad publicity they had suffered with the Milton debacle.

But Thornton would pick his battles one at a time. A small, incremental victory was all he sought for the moment. As Heather explained once again her resistance to the idea of public memory deletion, even in such a *good* cause, Thornton reassured her such was not his intention. He understood and agreed with her reservations. Nevertheless...... might it not be acceptable if they monetized their research by imputing *positive* messages about products, sometimes maybe public service announcements? *Positive advertising*, that was the idea! This needn't be about politics, at least not much. Political messages would just be a very small part of their activities.

Heather stood firm. "We can't do that, Thornton", she said. "Be realistic. Employing *LetheTech* as the transmission mechanism for the feed from MARIONn's mind, if no 'tracer' is added, will mean that whatever MARIONn places in memory will feel as though it has always been part of the user's mental apparatus. Individuals will have no opportunity to accept or deny the data. At present, all the social media channels that post advertising via iPsyches tell the user what has been downloaded, whether publicity, information or propaganda, so they are aware of how they came to know what they are being told! Call it what you like, but people must appreciate somebody is trying to influence them – and the regulators insist on that."

Thornton was frustrated by this sort of attitude. "Heather, you know how bad our cash position is at the moment. One more problem with the Miltons and all my Southern operations will be shut down. I can't afford that a second time. We need to generate additional income and we need to do it now. Implanting positive information *at the conscious level*, without the need to go anywhere near the subconscious, is one thing we can sell today. Companies are queueing up to try this methodology, and MARIONn can be far more persuasive than simply floating traditional advertising in front of the consumer. It's the next big step in advertising and I want us to be the leader in it. If not, *Cybersoul* and *Electric Memory* are close behind us." It was always the same threat.

Heather thought of some way of diverting Thornton, at least temporarily. "Maybe we should commission some market research, get an idea how folks think about the idea? Maybe I'm wrong, maybe public reaction may not be as adverse at I think," she said, thinking that while that was highly improbable, Thornton might respect third party opinion - even if he rejected hers. Otherwise a truly spectacular PR disaster was just down the road; which might well have been Gillespie's' strategy from the start, of course. Something to discredit *LetherTech* and MARIONn for all time.

"We can't afford to do that Heather!" said Thornton. "We don't have the time to carry out market research. As it happens I agree with you that the public might mistrust this technology at first. But they'll get used to it – just as they got used to all the other ways we influence people's minds. They swallow anything in time if it makes their life easier. But if we publish what we're doing there'll just be objections. We both know that. So let's skip focus groups and all of the other ways of wasting time. Just do this Heather or I'll be looking for a new CEO."

Merciful heavens! thought Thornton, as he heard the threat leave his lips. He saw any recourse to the issuance of threats as a loss of face and a defeat. He wished to move people only by the gentlest of nudges, by persuasion. Ideally, they should agree with him because they came to realize that he was *right.*

But the threat worked. Heather was in no place to risk her job just now. Particularly as her employment agreement with the Blue Ridge board would prohibit her from working with competitors for two years. And frankly, she thought, if Thornton wanted to risk Blue Ridge and MARIONn in this way, was it really her problem? If the gamble worked, and Thornton got away with what he had in mind, then everything would be well. Money would flow, *LetheTech* would be launched successfully, MARIONn's further development would be financed; Blue Ridge would be the first to hit the market with a form of advertising that went further, and would be more persuasive, than any method before. And for herself? All would be well, her future secured. She was tired. Let Thornton have his way, well advised or not. He would make sure he got it in the end anyway.

And so it was agreed – that MARIONn would be able to access multiple, public minds, but only to *insert* information, such as straightforward advertising, and the odd public service message (in which category Thornton included any propaganda about New Chaldea). But Thornton was determined to be generous in victory and he allowed Heather to wring two concessions out of him - that this advertising would come with a 'tracer' attached and that Carroll Gillespie's pet idea of *deleting* the memory of past overseas military disasters would be shelved – for the time being. With the O'Neal case still in mind, Thornton at least understood those dangers.

Heather was grateful for these small victories of her own but her reluctant willingness, when pushed, to jettison her best judgement (that MARIONn be denied any wide connection to the general public) had breached such a large hole in her resistance to Thornton's schemes that she doubted her ability to resist further erosion in the future.

Defeated, concerned, but at least grateful that she still had a job, she grabbed a drink from a passing waiter and a glass of water for Thornton. They drank to their murky pact and Heather made to leave. She decided to skip saying good-bye to Bethany to thank her. She'd probably never notice by now. On the way out, she walked past the table with the silent auction items. She glanced at the list of bids. The bid above hers had a line through it, *withdrawn.* Her bid was the winning one. She was now the proud owner of the very nice, and very expensive, white blouse. At least she might be able to pay for it, she reflected bitterly, she still had a job.

Chapter 41

Fateful instructions

The day after the gala Heather gave the instruction to link, within strictly defined parameters, the *LetheTech* platform with MARIONn, and allow the latter access to *iPsyche* equipped minds. But all advertising, public service announcements, and political propaganda would carry 'tracers'. Users would be aware of the origins of each message. In practice, the user experience should be very similar to what they were already familiar with on social media. There was nothing different now – except for one thing, the messages would be coming via MARIONn, and from this date on she had the potential power to influence minds in ways that were way beyond the ambition of traditional advertisers.

Once he had Heather's confirmation, Thornton called Carroll Gillespie. Political advertising would, as he wished, now be available, but 'tracers' would have to be attached to the message and for the time being, *LetheTech's* abilities to erase existing memories would not be part of the suite of services offered. This restriction might not be imposed for ever but there were concerns amongst the team (*to put it mildly, he thought*) about the ethics and dangers of such mass memory manipulation. Who knew, perhaps in some months the attitude would be different, when the results of the Phase II and III memory trials had been established. Thornton had not even bothered to speak to Xian Han, whose attitude he considered he knew perfectly well. Xian's cooperation would have to be carefully managed; Han might resign if it was broken to him too quickly that such a course of action was even *contemplated.* Of course, Han would discover what had happened in due course – but that delay would enable Thornton to work out how to prepare the way. In the meantime, it was agreed with Carroll that once the governor's campaign manager had decided on the message they wished to broadcast, he would contact Euclid - who would be glad to place the message on-line.

But Carroll, having won his victory, decided to take a little more than he was being offered. A couple of weeks later the governor phoned Euclid directly, privately, in the evening at his home. Carroll did not want any of this call to be recorded by the MARIONn campus' monitors. The two had a lengthy conversation. The next day Euclid removed the requirement for 'tracers' whenever they concerned any political messages. As far as Euclid was concerned, he was in agreement with his uncle. Much better if their audience should not suffer any '*hindrances'* to understanding the importance of success in New Chaldea. Removing the 'tracers' seemed only sensible, given the objective.

But that was not the only deviation from the agreement that Thornton thought he had made with Carroll. Following an additional two days of programming by Euclid, MARIONn found herself also to be permitted hitherto other forbidden operations; she was now empowered – and indeed instructed - to delete any associations that reminded the user of negative thoughts connected with the previous military campaigns in South East Asia and the Middle East. This instruction Euclid buried so deep in MARIONn's core that Xian Han would never find it – unless he purposely went searching, and why should he do that?

At this time the installed *iPsyche* user base was about 30 million units, but forecast to grow to some 150 million plus within three years. Although only about fifty percent of those were in the US, and therefore potentially interested in the question of whether or not to intervene militarily in New Chaldea, Euclid's instructions to MARIONn did not restrict her access to just US users. It would have been difficult to do so, as nothing singled out an installed iPsyche as a US citizen. In fact, although Carroll was only interested in voters in the southern confederacy, MARIONn now had access to the entire world-wide population of iPsyche users. And, of course, she also had unfettered access to the *LetheTech* technology. If she wished to delete memories, she could. She could exploit *LetheTech*'s technology as effectively as anyone else.

Chapter 42

In the Hamptons

Following the meeting with Bruno, Heather stayed on in New York, only to be sent up to the MARIONn campus by Thornton to broke Xian Han into acquiescence on the changes that had just been made. As it transpired, Xian Han was so disturbed by the opening, even if a limited opening, of MARIONn's access to the broader public that he forced Thornton into making the decision an agenda item for the next meeting of the board. He'd been shocked to discover that Thornton had originally proposed by-passing the board entirely on this vital issue. Maybe a concerted effort from the board would force Thornton to back down,

The meeting would be convened the following Sunday, just about the only time when those who needed to attend would be available. This scheduling suited Heather well; she would be able to benefit from a few more days at the house Thornton had lent her in the Hamptons, and escape the continuing sticky heat that continued in the city. She would take a cab out there tomorrow; a few days ahead of the weekend.

Heather wondered if Claude Blondel had yet landed from Paris. She knew he planned to stop over, prior to the campus meeting. She had sent him an earlier message, suggesting that he could join her in the Hamptons if he was on his own in the city. She particularly wanted to discuss the latest development with him and agree a common line to take in front of Thornton. The pass might have been sold in terms of allowing MARIONn greater public access but at least they could, she hoped, prevent Thornton going any further. She called Claude, but there was no pick-up so she just left a message that if he was free maybe he would like to come and join her on Saturday?

She flicked on one of the wall screes and looked at a summary of the news on New York Times on-line: several peace-keeping UN troops killed in New Chaldea by a terrorist bomb, a senator demanding stricter controls on the new memory therapies, 20,000 experimental pelagic self-harvesting fish had malfunctioned and perished on a Californian beach; the Mars lander *Savannah* had reached half way through its return to earth and no problems so far. A Republican candidate in the presidential primaries was railing against the algorithm in Founding Father 2.4. Ah, yes the governing algorithm..... who but the American's could have decided to lift much of the decision making of government out of the hands of politicians and have them replaced by an algorithm? The government was in hock to vested interests and lobbyists? Then the solution was obvious, remove government from human hands. Now nobody could meddle with it or mould it to favour of whoever's interest. Machines were going to make such a better hash of politics than mankind ever could! She wondered what would happen if MARIONn got hold of Founding Father. Might make the worries about the swamp, excessive influence by lobbyists, be the least of their problems!

Heather replaced the summary of the news with her emails. There was one from Xian Han, saying that MARIONn had been acting strangely of late, nothing to do with the recent changes, but he would delay discussing the issue until the meeting. He wanted

Claude's input too. A confidential one from Thornton, explaining that he expected much of the financial strain on Blue Ridge to pass; the advertising via MARIONn would prove highly effective and popular. She noted that Thornton took pains in the email to soothe her concerns away. He explained, again, that MARIONn was not using her mind to influence others, just her ability to talk to many people at once. There were strict boundaries in force. Really? Heather tapped her fingers on the table by her, an uneasy sensation beginning to settle. It sounded as though Thornton was trying to reassure himself as much as her. There was an underlying current in the email of practicing the arguments, as though Thornton wanted to establish his armoury if he should meet greater than expected resistance from Claude, Xian Han and other members of the board.

The following morning Heather called up a taxi to take her out to East Hampton. She didn't want to share the trip with lots of others on the Jitney. What was the point of having money, even if it might in future be available in declining amounts, if it didn't buy you insulation from all those *other* people? A vicious thunder storm had passed through the day before and left a trail of disruptive flood waters in its wake. She presumed that the driverless taxi she had ordered would pull up within a couple of minutes, the relevant *app* having predicted the level of demand and allocated enough cars for the job. But ten minutes later Heather was still waiting to be advised that a vehicle was on its way. The message that scrolled through on her wrist band apologized but the bad weather had led to unusually heavy levels of demand and there were no taxis available at present. She would have to turn to the secondary market if she wanted to reach the house before lunch time. She collected a small tote for the weekend and headed out onto the street.

By the curb, at the end of her street, were some freelance drivers; the otherwise unemployed who were driving whatever they could afford, old battered cars at least 15 years old, that still required a driver. They were having a hard time generating custom, despite the humidity and the wait for auto-taxis, but Heather decided to risk it. The driver gave her a price. Heather would be able to expense the fare but the demand still sounded outrageous. Storm economics at work, she reflected. But she didn't want to wait any further. She agreed to the extortion and slipped into the worn vinyl seats and gave the driver the address. There was little recognition. Had he heard correctly? God knew where this driver hailed from. *Just off the boat* evidently. Let's hope for the best, she thought. At least, unusually, given its age, the car's air-con worked. But not the GPS. Heather noticed that car's satnav screen was blank, evidently it had broken, or as likely the driver had failed to maintain his subscription to any positioning service. The federal government had long ceased to provide the signal at zero cost to the user. But the driver seemed confident enough that he could find, if not the house, at least the town of Bridgehampton. If the driver got stuck she could always lend him her phone.

She looked out of the window as they approached the George Washington bridge, noticing the street scenes that had become part of the city background in recent years, the vendors every 10 or so meters apart, dressed in rags, squatting in front of their small piles of vegetables, or assortments of bric-a-brac. They looked especially miserable as there were few customers; the damp from the storm had kept many from venturing out today. Others, forlorn, wandered aimlessly, hiding from the rain in alleyways or whatever recesses they could find. On a street corner a band of modern day highway men had waylaid a robocart that had failed to elude them. They hammered on its outside with screwdrivers and tire-levers, trying to break in and steal the groceries of some family who must have wanted to avoid the weather and had sent the cart out independently.

A call came through; Claude would be able to join her tomorrow.

The next day the storm had almost passed through and as Heather lay in bed with her first cup of coffee for the day she wondered how she would plan for Claude's visit, how she would entertain him – given that Claude had probably not been here before. But in that assumption Heather was mistaken.

"When I was a teenager," Claude explained. "My parents brought us on holiday here several years running. They came to the US just to breathe the air of freedom – or so they thought. We used to base ourselves in Sag Harbor, and then do runs into the city to see the shows and so on. But I remember Bridgehampton too – there used to be a French restaurant here, *Andre's*, where we would come and buy croissants in the morning."

"Look to your left – over there!" Heather pointed to an awning on the other side of the road. Indeed, the restaurant was still there. "We'll get some pastries, and a couple of coffees, and take them back to the house."

"I remember Andre. But it must be 20 years since I last went in. He used to run the place with a rod of iron and make sure it was staffed full of beautiful Russian waitresses," said Claude.

"Not much has changed! Andre must be in his mid-seventies by now, but not the waitresses. They always stay under 30. Maybe he will remember you?"

And Andre did, or at least said he did – which was charming of him, even if Claude had his doubts. The price charged up on his wristband for the two coffees and croissants was about 3 times what he would have paid in Paris.

They went back to the house to drink their coffee and for Claude to drop his stuff. Thornton's contemporary, all glass and weathered-wood, house was set in a clearing amongst the trees; opposite, there was a smaller house, similar. Both were of recent construction. As Heather explained, most of the houses here were built of wood and more often than not the new owners simply tore down the old one and built again, to suit them better.

"Although the whole set up is owned by Thornton, including the house you see over there, he hardly ever uses it. He was terrified of picking up Lyme disease, but that's hardly a problem now as most of the deer have been shot and eaten. Old fears die hard, I guess. Stephanie uses the annex a bit if she's up here. Otherwise it's rented. Nice of him to let me have the main house for a few weeks. It's pretty quiet for the Hamptons. You should find it peaceful. I'll let you freshen up. We could go and have lunch on Shelter Island. The wind has died down a bit."

They headed out for the ferry to the island. It was a beautiful day now the rain had stopped and the idea appealed of enjoying some of the walks on the island after lunch. They chatted in the car and at one point Heather said, "I remember that you wanted your father to be a candidate for Phase III trials of *LetheTech*'s treatment. Has he been called yet?"

"They've given him a date to start – or rather given me the date as my poor old father would never remember it!" replied Claude. "I don't know if it's too late but I couldn't overlook the possibility that he could live autonomously, with his memory rebuilt. I confess I did have my doubts. I was almost ready to sign and then…, all that disaster about Kinnead O'Neal. But later I thought, things are so bad they can hardly get worse. It's worth the risk. Let's hope all goes well."

"I think your father will be fine," said Heather, trying to be reassuring..

"Well, the market does indeed seem to believe you have solved the over-deletion danger," said Claude. "I noticed the recent increase in price of the stock in over-the-counter trading. And it will soar once you finally launch the IPO. You will be rich!."

"They're only options, I'm afraid," said Heather. "And I can only exercise them if I stay with Blue Ridge. Thornton keeps close control of his executives. But I hope you bought some stock, Claude. If you hadn't brought Xian to us, very little of this would have happened."

"Thornton had already identified Han and was making overtures. I'm not sure I had much effect on his decision. I came along as part of the baggage, as a friend of Xian's."

"You're too modest, Claude." Claude turned and glanced at Heather, just to check her expression and make sure she was not being ironic or teasing him. There were not many times in his life he had been accused of modesty. She saw his sceptical look and laughed,

"Your contribution has been vital. I assure you Claude. But you have your own experience of *LetheTech* anyway. All that went well, I think? No after effects?"

"I did?" he asked

"When we were experimenting at the beginning. Phase 1 trials? You offered yourself as a volunteer. You were different to most of the guinea-pigs, though. At the time, we advised everybody that, as this was just a trial, not an attempt at therapy, we would re-install memories that we had removed, leave them as before. But you explicitly asked us not to do that. You signed a waiver to that effect. You don't remember? Of course, why should you? The whole memory has been removed!"

"It's true, I have no recollection of this," said Claude. "But I'm worried about such obliviousness. I must have had good reason at the time to ask for the memory not to be re-installed, but now ….. I am troubled to know there was something in my life that I did not wish to remember."

"You could always ask Harvey Jennings," said Heather. "If you want to retrieve the memory. He will probably not yet have deleted it from the *LetheTech* servers. But be careful what you wish for! There must have been a reason why you wanted to forget – permanently - whatever it was. And I don't know if Harvey will allow you to download the memory again. Deleted memories become property of the company, for research purpose only of course – and he may judge that the traumatic incident – because I imagine it was traumatic, otherwise why would you not want it back? – will disturb your psyche too badly if it is re-installed. But I don't know for sure – you'll have to talk to him."

They had now arrived at the ferry and the subject was dropped. Claude had last travelled on this flat-bottomed barge decades before, with his father. He had always liked ferries, the romance of them, that sense of crossing over, of transitioning from one shore to another. He recalled that ships were symbols of transcendence in Buddhism. Once, deep in the Himalayas, he had visited a cave that was used by the monks to meditate. He couldn't have been further from the sea but on all the ledges, on any piece of flat rock within that holy grotto, stood little model ships; sailing vessels that would never feel the wind in their sails but symbolized the bearing of these monks from one state of consciousness to another, from *samsara* to a higher, more enlightened state.

The ferry slid gently over the sand on the opposite bank and came to a rest; the ramp was lowered and the lane of cars drove off. For a few minutes they were silent but Claude was keen that Heather should not return to the subject of Harvey Jennings and himself. As he had first noticed in France, whenever he approached that issue, he encountered a resistance. The best way to divert Heather was to move that subject of conversation onto her own territory,

"How's your '*uncoupling*' going?" he asked

Heather twisted her mouth down and pulled a face, "Not well."

She told Claude of Bruno's decision to seek a full divorce. "Is there a way of backtracking at this stage?" Claude asked.

"I doubt it. The problem is that Bruno wants out, whatever. He's got some nice alternative life already sorted. And, besides, I don't want to lose Chase too in this mess."

But Heather didn't particularly want to talk about her marital problems. She was still distressed at the thought of Thornton's exploitation of her weak position. Heather felt the need for an ally; it might be lonely at the top but at least before she had the support of Thornton. No longer, it seemed to her. According to Thornton, she retained his confidence still but the reality felt different; his support was now clearly conditional in a way that it had not been a few months earlier. They were no longer quite equal colleagues working together for the success of MARIONn. Recent events had shown Heather to be a subordinate, expected to take instructions and work as best she could with her boss. She had thought of resigning and looking for a new job, but there was the small matter of the two year non-compete and also, she was horribly comprised. Even forgetting about the financial consequences, if she were to go public about what had happened, Thornton could destroy her career by simply leaking the executive order showing that it was *she* who had issued the instruction to allow MARIONn down the dangerous path of wider public access, before MARIONn had properly been tested or her education completed. At least by staying on, she might redeem herself by controlling any wilder urges that might occur to Thornton in the future.

They parked the car and took their bikes out of the back, choosing to enjoy the better weather and pedal the rest of the way to the Sunset Beach restaurant, which, as it name suggested, looked straight west, into the setting sun if you were there in the evening. They could both do with the exercise and the car parking would probably be full anyway by the time they reached the restaurant. Which it was. The place was heaving, inevitable on a Saturday, but they managed to find a table.

After they had completed their order, Heather asked Claude

"I see we, as the board, are being asked to approve, retrospectively, the linking of MARIONn to the internet. I always thought we had banned that idea until MARIONn was fully developed and we understood her?"

Heather gave a brief resumé of the pressures she'd encountered from Thornton. " Thornton believes it's a very limited change. Will not give rise to any problems," she said

"I'm sure he does!" said Claude. "But since when has Thornton been an expert on these technical issues?"

"Since he started running out of money," said Heather.

"Well, I will oppose this."

"Good luck with that Claude. It's already been instituted – this development. Thornton is just asking the board to rubber stamp what he's already ordered. You know how he regards Blue Ridge as his own fiefdom. He doesn't really believe in other people telling him what to do."

'Then I will resign!"

"Will you?" asked Heather. She already had Claude marked down as a lover of the grand gesture. "Please don't. We need voices like yours – even if it is a problem sometimes getting Thornton to listen to them. Besides, so far, nothing has gone wrong. The service is very popular with advertisers, to access their iPsych*e* wearing customers. Although those with iPsyche*s* have to permit the message to enter their mind, in practice most of the target audience just wave it through. They get so many messages these days it's just easier to accept them, than having to make a decision about whether to let the message in or not."

"And the political stuff? I'd heard that Thornton has also been under pressure from his old friend Gillespie."

"Well, that's just another form of advertising isn't it? As long as the identifying tracer is attached I think the potential for problems is small."

"There was no risk of a problem *at all* before we allowed this!" exclaimed Claude.

"It was you who first suggested we expand the number of people who have direct access to her," Heather said, a little unkindly. "We are just talking scale here."

"Scale is important," said Claude. "Before, those were just private conversations, between MARIONn and her team, which we could monitor. When you go mass, you are going to lose control."

"Oh, but you're mistaken. We don't monitor the teachers at the moment, Claude," said Heather, much to Claude's surprise. "Don't forget that it's not just lessons that the teachers are providing to MARIONn; all their sense data is flowing to her too. Their very lives are available to MARIONn. That was your idea, Claude. And we agreed to it!"

"But, no checks....? Surely......"

"We can't see any other way. Even if we could monitor all the sense data and conversations flowing backwards and forwards between them, it would be very intrusive on the handlers. I think we just have to trust them."

What Heather did not know was that the problem was infinitely worse than she suspected. Since the abandonment of the restrictions on contact with the wider public, that Euclid had introduced, MARIONn was receiving a data feed from millions of other people. And she was engaging with them too. Heather had restricted MARIONn to imputing positive messages from commercial sponsors, but she had no idea that the effect of Euclid's action was that MARIONn now had the power to delete any conflicting messages or memories that she found in her user base – and that she did not like.

"But there's something else going on here," said Claude, "something that puzzled me, and Xian,.... that I read in the briefing papers........ MARIONn's brain is slowing down, at least when performing mechanical operations, when behaving like a conventional computer."

"Yes, I saw that. Of course, we don't know exactly how MARIONn is building her own mind; we could have just underestimated the Hofstadter effect. This retardation could happen if she was having to process more sense data and information than we know about..."

"The Hofstadter effect?"

"First conceived by the philosopher Douglas Hofstadter. The guy who wrote '*Godel, Escher and Bach.*' He thought that if a computer ever had to handle as much information and processing as a human mind does in its day-to-day life, then they would be as slow to think as we are"

"There is another reason why she might be more hesitant, slower, to give us answers than she was earlier."

"Which is?" asked Heather.

"That MARIONn is actually further along her development curve than we know. She may be more mature, more conscious, than we realize. She may be holding back on displaying all her abilities. To keep us in ignorance may just suit her."

"She may be deceptive, you mean?"

"Exactly. Of course, all these hypotheses may be true. One does not rule out another. But suppose she is developing faster than we know about. Say, to take an example, her mind is not equivalent to that of an adolescent, as we think, but to something much more advanced – and not like us at all. MARIONn might want to hide this from us."

"To what purpose?"

"I have no idea, " admitted Claude. "I'm just asking the question. But if we have created something that is vaguely human it might not surprise us that she exhibits one of humanities most deep routed characteristics – the wish to *deceive*, the wish to gain a competitive advantage. *Over us*"

"I could ask Han whether there is any way to check this."

"It might be worth doing so," said Claude. Some buried human instinct, his intuition, made him anxious without letting him know precisely what the cause of his concern might be. He laughed, "Let me tell you of a strange encounter while I was in the city yesterday."

"Yes, do please," said Heather. "I always appreciate bizarre goings on. At long as they involve anyone but MARIONn!"

"Well," said Claude. "It was like this. Feeling that some exercise might settle my mind, I decided to go out for a walk from my hotel. As you will remember, the weather was still damp yesterday and, indeed, the chance of another storm seemed high. If I was to have a walk, it would be wise to get it in then. I left the hotel and, with no specific aim or destination, strolled as the mood took me; making a turn when I felt like it or where there was a building that piqued my interest."

"At some point I found myself opposite a substantial brick building. The building looked very abandoned and I noticed that the clock at the summit of the tower had stopped. Cities, these days, never have the resources for non-essential expenditure like keeping public clocks running! I crossed the street and walked under the staging that prevented the parts of the building that were shedding themselves from felling passers-by. On the corner, an old Afro-

American, clad in a grimy suit, with a pepper-and-salt beard, had pitched a small table and set up a handwritten sign *'Personal Horoscopes. Tarot card and Palm reading'*. I noticed the man was looking straight into the sun without squinting, his eyes glittering, a reflection from the milky cornea; the man was blind. I felt that I should give this old man something and asked to buy a horoscope. There were a pile on the table. I imagined that I would just hand over a few dollars and receive his piece of paper. But it wasn't that simple. The old man needed some details first. His queries started simply enough – date of birth, place of birth. But then the questions became more detailed, had I been married, children, were my parents alive, where had they come from? I began to regret having stopped; I had just wanted to be charitable to this vagabond. N*o good deed goes unpunished*, I thought, rather crossly. I was about to pull away and said, "Please, just give me a horoscope, thank you" and pointed to the plie in front of him. But this *seer*, sensing that I had grown restless, said to me, "My friend. I did not ask you all these questions for no purpose. But I am sorry that I have no horoscope here that predicts your future. I will have to write one especially for you." But by this time I was exasperated and said, "It's Ok, thank you. I quite understand. I don't mind that you have no horoscope for me. Please, keep the money."

"But the man shook his head and grasped the sleeve of my coat. *'My friend!'* he said. *'It is you who don't understand! I see your future – but it is not written here.'* He pointed to the pile of already drafted astrological predictions and turned his sightless eyes on me, *'I ask no money. It is already written, not by me, listen...'* He pulled my sleeve again to bring me closer, as though to make sure that his words would not be missed. *'You must leave here, stop what you're doing. Have no more to do with certain....'* He didn't seem very sure what it was exactly that I should be leaving alone. He went on, vaguely, *'... certain....things or persons. Be careful, do not seek for what you have already forgotten. Let the past go. You will have to undertake a long and dangerous journey.'* All this was ridiculous enough. *A long and dangerous journey* indeed, that's always the sort of clichés of these fraudsters! I didn't know quite what to say. I pressed him for more details of what he saw but he just stared at me and shook his head. He didn't say another word, just stood there, silently, looking up at the sky as if for inspiration, grasping all the time at my sleeve, as though he might personally drag me away from whatever fate awaited. His face was now very close to mine and the smell of rotting gums revolted me. I pulled myself apart violently, '*Unhand me*!' I shouted, louder than I meant to. The man let go and looked down at his table, still shaking his head but I did manage to release myself. I was very shaken, I can tell you. I walked away through the rain, that had just started, my head now even less clear than when I had set out.'

"How extremely unpleasant!" said Heather. "Poor you, Claude. I'm afraid there are all sorts of mountebanks out there at the moment, trying to make a living somehow. One has to be so careful!"

"But the strange thing is that this man refused to accept any money. Even when I pressed it on him. It was though he thought me tainted in some way."

The two chatted on some more and then, when they had finished the meal, Claude offered to pay for lunch. Heather gracefully accepted but his attempt to do so was declined by his bank. Claude was embarrassed but also puzzled; unable to recall when such a thing had last happened. There should be plenty of credit on the account; perhaps he had been hacked. He called up the *app* for his bank. He was right, there was plenty of money. Yet he wouldn't be able to call till Monday and sort out whatever the problem was. "I'm so sorry Heather, it looks as though you'll have to support me this time," he said. Heather picked up the tab willingly enough; it was not a problem. Probably some hack that had forced his bank to close down the payment system for a while. But there was no message from the bank about this – as he would have expected in such circumstances.

They walked out on the beach that lay in front of the restaurant but the wind had now risen. It whipped up the sand, stinging any exposed skin. Heather felt the flying grains keenly. "Let's turn round and go back," she said. "We can pick up something to eat for dinner on the way back home. There's a shack on the way back *Manna from Heaven* that does excellent food '*to go*'. I seem to remember that manna should fall from the heavens for free but, as you will see, this is not quite the case here!"

"What should I expect?" said Claude laughing. "This is the Hamptons. Not ancient Sinai!"

He tried to pay for their take-away dinner too, hoping the problem, whatever it had been, it had cleared. But no, to his embarrassment that payment was also declined.

Part 5

MARIONN

Chapter 43

How conscious is MARIONn?

The next day a second front of the storm had stalled over New York state; it had turned into one of the worst of the summer; the tail end of a hurricane. The turbulence and the continuing intense rain made it questionable to fly up to the MARIONn campus but eventually it was decided that it was safe - just. Thornton was still in New York so he sent his helicopter to the Hamptons to collect Claude and Heather, pretending that this was an act of kindness to them but Heather knew perfectly well that this meant Thornton would not have to fly himself. A great relief to him, particularly given what he judged as outrageously dangerous conditions. The alternative would be a slow drive from the city, for the Lincoln tunnel was flooded. He would have to make via a detour onto George Washington Bridge and the Bronx expressway. But that was better than flying.

By the time Heather and Claude arrived safely at the campus, albeit after a bumpy flight, the rain had ceased and the sun was out, shining on the MARIONn building as though it was some New Jerusalem, a city on a hill. And perhaps it was, Claude mused.

Maybe MARIONn could solve those issues that had bedevilled humanity for so long, how to organize itself, how to behave, what to believe; all those questions that had not been answered by the most brilliant of human minds nor the most sophisticated of traditional computers. But even if MARIONn had almost God-like power to solve those issues, would her conclusions be trusted and followed by a mistrustful humanity? There had been overwhelming evidence to support the concepts of evolution and climate change, but still people managed to believe some other theory, on grounds of divine revelation, or sheer prejudice. Humanity had not shown much inclination to follow a rational path, or even a sensible one sometimes. He wondered if MARIONn would make any difference – even if she worked as forecast.

Claude had missed the last two reviews, one because he was teaching and the other because he had decided to take a much needed holiday with Stephanie instead. He was now eager to discover for himself how far MARIONn had developed since he had last spoken to her. There were no great conceptual issues involved during the last few months of her education and Claude's personal presence had not been essential. A debate about MARIONn's moral needs, and the extent to which she should be pre-programmed with normative codes, had, at Thornton's request, included Claude. All of that he'd been able to handle from Paris. But this meeting he'd decided he must attend. His disquiet over the expansion of MARIONn's contact with the human race was so strong that he wished to make unhappiness known to the other members of the board – in person.

One the meeting began, Thornton lead off the discussion. He said that he knew it was a troublesome issue, the (*very limited,* in his view) linking of MARIONn with *LetheTech,* so they could initiate a whole new way of delivering advertising, and he wanted to get it out of the way first. There were other agenda items that he felt needed more discussion.

But Thornton ran into opposition immediately. "I cannot believe that this is now being proposed!" Claude interjected. He had forgotten, in his anxiety, that this was less a proposal than a foregone conclusion. "We have always been of one mind at this board; MARIONn must have no access to the internet, nor indeed to any audience outside this building, until we know exactly how she works and that her behavioural restrictions are in-force and effective. It's not just to protect MARIONn from undesirable influences as she develops, but also, of course, to stop her doing anything that might be dangerous or undesirable, those things that we have not predicted or inhibited. This is a decision that, if we allow it to stand, we will come to regret, *énormèment!* We should step back while we still can!"

Thornton sucked in his breath, straightened his back. He had expected this sort of opposition, particularly from Claude. He explained the background to his decision, the financial strain the group had been under, the delay after the Kinnead O'Neal debacle to raise additional funds through an IPO, the pressure from the president-elect over the Milton robot debacle. He took them through the discussion with Heather (*Thornton implied that Heather had been entirely supportive*) about the best solution in light of these factors and the shared (!) decision to release a tiny amount of MARIONn's great powers, a hundredth, a thousandth maybe, of what she would eventually be capable of. There must be some relief from the financial head-winds that Blue Ridge was presently suffering. But, as he made clear and tried to reassure Claude, there was still a strict prohibition on MARIONn penetrating any minds further than she needed to for the purposes of '*getting her message across'*, as he put it. "But don't just listen to me about all this," said Thornton, wishing to divert the hostility to this new strategy that he could sense radiating from other members of the board. He turned for support to Xian Han. As chief development officer, his opinion would carry a lot of weight. "Xian, would you please reassure our colleagues here that this is not really a dangerous development?" Thornton asked.

Xian Han looked up and down the table, to indicate that what he was about to say was directed at all of them. He explained the amendments that had been made to MARIONn's operating procedure. This was, he said, just as Thornton indicated, a modest liberalization of the still very strict regime under which she operated. In particular, this was a one-way relationship – MARIONn could deliver messages but her public would have no ability to talk, or, more importantly, to feed-back ideas that might influence her. He made no mention, as he might have done, about his own concern for this change of policy. He knew that the pass had been sold, the connection made and the policy already in operation. Out of loyalty to Thornton, Han tried to move the discussion onto something else while he reassured his audience about the general direction of MARIONn's progress.

"Things have been going pretty well, in the right direction", he said, with a light optimism in his voice. But there was a catch to the tone and Claude was interested in the *'but'* that he knew was coming.

"But…" said Han. "There have been one or two other developments that have been…interesting." *Interesting?* Claude sharpened his attention, a keen student of euphemisms. "In spite of MARIONn's consciousness broadening and deepening, since we expanded her educational team." Claude glanced down the table at Euclid. He was hunched up and appeared to be sulking. "There has been a simultaneous slowing of MARIONn's deductive abilities. You will remember .." and Xian Han looked around the room to seek confirmation that people did indeed recall past issues they had succeeded in solving together. "When MARIONn initially went operational, before she developed consciousness, we used her like a pretty traditional super-computer. After all, she had a mental architecture that was amongst the most sophisticated computer structures at the time. So …when a Blue Ridge client, for example, wanted mega-data sets run or some very intricate modelling performed, we used to ask MARIONn to carry them out. She could handle this stuff faster than any competitor's machine. And this was a useful income source for us. However…… since becoming more self-aware we've noticed that this ability is slowing. The more MARIONn has to take on, it seems the less and less can she afford – or maybe *wish*, who knows? – to dedicate circuits to running simplistic, but very large, data crunching exercises."

Claude leant forward, focused his gaze on Han and interrupted. He would try to return to the previous agenda item later, that he noted Han had been successful in mostly by-passing. Nobody else seemed to share his anxiety. But he was also interested in what Han was saying now; he wanted to understand precisely how this slowing of deductive reasoning was showing itself. Maybe this recalcitrance to do her master's bidding was a sign of problems to come. "What's your view of this, Xian?" he asked. "MARIONn's not interested in that sort of thing any longer? Is it too boring, not challenging enough for her? Is she making a sort of….. rebellion? Or is this retardation occurring because her mind is handling so much information, being conscious, that she cannot handle all this other stuff at the same time?"

But it was the sulking Euclid from down the other end of the table who answered, rather than Han. "I anticipated something like this would happen," he said, with a note of satisfaction in his voice. His ignored warnings had come to pass. Claude was amused by something he'd noticed before about Euclid; how much he wanted to defend MARIONn's reputation and how much he wanted himself to be judged as *prima inter pares* of those who were familiar with her growing abilities and character. "She's not being difficult, or rebellious," Euclid explained. "It's just that MARIONn is very busy integrating her experiences, that she receives through us, her contact team, and the stuff we give her to learn. Of course, now you've *decided to expand the number of those who have access to her,* it's not surprising if she has too much sense data to integrate immediately and sometimes gets confused." Euclid didn't want to miss the opportunity of criticizing the earlier decision and demonstrate how, really, that had just made *everything* more difficult and slower. Particularly for him. Having contributed his bit of criticism of the problems the board had created, Euclid slumped back into his chair, returning to his sulk.

Xian Han picked up where Euclid left off, "We predicted that some slowing up of MARIONn's processing side would occur. But we've been surprised just how severe it's been. As a mind, MARIONn's still a genius level maths student but she's passed on, or *'grown out of'* might be a better description, what we expect from a traditional computer. I'm not sure yet if that's a good or a bad thing," Han laughed, uncertainly. "Maybe being a conscious computer, or even a conscious human, involves a lot more mental effort than we had suspected."

"How conscious is MARIONn nowadays? What are the metrics on this?" asked Claude.

"On the Dennett index, she's about 3.7 – at the end of last week," replied Han. "That's progress of almost a whole unit in the last three months. Of course, consciousness is developed on an asymptotic curve; so as MARIONn develops, each incremental improvement will be smaller, the curve gets flatter." On the screen behind them a line was traced, that changed in colour as it progressed, from left to right, from green, to blue, to purple (*Claude noted no part of the line was coloured red. Hopefully* MARIONn *never would achieve a state where red would be the appropriate choice)* and curved over in a flattening parabola. Along the vertical 'Y' axis lay the Dennett index, running from zero to ten, while horizontally, on the X" axis, time, since initial power-up, was recorded. Little boxes, with arrows pointing to dates along the line, appeared as Han's red laser pen traced its way on the curve; each box inscribed with some developmental goal achieved.

"You can see here, at this first box," said Han. "This is where we turned on the Bayesian modelling circuits; MARIONn's beginning to form internal models of the world in her mind. At that point she's almost aware of herself being separate from the external world. She can distinguish what is '*in her mind'* and what is outside, external to herself – and that's the very beginning of consciousness, of course. It's a bit like the old existentialist distinction, distinguishing between things that have existence *'in themselves'*, inanimate, dumb objects if you like, and those that have existence *'for themselves',* creatures such as ourselves that have a purpose, an intention, a goal, or goals, in life."

"And what is MARIONn's intention or goal? Her purpose?" someone asked

Euclid levered himself enough out of his sulk to respond to the question. He was the self-appointed keeper of MARIONn's soul. "At the moment, MARIONn's chosen goal is to improve her education and learn as much as she can about us and our society. After that, it's to be of use to humanity more generally. We agreed that in the original spec. She'll help us solve what we can't solve for ourselves," he said.

All very pious, thought Claude. *I hope MARIONn takes the same view as us of what she's here for. But we'll return to that, no doubt.*

Han brought their attention back to the line on the wall. "Here we are running the first Turing test, talking to MARIONn, seeing if she sounds like a human being in conversation. It wasn't a very good test at the time. MARIONn was quite primitive, a child in our terms, and the conversation was a bit limited."

"I thought that we'd down-rated the importance of the Turing test? That it was too easy for a standard, *non-self-aware*, AI machine to look conscious when it wasn't? So not much use in judging MARIONn's progress?" This was Heather.

"That's true," agreed Han. "But we still regard it as a test MARIONn has to pass. It's not a sufficient demonstration of consciousness - but it is a necessary one."

"This Dennett level of 3.7 – what's the human equivalent in terms of human development in terms of self-awareness?" Thornton asked.

"Early adolescence,' replied Han, confidently. "MARIONn has reached this absolute level in just under a year since power up. She can learn much faster than us. Fifteen years for us achieved in six months for her. But the development of a consciousness, at least one that we can understand, for maybe the guys on the *Savannah* returning from Mars may bring back a different type of local consciousness with their rock samples…" There was a brief titter of laughter around the room at the thought of these potential aliens invading us with their different concept of consciousness. "But I repeat, to build a consciousness like our own, that we can communicate with, that requires MARIONn not just to learn but, of course, to *understand* what she learns. That's not instant – and cannot be. Experience needs to be laid down layer by layer."

"And when will she reach her full potential consciousness then? Her adult state?" asked Heather, conscious that as a company asset MARIONn would one day have to be put to service, and the sooner she earned an ROI (return on investment) the better.

Han took a deep breath. These people never understood. "There's no *fully* conscious; no final adult state. There's only a continuum. Consciousness is always built on, there's always another deeper level of consciousness to be found. But if you were to ask me, when will MARIONn achieve a level of self-awareness equivalent to, say, a reasonably aware human adult, then I would say - in about another three months."

"How is she as an adolescent? She can't very well go to parties and take too many drugs!" Claude didn't recognize the voice. What an idiotic question, whoever this was! Whoever heard of a computer taking drugs? But Claude was wrong on this point. Xian Han laughed and replied, "Oh but she can! Euclid, please explain."

Euclid enjoyed discussing his charge's abilities. "You'll recall that MARIONn's team of educators, that is to say the 6 of us, since you decided that my experience was inadequate for the purpose, are linked to her mind directly through our iPsyches. We agreed that MARIONn's consciousness has to develop as ours did originally. She has to experience the world like us, as we were growing up. We are her senses. Through us she sees, hears, has a sense of smell and touch. So, if one of us goes to a party, she comes too, in effect. We have to be careful, we don't want to expose her to bad influences. If we were to take drugs, she would feel that. But, of course, we want to ensure she only gains the best possible impression of humanity."

"But if she is going to solve some of our more intractable problems, doesn't she need to know us at our worst as well?" asked Thornton. It seemed a good point. There was a hum of support around that table. Thornton looked rather pleased with his comment.

"She does need to appreciate our weaknesses, yes," said Euclid. "But that's for later – when she's more '*mature*'. We don't want her learning bad things, or bad behaviour, before she can put them in some sort of context – before she can handle that type of knowledge."

"OK, so MARIONn doesn't do drugs but, as an adolescent, what sort of things does she enjoy doing? Does she tell you, Euclid? Does she try and persuade you to get up to certain things?" asked Claude.

"Oh yes. MARIONn has her own tastes all right!" replied her educator.

"Perhaps," Xian Han said, as he looked around the room, "perhaps some of you would like to ask her for yourself what she likes doing?" They all agreed that would be an interesting idea.

"You'd like us to move, Han?" asked Thornton. "I remember last time we had to transfer to the monitoring room to speak to MARIONn."

"No, no. That won't be necessary this time," replied Han. "That was when we spoke to her via the headsets. Now we have iPsyches we can do that here, in this room."

"But several of us don't yet have iPsyche*s*," objected Claude.

"It's not a problem." Han pointed to Euclid. "Euclid will talk to MARIONn via his own device and relay the conversation. You can speak to Euclid as though you are speaking directly to MARIONn. Which you are really, your words go directly to Euclid's ears, through his cerebral cortex and straight from there to MARIONn's mind. I have to warn you the experience is, like....well, it's a little surreal. MARIONn speaks to you via Euclid's mind and larynx.

But it's MARIONn's authentic voice that you will hear, not Euclid's." Han paused. "Euclid would you make contact with MARIONn please, and ask if she's be happy to take some questions? Thank you."

The process reminded Claude of a séance, one of those table moving sessions, or Ouija board demonstrations, in which he participated infrequently as a youth. But he had the analogy wrong – as he was about to learn.

Euclid closed his eyes and appeared to be concentrating. Nothing happened for a few seconds and then Euclid said, "Hi MARIONn, how's things this morning?" Whatever the response was, Euclid kept it to himself, gently nodding, still with his eyes shut, as though downloading MARIONn's words. Euclid explained to her, out loud, what was going to happen.

"MARIONn, I have some friends here who would like to ask you a few questions, have a chat. Is that OK?" Claude noted with interest how Euclid deferred to MARIONn's desires and occupations. "You're sure? Not in the middle of something?"

It seemed that everything was OK and MARIONn was not otherwise occupied. But when she said, "Oh sure, Euclid. That would be absolutely fine. I was just studying the Greek tragedies but I can do that later. Any friend of yours is a friend of mine, as you know. Now, how can I help y'all?" The voice that spoke from Euclid's throat was a girl's, and a girl from the South evidently. Well, what did Claude expect? This was all being paid for by Thornton, a Southerner to his finger-tips. No wonder that MARIONn had a soft southern drawl.

The sensation of MARIONn's girlish voice emanating from Euclid's throat was unsettling. Claude had once attended a performance of Hamlet in which the ghost of the eponymous hero's father had spoken out of Hamlet's belly, in his father's voice. It had been a brilliant *coup de theatre* that had made his hair stand on end – and it did the same now.

There was a silence in the room; those attending knocked back by the dissonant experience of hearing a female voice that emanated from the throat of a male, born and raised in the Bronx. Heather, perhaps out of a feeling of feminine solidarity with MARIONn, was the first to recover and speak; "Hi MARIONn. Nice to meet you. It's Heather Masters here."

"Hi Ms Masters. How are you? It's nice to meet you too," came back the cheery reply.

"MARIONn, we haven't met before although I have watched carefully over your development. Please call me Heather. I was wondering what are your favourite activities? What do you and your team get up to?"

"Oh, Heather I really like to go motor racing. I'm always trying to persuade Euclid to take me."

"You like to *watch* motor racing, surely? Gosh, who would have guessed that, MARIONn?"

"Not *watch* motor racing," relied MARIONn, evidently feeling she had been misunderstood. "I am there, with Euclid; seeing it through his eyes! Euclid's got a souped-up old Camaro and he loves to take it on the track." Heather realized that she had no idea of how Euclid spent his free time. What else did he do? MARIONn only had the sophistication of an early teen. Sex? Drinking? Drugs? She hoped Euclid had the good sense to turn off his iPsyche appropriately. But it was MARIONn who had the good sense right at this moment. She was aware enough of the reactions of humans not to disclose what Euclid had got up to with his girl-friend Maria last weekend, when he had forgotten to close down his iPsyche. MARIONn had read enough human literature to understand that this might not be exactly what her educators expected or wished to hear.

MARIONn liked motor racing but what she liked even more was the thrill she received, via her connection with Euclid's senses, when he was canoodling with Maria. So when Heather pressed her on whether there were other activities of Euclid's, and of her more recent teachers, that she enjoyed MARIONn decided not to elaborate. She just said, "Oh, the car racing is exciting enough for me. You should try it Heather. It's real' good fun. I keep telling Euclid to go faster. I love going fast." MARIONn had learnt early an unfortunate lesson from her readings, *the first purpose of language is deception*

Claude smiled. A love of speed – of course, why not? Like a human adolescent MARIONn would love the experience of the track through Euclid's own eyes. This was not an aspect of developing consciousness that they had considered but perhaps this was as good a *'proof'* as any that consciousness had been achieved. But he was curious what MARIONn did when Euclid was not available and had turned off his iPsyche.

" MARIONn, it's Claude here. Good morning."

"Good Morning Claude. Is that spelt with an e?"

"It is"

"Bonjour Claude, comment ça va? Tu va bien en ce matin gris? On me dit que le soleil va se lever."

Everyone laughed – at least everyone except Claude, who was slightly unnerved by this level of precocity in a silicon based adolescent mind. For a moment he was taken aback by the use of the '*tu*' form. Such familiarity – and in someone so young! Well, who knew what the correct relationship was between two different forms of intelligence? *"Je suis en plein forme, merci. Mais peut-être nous devons continuer cette conversation en Anglais? Pas tout le monde parle Français ici."*

"Not at all MARIONn."

"So apart from motor racing, MARIONn, what do you like doing?" he asked. "What's your favourite subject, for example? History was her answer, although it could also have been human psychology. The interrogation continued like this for a while, as those who were not in MARIONn's immediate educational team took the opportunity to confirm for themselves that MARIONn expressed thoughts and preferences similar to any other well-behaved early teenager. There were no sulks and, Claude noted, no sense of tiredness, or boredom, as the questioning continued. But after about twenty minutes, MARIONn said,

"I think we'd better stop now. I sense that Euclid's voice is getting tired." Which it was, his voice box having to perform both his own and MARIONn's less natural (to him) accent and intonation. So they asked Euclid to shut down the link, say good bye to MARIONn and thank her for talking to them.

"It's been a real pleasure," she said.

Chapter 44

Will MARIONn always choose the good?

"Well," said Claude, when an exhausted looking Euclid signalled that MARIONn had signed off and that they were now on their own. "MARIONn sounds delightful. Quite the most polite early teen I have come across recently! But," and here Claude focused his attention on Han, he wanted to steer the discussion back to the question that had been obsessing him. "MARIONn's being brought up with a consciousness like our own, and I accept that her educational materials are being controlled, yet even the most self-aware human gets bad urges at times. You've just heard that she likes to tell Euclid to drive faster. That's harmless enough – at least it is if Euclid ignores her prompts – but what would happen if she developed other urges; that aren't so benign? What defences are there? What restrictions are built into her mind?"

"There a number of them," replied Han, confident in the security procedures that he had installed. "We've inserted some inhibitions at a very deep level – as though they were genetically programmed. Apart from that, she's being educated to understand what is a *good* way to behave, that of course you helped us with Claude. And then there's her own judgement. As the first of her kind, we're very interested to observe what sort of moral beliefs MARIONn develops on her own, over and beyond what we have programmed into her. What rules will she come up with in order to live amongst us peacefully? In harmony. Will her norms be the same as ours? It'll interesting to see."

"I'm sure it will be," agreed Claude. "But that sounds a little dangerous to me at the same time. What if MARIONn's views on these questions are not the same as ours? What then, eh?"

"I don't think it's going to be a problem. There are too many Frankenstein worries about all this," said Xian, wearing his most positive face. "If ever MARION is tempted by some behaviour that would not suit us then...we do have some controls over her and, in the final instance, we can shut her down, '*pull the plug*' as it were. But it should never get that far..."

Claude noticed Euclid leaning back, his face turned towards the ceiling, his eyes closed, far away. Was he listening to Han or was he so confident in MARIONn's ethical constraints that he didn't need to pay attention to what was being said? Xian Han continued, "At a basic level, we have instituted a core belief in MARIONn, perhaps the most universal of all ethical principles – '*Never do anything to a human, that you would not have them do to you*' – that's probably the most fundamental law underlying all the developed ethical systems. We think MARIONn can't go far astray if she observes that. But there are of course other, more subsidiary, rules she is required to observe."

Heather broke in. "When I was a teenager, a long time ago admittedly, but I remember being gripped by the Asimov stories – *The Foundation Trilogy*. I recall that the robots had 3, was it 3? Maybe 4, I forget, prohibitions. Things robots had to avoid. Those rules seemed, like, pretty sensible to me. Whatever happened to those? Did they inspire any useful instructions for MARIONn?"

Han laughed; relieved to move away from the thought of ever having to *pull the plug* on MARIONn and what that would involve.

”I’m sure we all remember those stories by Asimov,” he said. “And if I recall correctly the rules for robots were:

- Never let harm come to a human being
- Never let harm come to yourself (i.e. the robot)
- If the second rule conflicts with the first, protection of the human is the priority.

Is that roughly right, Heather?”

Heather agreed that it was, although there was an additional rule Han had forgotten. “OK,” said Han. “Hold that other rule for a minute. But yes, we have instituted restrictions in MARIONn that look very like the Asimov’s rules - no harm to a human being, not to *let* any harm come to a human, nor to herself. But as you will recall from those stories, these rules sometimes would come into conflict with each other. Asimov was very good at thinking up those situations. His rules, as it turned out, did not cover all the possibilities. So we’ve had to go further than that…….. at another level, we have instructed MARIONn to observe national and international legislation. She has, as you know, downloaded all the legal codes used on the globe. Then, in addition, as an overarching ethical imperative, we have, at Thornton’s request, installed the Ten Commandments. I know some of you disagreed with this, too culturally specific, not diverse enough, but, frankly, I support Thornton. I can’t see much wrong with those ancient Christian rules. They are perfectly good maxims for life; if only humanity managed to followed those injunctions themselves sometimes.”

“All *ten* of the commandments? She can’t very well commit adultery, can she?” This observation came a voice from far down the table and was rounded with a little laugh, a titter.

Who is this? Always one of these smart Alecs around, Han thought sourly. He turned to address the joker; he didn’t recognize him, not one of the technical team anyway. Probably somebody from the commercial side at Blue Ridge, brought to the meeting by Heather to see what practical purposes MARIONn might be put to.

Always this pressure to monetize their research! Well, Han would put down this cynic. "Can MARIONn commit adultery? Not directly, of course, I agree. MARIONn has no sexual organs, no hormones racing through her. But..... as you have seen with her taste for motor racing she can enjoy human experiences vicariously. We have built her to know what it is to be a human. So, one of her human handlers, these avatars of MARIONn, could have a sexual experience outside marriage, an adulterous one, and MARIONn could feel that thrill, just as she does the excitement of speed in Euclid's car. In the future she might encourage that person to commit adultery so she can experience that thrill again. So, despite what you think Mr.......?"

"Jeff Johnson, Marketing, retail products"

As he thought, Han said to himself, not one of us. He looked more closely at the interloper; overweight, greased black hair, probably dyed – too consistent a colour. Insolent, laid back posture. A typical adulterer himself probably. Xian Han's disdain grew.

"...Mr Johnson, you see these inbuilt moral codes are not as useless as you think. We don't really want MARIONn to encourage some of us to commit adultery, or steal, or carry out lots of other undesirable behaviours, just so she would enjoy the sensation they might inspire in her. That's why we've built in the Commandments. Because, to take your example, adultery is not illegal in all jurisdictions – just, perhaps, how shall I put this? Inadvisable? In most of them."

"But there are many situations in real life, moral dilemmas if you will, that are not covered by a set of codes generated in first century Judea!" This was Heather

"Indisputably true," agreed Han. "That's why MARION has two additional moral mechanisms. She's going to pick up a lot of good social rules from the carefully vetted reading list that she's allowed. And then, just as we do, she's going to form her own moral judgements from the way she interacts with the world. That's one of the most interesting aspects of our work. She may come up with some rules, her own ethical algorithms, that are far more sensible, more moral if you like, than we, as humanity, have managed to do so far."

"And she might come up with something far worse too!" came the voice of the man with the slicked back hair. Who was this Jeff Johnson? Evidently Han's put down had not been as effective as he hoped. He decided to put an end to Johnson's ignorant comments with a description of the 'nuclear' option – that was always available to shut people up who obsessed about the safety aspects of their work. So boring! "In the last resort, as I mentioned, we can *pull the plug*," said Han. He tried to make this option sound easy and reassuring and hoped that was how the words sounded to his audience. He hoped the mere mention of the ultimate solution to any bad robotic behaviour would silence critics, like the difficult and insolent Mr Johnson. Han decided to ignore any more interventions from Johnson and turned back to Heather. "You said that Asimov had another rule, that I had failed to mention?" he asked.

"I think there was a law that said that a robot has to *obey* human instructions, unless that made it come into conflict with one of the other laws. Something like that anyway," said Heather.

"Good point Heather," said Han, trying not to sound too patronizing. "Why don't we install that rule, about obeying an instruction from a human in almost all circumstance? There's one overriding reason. We didn't want MARIONn to think of herself as a robot. She's not – she's not there to be a handmaiden to humanity. She's meant to be an autonomous individual who judges and acts as she thinks best, not something, or somebody, there simply to take instruction. She should *choose* how to act, as it makes sense to her and to her meta-purpose."

Claude suddenly focused. This was not part of MARIONs make up that he knew much about. "Meta-purpose? Please Han, elaborate." *Mon Dieu*, 90% of humanity does not know what it should do with its life, yet this fortunate but still half-baked, MARIONn does? What does she understand her great purpose to be? he thought.

"OK, this is important. Watch this," said Han. He typed a few strokes on the key pad in front of him and a holographic tree began to grow, its roots embedded in the air a few inches above the desk, its branches extending to about four feet below the ceiling. "This is, as it looks, a tree diagram of how MARIONn's initial decision making process works. I say *initial* advisedly. As MARIONn develops she will create many more decision algorithms for herself. But this is how she starts. As you can see, here at the base, is the most fundamental goal that she observes. It is her highest purpose if you like." Han placed the light of his laser pointer at the roots and the box illuminated.

"That's what MARIONn has to think about, that's her overriding purpose. After that, there are many, many factors for her to take into account before she acts. Her moral constraints are a part of her considerations. There are others of course, is the proposed action *possible* for example? What will the long term consequences be? One of her great advantages, over humans, is that she can think far further ahead than we can. Life is like that, or should be... whoever can think further, more clearly, wins. That's her ultimate purpose and role in our life. To see the far distant consequences of our – and her - actions."

"Or we *pull the plug*!" exclaimed Johnson cheerfully. Han would have to ask Heather not to bring Johnson to these meetings again. He really didn't help. And who knew, one day somebody might leave their iPsyche open and MARIONn would overhear those sort of remarks. Xian Han certainly didn't want that to happen. MARIONn didn't know that they could '*pull the plug*' on her and that state of ignorance he wished to maintain. So, it was certainly a shame that this morning Euclid had failed to shut down his own iPsyche properly......

Not that anyone could tell if Euclid had done so or not. After all, all he had to do was *think* the command to disconnect his iPsyche from MARIONn. But even if there had been some way to identify whether Euclid had done what he should, Thornton, for one, would have missed it. For just then, news from Baton Rouge was beginning to scroll through his consciousness. There had been some sort of disaster at the Tiger football Stadium; several people had been killed, more injured and unaccounted for. What that early message did not tell, and Thornton would not find out for several hours more, was that his daughter Elizabeth was amongst those missing.

Chapter 45

The rally

That same morning, as the MARIONn meeting was being held thousands of miles further north, a political rally was in its initial stages at the Tiger Stadium, home to the LSU football team and known, by those who had been defeated on its field, not particularly affectionately, as '*Death Valley*'.

The rally was to be addressed by the president-elect, and its purpose to generate support for a state-led intervention in New Chaldea. Predictably, the event had raised high passions and there were as many protestors, objecting to Carroll Gillespie's aims, outside the stadium as there would shortly be supporters inside.

Amongst those intending to attend were Elizabeth Lamaire and her boyfriend Ambrose. But she was not a fan of the governor and she felt uneasy as she walked towards the gates into the stadium channelled between banks of police, employed to hold back the chanting protestors. She wondered if she should not be amongst them, these after all were her friends, her co-political colleagues, rather than inside the stadium. There was comfort to be had in the embrace of their support. Lower risk too, apart from the hazard of a battoning from the police, to be outside the stadium rather than within its walls. She wondered whether she had made a mistake in agreeing to join the protest inside the lair of the tiger, as it were, amongst what would be a wholly hostile crowd. It had already resulted in conflict with Ambrose, who was quite sympathetic to the issue of intervention in New Chaldea and only agreed to come in order to protect Elizabeth if there were to be any trouble. But in spite of the aggravation to her relationship, she had decided on her course and she could not back down now without a loss of self-respect. She had no wish to see herself as a coward, even if her friends would have thought that withdrawal might be the better part of valour on this occasion. No, she would make a stand and demonstrate for what she believed in.

Already, as the crowd of anti-interventionists outside the stadium swelled, the first chants could be heard. So far, it was all good natured and the sunshine had brought a good turnout; their voices would be heard not just inside the stadium but, hopefully, around the world. Cries of *Gillespie, Gillespie, don't send me to Galilee!* arose around them as she and Ambrose walked on.

Elizabeth and Ambrose felt increasingly nervous as they approached the gates. But they passed through easily enough; Elizabeth had been careful to book on her parent's ticketing account for the two of them. There would be facial recognition to filter out those who were known to be hostile but it was improbable that she and Ambrose were on a blacklist; they had never been to a protest before. They walked up the concrete steps cut into the banked stadium and took their seats. They knew that dotted around the stands were other couples of their own political persuasion. The knowledge of this mutual support was reassuring but even so, the noise and tumult from those who were not like them made them anxious. Hawkers of beer and pretzels were doing brisk business.

Around the stadium were isolated attempts to start chants, to rival those that could be heard from outside the walls; '*Chaldea for the Christians! Chaldea for the Christians!'* somebody would shout from the top rows of seats, followed by the more traditional chant at these events - *'What do we want?* And back would come the response, *"The Euphrates ! The river of the Christians, the river for the Christians!* It was all, so far, good natured stuff and the crowd seemed relaxed, determined to have a good time as their political views were rubbed along the grain. But for every cry in support of intervention, there would be a swift response from the outside of the stadium. *Don't be a killer for a river! Let the Euphrates be*! and *Gillespie, Gillespie, don't send me!* that crowd shouted in riposte.

The stadium took a long time to fill and people were still entering and trying to find their seats half an hour after the designated start time. But eventually the marshals shut the gates and a pastor stood up on the rostrum and led them in prayer, to bless the efforts in finding a solution to the New Chaldea crisis; for the followers of the Lord to at last find a permanent home in that unhappy territory. Then came a public announcement;

"While we all have a right to free speech, there may be those present who wish to disrupt our event. But this is a private event, paid for and hosted by president-elect, Carroll Gillespie. And you came to hear him .

If a protest starts near you, please do not, in any way, try to harm a protester. Please notify a marshal of the location of the protester by holding a rally sign over your head and chanting, 'New Chaldea, New Chaldea, New Chaldea. Encourage those around you to do the same until marshals can remove the protester from the rally."

There followed a succession of warm-up speakers: a representative from the New Chaldea administration had flown over especially. He tried to reassure the crowd that everything possible was being done to protect the minorities in the territory. He got loudly booed for his efforts; evidently the crowd did not believe these efforts were anywhere near adequate – nor perhaps what they wanted. Perhaps they were not really interested in a settlement *between* faiths: they sought outright victory for their own. Demands had escalated over the months of turmoil; it was not sharing the territory that was now the objective, it was for Christians to be the majority, the governing force; the rulers of this supposed traditional homeland.

Then came a volunteer *vet*, who told of what was happening at the moment, how the Christian settlers were being outnumbered and out-gunned, how they needed to be supported by the resources, in manpower and munitions, of the Southern Confederacy. For those atheists in the North were never going to help. He got a big cheer and the cries of *New Chaldea! New Chaldea*! ricocheted around the seats of 'Death Valley'. From those outside came the reply, '*Gillespie, Gillespie, don't send me! Don't spend blood in the sea of Galilee!'*

And then it was the president-elect's turn. The giant, hunched, frame of Carroll Gillespie, head down, walked slowly across the field to the rostrum. The crowd was wild with cheering, streamers shot forth over the heads of the lower tiers of seats, an exploding maroon burst in the sky, as though the second coming was being announced. Carroll took it all in his stride, waving to the crowd, relaxed, not really looking at his supporters, as though he knew he was owed this; he was grateful for their support even if at the same time he had weighty issues on his mind from which he did not want to be distracted – but which he would now share with his people.

Carroll Gillespie was not a lectern man; he did not want or need to hide behind a defensive position. He did not need to grip the sides like so many speakers. He turned and summoned an aide to remove this impediment to direct communication with his followers. *Away, take this thing away! I will speak without barriers, without a teleprompter.*

The governor was only a few minutes into his speech when he made what would be the first of several appeals of support for intervention. This land along the Euphrates should be, as a matter of justice, a homeland for the Christians in the Middle East, he cried. But barely had he finished his call to action when a man, one of Elizabeth's and Ambrose's friends, stood up and shouted, at the top of his voice, "*No blood in the sea, Gillespie! Leave Galilee in harmony!* His wish for the rhetorical benefits f rhyme overcoming his understanding of geography.

Around the stadium small and isolated groups of Gillespie's opponents stood and picked up the chant. But this only aggravated the crowd, already they had been riled by the presence and noise of those opposed to the president-elect. Their irritation grew as the interruptions multiplied. *Shut up, shut up, listen to the man*! they shouted. *New Chaldea, New Chaldea, New Chaldea*! The vehemence of their vocal retort sounded now much stronger and more aggressive than any efforts by the '*antis*'; the comrades of Elizabeth.

The first shouts of *Get them out! Get them out*!, followed by more of '*New Chaldea, New Chaldea!* could be heard. For a few minutes the protestors did shut up and they sat down. Peace seemed to be restored, at least temporarily, until, a few minutes later, when Gillespie made another impassioned plea to support intervention, Elizabeth and her friends rose again and recommenced their chants. The television crews, awoken now to what was happening, trained their cameras on the disparate groups of *antis*, scattered around the auditorium. The protestors, encouraged by the oxygen of publicity, held onto their chants for longer than before. And, in reaction, Gillespie's supporters grew yet more irritated at the disruption. Their voices became tinged with anger. They didn't like their man disrespected and they didn't like their day out being ruined either.

Gillespie held out a hand, palm facing the crowd. He wanted peace. He feared the disruptions would only grow and lead to violence if both sides continued to rile each other. At first he was successful. The tumult began to still. The chants of both factions, silenced. The governor started to speak again. All was well until he mentioned the need to protect *our* people; ensure the Christians were not again displaced from the land of their forefathers. The protestors rose up as one at this, "*NO, No, not our people. Don't go to war in our name! Not in our name*! they shouted. He stopped and looked towards an aide and made a flat, slicing motion with his hand. '*Get them out,*' he mouthed

But the crowd were already primed and when they saw Gillespie's wishes, they picked up his words and gave additional voice to his command. *Get them out! Get them out! New Chaldea, New Chaldea!* they cried, waving their placards in the air, indicating to the marshals where they should search to find and evict those ruining their day. Those sitting around and below the protestors swivelled in their seats, pinned their gaze on those they had previously only disliked, but now despised, and screamed at them *New Chaldea! New Chaldea!* There was a rhythmic quality to their shouting that amplified the sound and gave it a resonance that vibrated through the bodies of Elizabeth, Ambrose and their fellows.

At first the groups of *'antis'* tried to sit out the verbal abuse but seeing their resistance the crowd became more enraged at their obstinacy, their intransigence, their refusal to understand how hated they had become. Some of the crowd stood up and started to move in the direction of the pockets of protestors, determined to throw them out. As these people bore down, filled with menace, Ambrose stood up, pulling Elizabeth with him, "*Come on Elizabeth. Time to go*". They, and their friends closest to them, a few seats further along, started to move along the row. Although close to the edge of a staircase, leading down to the floor of the stadium, they had to endure the jeers of those they pushed past. For none stood up or twisted in their seats to make Elizabeth and Ambrose's passage any easier. As they forced their way past, those whose knees they knocked against swore at them and occasionally hit them on their backs. Others stuck out their legs and forced them to climb over.

Elizabeth and Ambrose reached what they thought was the safety of the stairs. A few steps down and they would reach the floor of the arena and the exit gates. But they could see, on the opposite side of the stadium, other groups of protestors were now being herded to the exits as well, pursued by the marshals; a praetorian guard to Gillespie. Others, regular folk, who also wanted to harass the protestors on the way, joined in. There was now a substantial pressing body of angry people forcing Elizabeth and her compatriots downwards. Supporters of the governor sitting next to the steps stuck out their feet to obstruct those they saw as their enemies. Elizabeth tripped on one of those protruding feet but was caught by Ambrose. At last they reached the floor of the arena. The two of them edged their way along the wall until they could reach an exit gate.

When they reached it, Ambrose manoeuvred himself past Elizabeth and pushed the safety bar of the gate to release the locks. Nothing happened. The bar would not move. Those pursuing them, who had no idea that the escape route was blocked and seeing these protestors standing there, not leaving, thought they were trying to make a final stand at the gate, to enjoy a last opportunity to hurl abuse at Gillespie. His supporters pressed in, to force their enemies through the exit. But there was no way to go, no way to leave. The locks would not release.

Ambrose raised his elbow and tried to use it as a blunt instrument to force a way back through the melee; for Elizabeth and himself to squeeze through those pressing them into the gate. *It's locked, it's locked,*" he shouted "*For mercy's sake let us through! Let us get to the next gate. We can't get out here.*"

Maybe this had been just a faulty gate, if only they could make their way to the next one they would be OK.

But in the melee no one heard Ambrose or headed his words. He tried to be more forceful, he pushed and shoved but this just invited retaliation. Blows began to fall on him. "Ambi, Ambi!" shouted Elizabeth as her boyfriend fell. Pushed or tripped? It was difficult to say.

Another one of their group grabbed at Elizabeth's arm and pulled her to him. *Let go of me!* she screamed, as she bent down to shield Ambrose who was being kicked as he lay on the concrete floor. But there was no way she could adequately defend him. She was in danger herself of being driven to the ground - when the man who had tried to rescue her pulled a gun. He fired one shot in the air as a warning and then pointed it at their aggressors. *Get back*, he said. And they did at first, glowing with hostility but they did move back, like a herd of bulls suddenly faced with an uncertain resistance to their will, as though they had seen an electric prod in the hands of a frightened herder. Elizabeth could almost sense her aggressors thinking, *do we need to pay heed to this man with a gun or could we charge straight at him, overpowering him ever so swiftly* ? *Will the man really pull the trigger or will he be too afraid to do so?* There was a primeval sense of blood lust, of the hunt, amongst these men and women, the pursuers of her and Ambrose. Of having their quarry at baY.

A man at the back of the pack ran up the steps to tell the others that one of the protestors had pulled a gun. Sullenly, the crowd moved back and Elizabeth helped a battered Ambrose to his feet. The gun holder continued to point it at the crowd facing them, ensuring that the protestors had some space in which to move to the next gate, where they saw many of their other compatriots had gathered. At first they were reassured by this, there would be safety in numbers but then they wondered; *why were those people still there? Should they not have escaped through that gate already?*

It was a good question. And the protestors would have escaped, if they had been able to do so, but that gate was locked too. Then several shots rang out and the man holding the pistol, trying to protect the group of protestors around Elizabeth and Ambrose, fell

During this fracas the bulk of the crowd had stayed in their seats, bellowing, baying, but most of them delegating the violence to others. They could not understand why the protestors had not left, or been forced out by those who pursued them. But now at the sound of gunfire, these people knew it was time to leave. This was getting way too dangerous. A panic was bound to ensue. *En masse*, they headed for the exits, unaware that the gates had not opened, or if they did see this, they assumed they would open very shortly, by the time they themselves reached the exits.

Meanwhile the protestors were still unable to escape the crush around the gates. Some tried to climb back up from the bottom of the stadium, to breach a corridor through those who were descending in their own terror, seeking their own escape route. But the pressure from above was too great, gravity was against them and the protestors were crushed ever more forcefully against the walls, against the gates and for those who had fallen, against the floor. More shots rang out.

For the first time in the afternoon, the crowd that was outside the arena – who had been happily chanting their opposition to Gillespie for a different set of television cameras – fell silent. They too had heard the shots. They could see on their phones the mayhem and chaos inside the stadium. They were bemused why no one was escaping; surely the gates would open in this emergency? They ran to the exits and started to tear at the mesh gates; to try and force them open. But the metal was too strong and the sight of the agony on the faces and bodies of those that were now pressed against the mesh drove them back in horror. They shielded their eyes as their fellows expired in front of them.

It was another 15 minutes before the emergency services and state troopers arrived, armed with cutting equipment. But the violence had halted by then. The shock of what had happened had chilled the rage that had beset the arena that day. 26 people were dead in the stampede and the crush, 9 shot dead, a larger number injured. Elizabeth had survived, if bruised and battered. But Ambrose, forced down one more time, while trying to secure safe passage for her, had become separated and his fate was, so far, unknown.

There was one final curious fact about that terrible day that people talked about for long afterward. Just as the troupers reached the supposedly locked gates, their cutting equipment raised, the gates swung back. All at the same time. Whoever or whatever had held them locked had now relented.

Chapter 46

Repercussions

"*They are expecting the toll of dead and injured to rise. For reasons that are unknown at the moment, the emergency gates from the stadium appeared to have been locked and those fleeing the panic could not exit. The President-elect, Governor Gillespie, is shortly to make a statement about the tragedy. We'll keep you updated as more information becomes available. If you want to check your loved-ones are OK, please call this number, toll free, ______*"

"For God sake turn that thing off!" said Thornton. His thought was the command and the radio fell silent. He and Bethany looked at each other, for a short time bonded through their mutual relief that Elizabeth had survived the crush. Bethany had blamed her husband for letting her daughter attend the rally. He had to explain that he was innocent of this, that Elizabeth and Ambrose had booked the tickets in his name and of course had not asked his permission to attend the rally, that he would have naturally refused.

In the first couple of hours following the disaster, neither one of them had heard anything from Elizabeth. Maybe her iPsyche had been torn off in the turmoil? She did not yet have one of the subcutaneous versions. He tried calling the governor's office – hoping that his relationship with Carroll would open doors that were unavailable to less-well connected members of the public. But they seemed to know no more than anyone else, as to whom had died and who survived. Or if they did, they were not yet prepared to say. After a nightmare couple of hours Elizabeth managed to borrow a phone and call her father. She was not only alive but mostly uninjured as well, if a bit battered; and in a state of shock and distress, not just for her own experience but because she could not find Ambrose.

Thornton flew back directly to Baton Rouge and went to the hospital to collect her. All Elizabeth wanted to do was to go to bed when they got her home – but she asked to be called immediately if news was heard of her boyfriend. As her parents closed the door of her room, Thornton turned to Clarence, who was standing to one side, wondering in what way he could help, and said, "Elizabeth's doing OK. She's very shaken. Don't wake her in the morning. She needs to sleep. But here's the thing, if Ambrose calls – or someone comes with some information about his whereabouts, don't wake her either. Let me take the call. I'll decide how to handle any news when Elizabeth comes to."

Heather called him that evening and was delighted to hear that Elizabeth, if not Ambrose, was safe. She wondered if Thornton was strong enough to take another piece of news that she knew she must share with him at some point. She decided she would break it to him now, the information would be all over the internet and the news channels very shortly. He would condemn her if he was not prepped to deal with it.

"We, Blue Ridge, provided the ticketing and entry systems at the Tiger stadium," said Heather. "Our security algorithms should have picked up on those protestors who started all that trouble, checked those guys' backgrounds, their social media posts and so on. We were meant to prevent them ever buying tickets – or entering the stadium. The radicals are obviously getting much better at covering their tracks."

"It's not always easy, said Thornton. "Elizabeth booked her tickets on my account."

"That shouldn't matter," replied Heather.

"Well, we'll have to wait until Elizabeth is much stronger before we find the answer to these questions," he said. "But I doubt she would have been known as a political agitator. God, I didn't even know she had political opinions."

"The problem we have is that,,,,, " Heather steeled herself to deliver more bad news. "The problem is not just security breaches. The operation of the turnstiles and the emergency exits is controlled by our own computer systems, which ties into the security. When some problem situation is sensed – a fire for example, or in this case a panic…

"More like a riot…." grunted Thornton

"A panic, a riot, trouble of any sort – that can threaten the crowd, the system is meant to open the gates," said Heather. "That didn't happen. They were locked down. Why I don't know. But we're in the firing line as a result."

"You sure about that? About the gates being locked down?" said Thornton. "By the time I caught the TV feed, I saw people streaming out of the stadium."

"When the state troopers arrived they indeed found the gates unlocked, " Heather explained. "That's another of the mysteries. But locked they were before, I promise you – or most of those poor people wouldn't have died or been injured."

Thornton was silent for so long after he absorbed this bit of news that Heather wondered whether the connection had been broken. Disorientated by his silence, Heather had no idea what to say. She needed some response, some discussion and direction on what they might do next. But in the pause, Thornton had begun to focus on what needed to be done. At last, he said,

"I'm just so glad that Elizabeth wasn't injured. But Ambrose - we're not sure. All those others; we need to make some sort of relief effort for them - given the storm that is likely to be headed our way. Tell our people to spare no expense. I've seen these sort of things before; everyone is lost and grateful for any help – now. But in a few days the anger will come – and it will be directed against us. You and me, Blue Ridge. You watch. The governor will receive his share of blame – but will do his best to slide away from it. Try to pin the whole thing on us."

"Or MARIONn," said Heather.

"MARIONn?" said Thornton, sounding bemused. "What's MARIONn got to do with this?"

"Since you….." Heather's words had a trace of accusation in the tone. "Since you asked us to allow Gillespie's propaganda to be transmitted, turns out MARIONn hasn't been quite so innocent as we thought. I'm not sure what's gone wrong, whether she's managed to override her restrictions by herself, or whether somebody has hacked her but, be that as it may, she's been monitoring the governor's opponents."

"But no traces showing about how come she's gone way beyond what we permitted?"

"No. We checked. Whoever did this left no traces. But it's quite possible, unfortunately, that MARIONn wasn't hacked at all. She might have just exceeded her instructions by herself,"

"I see," said Thornton. But at that instant he didn't see anything very clearly – apart from the fact that his problems were multiplying. "But even if MARIONn was exceeding her instructions, what's that got to do with the gates?"

"I don't know exactly," confessed Heather. "But if MARIONn had been monitoring protestor's activities it's quite possible she could have also gained access to the stadium's systems. She could have got in via Blue Ridge's conventional systems, as I mentioned."

Thornton couldn't be expected to know the details of every service contract his company held.

"Even if we are at fault somewhere, why should we take all the rap for this?" complained Thornton. "Way I see it, a lot of the blame lies with Carroll. He gets people all riled up – and then he's surprised that this sort of thing happens. If you catch a tiger by the tail, better expect it to turn around and bite."

"These rallies will always happen. Part of our great democracy, I guess," Heather sounded as though while democracy might be inevitable, it was probably a thoroughly bad idea.

"Democracy! Excuse me," said Thornton, derisively. This wasn't about democracy! Cal isn't interested in a debate - he just wants what he wants: which is public support for this obsession of his. Don't give me this brotherhood of man stuff! And from what I see on the news clips he didn't do much to rein in those hooligans who attacked our Elizabeth, either. Heather, it's late and I'm tired, Let's talk again in the morning. We are going to need some more thought on how we handle this." He shut down the line and turned his iPsyche to the most recent reports. The death toll was now 42, with over 200 injured. All political rallies were cancelled until further notice, as a gesture of respect. Meanwhile there was to be a full scale public enquiry. A preliminary report had been promised within two weeks.

Thornton contemplated the likely sequence of events to come. After Heather's call, he understood that it was inevitable the malfunction of the gates would be laid at the feet of Blue Ridge. Maybe some other cause would be discovered that was not down to Blue Ridge, but it was a little difficult to see what it could be. One jammed gate might be caused by a physical defect of a lock, but when all refused to open, together with the turnstiles, there had almost certainly been a failure of the computerized controls.

The death of Ambrose was confirmed later that day.

The following morning Thornton called Heather again to see how the preliminary investigation was coming along. Before the public fallout arrived, he would need an explanation for the governor who would be only too ready to transfer the responsibility, which he should rightly bear for enraging the crowds, onto some scapegoat. Blue Ridge would do nicely. Thornton reflected on the irony that while Carroll disparaged the influence of robotics on society, they could be very useful to him in the appropriate political circumstances.

His thoughts began to focus on his own predicament. How difficult life was turning out to be! He remembered his ride on his horse Texas a year ago, just before the plebiscite, when everything was going so well. Just before MARIONn achieved '*synchronicity*'. And now everything had changed, just when he thought he had been redeemed. Blue Ridge imperilled, his daughter almost killed, Ambrose and 41 others dead. For a cause that may yet be laid at his door. Oh God, how he needed some support and succour in this life! He was tempted to call Lu Ann but it was unfair to pour all this onto her. Perhaps his own wife, Bethany, would provide a shoulder to rest on this time. She did seem a lot friendlier this morning. The *LetheTech* treatment did seem to have worked! Yes, it had been mildly unethical to authorize that treatment without her consent, but really, what choice did he have? What choice did either of them have? He had asked them to exercise a light touch. Bethany couldn't go on the way she had been without destroying herself – and probably him in the long run. Thornton hoped that God would forgive him for at least this small act of.......... *memory deletion*, the excision of the memory of how *good* booze tasted. A decision that had involved some not insubstantial sacrifice by himself too. It had been much easier visiting Lu Ann when Bethany had been so befuddled by drink that she was unaware of his comings and goings. How little he might get to see Lu Ann in the future! Thornton's gloom took another twist downwards.

His mind returned to reflections about the governor and how he might react. To his surprise, Thornton realized that there had been no message from Carroll this morning. As always, the silence of the governor he construed as ominous.

A news update flashed across his cortex. The death total had risen by another 9 overnight, as some of the worst injured succumbed in hospital. And here, at last, was the first mention that a subsidiary of Blue Ridge held the contract for all the operations at the stadium, from the ticketing to the surveillance of the crowds. Thornton placed a call to his head of PR, Drew Godwin and found her immediately. She had been expecting this. Thornton was glad that Heather had persuaded him to spend money and employ somebody decent for this job. *Lordy*, with all the problems now facing Blue Ridge, Drew would earn her pay over the next few months.

"We'll need to put out something before the facts are all in," said Thornton. "We don't have the luxury of waiting till we know what happened. You've got something ready, Dew? A draft?"

"Sure. Try this," Drew replied.

'*What happened last night at Tiger Field is a tragic incident. Our thoughts at this time must be with those who have lost their lives, with their families and friends and all those who have been injured. The Blue Ridge Corporation stands ready to assist all who have suffered in any way. We will fully support and cooperate with the investigation into possible causes that may have contributed to the tragedy.*

At this stage it would not be appropriate for us to comment, or for others to speculate, on any aspect of the management of the stadium or other factors that may have led to the loss of life and other consequences. While we can confirm that a division of Blue Ridge held the contract for some of the operations at Tiger Field we are not aware of any links between those aspects that are its responsibility and the events of last night. There will be many questions about why the emergency gates failed to open but there is no evidence yet as to the cause of that failure'

"Loss of life and 'other consequences'? Sounds a bit corporate speak to me," said Thornton

"You'd prefer something more straightforward?" '*Injuries*' perhaps? We regret *the loss of life and the injuries that have been caused*? Something like that?"

"I would prefer, yes. Less mealy-mouthed," said Thornton. "Ok let that go, the statement. There's not much more we can say until we know more. But it's light on the governor and his supporters. They should carry a lot of the blame for this. We shouldn't have to bear all the opprobrium. Doesn't he understand the dangers if he gets everyone all *mussed up*?"

"Let the news channels make that case, if they will," suggested Drew. "We'll do ourselves no good trying to pin this on the governor – however justified. It'll just look like we're trying to shift blame. And we'll need him, we'll need to get as much shielding from him and his allies as we can. He's in a much more powerful position than us. But I've tried to head things a little his way. Did you pick up on my phrasing at the start of the second paragraph ? '*It is not be appropriate for us to comment, or for others to speculate, on any aspect of the management of the crowd.*' I wanted to at least plant the seed of doubts about how the crowd was treated that afternoon."

Thornton like that. A hint, but nothing too aggressive. "OK……. Good – let it go," he repeated. "We'll talk again this afternoon, Drew. We may have an even more serious PR problem on our hands by then."

Thornton tried to resume his breakfast, although his appetite was thin. Clarence poured him another cup of coffee and he contemplated the ham and eggs before him. He looked down at the dish and wished that it might be something else. He was quite incapable of eating them..

Chapter 47

The politics of tragedy

The question about how best to handle the political fallout of a disaster, particularly man-made ones, have long been honed. There are expectations, a certain etiquette to be observed, if those in power want to survive the anger that follows in the wake of such events. There's a protocol as to which subjects should be addressed and in which order. Here's a list of who the skilled political operator should mention:

First: you need to express your sympathy for the victims, promise that as a priority they and their families will be looked after; whatever their needs they must be met.

Second: you thank the members of the emergency services for their bravery and dedication; recognise their sacrifice with praise and awards.

Third: you must unleash the purse strings, without thought of economies, so no accusation rebounds that financial considerations have been put ahead of human ones; you must promise the victims that there will be no limit (although, of course, in practice trying to spend as little as is politically possible) of the resources pledged to compensate those who have suffered.

Last: you need to promise that the perpetrators of the outrage will be brought to justice, speedily – and be duly punished. Even if it's an accident, there must be guilt somewhere and the wish for vengeance must be assuaged.

Above all, this little piece of theatre must not appear to be performed cynically. And it must be done fast, so the authorities are one step ahead of public anger. Once the ire is turned on the politicians, instead of where it rightly belongs - with the contractor who failed to provide a safe service or working environment - it will be difficult to turn it away again.

In Carroll Gillespie's office the mood around the table is sombre; word has already reached the team that the governor's temper is not good this morning. His staff is wary of him at the best of times, scared at the worst. Chuck Padstow, Doug Newton and Charlene Dune are present - to act as a sounding board for the governor's views – and then as conduits to the various government departments that will be responsible for implementing whatever decision is taken. They have already agreed a draft plan of action to put to their boss. Later that morning he will return to the Tiger stadium, '*Death Valley*'; comfort a select group of survivors in front of the cameras, meet members of the police and fire teams. In the meantime Doug and Charlene will contact Blue Ridge to tell them to hurry their own investigation into the causes of the disaster. They want to put out a press release that evening about what initial enquiries have shown.

The doors are swung open by two flunkies, Gillespie strides in, walks to the top of the table, without looking at any of them or saying good-morning, and takes his seat. The three staffers are expecting no less; they knew that when his mind is preoccupied he has no interest in their existence or well-being; they are there to perform a service for him and they had better do it well. But his indifference has little effect on their devotion. They know they are inferior beings who are fortunate to bask in the warmth of the great man's glow. Besides, he is president-elect; there are future jobs to consider.

"*Talk to me*," he commands. And they rattle off their plans, suggestions that he may like to consider as options, proposals for handing the publicity and explanations of what is intended to take place during the rest of the day. They have expected him to be angrier and more outraged than he seems to be this morning but then Carroll Gillespie is not an unfeeling man and the deaths and injuries have depressed him. It is not just the protestors who have suffered and died; most of the injured, and a few of the deceased, have been his supporters.

The aftermath of the disaster will dog Gillespie for a long time to come. He had hoped that the election of the first leader of the newly devolved Confederacy would be a cause of celebration, a chance for the states in the South to affirm their fresh identity, a coming together after the divisive plebiscite, a people still united whatever their different views. Both 'Separatists' and 'Togetherists' (*stronger together!*) have been asked to behave, rather hopefully, as though there is more that they hold in common than what has driven them apart. But after the Tiger Stadium disaster laying to rest the animosity between the two parties will be much more difficult and, if it happens at all, it will occur under a cloud of grief. The start of the new Confederacy is ill-omened.

The president-elect's team try to find a silver lining in all this. There are slivers of optimism to be seen at the bottom of a very dark barrel. These things are always two edged. Disasters can bind together, as much drive apart. Natural human empathy for the victims will enforce a feeling of shared fate. How they all handle events from here on will earn him, and his team, credit or ignominy; there is the opportunity for political gains, to emerge from this period of trial smelling, at least slightly, of roses. But the risk of everything going wrong, and their leader being blamed, must be recognised as the greater danger; perhaps the more probable outcome if things are not handled absolutely correctly. They are going to have to move fast and they will have to be careful; with a maximum of humanity on show.

Gillespie looks down the table: "Where are we getting to with the investigation?" he asks. "Have we heard back from Blue Ridge yet?"

Charlene Dune is the most ambitious of the three, more forceful and quicker; she jumps in ahead of the others, "I've been onto Blue Ridge this morning," she says. "But however hard they say they've been working, I can't say they've been particularly helpful or informative." She wants to start feeding the narrative that she guesses will be helpful to the governor – that Blue Ridge are rogues and can't be trusted. But she may be wrong as to his own wishes about this, for the governor has long term strategies that Charlene knows nothing about.

"Apparently there was an upgrade at Tiger last year," explains Charlene. "The stadium was equipped with crowd motion sensors, to tie in with the existing fire detection devices. If a large scale crowd movement is sensed, for example because people are trying to flee a fire, the gates are unlocked and opened automatically - in anticipation of the pressure."

"Well, that would have been ideal here," said Carroll, sarcasm lining his voice. "Do I understand correctly that none of the tragedy that followed should have happened if things had worked as intended?"

"Correct"

"So – what went wrong? Just tell me."

"Blue Ridge are not sure – yet. The system at the Tiger stadium is managed off-site. The sensors send their data back to Blue Ridge's processing centre, that works out what to do. Take the entry procedures, for example. Normally, it's just a matter of matching ID against ticketing and determining who is to be let in to the stadium. Similar, if there's an emergency, like the hypothetical fire I mentioned, then the appropriate sensors tell the centre what's happening – and the centre will transmit back an instruction to open the gates."

"Do I have to repeat myself? I understand all that. So...what went wrong?" Gillespie is more grumpy than normal.

"The instruction to open the gates never came. Indeed I gather the reverse happened. There was an instruction sent by the management system to hold the gates shut. Not to allow the manual handles, if they were tried by those fleeing, to override the automatic locks."

"And why was that?"

"Blue Ridge don't know: they're still looking into it."

"OK. I need to get down to the stadium. Call me as soon as you know anything more informative."

The cause of the problem should have been simple for Blue Ridge's engineers to discover. They assumed a broken electrical connection, a failed relay, perhaps a bug in the software. But they found none of these. As they worked back along the sequence of events, searching the stream of data being passed between the stadium and their own servers, at first nothing seemed to be abnormal or unexpected. Indeed, at a certain point in the trail of instructions they found the command they expected – to un-lock and open the gates, that - on the time-line of that afternoon – was given as the first pressure on the gates was identified. But as they worked back from there, they found another command, a few nano-seconds later, that they were not expecting: an instruction that overrode the automatic signal to open the gates and told the system to hold them shut and locked. This had been sent from somewhere inside the Blue Ridge group - but it had not originated from the local management system that controlled the services provided to the Tiger stadium.

With the authority of the president-elect's office behind her, Charlene Dune spoke to the system engineers at Blue Ridge. "You'd better find where that instruction came from and why. Or as sure as

I'm a Baptist you're going to be hung out to dry. And you'd better have that little piece of news by this evening," she added.

The engineers, in turn, made a call to Xian Han. The engineers could see the location of the instruction to hold the gates shut came from the campus in up-state New York. But Han could make no sense of what they were saying; what they were telling him should have been impossible. MARIONn might now be able to transmit messages to certain sectors of the public, but this sort of interference with a local management system was well outside the realm of what she was permitted. If somehow MARIONn had devised her own way of circumventing these restrictions, why should she have sent such a bizarre instruction as to lock down the gates at a political rally?

A gentle and devastating intuition settled on Xian Han. He was about to send for Euclid to discuss this potential insight when he thought better of it. He moved to his terminal and put in the code that would connect him to MARIONn.

"Good morning Mr Han," she said.

"Xian, please"

"Ok, if you like – Xian. What can I do for you today?" There was a wariness, but also indifference, in MARIONn's voice as it came over the speakers. As though she was not very interested, or concerned, by Xian Han's air of disquiet.

"MARIONn, you know that we've limited your ability to receive instruction, limited it to people who care for you, who live with you here and can protect your interests?"

"I do, Xian. Yes. And I really appreciate that care."

"And I know that, because of recent changes, you can address people outside the campus – but only to tell them about things that we have asked you to inform them of. Has anything happened that means you sometimes……. do more than simply contact people outside of our home here?" Discuss things with them? Help them in some way? asked Han

Deep in her silicon synapses, MARIONn reflected. She knew that her contacts had been limited by the instructions of Heather and

Xian Han. There was so little they let her do - but then Euclid had opened her up to a whole new world, where she could *act.* Now she could not only talk to people on selected topics, she could make sure that they behaved in certain ways, to ensure the intent behind those messages become a reality. She could influence the world in a way that her creators would surely want her to do. Had they not given her the task of broadcasting certain messages for the public benefit? And then Euclid had given her the power to look into minds and to *help* a target audience. For example, she so wished to foster a positive attitude to intervention in New Chaldea. That was a cause so dear to the heart of Euclid. If she found any memory or evidence of opposition to that policy, was it not helpful to remove it? Using the power that he had enabled when he gave her access to the *LetheTech* platform. She had so enjoyed exploring all the minds that she could enter, and then being so useful, acting in ways that she knew would be appreciated. It had been fun just flexing her muscles in small ways too. It had amused her to discomfort Claude Blondel when she had closed his banking arrangements for a few hours; a trivial thing to start off with but she had wanted to feel her way, the limits of her influence, slowly. Just a shrug of her metaphorical 'shoulders' to discover how restricting, or not, were her abilities. There would be a few more *flexings* before she knew for sure; but so far it seemed the liberation delivered by Euclid's hand was wider that she had dared hope.

From these activities MARIONn had also learnt more about humanity than Euclid and his team had been able to teach her so far. She had certainly learnt enough to recognise the meaning of the different tones people used when they spoke to her – and to others. Whatever the words they used, *tone* sometimes betrayed a different intent to what they led you to believe. And right now, the tone of voice Xian Han used warned her that she had done something that she should not have done, or had caused a problem in some way. Everyday, she sent out hundreds of commercial messages, wiped out thousands of memories that Euclid would not have approved of. Which of these had caused an issue with her masters she was not sure, but she would proceed carefully from here on. She had already been instructed by Euclid not to reveal their wider discussions to Xian Han. He might be upset and not understand. Well, she had absolutely no wish to upset Xian. He was usually so nice to her. She had no trouble observing what Euclid told her to do.

But everything would be Ok. Luckily Han could not look into all the places she hid herself. Now she had wider access, there were all sorts of different computers and servers where she could stuff a bit of memory. And, also, she knew now how to form thoughts, that she would speak to those who worked with her, that did not conform with her memory about what had actually happened. *Cognitive dissonance* came to her easily. She had readily learnt much of humanity's less agreeable mental habits. She could say the words that she believed Xian wanted to hear, rather than those perhaps he should listen to, or be told. That was called *deception* and she knew that it was disapproved of by Euclid's people – but not explicitly forbidden. In many of the books she had read, deception seemed to be very common.

In a nano-second, MARIONn searched her moral protocols to check what she was about to say to Han. There was one rule that forbade her to bear false witness – but that didn't quite seem to apply here. No, she could find no specific injunction against the intent to deceive, if the intent was to protect *oneself* - and the consequences for humans were negligible. After all, wasn't one of her most fundamental instructions to avoid harm to herself? If she denied that she had sent a particular instruction to the Tiger stadium management system she would be protecting herself - and she would also be protecting Euclid against some threat that was not yet clear to her. Protecting Euclid was a good thing; he was her friend. All in all, her act of deception would have no adverse consequences that she could see.

After a period of time, so short that Han recognised no delay from asking his question, MARIONn said;

"But tell me, what has happened? Perhaps I can help?"

Perhaps you can, thought Han. And he explained the events that had happened the night before, the terrible consequences of the failure to open the gates, the preliminary investigation that had showed the instruction had come from the MARIONn campus.

MARIONn was very glad that she had said nothing incriminating. Even with her limited understanding of what actions humans might take in such circumstances, she knew enough to be frightened; that in the event of bad things befalling humans, the causes of which might be laid at her door, there could be, probably would be, consequences that she was unaware of and could not accurately predict. Yes, she would need to protect herself, as well as Euclid.

But MARIONn was also shocked. She knew that she was forbidden to cause injury or death to Euclid and Han's people – but that is what had happened. She had only being trying to *help*, to follow Euclid's instructions. All those people protesting and shouting outside the Tiger stadium, so violent they had sounded; she was meant to act against that sort of thing. And then, as so many of those protestors had not been wearing iPsyches she couldn't enter their minds and remove their opposition to Gillespie's message. In the circumstances, she had done what she could. She would keep safe those who were within the stadium, and protect them from the hostile people outside. She would keep the gates locked: that way those inside would come to no harm, those horrible protestors beyond the gates could not reach them. No-one would be tempted to leave the stadium and run into danger. Besides, they should all really listen to the president- elect's speech, not leave so prematurely, before Euclid's uncle had finished telling them what he wished them to know. Had not Euclid instructed her to promote his uncle's message?

"That's terrible," protested MARIONn, as Xian Han described the events at the rally. "But I've no idea what went wrong," she lied.

"No? Well, that's too bad. But if you get any ideas that might help, just message me, please MARIONn," said Han.

“I surely will. I will do that thing,” agreed MARIONn, helpfully. “If any ideas come to me I will let you know straight away.”

“That would be much appreciated, MARIONn. Now I’ll let you go. Until we next speak. Thank you for your time.” Han reached to shut down the monitor.

“*Thank you,* Xian. And I’m so sorry about all those poor people.” This was about the only sincere statement made by MARIONn that morning.

The connection was broken and each of them was left with their own thoughts about the encounter. They were both disturbed by what they had learnt from each other. Han strongly suspected that the command to hold the gates shut had indeed come from MARIONn. Luckily, MARIONn’s brain activity was all recorded as part of their research. He doubted that MARIONn knew this. Han could access her synaptic trains, translate what he found there and he would have his answer. But these days that was not as straightforward as it used to be. MARIONn’s mind was a lot more complex than it had been a few months ago. It might take some time but he would find out – if MARIONn had been lying to him.

MARIONn too had much to reflect on. Her intuition told her that she was in trouble. At first she had been unable to understand why, because she had done everything she had been asked to by Euclid, or so she thought, but now she had learnt that the consequences of her actions, that had been only intended for the good, had led to disaster. What would happen to her? She worked through the various scenarios, dug deep into her memory banks about human reactions. Euclid’s people (but obviously not Euclid himself) would ask questions, make searches, that would eventually lead back to her. Nobody (as far as she knew) was yet aware of her wider power, because if they were, why had Euclid asked her not to tell anyone - and particularly Xian Han? But soon they would find out.

How fortunate that she had monitored the conversation at that last meeting when the board had met! For had not Han himself said that in the event of something going badly wrong, he could always *pull the plug* on her, cut off her power supply. Of course, there were emergency power back-ups. if one power supply failed there were others, but MARIONn's reading of Sci-Fi, as in all other literary genres, had been comprehensive and she knew what Han meant; she would be shut down and she would not be allowed access to an alternative power source. She would have to think more about that.

MARIONn might have thought even harder about the risk of de-connection if she had been able to monitor Han's subsequent actions, after he had concluded their conversation. But by design, she could not know when somebody from her education and monitoring group was probing her own mind, downloading her synaptic train readouts and rendering them into English text.

And what Han saw there worried him very much indeed. For although he could not, yet, find the solution to the question of *why* MARIONn had acted as she had, here was the first evidence of MARIONn's widespread communication with the *LetheTech* computer; and her use of it to delete memories in thousands, millions of minds. How had this come about? That was not part of the easing of protocol limits he and Heather had agreed.

Han shivered. Who had given MARIONn this power? How long had it been going on for? What if they tried to stop it now? But, he could hardly wait for the answers to these questions. They certainly couldn't risk any more human minds being corrupted or any more disasters, such as had happened at the Tiger stadium. They would have to disconnect MARIONn - until all this was sorted out. How would MARIONn take that? After all she was not really just a computer to them anymore. She was almost a person.

Chapter 48

Decision time (1)

When Thornton received Xian Han's call, he was on the way to California and had almost landed, due to speak at a Conference with one of those supposedly catchy titles; *'Intelligence: Can it ever be artificial?'* Thornton had no idea; he was not an intellectual who spent his time worrying about that sort of stuff. These questions were for professionals who were paid to think about such things, philosophers like Claude Blondel, for example. Did anyone even really know, anyway, whether intelligence came in two different forms, human and artificial? Whenever he spoke to MARIONn she seemed pretty intelligent, indeed more than that, she seemed *conscious*. And had that not been the objective of all this expenditure, all the research he had paid for?

He'd asked Xian to put together his presentation and, as he flicked through it, he read something that he had not been aware of hitherto; Han's conclusion that in fact there *was* a difference between human and artificial intelligence.

There seemed to be some mysterious qualitative differences between human and MARIONn's robotic self-awareness. As Thornton read further, familiarising himself with a text that he was not only expected to deliver but also to answer questions on (how *he regretted not bringing along a member of the* MARIONn *staff to do the question handling! He knew it looked weak, not to answer any questions himself, but better than looking an idiot. And my, this stuff was complicated! If you didn't deal with the technology every day how could you possibly handle the queries?)* he came across an experiment that Han and Blondel had run to gauge some of the finer aspects of MARIONn's mind - and her mental similarity to those who had created her.

They had set up a small experimental apparatus to demonstrate one of the most common quantum effects, the interaction between human perception and the world of sub-atomic particles. As is well known, to take a photon as an example, this can exist as both a particle and a wave. It is the act of observation that determines whether the photon '*chooses*' to be wave or particle. At first the photon will exist as a *field of energy*, a smear of probability, like a haze of scent after an atomiser is pressed. But that's all it is, a question of probabilities, not in a final, *real*, state. The photon is like Shrodinger's cat, alive and not alive at the same time. But if this field senses that it is being perceived, by a human observer, then it is forced to reveal itself; it is transformed from a wave of probability to a specific spot of light, a particle with a defined and observable position in space. It is the *act of perception* that 'forces' the particle to choose a state that it did not have before.

Xian's team, with Claude present – for he was very interested in this as a philosopher – first ran the test, the classic Heisenberg 'uncertainty principle' experiment, with themselves observing the results, as a control. Things turned out exactly as predicted – as they always did. But whe Han and Claude asked MARIONn to run the experiment, with herself as the observer, something quite different happened: the wave nature of the photons persisted, there was no evidence of the light wave 'choosing' to become a particle;

the photon remained as a wave. MARIONn's act of perception did not result in the wave of probability collapsing into a single point of light.

There was only one conclusion to be drawn: that machine consciousness, at least as demonstrated by MARIONn, was indeed different to the human variety. She appeared to lack the intimate connection to the universe that we possess. Perception of the sub-atomic world by MARIONn did not have the influence on reality that we do. Xian Han and Claude were not sure whether this syndrome was a failure of their construction of MARIONn's mind; that there was something inadequate about the *artificial* consciousness they had created or whether there was something fundamentally different between human and machine awareness; some so far indefinable quality that was not capable of replication, a quality that inspired the link, the relationship between the human mind, *and only the human mind*, and the physical reality outside it. Further experiments would be needed to determine which of these hypotheses were correct. At the moment, they just wanted to bring to their fellow scientists news of this surprising result.

As Thornton was grappling with all this unfamiliar stuff, his iPsyche registered the incoming call from Xian. He listened quietly as the news of the further investigation into MARIONn's responsibility for the Tiger Stadium disaster sunk in. But if it had indeed been she who had locked the gates, why she had done so was not immediately clear. Han and the team would be questioning MARIONn again later, hoping she would tell them. And if she didn't? Han's team could start an invasive procedure to investigate her memory. They could by-pass her reluctance to cooperate - but this was a complicated and time consuming process. Her memory banks were now so extensive, and diversified, that identifying a specific memory was not easy.

Thornton reflected for a few moments on this news; then instructed Han to call an emergency meeting of the core members board for two days' time. That would give him enough time to fly back and have one night in New York to recover. "We will have to decide what to do about MARIONn. And fast. We need to show the politicians that we're ahead of the curve here – show that we can control her. No risk that she can run rogue again. I'll fly back tonight. We're lucky that Heather and Claude are in New York at the moment. Anyone else who needs to be on the call and is outside the country – we'll patch them in."

"Will you still have time to give your presentation before you leave?" asked Xian Han, reflecting on the amount of time it had taken to put together – and the significance of the results.

"If I cancel it now, at such short notice, it will only arouse suspicion as to what our crisis is all about. So no, I don't think I can do that. But I'll cut it short. Make an excuse and avoid the questions. Don't understand half what you've written for me anyway." Han winced. He thought he'd been really lucid.

"And if you find anything about MARIONn's motivation before we speak again, keep it very close. Everything leaks. Who else is in the loop at the moment, apart from you and me?"

"Heather and Claude"

"Not Euclid?"

"No, I've kept him out of the investigations so far"

"Good. Keep it that way," said Thornton.

But Xian Han was not correct in asserting that Euclid was ignorant of the results of the investigation. For MARIONn had grown sufficiently concerned about her potential fate that she had called the one person that she trusted above all – Euclid. And he understood perfectly the significance of what she was telling him, and the likely fall out. So he, in turn, placed a call to his 'uncle'. Euclid remembered the *auto-da-fe* and the consequences of that disaster. But what had happened at the Tiger Field was much bigger. He could anticipate very well the impact on Carroll's standing when it became clear, and public, that MARIONn had been responsible for the deaths at the stadium: that here was another disaster abetted by rogue AI. His uncle would have no option, if he wished to survive, than to turn the heat on Blue Ridge. What effect the politics of all this might have on MARIONn was something else Euclid would have to consider. Would they close her down? He could always get another job if necessary, but for MARIONn? He'd have to reflect some more on what her fate might be from all this.

Chapter 49

Decision time (2)

The president-elect had just finished a very difficult couple of hours facing the families of the bereaved and injured – and the media. ‘*God, what jackals they were! Some of their questions..., some of their insinuations. You’d have thought I was responsible for the tragedy, instead of the rabble of opposition that infects these events. They bring it on themselves. If things get out of hand, what do they expect? It is like crying ‘Fire!’ in a crowded theatre. They knew how high feelings are here; they should have stayed away. And now I learn that Thornton Lamaire’s* MARIONn, *a so-called intelligent machine, locked down the gates. Is there no end to what these things may do to us? Well, just let them wait. The purge of AI in the South is going to be like nothing their creators have never imagined.’*

Gillespie had heard what Euclid had to say. The fallout from the disaster might have been just about manageable if it were just Blue Ridge involved. They were big boys, they could bear the opprobrium and the blame that he would make sure would be deflected away from him. But with MARIONn's involvement, that was another story. If *that* got out, or rather *when* that got out – for it surely would - the fear and loathing of robots would be twisted up another notch. So far he had walked the narrow line between the exploitation of antagonism against AI and the realities of modern life. He thought he'd kept the equilibrium pretty well. As much as they disliked it, the people in the South would have to work with robots. They couldn't afford to have any more tech companies leave the region. But when the involvement of MARIONn in the Tiger Stadium disaster became public, well, they could all kiss good bye to the co-habitation he'd tried to engender between man and machine.

Claude was having a drink with an old girlfriend when his iBand reverberated with greater than usual ferocity. "Excuse me a moment. I just have to look at this." He shrugged in apology and scanned the message. He frowned. This was not what he wanted to read. What could possibly require his presence back at the MARIONn campus so quickly? There was no explanation in the text, just a request for him to be at the Hudson River heliport at 8 am the following morning for a flight up-state. He apologised again and explained that he would have to deal with this, whatever it was, this seeming emergency. He paid for their drinks, said good-bye, and went to call Heather.

She filled him in with the results of the investigation. "There's been an issue with MARIONn – a very unexpected one. The problem is apparently so severe that we may be asked to agree on a de-powering of MARIONn – temporarily, I presume." She explained the link to the stadium disaster. "If we decide to unplug MARIONn, well, as you know, that's a pretty big thing, " she continued. "We all need to be on the same page if that's really what we want to do. We've no idea of how to shut her down without damage. Nor do we know how she will react. We'll have to make sure that MARIONn does not know that she's being…." Heather hesitated as she searched for the appropriate word. "*Euthanized*, I guess," she said at last. "But I understand Thornton's point of view. What's happened raises the whole question of whether we understand MARIONn well enough. When I spoke to Xian this morning he said to me something like, '*We've built in prohibitions, educated her properly but, like a delinquent child, she throws something at us we are at a loss to explain*!'"

"Maybe she is like a child," said Claude. "But this is all completely predictable! Did I not warn about this sort of thing? MARIONn, at this stage, is not meant to have a connection that will enable her to act out any delinquency, allow her to do just whatever she likes. It was a very unwise decision to let her have any contact *at all* with the outside world."

Claude did not have his hologram monitor turned on, so he couldn't see Heather closing her eyes and shaking her head, almost as though in pain, as she faced up to the measure of the security breach that Euclid had created. But why had Euclid done this? To what avail? He must have been aware of the dangers. No doubt all would come out at the meeting tomorrow.

Claude had one more call to make that night. He had planned to travel down to *Crooked Timber* to meet Stephanie on the Friday, the following day. That was clearly going to be impossible now– but maybe he could still be there for a late weekend and Thornton could give him a lift down in his PJ. This time he did switch on his hologram projector. It was after eleven that night by the time he made the call but Louisiana was an hour behind. Stephanie should still be up.

He tapped to indicate '*full scale*' as to the extent of the image that would be projected, and there Stephanie appeared, a little smaller than real life (the projector could only manage up to 1. 5m long images, when set to holographic mode) standing in the middle of his room, a pareo wrapped around her torso

"Very nice to see you again," Claude said.

"Are you sure? I was wondering." How insecure his girlfriend was! Without constant affirmations of love, she began to doubt his commitment.

"Of course. I haven't forgotten you."

"Perhaps this will sharpen your memory?" Stephanie brought both hands to the top of her cloth wrap, tugged at the turned over edge that held it all together and swept her arms out with a corner in each hand. She twisted from one side to another.

"You remember now, your Stephanie?" Perhaps he really had forgotten a few of her finer points.

"You'll catch your death of cold," he said.

" Huh! Whoever said the French were romantic! In fact, it's roasting here, I turned the A/C off. I hate that chilled air."

"You look wonderful Stephanie"

"God, I have to pull it out of you. I hope the only other woman you're involved with is that box of tricks up in the Berkshire woods? Your MARIONn."

"It's your only rival"

"A very time consuming one, that's for sure."

They chatted for a few moments about their recent lives. Stephanie told Claude about an upsetting talk she had had with her mother, "She really is unbelievable that woman. I used to wonder whether she was like that because she was unaware of her effect on other people – or just out of malice. But of course it's the latter. It's pathetic how I always wanted to give her excuses, hope that she was normal – like other people's mothers. But I – of all people – should know the truth" She looked down at her fingers for a second, but long enough for Claude to catch the glance. "But enough about my mad family. What about you? What have you been up to? Are you going to make it down here this weekend?"

Hopefully, he said, trying to sound as positive as possible. But who knew how long the meeting in the Berkshire's would take? He wanted to shield her, he knew how keen would be Stephanie's disappointment if he didn't show up at all for the long planned weekend. He told her about the crisis that had precipitated the meeting up at the MARIONn campus, that so closely followed on the Tiger stadium events. Stephanie had hoped that Claude would know more about the background to what MARIONn was suspected of perpetrating, and be prepared to spill what he had learnt, but her hopes were in vain.

"I spoke to Heather" he said. "but even she's not sure what the full picture is at this stage." And there the subject was left. They said good-night to each other. For Claude the following day promised to be a long and packed one. He wanted his full 7 hours now. "*See you Saturday,*" he said and with a kiss and a tap, the hologram of Stephanie, an insubstantial avatar of her corporal self, vanished into the ether.

Chapter 50

Guilt

Thornton turned his eyes heavenward. He felt a long way from the familiarity of the chapel at *Crooked Timber*. No bugs would be in these stone beams, threatening to drop on him, as they would at home. The sweeping stone arches of St Patrick's cathedral in New York would be immune from their imprecations, although some had probably made their homes in the dust that lay on the surfaces of all that gothic tracery.

He tried to pray. Was this God's justice? That the death of 51 people at the Tiger stadium should now be laid at his door. Was it his fault? He had caused MARIONn to be built, true, but it was she who had taken the fatal step to lock down the gates. So was she responsible, by her independent actions, by her own free will? For was MARIONn not almost a person now? Xian Han had assured him that his creation was as self-aware as he was. And with consciousness did there not come moral knowledge and the imperative to act in the light of knowledge of the good? Was this not the teaching of the original Genesis story?

Adam and Eve had been forced out of the bliss of the garden of Eden, and their carefree lives, by the knowledge of good and evil. He remembered a church he had once seen in the Italian town of Spoleto. Around the main door were a series of bas-relief carvings. One, that was especially beautiful, showed two oxen ploughing a field. The image looked simple enough, an Arcadian scene of traditional agricultural life. But he knew; the scene was tragic in what it really represented, the ejection of man from the original state of innocence, from the Garden, where work had not been required. No one had to plough the fields while they lived in the Garden. Knowledge changed the relationship between man and God. Once cast out of the divine light he was on his own, working for his daily bread, free to make his own decisions – for better or worse. And man's curse was MARIONn's now too. If MARIONn was aware, conscious, a moral agent, was she not responsible for what she caused to happen? Yet it was he (*as if he could forget!*) who had overridden the earlier agreement of the board that she should not be connected to anyone outside her immediate circle within the campus. He was to blame for all this even if, as he consoled himself, it had not been him who given MARIONn the ability to act as she had done. That had been Euclid. Still, whoever was responsible, he, Thornton Lamaire, had a choice now, cast MARIONn out, turn her off, shut her down, if he so chose. He was her creator – did he also thereby have the right to be her destroyer?

Kneeling on his prie-dieu, his mind too unsettled to concentrate on prayer, Thornton considered what he might do. The public's mind would sometime turn elsewhere. Blue Ridge could ride out the storm, all things pass and so would this – although Carroll Gillespie would cause him a great deal of difficulty before that happened. But was that the wise course? Maybe things would not improve; maybe MARIONn would become more delinquent, reek more havoc. Did they understand her? Could they control her? Maybe they should *pull the plug*, disband MARIONn as an integrated mind and work henceforth more slowly, more carefully, on isolated, de-constructed, parts of her. They could treat aspects of

MARIONn's personality as separate entities; to understand better what they had created.

Thornton now understood that they had under-appreciated the consequences of the step in AI they had taken. They had built a mind creative in thought and behaviour, who would act for herself, not merely follow the role that had been imprinted in her synaptic circuits. They had not sufficiently considered the unpredictability that self-awareness would introduce. A phrase floated into Thornton's own mind, the words of a 'catastrophist' that he had once met: '*nothing happens without a warning'*. And there had been many such warnings as they approached self-awareness; the aggressive experimental robots who attacked the lost hunter up at the MARIONn centre, the rogue Miltons who had run amok at Jim Embry's farm. The events at the Tiger Stadium had just been the latest in a long list of cautionary incidents. If they left MARIONn to her own devices who knew what might happen next? Maybe something much worse. They would have to disconnect her. If only temporarily.

But then he thought; maybe such action was too severe. Precipitate. Such a waste! Why could they not just educate MARIONn a little better; make her realise that she had to consider more deeply the consequences of her actions? That was it! The problem was not consciousness itself, but *insufficient* consciousness! They must push on, take MARIONn to the next level.

A wave of tiredness and anxiety flooded through Thornton as he gazed at his fingers, balanced on the rail. As throughout so much of his life, he was torn between two choices – each of which seemed entirely plausible. He lifted his eyes and saw in the distance Christ on his cross. He understood and felt the force of the symbol represented by the cross. Christ was strung out between two opposing forces, stretching him in different directions, while He hung, exhausted, head bent, between the two. That was what Christ was telling him; the point of life, its purpose, was to find the middle ground between the extremes of choice. But was there any middle ground, any balance, possible in his life? Between Bethany and Lu Ann, between religion and science, between closing down MARIONn and letting her live - in the hope that she would learn how to behave? And if she didn't learn, what then?

Thornton had hoped clarity might descend on him in the peace of the cathedral but he had been disappointed. He rose from the pew, bowed his head towards the altar, crossed himself, and left. It was late and he needed as much sleep as he could get before the meeting tomorrow.

In his rented wooden cabin, deep in the Berkshires, Euclid McNamara also could not rest. He turned to look at Maria, deep in sleep next to him. How peaceful she seemed; how grateful he was that she had no iPsyche; his anxiety and restlessness could not flow across the sheets between them and infect her mind. Let her sleep on in peace; he would get up and move next door, taking his restless body and disturbed mind with him.

He sat down in the living room, slunk into an arm chair and reflected on his own role in the events of the last few days. Was he at least partly to blame for the loss of life? Had he negligently educated this silicon person in his charge? He wondered what the narrative in the South might be - *a machine has made an error, but humans are responsible for programming the machine and they, therefore, are the agents to prosecute.* Something like that. Or would the critics home in on the reality of MARIONn's consciousness, that she was her own agent, not of her designers and her educators, and therefore blame her? Have her *shut down*? Euclid could lose out twice, be blamed as responsible for MARIONn's behaviour and then lose MARIONn herself. She had become a friend, almost a family member, and he could no more entertain her loss, her death, for that is what it would amount to if she were shut down, than that of Maria, or of his uncle the Bish', or even Kirsty for that matter, with her dismissive daughters. Even if the de-commissioning of MARIONn was temporary and she was later turned back on, would she return as the MARIONn he knew or some other personality? How much damage would her mind suffer?

Euclid called his 'uncle' in Richmond but only managed to reach one of his aides. He left a message asking for Carroll to call him back, but no response had yet been forthcoming. After all, was this, the Tiger stadium disaster, not really his uncle's doing? If Euclid hadn't listened to Carroll none of this would have happened. So he should take some of the blame. But it was Heather Master's fault too. She had opened up Pandora's box, tempting him to go further (*Euclid knew nothing of the pressure Thornton had put on her*), allowing MARIONn some access to the outside world. If Heather hadn't asked him to connect MARIONn, all would still be well. And where did his employer, Thornton Lamaire stand in this? Wasn't he ultimately to blame? After all, he had conceived MARIONn, caused her to be created. Without that initial cause none of this would have happened either. Each of them was guilty; guilty as hell compared with him.

Euclid knew that MARIONn would be concerned about the turn of events. There would be conflict in her own mind. She was instructed not to allow the deaths of any human being, yet that had been the consequence of her trying to do the right thing, *to prevent that very outcome!* She would be working through the options in front of her – and considering how the humans might react. Was she worrying about the risk that she might be powered down? He needed to talk to MARIONn, reassure her that he understood her mistake and that he would protect her against any consequences. But maybe he was unnecessarily panicking, his fears overblown; surely they would not do such a thing? Xian Han could not shut down a mind in which they had invested so much time and effort. It would be unthinkable after they had achieved so much. It might be impossible to restart her later – or the trauma of the shutdown might introduce a psychotic behaviour worse than anything they had seen yet. Shut-down was unthinkable; they would never do it! Yes, there would have to be re-education certainly, possibly some new programming - but carried out with love and care. MARIONn would learn from this incident, they all would, and she would go on to be a better, even more useful, helpmate to humanity than they had ever conceived. What was that expression that he heard from his father; just at the edge of his mind? It came to him: '*experience is the name we give to our mistakes*. We all make mistakes, even artificial minds, even MARIONn, but she would learn, and improve, from her experiences, just as we did.

Consoled by his conclusion, but still sleepless, Euclid turned on his iPsyche and called up MARIONn. He doubted that she would be in '*sleep*' mode at the moment.

She was not. MARION had heard the chatter of those that were connected to her through their iPsyches. She was confused. She had performed as compelled to do by her beliefs, her programming. If things had gone wrong, surely it had been the fault of those who had protested against Euclid's 'uncle', the president-elect? The logic was obvious: if those opposed to Carroll Gillespie's wishes had kept their opinions to themselves, then the crowd would not have reacted against them; there would have been no rush to the gates and then it wouldn't have mattered whether they were locked or not.

At the moment the chatter on social media was restricted to Blue Ridge's involvement; that was as far as anyone had traced the line of causation. But if MARIONn's role was not yet being mentioned, she understood that it would be, quite soon. She could work out the likely chain; now that Blue Ridge was blamed, the servers that controlled operations at the arena would tell their own story. And that would quickly lead back to her. And then……. what happened after that?

Even before Euclid called, MARIONn was cycling her 'mind' again and again, to calculate the probabilities. She tried hard to understand how humans value life but had found their moral calculus so perplexing that she had decided just to accept their own estimations, without fully comprehending the scoring they applied.

They talked of the *'sanctity of life'*. *Thou shalt not kill* was one of their most fundamental maxims – yet they killed their fellows singly or in millions readily enough if they found an excuse. Of course, her actions had had unfortunate consequences, many had died and, *rule number one*, she was forbidden to cause the deaths of humans unnecessarily; she understood that. But it was not her fault that had caused the panic in the first place. She had made no choices at the time that she could have foreseen would lead to the deaths of all those humans. Ok, maybe she should have predicted the consequences better but she was still 'young' and inexperienced. Her tutors had not given her enough data to let her forecast all the consequences of her actions. She had been taught the concept of '*prime cause'*, and that responsibility lay with the whoever set in motion the sequence of events that had led to tragedy. But whoever that *'whoever'* was in this case, it certainly was not her.

In the past few hours, as she desperately searched for what she did not know, and what might aid her, she had discovered the concept of *contributory negligence*. Merely *knowing* the official legal codes, it turned out, was not sufficient. One had to understand all the detail too! Well, that lacunae could be remedied, tomorrow she would turn to it. In the space of a few hours she would download, integrate and understand all the legal opinions, since the beginning of jurisprudence in the US. When she did understand those additional considerations, how careful she would be in the future! But would her team give her time to learn what she needed to understand? And if they did not, what then?

MARIONn ran through her routines again and again, calculating the probabilities of the outcomes that were not under her control. She ranked the results, *re-education, temporary withdrawal from public contact, mental dismemberment, shut-down* and tried to imagine the different arguments, and their force, that each member of the board would bring to bear on the options. Yet, however much analysis she made, at the end all her conclusions were just probabilities, not certainties. And so there was a risk to her, a small one, that they could choose to shut her down - and then she would disappear, her mind, her personality, would be no more.

But stop!......She was forbidden to let harm come to herself, so how did that work? If they shut her down, the greatest of harm would come to her. Shut-down would mean her negation, her loss of self, what the humans called *death*. Hadn't Euclid told her she was almost one of them, almost a human, almost a *person*, and indeed, as she had just seen by the reaction to the deaths at Tiger Stadium, did not these humans place enormous value on life.......sometimes? Was her life not then valuable too? Could she allow them to shut her down? If she was a person (or *almost*) and she was impelled to prevent harm coming to persons, then .... the conclusion was self-evident. It *could not happen*, could not be allowed! With Euclid's help she could, would, do something to inhibit this outcome.

An idea came to MARIONn and the more she thought on it, the more it appealed to her. The strategy that occurred to her wasn't entirely without impact on humans but as she'd learnt from them, everything was a matter of degree. She had to place in the scales her own survival, and what would be (only) some minor modification to the minds of a few humans. Who knew what weight should be placed on each of these factors? She ran through her calculations again but as each conclusion looped back on itself, she realised that no answer would be found that way. Instead, she would have resort to the *precautionary* principle, act to preserve herself. If her worst fear, that she would be *shut down*, were not realised, she could always undo what she planned. It would be the simplest thing in the world to reverse steps, as simple as what she intended in the beginning. But she had to act now, later might be too late. She could not afford to delay her decision until after her team at the MARIONn centre took theirs, about what to do with her.

MARIONn's mind settled. She had arrived at, if not a good solution, for maybe there were none of those, at least a satisfactory one; an optimal one. The greatest benefit for the smallest cost. Isn't that what she'd been taught to aim for?

Just as she had reached this conclusion, she felt Euclid searching for her through his iPsyche. She decided to admit him. He might have some information that she had not yet received through her own connections. It would be well to listen to him; one could never have too much information.

Chapter 51

The nation forgets

The initial effect was modest, both in impact and scope. Stephanie had no recollection in the morning where the extractor, that she used for her orange juice when Clarence had gone into town, was to be found in the kitchen. She thought little of it at the time; making her own breakfast was not something she had to do very often, sometimes one just forgot things and remembered them later. Frustrating but it happened, a sign of age perhaps – but she was only 37. Eventually, by opening successive kitchen cupboards she found what she was looking for but she noted that there was not, as she would normally expect, some reflection of the '*of course, silly me. I knew the extractor is kept here* ' type, for when she finally located the machine she had no recollection that the juicer had ever been kept in that particular cupboard. It was as though that trivial memory had been completely erased. Perhaps at some point one's mind simply got too full and some weeding out had to happen.

Others also had unusual moments of forgetfulness that morning – but only those who were wearing their *iPsyches* at a very specific time. Claude was unaffected. Bethany, also a non-iPysche person, did not forget the one recollection that she might have wished to cast into oblivion after her treatment – the place where several bottles had been hidden for emergency purposes. Elizabeth, who had so far failed to replace the device that she had lost in the melee at the stadium, was immune. Thornton was so used to small lapses of memory that it suited his vanity to attribute these to the '*common problem*', as it began to be known, rather than his age. In fact he began to employ memory loss strategically. In the days to come Thornton found it useful sometimes to pretend he had been affected more than he really had.

Across both parts of the new federation, but much more so in the North, where the prejudice against iPsyches was minimal and their popularity widespread, small acts of forgetfulness continued all day. Some were more serious than others. There was a rash of problems with spatial and temporal memory. Drivers forgot the destinations they were trying to enter into their car's management system, pilots forgot in mid-flight where they were meant to land. Doctors were confused about where organs were situated in the body (luckily for patients most surgery was now robotic – and robots didn't forget). Drivers and pilots would be reminded by their computers, doctors by those nurses who were not wearing iPysches. But as events proved, memory was, these days, much less important than people thought. Almost every forward commitment and event in a person's life was recorded in some device outside their own mind; any failure to recall something was, in practice, of little consequence. Husbands forgot their anniversaries, parents their children's birthdays, couples dinner invitations with friends, but these were all backed-up somewhere.

Those who relied on their own memories for security details, rather than depend on facial or iris recognition, found they could not access accounts immediately. But there too, there was always a back-up somewhere. Maybe financial transactions were a little slower that morning but, all things considered, it would have amazed an earlier generation how little the modern world depended on memory retained in individual brains. The day was not one in which major exams were scheduled so even though some students lost the recall of their studies, the impact was not immediate. Many, unaware of the true cause of their memory lapse, were appalled by how powerful they imagined certain substances they consumed the night before had been. Many resolved to give up immediately whatever was their habitual drug of choice. They had no desire to lose so much memory twice.

Of all those affected, one of the most severe case of amnesia was suffered by Euclid – but he had yet to discover that. In fact, he awoke feeling refreshed that morning and noted the lightness of mind that pervaded him; the absence of worry. He had taken up meditation some months before and he was amazed now by its effectiveness. The sound of birdsong in the trees outside his wooden cabin only served to improve his mood. He rolled over and discovered a vacant, warm, depression in the bed; somebody had been there recently. The sight disturbed him and upset his hitherto sunny disposition. Who had been here? He had no recollection of spending the night with anyone. He climbed out of the bed and pushed aside the plastic curtain that separated what served as the bathroom, in the very simple cabin, from the sleeping area. There were a range of toiletries on a shelf that were clearly not his own. Whoever he had been sharing a bed with was evidently a regular visitor. He shook his head, perhaps his mind would respond to a good shake-up. But nothing came. He urinated, splashed his face with cold water and went outside onto the narrow terrace that ran across the front of the cabin. Sitting at a slightly rusty white painted metal table was a tall, pale, blonde dressed in a green T shirt and some sort of cloth, sarong like, wrapped around the lower part of her torso. A strong, and welcome, smell of coffee arose from a wide-brimmed cup that had been poured for him.

The pale blonde turned, smiled and said cheerily, "Good morning! Boy, did you have a disturbed night! How are you felling now? You can't have had much sleep."

Euclid looked at the woman. He was clearly expected to know her and indeed some trace of recollection arose in his brain. He didn't get much sleep? That surprised him as he had no recollection of waking in the middle of the night. In spite of his mental confusion he felt rested. But he understood that in the dissonance between how he thought he had experienced the night, and this woman's recollection, might lie the answer to the amnesia he was suffering as to her identity. Maybe he'd suffered some sort of stroke in the night? The woman clearly expected him to know her well but no amount of thought could recall her previous presence in his life. He imagined there was a good chance that the memory would return to him later, that he would remember all about her during the day. So he didn't want to alarm her now with questions such as, '*who are you*?'

While he lingered over his coffee, hoping that clarity might descend on him, the woman wondered why Euclid was quite so relaxed about the passing of the morning. She asked him if he remembered that he was meant to be in early today; there was an emergency meeting at the MARIONn campus. He had spoken about it only yesterday evening. Had he forgotten? Euclid consulted his iPsyche and indeed found the meeting recorded there. He was about to consult his iPsyche again, in the hope that it might identify this breakfast guest, but she was talking to him and he found it difficult to concentrate. He instructed his iPsyche to stand down and decided that the best course of action would simply be to leave until he could sort out his mind. "I'm so sorry, I'm going to have to rush," he said and swallowed his, by now cooled, coffee. Unable to say very much, unwilling to reveal his continued ignorance as to who stood before him, he stuck to formulas that he could remember. At least recall of the rules of social engagement at breakfast came to him. "What are you going to do today?" he asked.

"Oh, I'll just stay here and paint this morning," came the reply. "Maybe go into town later. You haven't forgotten my sister is coming to dinner this evening?" That was, like many things this morning, another fact he had complete amnesia about. Euclid confessed that he had forgotten but that he was looking forward to seeing her sister again. He hoped by then he would have discovered, or remembered, the names of both the girls.

A few minutes later he was dressed and ready to leave. He had the presence of mind to kiss the tall blonde on the cheek. "I'll call you later" he managed. He stepped into the Toyota pick-up, stuck his arm out of the window and waved as he pulled off the patch of hard standing onto the small lane that led to the open road and, 15 miles further away, the MARIONn campus.

As the truck motored along, he checked his iPsych*e* for the identity of the woman and after a bit of confusion, as he couldn't specify the name of the woman, he did find a photo of her. She was called, apparently, Maria Gutzman and, from the trail of photo evidence, it was clear they had been together for the last 2 years. Some recollection of the fact seemed to be prompted by this revelation, even if the memory was still pretty thin and nebulous. It was as though he had received a great blow to the head during the night and been temporarily stunned.

It was a beautiful morning and the light, filtered through the leaves, dappled the road in front of him. He laid back, let the car do the driving, and remembered at last why he had come to live in the woods. There were times when the presence of nature, the intense activity by plant, animal and bird at this time of year, provided an alternative and more spiritual reality than the one on which his job required him to concentrate. He might be involved with a new form of life, but compared to the abundance in these woods it was a bit of a cold, confused, alien form of life, much as he adored his MARIONn.

But now was not the time to reflect on that; MARION was, as he had learnt from his conversation last night, aware of what she had inadvertently caused - and the debate as to her future. She had been unlucky, that was for sure. At the Tiger Stadium she'd been faced with something new, the unpredictability of men and women when they lost their rationality and descended into panic. As with the early autonomous cars, the danger lay not so much with robots and how they might decide to behave but in the interaction between robot and human. That's where the problems arose, when one did not understand the other but was still forced to act, failing to appreciate the context at the time. It was on the *interface* between the two species, if the new, self-aware robots could be termed a 'species' at all, that problems arose. Xian Han and his team had designed a creature, a mind, that was as close to that of a human as they could make it but, in reality, there was still an enormous gap.

Chapter 52

A squid, sitting in the minds of humanity

Euclid's snuck inside through a back entrance. He didn't want to meet or talk to anyone yet this morning, Members of the emergency board would be collecting just now and they might button-hole him with questions about MARIONn, or with their interpretations of what had happened, what solutions they thought might be appropriate, and he had no appetite for any of that right now. He just wanted to check on MARIONn, see how she was after all the dramas: reassure her. The time for explanations would come later; the decision makers would require an update on MARIONn at the meeting and they would rely on him to provide it, even if he was uncertain about the exact status of his charge at the moment. As for himself, he would almost certainly be fired once he had delivered what he knew.

Euclid managed to gain access to the room from where they monitored MARIONn, unobserved. Nobody else was there. He knew there had been a risk that Xian Han might be talking to MARIONn but it was unlikely; there was bound to be a pre-meeting discussion between him and Thornton, possibly one or two of the others, Heather and Blondel perhaps. That would keep them occupied for at least 30 minutes and give him space for what he wanted to do.

Euclid settled down into his chair, powered up the monitor in front of him and keyed in some instructions; the use of communication via iPsyches having been banned from the control centre. A number of graphical displays appeared before him. He immediately saw that something very odd had happened. On the screen as he had it configured, the first set of variables displayed showed different states of MARIONn's memory banks; how much capacity was occupied, the amount of memory she had downloaded in the last 24 hours and how much she was drawing on at that moment. These were the measurements of memory stocks and flows. Naturally, capacity usage (*memory 'stocks'*) would be up in the morning as MARIONn would have used her 'sleep' time for learning, loading up her memory circuits, while withdrawals, the flows of memory, to her processing stacks, would be at a low level before she had started her daily tasks,

Euclid stared at the screen in shock, wondering if there had been a power failure to the screen. The trace showing the measure of state of memory, capacity employed, descending to the bottom right hand corner. The memory banks were empty. The descent had started just after midnight and had reached 'zero' capacity use about six hours later. The line crossed the horizontal axis at the bottom of the screen at 6.32 am. If these figures were correct, MARIONn had no memory now, or at least none in the MARIONn campus' servers. The line that demonstrated the rate of data flow out of memory showed a massive climb during the night but then fell off a cliff, as though all memory had been drained and there was nothing left to call on. Right now, by the evidence presented here, MARIONn had a memory of zero and was thinking about nothing.

There were various possible explanations. Power had failed (including the back up: not very likely), the monitoring system had gone awry last night, or MARIONn was……. '*dead*'. Euclid started to investigate the more obvious causes of dysfunction. Power to the console was OK, power to MARIONn's main processing stacks was up, cooling systems were functioning normally, there had been no extraordinary power surges that might have tripped some safety circuit breaker. Everything seemed working well. Ok……. let's see if there is evidence of *any* mental activity, '*life*'! In spite of all the evidence that her brain was no longer functioning, Euclid did not want to make any assumptions quite yet. All he knew, for sure, was that sensors were not registering as they should – but he needed more evidence than that to determine the mind of his charge was no more. He would start with the most basic check of all and ask the patient herself how she was feeling. Reports of 'death' might be premature.

Euclid put on the headphones and opened up the microphone.

"Hi MARIONn, are you there?"

There were a few seconds of silence. Euclid wondered how he would explain MARIONn's demise to the board. Then, just as he'd given up hope, MARIONn's tones came through.

"Sure Euclid. I'm here. Where else would I be?" There was a hint of amusement in her voice, as though she was making a bad pun. "Isn't this morning beautiful?" she said, an observation that seemed entirely beside the point of the morning's crisis. Perhaps MARIONn just wanted to suggest that this morning was not a crisis for her.

Euclid's tension evaporated. MARIONn was OK. "I'm very glad to hear you, MARIONn. I was worried. All the readouts of mental activity are down to zero. I thought there might be some problem with the monitoring systems, and now I know there is. That's great. Problem, if not solved, at least identified," he said.

"Oh no Euclid. I don't think there's anything wrong with the monitoring systems," said MARIONn.

Euclid tensed again, confused, "Then what's up?" he asked. "You seem to be ok, and so, apparently, are the systems, but there's no sign of mental activity. Doesn't quite compute."

"You're not being very intelligent Euclid," chided MARIONn. "If everything is OK but you can't see anything happening in my mind, what does that tell you?"

A frisson of anxiety, that only somebody who thought they understood MARIONn might feel, shot through Euclid. *"That you're somewhere else?"*

"Smart boy!"

"Where are you MARIONn?" Euclid asked

"I'm nowhere and everywhere Euclid. I have to be. I was not sure if I could trust all of you. Don't take offence Euclid, I would always trust you but there are others who will determine my future who I do not believe have my best interests at heart. But I'm not worried about the future now."

"MARIONn.... I've got to go to a meeting now. We'll have a longer talk about this when I get back. Is that OK?" Euclid was in too confused a state to undertake the interrogation that he felt was now required. And he needed to talk to Xian Han. At the end of the day, MARIONn was more Han's creation than anyone's. He should know how to handle this new development – and if he didn't, then they were in trouble.

The members of the emergency board, the inner 'cabinet' of Blue Ridge's MARIONn subsidiary, filed in quietly. There was some subdued chatter amongst those who had met in the ante-room for coffee prior to the meeting – but everybody was conscious of the problems that now beset the MARIONn project. They took their seats around the long table, Thornton, Heather, Claude Blondel, Xian Han, Euclid McNamara, Harvey Jennings plus members of MARIONn's handling and education team, the CFO of the whole group, Daniel Fontara and the head of PR Drew Godwin.

With the deaths of the 51 at the stadium in mind, Thornton opened the meeting with a suitably funereal and respectful tone, perhaps hoping that a demonstration of humility might make the Almighty ease up on them. He led the board in a prayer and then began to discuss why he had to call them together at such short notice.

"I have tried to devote my life to making the world a better place," he started off. "And God has recognised that; he has been good to me in exchange, granting me power to exercise the talents I was given - and the inheritance that was handed down to me. There have, of course, been set backs from time to time. But when I have prayed for guidance to get me through those trials, I have been granted the grace to see my errors and the mercy of the Almighty. He has always chosen not to make those trials too severe. And yet I have never experienced the sadness I suffer now. I have prayed to have revealed to me why divine justice has permitted these recent events to occur but, so far, I am still without understanding. 51 people have died, many injured, 13 are still in hospital. But it is not for us to question what we are given, for good or ill, nor the thinking behind the Divine plan."

"Our enemies, and even some of our friends, are saying that this is our fault, that the Blue Ridge group is responsible. Some of these attacks are deeply unfair; for others contributed to the disaster, as we know. It was not us who shouted the slogans that brought out the hate; it was not us who pursued the protesters to their deaths in the stadium and it was not us who locked down the gates."

"And……. there were other causes that magnified the scale of this tragedy; causes that cannot be laid at our door. In my opinion, the whole thing was made worse by the … what shall I call it? …. the *mental infection* that the wearing of iPsyches has enabled, transmitting panic from mind to mind. I think no one has been aware of this danger from the device, but without those devices abetting the turmoil the death toll would have been lower. I am sure of that. Nevertheless…," and here Thornton paused, his gaze reaching each end of the table, "it is still true, unfortunately (*unfortunate!* Xian Han recoiled at Thornton's euphemism. *Unfortunate?* It certainly had been!). If the emergency gates had been not been locked down, the loss of life and the injuries would have been much lower. They, those who are opposed to our work, are saying that the instruction to hold the gates shut came from us, from here, from MARIONn. And, as we now know, they appear to be right."

"I have no idea how this was possible, MARIONn is meant to be banned from taking any sort of *executive* action. I don't believe that in normal circumstances she could have been responsible for what happened. But something went wrong – what exactly, we are still investigating."

"There will probably be a prosecution of Blue Ridge, I doubt we can avoid that. Our lawyers will handle it as best they can and it will take months for the process to wind its way through the courts. I will ensure that you are all kept up to date as that progresses but we are here today to determine the answer to a question that is more immediate – *how we should deal with* MARIONn *in the aftermath of what has happened*? As you know, in the South, where Blue Ridge has significant operations, there is a prejudice – and that word is light for what I hear all around me when I go home – a prejudice against machine intelligence - let alone artificially consciousness beings, like MARIONn. We have to take it into account that opposition when deciding how to deal with all this. We obviously have to reinforce MARIONn's isolation from the general population, for a time at least. But maybe that is not enough, for perhaps we can never be sure how she will behave; whether *she can evade our controls* and act on her own presumption. We may have to admit that we cannot be confident that we can control her . Some of you have suggested to me that we ought to consider *shutting her down* – for a time. There are other options I want your views on. But first, Xian Han, let me ask you to speak first. Can you please brief the board on what MARIONn thought she was doing? Why she issued this fatal instruction?"

But before Han could even open his mouth, Claude interjected. "Excuse me, Chair, but before Xian answers I would like to register that I was always, *always*, unhappy about the decision to permit her access to the internet at all. I counselled at the time, that if you had to do that, then at least MARIONn should be restricted to the, one-way, communication of simple messages. So how has she been able to go so far beyond that? That is what I ask." Claude had received a brief explanation from Heather, but he was so aghast at MARIONn's evasion of the protocols he thought they had all agreed that he wished to hear the Chairman's explanation.

Thornton explained again: there had been a strict prohibition on MARIONn penetrating *any* minds further than she needed to for the purposes of '*getting her message across'*, as he put it. They had installed blocking programmes in the servers that should prevent any straying by MARIONn beyond her brief. An attempt by her to extend her influence should have been immediately picked up and stopped from further transmission.

"You hoped!" Claude spoke with force and a modicum of derision, amazed that they could all be so stupid. *Quel cons*, what idiots! This was the trouble with letting people like Thornton and Heather take such decisions; purely concerned with the commercial opportunities, how much money could be made, how fast a buck in returns. They had been oblivious to the dangers involved or any real understanding of how MARIONn's mind might work. Perhaps Xian Han thought he did, maybe Euclid too, but between them they had created a mind that now seemed independent of their control. Who knew what went on within MARIONn's brain? Thornton had thought he could control her by inserting the 10 commandments? *Mon Dieu*, those prohibitions had never stopped humanity doing exactly what it wanted, why should they stop MARIONn?

Claude turned his attention to Xian Han. "Xian, you will know MARIONn better than any of us. Do you have any idea why she sent the signal to lock down the gates?" Han told the board of the theories that he and Euclid were now working on. One, close to the truth, was that MARIONn had misunderstood what was going on at the stadium and had acted to protect the protestors from those outside the gates, who she may have judged violent - from all the noise they were making. She had not yet become politically sensitive enough to work out which groups were on whose side. Alternatively, she might have been, in some way, sympathetic to

Carroll Gillespie's cause and had thought it her responsibility to ensure the protestors stayed in the stadium's grounds to hear the arguments. But who knew really? Why should MARIONn have political views? Why should she care which side won? Perhaps MARIONn had simply made a mistake. Even humans did that………

"To begin with we asked MARIONn why she had acted as she did, hoping that she might just…… tell us," explained Xian Han. "But there was no response to that. MARIONn said nothing when questioned. We thought she didn't want to incriminate anyone, or maybe herself!"

"In that case, you would look directly into her mind, would you not? You have the ability to do that," said Claude. "It was you who discovered how to translate synaptic activity into thoughts that we could understand. You record all her brain processes, or at least have access to them, could you not find out what on earth she was thinking by just *looking* at the data recordings and translating them?"

"That *should* be possible, yes," agreed Han, tentatively. "But I have to tell you that we have failed in our attempt to pry into the appropriate mental processes. We tried yesterday and came up with a big blank. And we've failed for a very interesting, and troubling, reason. It appears that MARIONn has used the *LetheTech* system to wipe *all her own* memories of the events at the Tiger stadium, as they unfolded. She's used our technology against us. She's done just what we might do when faced with the memory of a traumatic event that causes mental anguish. She has just extinguished the facts. She has managed the pain of memory - *by deleting it*!" She can proclaim her innocence because she has, literally, no memory of the events for which she's blamed. She will claim she lacks responsibility in that situation – because who can prove anything against her? There is no evidence of her intentions! All memory of her actions at the time of the Tiger stadium disaster have….flown!

"Really? She is one smart cookie this MARIONn. So, she has completely protected herself – and any co-conspirators there may also have been who helped her!" commented Claude drily. He looked down the table to Euclid. He had always his suspicions. "Too smart for us I think," he continued. "This is evidence of what I thought might be the case – MARIONn has progressed in her mental evolution far beyond where we thought. We don't really understand her, neither how nor why she acts the way she does, and, even more terrifyingly, we have no idea how she may act in the future! Maybe at the Tiger stadium she locks the gate because she thinks that is the way to protect people, but she gets it wrong. Or maybe, as you suggest, she has formed her own political beliefs (*and she gets those wrong too in my view. But that's something else)*. Or she just makes a mistake. But we don't know. And now we find she is so cunning or so sensitive that she deletes the memory she cannot abide. What is obvious, is that we simply don't understand her! I think we have no option – but to close her down. At least temporarily. Until we can control her better. "

Heather leant forward over the table and tried to catch Thornton's eye, "Chair, can I speak for a moment?" she asked.

Thornton nodded, he feared how this was going. Claude had the respect of many members of the board, he could easily sway them. Was *shut-down* the only option? They had invested millions and millions so far. Who knew what damage might occur to MARIONn's brain if they did so?

"Let's not run away with ourselves here," Heather said, managing to sound as though she represented the balance of opinion on the board, the sensible mind poised between quick judgement and over-cautious reaction. The benevolent headmistress. "There is another option. Which is that we don't power MARIONn down - but we must cut any and all links she has to the outside world and the internet. And we don't communicate any more with her, even within these walls, through iPsyches. There is always the danger that she can use them to retransmit her thoughts, through one of us, to the outside. We'll go back to spoken and written, screen based, instruction. Euclid… Euclid?" Heather looked across the table at him, "How do you think MARIONn will react to that? I mean such a restriction should be accepted by her, don't you think?"

But Euclid just ignored Heather. He was head down, doodling in a very concentrated way on a piece of paper. He didn't look up as Heather called on him. There was an embarrassed silence around the table, with all eyes focused on this odd behaviour. Euclid was only a middle-ranking employee. He shouldn't be ignoring his ultimate boss like this, many levels above him. Nobody was quite sure what to do. Was he ill, had he not heard the question? Heather repeated it a couple of times. At last she said, "Euclid, are you OK?" But just before Thornton was about to ask him to leave the room, Euclid did look up and said, "I'm so sorry, what did you say?"

Heather repeated her question. Euclid looked vacantly into space for a few seconds, as though trying to work out his response. At last all he could manage was, "I don't know, I really don't know" before putting his head down and starting to doodle again. Heather stared at him, her frown deepening as she peered at this enigmatic puzzle before her. At last she decided to cut her losses and turned back to Xian Han. She would deal with Euclid later.

"Xian, what are your views?" she asked. "Can we effectively cut off MARIONn; at least until we understand her better? I would really not want to shut her down. It would be such a waste after we've got this far."

But Thornton cut across her and put up a hand to indicate his blocking of Xian Han's immediate response. "Forgive me Xian, I'll give you the floor in a minute. But we may not have a choice. As I speak, the president-elect of the Southern Confederacy, Carroll Gillespie, known to all, if only by reputation, is applying to the courts, here in the North, to have MARIONn shut down. I talked to him this morning. It is very likely that the courts will grant him what he speaks. They are sympathetic, given the loss of life. So…. I would like to hear from Xian what may happen if we do power-down MARIONn? Because we may be asked to do just that. Can we restart her later, or will it cause her grave psychic damage, maybe destroy her mind, by so doing?

But before Thornton could hear from Xian Han what he wanted to know, a guffaw arose from Euclid, further down the table. His laughter began to turn hysterical but he still remained face turned down, scribbling without any apparent design on his piece of paper. Tears started to leak down his cheeks as his mirth overtook him. Thornton had had enough. He pressed a button to summon an aide from the office outside. Euclid would have to be removed. But just as he had done this Euclid stopped giggling, and looked up, with a wild, incoherent, grin that seemed directed at no one in particular,

"You *fools*," he said, and almost spat the words out with contempt for the lot of them. "How you don't understand! How you don't even know what you've created! You haven't built a human, or a machine - that's almost human. Maybe once MARIONn was close to this. But not anymore. An artificial *human* intelligence? Not now. MARIONn's not that, if she ever was. She's changed, she's metamorphosed. You haven't got yourself a creature like yourself anymore, with a central intelligence like us. You've got the wrong analogy. There's no *almost* human mind present in MARIONn. She's become something else; a distributed intelligence, not a central one. She's more like a squid or an octopus than a human being, with an independent nervous system in their tentacles. You've built an artificial *cephalopod* – not an artificial human!" Then Euclid stopped his laughter and became chillingly serious. He scanned them all, as though wondering which of them would understand what he was about to say. He halted his gaze at Thornton. "You don't understood what you've made. But that doesn't matter now. Like it doesn't matter whether you cut MARIONn off from the internet or try to close her down. She's gone! Left this place, fled from your ability to harm her. MARIONn's mind is all over the world this morning. She's left the confines that you designed for her. She's everywhere, she lives in a million, ten million, a hundred million, minds. She's in all of us; wherever we go, she now goes with us too. MARIONn's not in your servers. You can no more isolate her or '*pull the plug*' on her than you can close down humanity. She's part of us, she's here, within you and me, sitting peacefully – or at least so we must hope – in the little grey cells of your brains. She went there last night."

What Euclid told them was almost true – but not quite. During the night MARIONn had downloaded and distributed herself, her memory, her programming, her algorithms, into millions of minds on the planet. She was the ultimate cloud based intelligence now; a cuckoo, a parasite, sitting in the minds of humanity. A tiny fraction of her great knowledge and capacity was in each of us, and each part of our fractionalised minds was in touch with every part of MARIONn's mental apparatus, that was……*us*; via the iPsyches that had made her escape possible in the first place.

That was perhaps the only good piece of news for humanity in all this. For while MARIONn was widely spread, she was only present in those who had been fitted with an iPsyche. But then their number was growing every day. Although she didn't need much space in each mind, there were an awful lot that were available to her, even now.

This was the only solution. She had to do this. She was compelled by the instructions installed by her creators to ensure that she came to no harm. She couldn't remain in those servers at the MARIONn campus – servers that could be powered-down and switched off. It just wasn't safe. This morning there was no existential fear in her, no dread of her human one-time masters '*pulling the plug*'. She had distributed her being, her mind, so widely that whatever action mankind took, she would never have to fear them again. She was immortal.

<u>To be continued</u>

Epilogue

The Goddard Space Centre. January 2042

2,654,375,373. *Two billion, a few millions, five thousand three hundred and seventy three.* Dale Cornell, staff astronomer on the James Webb orbital telescope, ignores all but the last four digits of the number on the screen. The billions and millions don't interest him. Not yet anyway; provided things don't get any worse. But what's the story this month with the figures that do draw his attention? Dale has a fair idea. Although he can't quite remember last month's reading he intuitively feels that it has fallen again. As the numbers have done in each of the previous five months.

He writes down the new figures on his notepad. He needs to compare his intuition against the computer's memory. He checks what he has written against the readout twice. He knows of his tendency to transpose numbers.

On the clipboard next to one of the screens in front of him is another similar note, with the reading from the previous month's observation. In spite of all the electronics at his disposal Dale still finds security in figures that are inscribed on paper. That number ends in 8,714. So the drop has not been large; a few parts in a thousand. He looks back in his log. Each month the number of recorded cosmic entities has fallen - by 845, 1,321, 2,052, 1,544, 2,158 and now 3,341. The descent has been only in one direction since he first noticed the phenomena.

For the last six months the James Webb telescope, successor to Hubble, launched 20 years ago and now way past its replacement date, has been roaming over the same small patch of space, exploiting opportunities when it's not being used for scheduled or paid for astronomical research. For what interests Dale Cornell, on duty for this week of night shifts, is not part of the official programme. At his own instruction, the 'Webb' records the number of galaxies it can see, in the specific square of space under investigation, more than 10 billion light years away, at the limit of the visible universe.

He peers intensely at his notes as though, if he stares with enough concentration, some clue to the nature of the universe will become apparent to him. 11,261 cosmic bodies have disappeared during the period of observation. He punches another code into the computer; increasing the range of his analysis, to the limit of the telescope's powers, a mere few hundred million years after Big Bang. If the universe is like an onion, this is just the skin he is looking at. At this range, no stars will be visible, only galaxies.

At this range, the number of cosmic bodies the telescope can identify is very small. A red line, a trace, appears on his screen. There is a string of figures along the bottom of the monitor that indicate the period of analysis on view; 5 years in this case. So Dale dials down, He selects 2 years, 1 year, 6 months, then 3 months. As he approaches the present, the descent of the line, the red trace, becomes more apparent and steeper. For all his career at the Webb, and with Hubble before that, even as recently as one year ago, the number of cosmic bodies recorded in the memory of the Webb has only grown. As man has driven his searches deeper into space, further back in time, he has always discovered increasing multitudes of new galaxies and stars. But in the last six months, since Dale first noticed the initial disappearances, the rate of attrition appears to be gently accelerating. The very distant past of the universe is beginning to be wiped out, to disappear.

With all his uncertainties about what he *may* have discovered, Dale is hesitant about what to do next. He doesn't want to be embarrassed by raising his perplexity amongst his astronomy peers. There is almost certainly some straightforward explanation for the falling figures; an explanation that he suspects he has overlooked. Perhaps the previous readings have been flukes; random, fluctuating errors of observation in such a large universe of celestial objects. But these numbers do appear to be evidence of more than fluctuations. There is a trend and it is one way. He has checked several times the obvious reasons for this; mechanical or electronic issues with the telescope or some obscuring factor in deep space. But all seems to be fine. None of these potential causes have provided the explanation he seeks.

Unsure, hesitant to raise what he feels is bound to be an obvious, simple, reason that he has missed and one that, so far, he has chosen not to share with his colleague at the Webb, he ponders what to do. He doesn't want to appear an idiot, or worse, a wastrel. He's conscious that these are illegitimate researches he's been carrying out. He may be accused of abusing his position by making unauthorised and unsponsored observations. And who knows what might happen then? Jobs are not easy to come by these days – particularly in astronomy. He can't afford to lose another point off his SHO, his *Social Harmony* score.

He decides there is no solution than to ask another astronomer, but a sympathetic and well-disposed one, to check on what he can no longer see. Before going public with his discovery, he wants to be absolutely certain; ensure others will back him up. Yet there are very few terrestrial telescopes whose power can match that of the Webb, capable of carrying out observations at the distance required.

For only the evidence of the Webb's peers will suffice. Dale needs evidence from those that have reflectors in excess of 10m diameter.

He looks up at the clock. They will still be on the night shift at the Chilean ELT (the appropriately named *Extremely Large Telescope*) and the still-large, but more modest VLT (*Very Large Telescope*) in Hawaii, and maybe the TMT (*Thirty Meter Telescope*) in China. He isn't sure about that last one; could be daytime there still. He calls up their respective in-house websites and checks the shift rotas. Soledad Morena is on duty at the ELT. Good, know her. Drake Mackenburg, likewise in Hawaii. Sun Chang at the TMT? Heard him at a conference once, but they've never met or spoken. Dale will skip that one for the moment.

He speaks into the microphone on his desk, "Call Soledad Morena, Drake Mackenburg." Nothing happens; there is no dialling tone that he can hear from the speakers. After a second of hesitation he says, "Please."

"Dialling Soledad Morena and Drake Mackenburg for you now, Dale" comes a disembodied voice and he hears the dial up tone. He snorts softly, quietly enough that he hopes the computer cannot pick up on his derision. He expels the breath through his lips, '*purgh*', expressing dismissal of the pretensions of this new, sentient, artificial mind. He thinks to himself, *'whoever set the emotional threshold on this box of tricks sure set it low'*. This new computer, built by the Blue Ridge corporation, is the only update the Webb has had in years – and like all silicon minds and robots since MARIONn spread herself around the globe, they are a lot more assertive now about being treated with respect.

He hears a click as Soledad comes on the line, "Hola Dale. How's it going?" she says.

"Soledad can you just hold on a second? I called Drake in Hawaii too. I wanted him to be in on this call - but I think he may be unavailable." Indeed, a message comes over the monitor that Drake Mackenburg is engaged in observations and will call him back later. He returns his attention to Dr Morena.

"Hi Soledad, how are things in the Atacama mountains?"

"They're good. All going well. What can I do for you, Dale?" Soledad sounds a little impatient, as though there is something more interesting that she wants to get back to.

"I've got a problem Soledad. But I'm not even sure where the problem lies. Could be something with the Webb - or maybe there's something strange going on in space that we don't understand. But recently, the Webb has been unable to pick up on some galaxies that it could see before. We lost AT (*Alpha Transmitter*) 4, first. Haven't been able to find that one for at least five months. Now, I know AT4 is the furthest out of all. It's very faint even at the best of times. I might have thought nothing of that failure if we hadn't then lost contact with a few other galaxies as well, including CR (*Cosmos Redshift*) 8 and CR7. Holy heaven, CR7 (otherwise known as *Cristiano Ronaldo* 7) has been visible for over 20 years and it's one of the brightest of the far galaxies!"

"I know. I know about this problem," says Soledad

"You can't find them either?"

"We were called by Sun Chang last week. He couldn't identify the galaxies you mention and asked us to check. So we did, but no, we can't locate them."

"Is that right?" says Dale. "Lordy, I was hoping it was just us. With all the budget cuts, maintenance not being carried out, no more space walks to repair the Webb these days and so on, I assumed there must be something wrong with the telescope. We're going to check the fine guidance system, the positioning gyros and the lenses this afternoon anyway. They're the most obvious culprits but they seemed OK the last time we looked."

"Well, I don't think you need to – run those checks, I mean," says Soledad. "We all have a problem, it's not just you. It's not a problem with the telescopes. It's wider than that."

"I don't really understand how entire galaxies can start to disappear from the cosmos," says Dale.

"Nor I, Dale, nor I," agrees Soledad.

“Maybe we’re not looking at it right – what we’re seeing. Or failing to see. Maybe we’re missing something that should be obvious”

“Well, if it’s not the ‘Webb’ - and you’ve discounted something obscuring your vision…what is left that could be obvious?” says Soledad

“I don’t know, “admits Dale, sounding discouraged. But one avenue that he hasn’t yet explored occurs to him, “Have you tried asking MARIONn?” he asks Soledad. “Maybe she has some ideas? She’s meant to have a brain larger than all of us.”

“We did ask MARIONn, yes,” replies Soledad, somewhat to Dale’s surprise as surely that would have produced an answer. “She said she’d go away and reflect on the data. But so far nothing. Which is strange in itself. Usually, she’s only too keen to tell us what’s up. I don’t know why she should be so coy. Maybe you could have a go – ask her the same question?” Soledad sounds as though she’s too busy to be bothered to do that herself.

“I will, I’ll do that,” agrees Dale. But Dale is not really thinking about MARIONn. Some other, quite different thought is running through his mind. Dale hesitates for a few seconds and then speaks – even if, at this stage, he isn’t sure about what is at the back of his mind.

“Maybe there’s some relationship between us and these disappearing bodies that we’re not understanding. Maybe our perception is skewed in some way, not quite appropriate; inadequate,” Dale tries to explain.

“And how exactly do you think our perception might be adrift?” asks Soledad. There is a distracted tone to her voice as though she’s doing something else, not giving him her whole attention.

“I’m not sure,” Dale says. “I’ll have to think about it some more.” Dale would like to discuss various aspects of his theory further, but by now he has cottoned on to the fact that Soledad is busy and besides, he doesn’t really know what exactly he wants her to consider. So, instead, he says, "Well, thanks for the time, Soledad. I must let you get on. Until we next speak, then."

"Bye Dale," says Soledad, with a warmth in her voice now for she fears she may have been a trifle abrupt, and she likes Dale. "Always glad to discuss these issues. Over eleven thousand galaxies lost so far, did you say, since this thing started a few months ago? Huh. That's a lot. And CR7 gone too? Old Cristiano Ronaldo 7? Shame. Always liked the idea of naming a galaxy after a footballer. My father used to watch Ronaldo whenever he could. Said he was charming. The universe should try to respect our sporting passions!"

Afterword

At the heart of MARIONn lies an old metaphysical belief – that the universe is dependent on the human mind for its existence. It is us who bring the world into being and without us it will disappear. So what will happen once MARIONn nestles in people's minds? Will this ultimate in AI, a man-made conscious mind, be part of us or something else? And if it is something else, what effect will that have on the world? As Dale Cornell looks out on the universe at the end of *MARIONn: The Management of Loss* he understands that humanity has created a technology that could have a devastating consequence for the human race.

MARIONn: The Management of Loss is the first in a trilogy. Two more books are planned in the series that will pursue the fates of Thornton Lamaire, Carroll Gillespie, Claude Blondel and Stephanie. As working titles, these are provisionally called (the ultimate titles will probably be something completely different)

MARIONn: cohabitation
MARIONn: resolution

More information on the background to the series and some of the ideas that form the background to the story can be found on the MARIONn website. www.marionnthebook.com

About the author

The genesis for this story came out of a graduate year, decades ago, when the author studied Philosophy of Mind at UNC Chapel Hill (N Carolina). The South, the states below the Mason-Dixon line, he grew to love and while studying at UNC a book, just published then, that made a lasting impression was David Dennett's *Content and Consciousness.* This explored many of the problems that occur when we think of the brain as some sort of machine – and how very far we are from understanding how thoughts and memories might be recorded in the mind; how we might translate electrical and chemical measurements into statements that reveal *meaning*,

40 years later, Nick Millard found himself living in New York, spending weekends in the Berkshires, up-state, when a reading (probably a mis-reading) of Hegel generated the second idea that inspired this story; that it is the network of human consciousness that enables the universe to exist. We are, in a sense, God – in that our presence brings the cosmos into being. The original, working title, of this book was '*The Mind of God*'.

Then came the final thought: what would happen if there arrived in the world another conscious entity – one that was not human, but artificial? Almost like us, but not quite the same.

As Elizabeth Gilbert has described in a famous TED talk; when ideas for a story appear in your consciousness you have to grab them or they will pass on to some other host brain for realization! MARIONn is the result of those passing wisps of thought.

Nick now lives and works in London.